Broken

Broken

MARIANNE CURLEY

.BLOOMSBURY

NEW YORK   LONDON   NEW DELHI   SYDNEY

First published in Great Britain in March 2014 by Bloomsbury Publishing Plc
Published in the United States of America in November 2014
by Bloomsbury Children's Books
www.bloomsbury.com

Bloomsbury is a registered trademark of Bloomsbury Publishing Plc

For information about permission to reproduce selections from this book, write to
Permissions, Bloomsbury Children's Books, 1385 Broadway, New York, New York 10018
Bloomsbury books may be purchased for business or promotional use. For information
on bulk purchases please contact Macmillan Corporate and Premium Sales Department at
specialmarkets@macmillan.com

Library of Congress Cataloging-in-Publication Data
Curley, Marianne.
Broken / by Marianne Curley.
pages   cm
Summary: When Ebony's boyfriend, Nathaneal, goes on trial in Avena for revealing his
powers to the enemy, Ebony falls victim to the schemes of Jordan, whose jealousy
propels Ebony into the treacherous heart of Avena itself, the perilous,
otherworldly realm from which she is descended.
ISBN 978-1-61963-168-7 (hardcover) • ISBN 978-1-61963-171-7 (e-book)
[1. Angels—Fiction. 2. Adventure and adventurers—Fiction. 3. Love—Fiction.] I. Title.
PZ7.C9295Bro 2014   [Fic]—dc23   2014005622

Typeset by Hewer Text UK Ltd, Edinburgh
Printed and bound in the U.S.A. by Thomson-Shore Inc., Dexter, Michigan
2 4 6 8 10 9 7 5 3 1

All papers used by Bloomsbury Publishing, Inc., are natural, recyclable products
made from wood grown in well-managed forests. The manufacturing processes
conform to the environmental regulations of the country of origin.

For the special girls in my life,
Amanda, Danielle, Jessica and Josie.
And for the boys, my two Christophers, and Zach

And for Missy,
my loving companion for fifteen years,
gone from this world on 21 August 2013.
May she have fun forever in puppy heaven

Broken

1

Jordan

I met her first. The connection was intense. She felt it too, and even after all that's happened since, she still does. They try to tell me it's not real love, that it's a supernatural bond that links us together, but the truth is there's only one thing standing in our way – the angel.

A Seraphim Prince.

Nathaneal.

He's convinced Ebony that the two of *them* should be together for eternity or some crap, and she's fallen for him in a big way, like it's her fate, or destiny.

It's ridiculous how much I want this girl. I *need* Ebony in my life. It's that simple.

Thane knew how I felt about Ebony from the start, and he still played his secretive games. He needed me to find her. Born in the same nanosecond, we are linked for life, and he knew the heavens would light up when we came close.

He knew everything, and he made sure I knew *nothing*.

I can't forgive him for that.

It's early on Monday morning and he's training us in his downstairs gym before school. It's our new training schedule since Ebony moved in. And it's rigorous. He's training Ebony to use her powers so that they can disappear off to Avena, the world where angels live.

I feel his piercing blue eyes on my back as I pound the boxing bag. *Wham! Wham!* I grab the bag with my gloved hands and turn round. He's looking straight at me, and I can feel him poking about inside my head, so I stare back. 'Do you have to?'

Ebony's working on the treadmill with earplugs in, but right away, her Guardian Angel alarm goes off and she stops. 'Have to what?'

'He's in my head again,' I tell her.

She raises her eyebrows at him.

'Jordan,' he says in his silky-soft voice that could turn horse shit into whipped cream, 'it's to protect you both.'

'Yeah? Well, maybe I don't want your so-called protection any more.'

'Jordan,' Ebony looks uncomfortable. 'Will one of you tell me exactly what's going on?'

I shove my chin in the direction of the angel with the guilt-ridden expression on his face. 'Ask *him*.'

Stepping off the treadmill she studies Thane's face, touches his arm and gives him a sad little smile that turns my stomach over. 'Do you have to listen to *every* thought?'

'Ebony, I can't hear *your* thoughts, so if you're in danger I will know through Jordan.'

'Oh. Because of our bond?'

He nods. 'Yes.'

'There you go,' I tell her, 'another perfect example of me being used again.'

He glares at me with darkening eyes. 'Neither of you is

2

safe. Danger could come in any form, one you might not recognise. I watch and listen, and I will do whatever is necessary to keep you *both* from imminent danger.'

'That's bull! You just wanna know what I'm thinking when I'm thinking about your fiancée.'

'Jordan, you're always thinking about Ebony. That's not new. What is new is your hostility towards me.'

Wham! Wham! I slam the bag, wishing it were his head.

'Jordan, we need to talk.'

Seething hot breath pushes out from between my locked teeth. 'So *now* you wanna talk? You could have told me Ebony was your fiancée a hundred times, but didn't. Why was that, Thane? Why now and not before?'

He flicks a glance away before bringing his eyes back to mine. 'I should have told you.'

'Damn right.'

'I'm sorry I didn't.'

'Too late for that.'

'Jordan!' Ebony scolds me like I'm a kid she's babysitting. 'Can we try to get along?'

I laugh. 'Oh, I get it. You're uncomfortable around me now.'

'No, I'm not. But *you're* uncomfortable around us.'

Us. US. I hate that word. 'Damn right I am!'

Her face collapses and she sighs.

'Ebony, I don't mean *you*. I mean *him*.'

'But it *is* me.' Her words rush out fast, like they're bursting to break free. 'If it wasn't for me, none of this would be happening.' She glances at Thane. 'If you two can't get along, I'll have to move out.'

'No!' I yell.

Thane moves in closer, shrinking the space between them. 'This is the safest place for you right now.'

'I'll be fine at Amber's. She'll love to have me back.'

'And so would her brothers,' he says. 'Twins, who recently turned twenty-two, presently away at university.'

What's with his anxious undertones? Can angels get jealous too? His eyes slide to mine, revealing that, clearly, they can. I laugh, enjoying the moment maybe a little too much. *See what it feels like, dude?* I turn to Ebony. '*I'll* move out before you have to.'

'You can't, Jordan,' she says, 'this is your home and –'

'And what? What do you think I would do? Where do you think I would live? I'm way too old for Social Services, and I can't afford to live on my own, but I'd rather be homeless than have you staying anywhere but in this protected house. It's why he built it. Don't be an idiot, Ebony. You're staying right here.'

'All right, I'll stay if you do, as long as we find an amicable way to live together under one roof.'

I flick a look at Thane. He promised to teach me how to block my thoughts, but that was just another lie. The sooner I learn how to do it, the more bearable it'll be living here. Somehow, I'll teach myself. I have an idea that might work. 'OK. I'll stay, on the condition you two stop doing that thing all the time.'

Her eyes widen, her face darkens with hot colour as she glances at Thane. 'But, Jordan, we haven't done ... er, anything like, er . . .' She stops and adjusts the ponytail at the back of her head.

'I'm not talking about *that*. Jeez, Ebony, I mean the way

4

you two are always, you know …' Damn, now *my* skin's growing hot.

'Making you uncomfortable,' supplies Thane.

I nod, and check what's next on my training schedule.

On my third cardio set, Thane glances at the wall clock and calls out, 'That's enough for this morning. Move into cool-downs.'

'Already?' Ebony says. 'But that's not even half as long as usual.'

'I thought you two might like some time to clear your heads before your exam today.'

'How thoughtful,' I mutter, working through the cool-downs as fast as I can.

Ebony keeps pace with me and we finish in no time. I grab a towel to wipe the sweat off my face while Ebony checks the clock and grins. 'We've got heaps of time left.' Playfully, she tugs on Thane's training T-shirt. When he leans in, she whispers, 'And the best way I know how to clear my head …' She leaves the rest unspoken, and he smiles meaningfully down at her.

This is exactly what I mean. The secretive looks between them, the way they radiate towards each other like magnets – they're driving me crazy. Only twenty minutes ago they had agreed to tone it down.

Bracing myself as I try to calm down, I throw the towel round my neck, and lower my eyes to avoid seeing the love-birds staring into each other's eyes. But the burning rage inside is not going away. I'm shaking with it.

Thane notices something's wrong and cuts me off at the door. I try to make my thoughts erratic by thinking of different things, switching ideas around as fast as I can. But nothing can hide my mood when Ebony joins him and they stand so close their fingers keep brushing together at their sides. Any second they're gonna run upstairs to Thane's room and start working on . . . on . . . *clearing Ebony's head*!

'You gotta be kidding me,' I mutter, balling my fists.

He frowns. 'Jordan?'

I keep scrambling my thoughts. Either he can't believe what he's hearing inside my head, or my scrambling concept is actually working. '*What?*'

'I think you've misunderstood what Ebony was referring to,' he smiles.

My head says to keep walking out, but my fists are tightening. 'I didn't misunderstand anything.' I can't let him work out what I'm thinking of doing, or he'll stop me.

So I just go ahead and do it.

Clenching my right fist into the firmest ball I can make, I swing fast and high. Right away I can tell I'm gonna come up short. But it won't matter. I'm still gonna hit something.

'Jordan, *no*,' Ebony screams.

My fist connects with the underside of Thane's jaw – and it feels as if I've hit the bull-bar of a moving truck! I drop to the floor in a crouch, instinctively cushioning my hand against my stomach. '*Argh, shit! Shit! SHIT!*'

'*Jordy!*' Ebony runs to my side and tries to tug my hand out for a look. 'How bad is it?'

The pain searing across every finger is such agony that I have to focus on breathing not to black out. Sweat is beading across my skin. Stars are flashing everywhere. Tears are stinging my eyes. I glance up at Thane with as much venom as I can muster. 'Are you made of steel or something? You could have warned me!'

He just stares at me, immoveable as a Greek statue.

'Nathaneal!' Ebony cries out, 'Is there anything you can do?'

He breaks out of his stunned trance and gets down beside me. 'Let me look at that.'

It's too embarrassing. I turn away and make myself swallow the pain, shoving it down, down, *down*! It's hard not to scream, but if I let go I'll scream louder than a girl would.

He tries again. 'Jordan, please let me see your hand.'

I stare at him, imagining my eyes are poisonous darts. 'Screw you.'

'Jordan,' he says in his calming voice, the voice that irritates me so much I would punch him again if I could find a titanium glove.

But I'm not a complete idiot, and since he's healed me before ...

He hears me giving in and skims the top of my wrist, gently tugging my hand out as he continues to feel me letting go.

'Jeez, Jordy, what were you thinking?' Ebony asks, digging her fingers painfully into my shoulders, her concern making them rigid as iron bolts. They're killing me. But I haven't the heart to tell her to stop.

Thane glances at me with a fleeting smile. Of course he's hearing everything now that I can't concentrate on scrambling my thoughts.

'You've broken every finger,' he says.

Ebony gasps, 'Seriously! Can you fix him, Nathaneal?'

'I can fix the *hand*,' he says with a lingering look at me before lifting his penetrating gaze to Ebony. 'But I'll need your help to keep it still. Like this,' he says, showing her.

Cupping my broken fingers, her touch is warm and feather soft. I'm sure Thane doesn't need her assistance, but if he thinks I'm gonna thank him, well, he can just forget it.

Thane's healing touch is still as good as when he finished what the doctors had started after Adam Skinner bottled me in the stomach a while back. And when the pain eases enough for my fingers to uncurl I notice Ebony grinning at me, her violet eyes sparkling as if she's trying to contain her laughter.

'What's so funny?' I ask.

'Riding.'

'What are you talking about? Riding what?'

'Riding Shadow is how I clear my head.'

Oh, man, I knew that!

I close my eyes while a burning flush creeps up my neck. Ebony pats my shoulders, her laughter completely mesmerising.

I just wish she were laughing *with* me.

2

Ebony

Angels exist. I know this because I've met them, talked to them. I've even kissed one of them! They call this an indisputable fact. What *is* disputable is that I'm supposed to be an angel too. I've always felt different, like I don't belong in my skin. For years I wondered who I was. But in all that time, not once did I think I was something other than human.

If I really am an angel, shouldn't I feel angel blood throbbing through my veins? Or feel the powers I'm supposed to have inside me yearning for release? Without DNA tests or something just as scientifically validating, I can't say for certain what I am, or where I belong.

Nathaneal wants me to trust him, but I didn't grow up on Avena. I didn't run down the halls of Angel School, or take Angel Biology for a subject.

I grew up on Earth. It's chaotic here. We clamour for peace and fairness, but never quite achieve either. Earth is a world with too many questions and not enough answers. Doubt, distrust, fear – these are the things I know. My parents raised me to question everything, to accept nothing without scientifically backed proof.

But I've seen things now with my own eyes – real angels with incredible wings flying through the air, emitting incredible power from their hands, or from their minds. I've had bumps growing out of my own shoulders, and once I sprouted a feather.

It's difficult for me to admit that I might really be an angel. The bumps on my shoulders and the feather that came away in my hand that day in Amber's bathroom have not reappeared. But there are still the things I can do that other people can't, like being the fastest runner in school (by a long shot) and hearing sounds I shouldn't, like hearts beating, and whispered words uttered in locked rooms.

It's Monday morning and still early enough to take Shadow out for a ride. After Nathaneal healed Jordan's broken fingers in the gym, Jordan ran up to his room, claiming he wanted to study for his exam today. I hope he was telling the truth, because it wasn't what his eyes were saying.

And reading eyes is apparently one of my special *angel* skills.

3

Jordan

Sitting on the shower floor with steaming water pouring over my head, I stare at the hand that Thane fixed. Man, he looked shocked when I slugged him, but even more so when he saw my five broken fingers. Why does every good thing in my life eventually turn rotten? And why can I think clearly when I'm alone, but when I'm near Ebony every thought is of her? I want that girl so much sometimes I think I'm going crazy.

Eventually I get out, dry off, dress for school, pack my bag and check my phone for messages. There are two from Danny and one from Sophie, reminding me not to be late for the exam in second period. It's like all we do as seniors are exams. At least school gives me something other than Ebony to think about.

I drop my backpack at the front door and head to the kitchen. It's strangely quiet. I glance at my watch. Ebony should be back from her ride any minute now. I'm not hungry, but should probably eat something so I pour myself some juice from the fridge, throw it down and start hunting for leftovers.

That's when I hear three powerful cars drive in. I've heard cars like these before. I peer through the living-room glass wall and see a familiar red Ferrari, silver Porsche and a sky-blue Aston Martin.

Yep, the angels are back.

My stomach clenches as I wonder what's going on.

The unmistakable golden angel Michael is first out. Trying not to look as shaken as I'm starting to feel, I jog over. 'Hey, Michael, what brings you back to Earth?'

My eyes do a double take when his colleagues start piling out.

Holy crap! These dudes are *massive*. How you'd imagine gigantic armour-clad gladiators would look.

They're fast and silent, making a pyramid formation behind Michael without stirring the air or fluttering a leaf. It's intense. *They're* intense. They look incredible in silver armour, with polished breastplates and fancy gauntlets reaching up to the elbow. But it's their helmets, revealing only intimidating ice-grey eyes, that give them that nightmarish otherworldly look.

The hairs at the back of my neck stand on end.

'Hello, Jordan,' Michael says, his voice bleak.

I get it. The fully armoured giant gladiators are some kind of elite military enforcement detail, like Special Forces cops or soldiers. Michael is here to take someone back with him. He wouldn't need these fierce-looking dudes to haul in a *human*. Or Ebony.

It can only be ...

'This is bullshit, man!' I give Michael an accusing stare. 'How can you do this? He's your friend. He's one of you.'

'Precisely why *I'm* here,' he says, as if that's enough explanation. It's not.

The soldiers suddenly look in the direction of the barn,

their heads moving in supernatural sync, like predators simultaneously picking up the scent of their prey.

The lovebirds swing into view as they lead the horses into the stables, and I fight the urge to run and warn them. Michael's withering look lets me know there would be no point.

'He knows already?'

Michael's nod is slight, just a fraction slower than a human blink.

'This is not right, Michael.'

'It's protocol.'

'You wouldn't be here with *them*,' I jerk my thumb at the giant soldiers, 'if it was only protocol. You're treating Thane the same as you would a dangerous criminal.' When he doesn't say anything, not only is my guess confirmed, but I get the whole picture. 'You're *arresting* him?'

'Jordan, you have a choice. You can make this more difficult than it is already, or you can help.'

'You think *I'm* being difficult? Wait until Ebony gets a whiff of this. Does she know yet?'

'As her friend, and because I know you care for her, I was hoping you would help her through this.'

'Do you think I'm OK with you arresting Thane?'

He doesn't reply, but looks at me with gold eyes that know more than they're saying. No. I shrink back and start pacing the pebbled driveway. He can't know about the message Skinner brought me from Prince Luca. No way. He can't.

Man, arresting Thane sucks.

I thought it was bad enough that I had to die to save my mother's soul, but Prince Luca's twist on our deal releases me from death as long as I break up Thane and Ebony before she turns eighteen.

Maybe this is not so bad after all. Maybe Michael and his soldiers are doing me a favour.

4

Ebony

My heart is beating too fast. It slows down for a few seconds before galloping off again as Nathaneal's words go round and round inside my head. *Michael is here to arrest me.*

We ride the horses back to the stables where Nathaneal insists on cooling them down. He puts his hand over mine to help me hold the brush when he sees how badly my hand is shaking. 'Everything is going to be all right, I promise you.'

We've already discussed how there's nothing we can do to stop this, how he has no choice but to go with Michael and answer the charges being made against him.

And now everything is moving too fast.

We walk outside to find Jordan racing across the yard towards us. Breathless and panting, he says, 'Michael's come to arrest you. I can't believe they're doing this.'

Nathaneal embraces Jordan, rubbing his shoulders with open palms and injecting calm pulses into him. 'You have to be strong now, Jordan. I'm counting on you.'

'What's going to happen to you? Those dudes with Michael are massive. Will they hurt you?'

Nathaneal gives him *that* look, the one that reminds us both of the power we know he has in his hands. It almost makes us laugh. But that's the point, I suppose.

Jordan has the same thought. 'Is that it? Are they here because you used your secret power to save Ebony?'

I inhale a deep breath, determined to stay strong. And then I see the soldiers. They bring me to a complete stop. I cover my mouth with my hand before anyone notices my shocked gasp. 'They make Michael look small.'

'Don't be alarmed by their size,' Nathaneal says, sliding his arm round my waist. 'They're an angelic order called the Thrones. One of the largest and strongest of the nine orders, they're trained to be soldiers from infancy. They have amazing stealth and are light on their feet. Try thinking of them simply as soldiers doing their job.'

'Nathaneal, is there something you're not telling me?'

He sighs. 'I had hoped, being away, the courts would hold off until we could return to Avena together.'

Except I didn't return and you wouldn't leave without me.

I glance up into his face. 'Are you saying you knew this could happen, and you didn't tell me?' This is hard to take. 'What else are you keeping from me?'

He turns to me and cups my face with both his hands, tilting my head up so he can look into my eyes. 'There is nothing else. Sweetheart, I didn't tell you because I didn't want to pressure you into returning to Avena before you were ready. And I wanted to save you from worrying about a situation that might not have arisen. I should have known the courts would not wait. I wanted to believe they would so I didn't have to return to Avena without you. It was foolish because I've made things worse. I'm sorry, Ebony.'

I lay my hands over his. 'I can see how you were trying to protect me, but if I'm an angel . . . You need to trust me to handle stuff like this. And humans live with disappointment too. But when you do something like this it confuses me.' Removing his hands, I take a step back. 'I need to know you believe in me completely or how will I make the leap from thinking I'm a human to believing I'm an angel? I'm trying, Nathaneal, but secrets don't help.'

He stares at me for a long moment before his face collapses under the heavy weight of remorse. 'I'm so sorry, my love.'

I can't stay mad at him when his heart is pouring out through those open and honest eyes, so I step back into his arms. A more comforting place to rest my head can't possibly exist. He plants a tender kiss on my forehead, and I tell him, 'I don't want you to go. Amongst your own kind, you'll forget me.'

His chest rumbles, but his laugh is more tragic than happy. 'I will send you a message at my first opportunity and you will know when you receive it that to forget you is impossible.' He lifts me off the ground so that we're eye to eye. 'I promise you, Ebony, my message will explain everything and dismiss all your doubts.'

'OK. Nathaneal, it will mean so much to get that. I'm trying not to doubt anymore. I really am.'

'I know,' he says, lowering me to the ground but keeping me close.

We start walking towards Michael again when Jordan asks, 'Do you know how long you'll be gone?'

'I'm not sure.' He glances ahead. 'Michael, do you know?'

Michael replies, 'That depends on how many witnesses give testimony. The Courts are still summoning them.'

'They'll back you up, Nathaneal. I remember you asking all the angels there that night for their permission to use your special powers.'

'And they will testify to that fact, Ebony,' Michael says.

'Except Jezelle,' I murmur, trying not to stare at the Throne soldiers who look even bigger and scarier close up. 'Michael, I remember Jezelle screaming that Nathaneal was making a mistake. Was it her? Is this why Nathaneal is in trouble?'

'Michael told me it's just protocol,' Jordan says, giving me a sad smile.

The fleeting look exchanged between Michael and Nathaneal tells me there's more going on here than just protocol, and my mind spins with possibilities – all of them bad.

'It shouldn't take more than a week,' Nathaneal says. Looking down at me, he cups the back of my head and tucks me into his shoulder. 'It will be all right, my love.' He lifts his head to include Jordan. 'But I'm not leaving you two without organising someone to come and stay. What about Solomon? He's a good soldier; his size alone is a deterrent.'

'He's away tracking.' Michael's eyes flicker to me, which makes me think Solomon is with the team searching for my parents. He reads my question before I ask it. 'I'm sorry, Ebony. There's been no word on your parents yet.'

'Jerome, then,' says Nathaneal, volunteering one of his brothers.

'He is also occupied elsewhere.'

'Doing what? What could be more important than protecting Ebony and Jordan?'

Michael stares at us for ages, switching from me to Jordan and back again. I feel my face grow warm under his inspection. 'Nothing,' he says. 'Nothing is more important, Nathaneal. It's just that your problems are not the only ones we're presently dealing with.'

Nathaneal lifts his eyebrows and Michael explains, 'Sixteen young Cherubim disappeared from a campout in the Drifting Fjords highlands. They haven't been seen for twelve days. It is now snowing. While on Earth, a landslide in Argentina has left thousands homeless with unknown numbers trapped beneath mud and concrete. Tectonic plates beneath a major New Zealand city are about to collide with possibly devastating effects. Humans are clinging to trees while floodwaters of the Yangtze River wash away homes in flood-stricken villages in China. A meteorite is heading for a major Northern European city – Dominions are working a plan to alter its course to uninhabited frozen wastelands. Shall I continue?'

Nathaneal throws a hand up. 'No, I understand. But you appreciate that for me to leave willingly I need assurance that someone will be with Ebony and Jordan before night falls.'

Michael glances at the soldiers behind him. 'Be careful, cousin, before you make *that* your final ultimatum.'

'What choice do I have, Michael?'

I interrupt gently, 'You know, we don't need babysitting. Really.'

Jordan looks surprised at first, but quickly backs me up. 'Yeah, man, Ebony's right.' He points at the big glass house.

'You built it to protect her. You said yourself that nothing can penetrate those walls. They withstood *your* power. And since you thrashed the Dark Prince now is a relatively peaceful time.'

'Nathaneal, we'll do whatever we need to stay safe.'

He relents with a short, sharp nod. Above my head he whispers, 'Still, *I* will find someone as soon as I can. It may take me a day or two.' He peers down at me. 'Try not to be too hard on them when they turn up at your door.'

I try to smile but fail. 'Why do you look so worried, Nathaneal?'

'I don't like leaving you without protection.'

'But those injuries you gave Prince Luca will make sure he's no threat for some time yet. What's the worst that can happen?'

Nathaneal sighs. 'Don't go there, Ebbie,' he pleads.

Keeping one arm round my shoulder, he puts his other round Jordan's. 'I'll say goodbye in private,' he tells Michael, and lifts us into the air.

But as soon as our feet leave the ground the big soldiers surround us. They hover a metre in the air, only their silent wings beating while pointing long spear-like weapons down at us. A light click and razor-sharp blades open out at the tip, forming lethal spinning discs.

'*Oh, shit!*' Jordan breaks out in a sweat.

Not being able to see their faces through their armour is incredibly intimidating, but their wings are something else. Nothing like Nathaneal's soft feathers, they have a sharp metallic appearance and gleam with the sleekness of blue steel.

But Nathaneal's reflexes are just as impressive. He sets us down and spins round, releasing all four of his wings to form a protective cage round us.

The soldiers blink. This must be the first time they're seeing Nathaneal's gold wings. Multiple wings identify a future king. It confuses them and gives Nathaneal the moment he needs to draw on his powers. Around us the air suddenly explodes into zillions of microscopic ice-blue bubbles that gravitate together to form a shimmering shield. I imagine how intimidating he looks with his eyes shiny black, daring them to try something.

Michael lifts both hands in the air, 'Hold, all of you!' He tilts his head at Nathaneal. 'This is unnecessary. No one is going to hurt any of you. The Thrones have their orders, and one of those is to obey my commands. You just surprised them. They're trained to react.'

'I'm not used to having to ask permission to move.'

Michael says, 'These are not normal circumstances.'

Nathaneal says through clenched teeth, 'Two minutes, Michael, that's all I ask.'

One Throne, whose spinning blades are almost touching the shimmering light of Nathaneal's shield, says in a deep voice, 'But, my lord, he may run, and it is said he moves faster than the speed of light.'

Another deep-voiced soldier, a female, says, 'My lord, it is also said that Prince Nathaneal is equally at home on Earth as Avena. He would have access to any number of escape routes and safe houses.'

Nathaneal grizzles. 'Look into my mind, Michael. I will not shield anything.'

'That's not necessary,' Michael says. 'Thrones, stand down. Prince Nathaneal will not be running faster than light today, or accessing any escape routes he may know of.'

Without waiting, Nathaneal dissolves the protective shield and carries us to the stables. Here, just outside the exercise yard, he turns us both to face him, lifts my right palm, and kisses it lightly. Butterflies flutter inside my stomach, and I feel myself on the verge of unravelling. My bottom lip begins to tremble, but I fight the tears and pull myself up as straight as I can. I need to tell Nathaneal what I feel for him, but he puts a finger to my lips and whispers, 'I know, my love. And I know why you feel the way you do, and why I feel exactly the same about you. But the explanation is long. It will be in my message. And then you will understand everything.'

Closing his eyes for a moment, he moans – a haunting, beautiful sound from deep inside his throat. Across both my arms, goose pimples break the surface, and my heart responds with a yearning flutter.

He then clasps my hand and Jordan's together. 'Jordan,' he says, 'for the duration of my absence, or until Ebony comes into her powers, I entrust her welfare to you. Be her second set of eyes. Keep her safe. Lock all doors. And obey this one rule – be indoors by nightfall. It's very important. Nothing can get to you once you're inside the house. Dark angels and demons are so used to living in a dark world they can't tolerate the Earth's sun, so by day you should be safe to go about your everyday lives.'

'So we should still attend school?' Jordan checks.

Nathaneal hesitates a moment but nods. 'If you don't,

the authorities will come looking for you. Just watch for anything suspicious. At the first sign of trouble get in the car and return home. I have protected the car like the house, although it's not as safe. Maintain a low profile in my absence. Make no unnecessary journeys. Take no detours. And always be home by sunset. Do you understand?'

'We get it, Thane. Don't worry. We can handle this. You just stay safe, OK?'

He ruffles Jordan's hair. 'OK.' He frowns. 'Something is troubling you. Your thoughts are scattered.'

Jordan says, 'Relax, I'm not about to slug you again.'

Nathaneal ignores his attempt at humour. 'What is it? Has something happened?'

Michael's voice rings through the air. 'We must leave now.'

Nathaneal doesn't take his eyes off Jordan. 'Talk to me. Tell me what's troubling you. Are you trying to block me?'

Jordan runs a hand through his hair. 'Is it working?'

'Well . . . yes.'

Jordan's eyes dart to Michael and back. 'There's nothing that can't wait until you return.'

'Are you sure?'

Jordan nods. 'Yep.'

The Thrones escort us to where Michael stands waiting beside the open Porsche door. As Nathaneal moves towards Michael, I grab his hand. 'Take me with you. I'll go to Avena now. I want to testify,' I plead. 'I'm the reason you're in this mess. Let the court see and hear me. I can help them understand why you used your powers. And –' I glance at the

Throne soldiers – 'there are enough of you here to protect me in the Crossing, right?'

But he shakes his head. 'Your wings have not reappeared yet and, besides your inability to fly, there is another reason you can't come to Avena at this time.' Peering down into my eyes Nathaneal says softly, 'Beloved, your heart is not in this.'

He sighs, and closes his eyes for a moment. When he opens them he says sadly, 'Ebony, it's too risky. The Crossing can be a treacherous place.'

'If you don't let me come with you, I'll follow you. I mean it!'

I realise I really do mean it and feel lighter suddenly.

'I have *Free Will*, remember? It's the law angels live by, right?'

'You would follow?'

'I would!'

'But it's a perilous journey without your wings,' he explains, 'and the Thrones will be watching *my* every movement, not yours. They wouldn't pay attention to your safety. Sweetheart, you don't know how I have longed to hear you say that you'll come to Avena, but … I'm afraid you will regret it.'

'No, I wouldn't,' I cry out, panic rising into my throat.

'Maybe not today, or tomorrow, or until the hearing is over, but one day you will wake up and realise you didn't say goodbye to Amber, or your beloved Shadow. And when you return …'

As he peers down at me with tortured eyes, from the corner of mine I notice Jordan's mouth break into a smile.

I turn to look at him, but he's rubbing his chin and I can't be sure of what I glimpsed.

'It's for the best, Ebony,' Jordan says. 'Thane will need to concentrate on his defence. You don't want him to have to worry about *you* more than his own problems, do you?'

Michael takes Nathaneal's arm and says, 'We have to go now.' He then tries to peel my fingers from Nathaneal's hand, but I'm not ready.

Two Thrones step up on either side of me. 'Might we assist, Commander?'

Nathaneal glares at them and something in his eyes causes them to step back. He lays his other hand over the top of mine. 'It's all right. You can let me go.'

Moisture hits my eyes again and my lips quiver, but I'm determined not to fall apart. Nathaneal cups my face. His hand is trembling and I catch my breath. I watch with my heart beating fast as a tear trickles down his face. And though he doesn't say another word, the look he shares with me is so intense it's as if he's lifting me out of here and taking me to another world where it's just the two of us.

I don't know how long we stay in our own little paradise, seemingly stretching the fabric of time around us, but ultimately two Thrones move in and split us apart, giving me the sense that I'm falling from a high perch.

I blink to reorientate myself, and see the Thrones walking Nathaneal to the Porsche.

Michael motions to Jordan and when Jordan's arms fold round me, Michael leans down and whispers, 'Take care, little one. I promise to bring him back to you.'

Anger spikes through me at the injustice going on here. 'Swear it,' I enunciate clearly, noticing a slight reddish haze around the edges of my vision. I blink to clear it, but it doesn't go away. 'Swear it, Michael.'

'Swear it?' he repeats, his head cocked slightly to the side.

'Yes. Make your promise real. Swear on your High King. I'll be your witness.'

Looking stunned, Michael stares back in silence for a long moment. Then his face softens. He lays a hand on my head and says quietly but with conviction, 'I swear on the High King of Avena, that I will do all that is within my power to return Prince Nathaneal to his betrothed, known on Earth as Ebony Hawkins.'

'Thank you, Michael.'

He nods, then slips into the Porsche beside Nathaneal with a small smile on his face.

The windows are too dark to see through, so Jordan and I just watch the cavalcade leave. When the last car's tail lights disappear from sight, I turn my face into Jordan's chest and sob.

5

Ebony

Jordan talks me into going to school to sit the English exam. 'I'll bring you straight home afterwards,' he says, 'unless . . .'

He figures keeping me busy is the best plan. In most circumstances he would be right, but there's nothing normal about this situation. Nathaneal hasn't gone home to visit family, or taken a holiday.

He's been arrested by angels.

And I have no idea how Avena's judicial system works. Nathaneal's explanations so far haven't covered that sort of thing. And I can't exactly Google it!

OK, realistically, of course I can handle Nathaneal's absence for a week. I'll miss him, but I'll focus on my schoolwork and take one day at a time.

But what if things don't go well for him? What if something happens to keep him there, and I never see him again? I can't seem to shake this thought from my head and it's scaring me to death.

'Hey.' Jordan tightens his arms round me as we stand looking down the now-silent driveway. 'It's going to be OK. *I'm* here, right?'

I nod, wipe my tears and take a deep breath. There's nothing productive in dwelling on stuff I can't change. After my house burned down, when I lost everything I owned, and couldn't find my parents, I forced myself to keep moving. After a while I realised I could function even with a heavy heart.

I go upstairs to my room, shower quickly and head to the garage. By now we're really late for school. We'll miss first period for sure. At least Jordan is ready and waiting behind the wheel. He sees me and tosses the notes he was reading into the back seat.

Inside Nathaneal's car his scent is everywhere. I close my eyes and inhale deeply. I feel him around me and it reminds me of how much he believes in me – *loves* me.

I know then I'll be OK.

Jordan starts the engine and lets it purr softly. 'Ready?'

I open my eyes and look straight at him. 'I'm ready.'

While reversing out he says, 'The exam today might help keep your mind off what just happened.'

'Maybe, but I doubt it.'

'Those two hours of intense concentration might help you forget – you know – that he left you.'

I raise my eyebrows at him. 'Left me?'

'I didn't mean it like *that*.'

'Then what do you mean, Jordan?'

He shrugs. 'Forget it. Just let me know if you want to leave after the exam, OK?'

'Sure. Thanks.' We arrive at the gates. I depress the remote control and we turn into Monastery Lane. 'It was just so unexpected.'

'A freaking shock, that's what it was.'

'If I had only known . . . Jordan, what if they find him guilty?'

He gives me a harsh look. 'Don't say that. Thane did nothing wrong.'

'We know that, but on Avena they call what he did treason.'

'What did you say?' Taking his eyes off the lane to stare at me with his mouth open, he inadvertently veers on to the shoulder. Gravel spins up at the rear. For the next few seconds Jordan concentrates on climbing back on to the firm road surface. 'Did Thane tell you they charged him with treason?'

I nod, not trusting my voice.

'Man, I didn't realise it was *that* serious. *Treason?*'

'His special power is Avena's secret weapon, one that was supposed to be saved for a more serious conflict. They're accusing him of putting his personal feelings before the realm.'

'But Prince Luca came close to taking you away forever. Don't they care about that?'

'Revealing his secret power has grave implications for Avena, and for peace everywhere, apparently. Nathaneal's action has disturbed quite a lot of voting court members.'

'Shit.' Jordan runs his fingers through his hair. 'I heard Jezelle say it could start a war, but I didn't think she was serious.'

'She said that?'

He nods. 'Do you remember how dead set against it she was? I just thought she was jealous of you.'

'It seems there was more to it.'

'Yeah, but . . . Ebony, she's still hot for him.'

'I know.'

He smiles grimly at me. 'There's nothing you can do from here.'

'I suppose not.'

'It must suck.'

I glance at him. 'What?'

'Knowing Jezelle's with him, supporting him where you can't, maybe even making her move while you're in another world.'

I swing my head round and stare.

Grimacing and lifting his shoulders, he says sheepishly, 'Not helping?'

'Not helping.'

We travel down Mountain Way in silence after that. It seems to take too long to get to school even though Jordan speeds all the way into the last vacant car-parking spot on the hill. His phone beeps and he checks the message. 'Danny wants to know where we are. He says we have, like, two minutes before they lock the doors.'

We run to the auditorium and find Mrs Jessop closing the entrance door. She shakes her head as she marks off our names, then makes Jordan wait while she walks me to my allocated desk.

All of Year Eleven is sitting in alphabetical order in rows that cover half the floor space. They fiddle with their pencils while they wait, until they spot the latecomers, then all eyes zoom first to me, then to Jordan at the door. Whispers quickly turn into a soft roar that follows me until Mr Crawford, standing out front, tells everyone to be quiet.

As usual my seat is in the row directly in front of Amber. Her warm smile is a welcome sight. She looks up, expecting me to smile back, but my attempt is pathetic and she mouths, 'What happened?'

Mr Crawford lays an exam booklet face down in front of me. When he walks away, I lean back in my chair, so glad that I've been keeping Amber informed on everything. 'Nathaniel had to return to Avena for a week.'

'Why?' she whispers back.

Mr Crawford spins round with his pen pointing at us. 'No talking, girls, or I'll separate you.'

'Tell you after,' I mouth the words.

A tap on my shoulder a few seconds later makes me jump, but it's just Jordan following Mrs Jessop to his front-row seat. He gives me a wink as he passes and the connection we share, the bond Nathaneal says we will always have between us, hums stronger than ever.

Two hours and ten minutes later Mr Crawford calls for pens down. Buzzing voices instantly fill the auditorium. Keen for details of Nathaneal's abrupt departure, Amber drags me to the front desk to hand in our papers. On our way outside we pass Jordan frowning at his cover sheet while holding a pencil above it. 'Hey, moron,' she says, teasing him with the sarcasm she seems to store up just for him. 'Are you just getting started? Got news for you, time's up.'

He scrawls his Student Number in the appropriate boxes and smirks at her, then whispers to me, 'Meet you outside.'

But when he joins us outside his mind appears to be elsewhere, his eyes flickering through the crowds of other students filtering out.

At first I think he's watching for his best friend Danny, who's been hanging around with us at lunchtimes lately, but when Danny arrives, joking about the exam being a 'piece of cake', Jordan continues to look around.

'Obviously, you smashed it, Danny,' Amber remarks dryly.

Sophie joins us then and, having heard Danny's cocky remark, adds her own cheeky comment: 'He should! He could easily do a higher level. He's just too lazy to do the extra work!'

A few strands of Sophie's silky blonde hair fall loose, so she pulls all her hair free, ruffles her fingers through it to spring the curls back up, and then re-ties it as our school rules dictate.

Sophie's not trying to be glamorous or sexy. She just is. No matter how she dresses or does her make-up, Sophie is just one of those girls who have that 'something' that makes heads turn everywhere she goes.

Apparently, even Jordan's! How have I not seen this before?

Since Sophie joined us out here, Jordan's eyes seem to have stopped wandering. They're glued to her! But then, so are Danny's. And, looking around, a few other guys are watching her too.

Seriously, though, a girlfriend is *exactly* what Jordan needs. I've never tried my hand at matchmaking before, but if Sophie likes Jordan as much as he seems taken by her, who knows?

Finding out will be my first step.

'What are you grinning about?' Amber asks. 'I didn't think the exam was easy.'

Everyone glances at me and I shrug. 'I'm just relieved.'

She doesn't believe me, but I'm telling the truth – I'm relieved that I've stumbled on to something that has the propensity to ease tensions at home. I'm bubbling inside with anticipation. If my little scheme works, Nathaneal will be thrilled too. When he returns, we might all be able to live under the same roof without the weighty blanket of guilt hanging over us.

'Oh, man!' Danny exclaims. 'When you two didn't show up we thought you were ditching the paper.' He includes Sophie with a quick look at her. 'Dudes, you gave us a scare.'

Sophie points at Danny. '*You* thought they were ditching. *I* thought something happened on the road.' She looks at Jordan. 'Did you get my texts? I sent two from my phone and two from Danny's.'

She cares enough to send *four* messages. She *is* interested. So how can I make this happen for them? They would make a great couple. Aesthetically, they'd be a knockout together with their matching blue eyes, especially if Jordan keeps training. He's starting to look seriously ripped.

But why hasn't he acted on this before now?

The answer sits uncomfortably on my shoulders.

Sophie says, 'I have to go to my locker.'

Beside her, Danny groans. 'Again? What did you forget this time?'

She shakes her head at him, pretending to be annoyed, then looks directly at Jordan. 'Come with me?'

Jordan shoots me a glance, reluctant to leave in case I want to take up his earlier offer to go home. But I don't want to go anywhere if there's a possibility Sophie might try to hook up with him. '*Go!*' Scaling down the enthusiasm a little, I add, 'I mean, I'm OK. Really. I'm just going to hang around with Amber and Danny until our next class.'

I watch them leave together with a heart full of hope.

6

Jordan

When Sophie asks me to go to her locker with her, I grab the chance because ever since I left the auditorium I'm seeing Skinner everywhere, fleeting images of him walking behind a group of students, or slipping suspiciously round a corner. Once, he stands still and stares at me from across the courtyard, hands in his pockets, a smug look on his face, and then suddenly, like a puff of smoke, he's gone.

If he's trying to get my attention, he's doing a great job. He's making me paranoid. But what is he doing here?

I take a good look around before I follow Sophie into B Block, where all the seniors' lockers run along both side walls with four horizontal stand-alone rows at the end. Sophie's locker is one of these, in the last line against the end wall.

Looking over my shoulder a couple of times, I wait while she grabs a book from inside. 'Hold this for me?' she asks, plonking the book in my hands as she locks up.

When she takes it back, our fingers accidentally touch. Her hand is as cold as ice. She takes a deep breath and exhales with a sigh, her eyes flitting away nervously.

I'm so conscious of Skinner suddenly appearing that I'm not taking in how agitated Sophie is getting. When it dawns on me, my first thought is she's gonna ask me out. Well, she's got my attention now.

'Hey,' she says, 'are you listening to me?'

'Yeah, of course I'm listening. Keep going.' I nod to encourage her.

'I'm trying to tell you something, but it's ...' She stops and frowns. 'You look distracted.'

I zero in on her eyes. They're blue. Really nice. Man, she is so hot. 'Sorry. I'm here now. Go on.'

'OK. Well, I know how close you and Danny are and I don't want this thing I have to tell you to wreck your friendship.'

'Whatever it is, it can't be *that* bad. Just tell me.'

Her eyes flicker to the ceiling as if she's asking for help from the heavens before she spills her guts. 'You've been really busy lately,' she says, like she's stating an indisputable mathematical fact, 'and, um ...'

Her voice drops so low suddenly that I struggle to hear her.

'... it just happened.'

A tingle starts up at the top of my spine. By the time she tells me everything that *just happened* the tingle is in overdrive, and I have a sour taste in my mouth.

'Say something,' she pleads.

'Like what?'

'Jordan, I'm so –'

As soon as I spot the pity tears, I back up quickly and plaster a smile to my face. 'Nothing's gonna change, if that's what you're worried about.'

'Really?' she sniffs, bringing her mega smile out.

'Of course, Sophie. I'm happy for you. Really.' The buzzer rings through the corridor ending the morning break and, even though my next class is a free period I'm supposed to take in the library, the buzzer gives me the excuse I need to leave. 'I gotta go. But I'll see you later, OK?'

I run through the corridor without glancing back, not sure where I wanna go next, but it should be somewhere Ebony can reach me in case she decides to leave, so probably the library.

But the moment I step out of B Block, Skinner is waiting and motioning with his head to follow him. This is all I need after Sophie's insightful revelation.

About twenty metres past the new Drama Block extension, there is an old white building made from cement blocks. This eyesore used to be the original school toilets, but today it looks a lot more like an abandoned convict prison. Since the school opened two new facilities about fifty years ago, the local council condemned the structure, fixing steel grid gates to both male and female openings. These entrances are both tightly secured with solid brass padlocks.

Skinner produces a key, unlocks the female entrance and walks in.

I stand outside and stare at him. Even though it's fifty years since the last kid peed in there, it still reeks of urine and, well, other stuff.

Right now, with pre-lunch classes underway, there's no one around, not even the usual bunch of Year Seven boys that congregate at the back sometimes for a smoke.

Skinner sits on a timber bench inside, stretching his legs out and crossing his ankles. 'Come in.'

'It stinks.'

'You'll get used to it.'

'I don't think so. I'm not coming here again.'

He gets up and stands right in front of my face. He gives me a condescending smirk, like he's privy to information so secret and important I could die from not knowing what it is. 'Is that how you greet your best friend?'

'No, but you're not my best friend. You're no friend at all. Not any more.'

He swings an arm round my shoulder. I don't see it coming and I flinch and try to get away. But his grip is solid, like he's been working out at the gym. He hauls me inside where it's grey and cold and damp. 'That's why I'm here,' he says.

'Huh?'

'To clarify the status of our renewed friendship.' His face is too close. It feels wrong on every level. I stretch my neck as far away as I can. 'We're going to hang out again, just like we used to.'

'Like when we were eleven?' *He can't be serious.*

'Exactly, dude.'

He releases me and I stumble backwards in my rush to put space between us. My back hits a stained cement wall. I'm not sure in the dim light whether the stain is a shadow or mould or something else.

'Too much has happened since then, Adam. We *can't* go back.'

He's in my face again, forehead to forehead, eyeball to

eyeball, nose to nose. He moves fast, and with aggression. 'You'll do what I say, all right, Jordy-boy?'

I try to shove him. 'It's not *all right*. And don't call me that.'

He pouts like I hurt his feelings.

'What are you doing here?' I ask.

He steps back, laughing. 'You're touchy this morning. Did my ex not give you the good news you were hoping to hear?'

I don't say a word. He laughs. 'Just relax, dude, I'm not here to hurt you.'

'No? So why are you bugging me at school where anyone can see you?'

He swirls his hands in the air. 'Take a look around. This is where we're going to hold our official meetings.'

'What are you talking about?'

He pokes his finger in my chest, his face turning serious. 'My employer is adamant I keep my eye on you to ensure you're sticking to the terms of your arrangement with him. So when Principal Eckard reinstates me into Year Eleven tomorrow, we're going to be friends again, meeting down here in our matching free periods two or three times a week for an update.'

My stomach drops. 'You're coming back to school just so you can check up on me?'

He takes his finger from my chest, points it at my head like a gun and makes a clunking noise in his mouth. 'You got it, bro.'

'Don't call me that either.'

'Why not? You used to like it.'

'In that other time before you tried to *kill* me.'

He waves his hand in the air dismissively. 'Oh that. Well, you killed my brother, so I say that makes us even.'

'Dude, it doesn't work that way. Whatever's going on with you, whatever you're on, keep me out of it. I'm not going to meet you here, Skinner. Tell your "*employer*" you don't have to check up on me. I have until Ebony turns eighteen to break them up. And I told you I would do it. I'm not backing down on the deal.'

I try to push past him to leave, but he doesn't budge. He sticks his chest out to block me while scrutinising me with narrowed eyes. Then he lifts his right shoulder and lets it drop. 'If you say so.'

Something's not right. Adam Skinner doesn't give in, not unless it's part of his plan. I go along with it for now, keeping wary. 'Yep.' I point to the exit. 'Now, if you don't mind, I'm leaving.'

He doesn't stop me. But before I feel the sun on my face he says, 'Of course, there is another way I can survey your progress.'

I turn round slowly. 'OK, so what's the other way?'

Examining his fingernails, he says, 'I'll just have to hang around with someone else who's close to the lovebirds.'

My mind races and it doesn't take long to figure out which friend Skinner means. 'No way! Leave Amber out of this. I mean it, Skinner. Do *not* go near that girl.'

In a flash he's grabbing my shirt, bunching it up in his fists and shoving me against the wall. 'Touchy, touchy. You're not carrying a torch for Amber too, are you?'

'She's just a good person. Leave her alone.'

'I can be *your* friend or Amber's. It's your choice, Jordy.'

It gets hard to breathe. I'm not sure why until I glance down and realise my feet aren't touching the ground. 'My friends will think I've lost it if I start hanging around with you. They won't accept you.'

He releases me, and when I drop to the floor, he says, 'You'll think of something.'

'Amber won't let you come near her anyway.'

His smile is nasty. 'I have my ways.'

And I have mine. Succumbing to this bully is not one of them. 'No. I won't do it.'

Surprise registers on his face. 'What do you mean, Jordy? You won't do what?'

'I'm not going to be your "friend" again, and you're going to leave Amber alone.'

He stares into my eyes for the longest moment, and then laughs. It makes me so angry that I push his chest with both hands. It does nothing but make his eyes flash weirdly like there's a fire burning inside them. 'One last thing I nearly forgot to mention,' he says, his voice dead serious. 'When your mother died it was Prince Luca who fought Solomon for her soul. We all know who won because she's now in Skade. But no one knows what happened to her *after* the King brought her to his palace.'

'What are you talking about?'

'You're smart. Figure it out.' He flicks my forehead with a finger and walks out the door.

'Adam. *Adam.*' He doesn't stop, but I gotta know what he means. '*Skinner!* What did that monster do to my mother? Tell me!' He keeps walking. Damn him. So I call out, 'Fine. I'll meet you here twice a week.'

He comes back, striding across the green grass and grinning like a great white shark. He puts his mouth close to my ear and whispers, 'He brought her back to life. She does things for him the other ladies – the souls – can't.'

I stand there, stunned. My mother is alive? She's living as a human in Skade? A realm only for souls and dark angels? 'What things? What things does he make her do?' I run after him and grab his shoulder. 'What you're telling me, is it God's honest truth?'

He stares at me for a long moment, then nods.

7

Ebony

The day passes in a weird kind of blur with my mind flitting from Sophie to Jordan to Nathaneal to Mum and Dad. By last period I'm over-tired, overwrought and seriously in need of unwinding.

Fortunately my last class is Physics, one of my favourite subjects. I love the sciences, and my craving to learn about life and the universe is encouraged by a great teacher – Andrea Paully. She's young and understands my need to learn; she says I remind her of herself at my age. And in a class of eighteen, where there are only three girls, it helps to have a female teacher to even out the odds a little.

Ms Paully is really nice, but she has a thing about tardiness and hands out detentions like Einstein developed theories. And for no good reason today, only that my head's in a daze and I'm walking slower than usual, Amber, Sophie and I end up late for class. I groan. Detention is the last thing I need. I'm *so* ready to go home.

But at the classroom door I get the shock of my life. Ms Paully isn't teaching today. Another teacher is – a man. He's writing his name on the whiteboard, but I don't need to read the words to know this man's identity. His distinguished look, polished foreign voice and expensive dark suit, are disturbingly familiar.

It's Zavier, the man who, according to Mum and Dad, organised my adoption.

Sophie runs into my back. 'Hey, what's up? Are we going in?'

When I don't answer, she peers over my shoulder. 'Oh, yeah, I heard Ms Paully had a car accident last night.'

Both Amber and I gasp.

'She going to be OK, but she broke her pelvis, her left leg and a couple of ribs. She'll be absent for the rest of the year.'

'Oh my God!' Amber says, clutching her books to her chest.

Sophie continues moving past me when she realises I'm not budging yet. '*Ooh-la-la!*' she sings after seeing the man writing on the whiteboard. 'I could get used to seeing *him* around the corridors. Suave and sexy, that's some combination. You know, girls,' she calls back to us, 'we should start sitting in the front row. I hear the view is better there.'

'Ladies, you're welcome to come in and take a seat,' Mr Zavier says without lifting his eyes off the board as he writes instructions under his name in stylish, eloquent strokes. 'I don't bite, though I can't speak for the rest of this rabble behind me.'

Fifteen boys laugh.

'Morons,' Amber murmurs, just noticing I've hardly spoken or moved since we got here. 'Honey, are you coming in?'

I know I should, and that I will have to at some point if I want to remain in this class, but it's the end of the day, I'm tired and I don't want to face this man right now. I don't want to ask him what he's doing here.

'Ebony, what's wrong?' She sees the teacher's name on the board. 'Oh my God, isn't that —'

I wrap my fingers round her arm. 'I can't go in there today.'

'OK, I understand. Do you want me to take you to the nurse?'

'No. I just need to find Jordan.'

'So you want to go home?'

'Yeah. Yeah, I do.'

She peels off my backpack. 'Let's get out of here,' she says, and hurries us away, leaving Sophie flummoxed as she watches us turn and leave.

We don't stop until we're outside and breathing in fresh air. In the late afternoon the winter sun is perfect to warm up my chilled blood. We sit on a bench and Amber pats my hands. 'Hon, you're as pale as a ghost. Are you sure I can't get the nurse?'

I don't want to lie to Amber. She's my best friend. She knows about the angels. But what am I supposed to say? How do I explain that the last time I saw that teacher he was standing in the burnt-out shell of my house? 'It's been a long day. I just want to go home.'

She pulls her phone from her skirt pocket. 'Mum will take you.'

'No, don't call your mum. Dawn's been so wonderful; I don't want to inconvenience her more than I already have.

Jordan has Biology in Mr Dawson's lab. It's last period. He won't mind.'

'OK.' She selects a digit on her phone and lifts it to her ear. 'Hey, moron, don't ask, too complicated to explain on the phone but she needs to go home – now.'

He says one word. I hear it clearly. 'Where?'

'Out front of the Science Block.'

I hear his footsteps bounding down the corridor before Amber puts her phone away. Running straight over without breaking his stride, he gets down on his haunches in front of me. 'What happened?'

Amber fills him in. 'We had a substitute teacher in Physics. Ebony recognised him and she didn't feel like going in.'

He swings his eyes back to me with a furrowed brow. 'Who is this dude?'

I take a deep breath. 'He says he's my uncle. As in my *real*, flesh-and-blood uncle.'

'You're adopted. How's that possible? How much does he know about your origins? Does he know you're an angel?'

Amber shrugs. 'That depends on whether he's been lying to Ebony, or not.'

'Lying about what?'

'My birth,' I tell Jordan. 'Amber and I checked his house out during our last semester break for proof that I was born there – like he'd told me.'

'So you've met him before?' Jordan asks, looking confused.

'He came to my house after the fire,' I explain. 'It was the first time I could walk through the remains.'

'I didn't see him there,' Amber says.

'He didn't stay long. By the time you came back from checking the barn, he was gone.'

I pluck at an invisible thread on Amber's blazer sleeve as memories of the day of the fire fill my head, how I went searching room by blazing room for Mum and Dad without finding a sign of them.

'You OK?' Amber asks, noticing my sudden withdrawal, and my watery eyes.

I nod and remember what I was about to say: 'I think Mr Zavier might work for Prince Luca.'

Jordan's eyes open wide. 'Then he *would* know your origins. He would know whether you're human or angel.'

Amber scolds him, 'But we already know Ebony is an angel. Why would you doubt that?'

'I only meant for certain – that's all.' He looks at me and shrugs his shoulders with a sheepish grin. 'I'm just saying, you know?'

'Well, I suppose you're right, if anyone knows the truth, it would be Mr Zavier,' I tell him.

'How sure are you that he's working for Prince Luca?'

'I have no tangible evidence, but when we met at my house he said some weird things.'

'Like what?' Jordan frowns.

'He wanted to know which one of my parents "cracked" first. He said it was important that he know whether it was Mum or Dad who admitted they had lied about my birth.'

'Oh my God,' Amber exclaims.

'And he wouldn't give me a straight answer to any of *my* questions. But there is something that proves ...'

I glance at Amber. 'Well, that I lived in his house when I was little.'

Jordan looks from me to her. 'What?'

She says, 'Ever since Ebony was a kid she dreamed of a big white house with shiny floors, fancy paintings, a polished timber staircase, a beautiful piano, that sort of thing. And when she saw Mr Zavier's mansion, she recognised it as the house from her dreams.'

'*What?*'

'There was one room in particular I remembered more than the others,' I explain. 'It had a distinctive mural hand-painted across the ceiling. It was always so vivid in my dreams.'

Amber says, 'I saw the mural too. It was exactly like Ebony described to me loads of times since we were kids.'

Jordan frowns. 'It looks like you did live in his house once, but that doesn't prove he works for Prince Luca.'

'On the night before the fire, my parents told me that sixteen years ago a man named Zavier offered them a baby to raise. He told them his young sister was my biological mother and had died in childbirth two days earlier.'

Jordan gasps, 'Shit.'

'Mr Zavier told me he would willingly submit to a blood test to prove he's telling the truth, and that he would answer my questions when I was ready to know who I am.'

Jordan leans forward and says gently, 'Ebony, if he's willing to give DNA, it's unlikely he's an angel or working for Prince Luca. In fact, he could be the real thing.'

I nod. 'I know. If this man is telling the truth, and he is my biological uncle, he's living proof that I'm *not* an angel.

It would mean Nathaneal has made a mistake. But if Zavier works for Prince Luca he could be lying about everything. Now he's my teacher and I don't know what to believe. I can't go into his class with my head full of so many conflicting images and ideas.'

'Fair enough,' Jordan says, then peers at me with an intuitive look. 'You don't want him to be your real uncle, do you?'

Once I would have been thrilled to be able to prove that I'm not an angel, but now? 'No. I wouldn't like that at all.'

8

Nathaneal

As always, standing before the northern gates of Avena quickens my heart. Majestic and wondrous in height and width, and created by the hand of the High King himself, they are a kaleidoscope of colour, an infinitesimal number of constantly moving atoms too small for the eye to see.

But even in beauty there is danger, for to touch any part of these gates can prove as devastating as a thousand bolts of lightning straight to one's heart.

It's this beauty that reignites my love for my homeland, knowing that once the gates open all the natural wonders of Avena will unfold before my eyes.

Michael commands the Gatekeepers, and, even though I know what comes next, my breath still catches at the sight of the gates opening inwards and revealing a thousand glistening stairs spiralling downwards in a spectacular arc.

Stepping through the gates, I inhale deeply, the air thinner but purer than Earth's atmosphere, and as I make my way across the arc each step allows my lungs time to adjust to the variance.

Arriving at the lower platform, which is still high above the land, Michael sends three Thrones on ahead to secure the road. They release their metallic blue wings, and plunge feet first off the platform.

I never tire of watching them. Such uniform precision is an impressive trait of this revered order. They land in soundless synchronisation, remarkable for their size, and immediately begin striding across the paved roads that lead to the city centre, checking buildings and side streets, their presence alerting the city of my return.

I take a deep breath as memories storm my senses. It's always, *always* the memories that break me at this point, memories of a moonless night, deep in the Lavender Forest, and the unanswered cry of an infant's first contact with the living world.

My parents were right to blame me. Even though I was only seven at the time, I knew better. Ebony's kidnapping occurred because, excited by what she had just showed me through a mind-link before her birth, and eager to tell my father, the captain of security, who had not wanted me to be there, I rushed.

The birthing chamber was a temporary, dome-shaped structure, purposefully created to protect the imminent birth of a future princess. The chamber walls consisted of hundreds of layers of pure silk, intricately woven to keep light from showing through it and inadvertently revealing the chamber's position. Security was high that night because the infant was already promised in marriage to a high-ranking prince, a future king.

But I foolishly allowed a splinter of light to escape the birthing chamber when I exited. That single glint revealed our secret location. And I will never forget the injured

51

soldiers' screams as they lay writhing in agony when the enemy's fiery explosions bore down on us, burning their skin and melting flesh off their bones.

Michael doesn't rush me as I prepare to reacquaint myself with my homeland. He sees my memories flooding in and out at staggering speeds, and slaps his hand down on my shoulder. 'Easy now, cousin, remember who you are.'

But . . . Michael, who am I?

Placing his hands down on my shoulders, he turns me to face him. 'You are Nathaneal, Seraphim Order's highest-ranking prince, a future king.'

'That's not what I mean.'

He frowns. 'What do you mean?'

'The legend told about me . . . is there any truth to it?'

'Oh, that thing written in hope and stardust before the Earth was born.'

'Are you saying it's nonsense, because I would be thrilled to know there is nothing in it and I can be free to live my life with my beloved Ebony.'

His gold eyes lose their playful light. 'The legend says hope and stardust, our king says blood on a wall of stone.'

I stare at him a moment. I haven't heard this before. 'Are you saying my name is written on a stone wall in blood?'

He nods slowly. 'As the *One* who will lead us in battle, defeat our enemy, and bring peace and unity to all the worlds.'

'That's *all*?'

He laughs, until I ask, 'Whose blood?'

'The blood of those who died in the great revolt.'

'The first angelic war.'

'Is it any wonder Prince Luca wants to eliminate you?' he says.

'But I've done nothing to justify being named this leader of angels who will unite the worlds in peace. That would be you, Michael. You've commanded Avena's armies for three thousand years. What experience have I had?'

He gives me a sympathetic look. 'You're still young, Nathaneal. Give yourself time.'

'What if I can't be this *defender*, this *champion of the people*? So far I have only been a burden to Avena. What if I don't have what it takes to be a king?'

He studies my face, golden eyes unblinking. A smile starts slowly and quickly grows. 'You will. You just have to trust me on this. Can you do that?'

I look to the horizon where the Lavender Forest merges into the sky. When I think of home my thoughts turn to Ebony. In those fleeting moments before her birth, Ebony understood how destiny had entwined our lives. She shared those visions with me in a mind-link from her mother's womb. But today she can't remember the images or their importance. I'm asking her to trust me, just as Michael is now asking me to trust him.

I take a deep breath and nod at him. 'I can do that.'

He thumps my shoulder. 'Good.'

'And you will be with me, cousin? Whatever happens?'

'Always. Don't ever doubt it. Just look to your left and I will be there.'

'Why my left?'

'Finally, an easy question,' he jokes. And grinning, he says, 'It's your weaker side.'

'What? I don't have a weaker side.'

'Yes, you do.'

'No I don't. Both sides are equal.'

'Spoken like a future king.'

9

Ebony

Jordan concentrates on the road as he drives us home. He hasn't spoken since we left school. He's gloomier than usual and I feel his sadness pulling hard on my heart, almost as if his pain were mine. Nathaneal would say this is the way the Guardian bond works, experienced more acutely when Guardian and Charge live in close proximity to one another. But if Mr Zavier is my real biological uncle, then I'm not an angel. In that case, could my feelings for Jordan be a form of human love?

I glance out the window. All this paranormal stuff is challenging my scientific way of thinking. Maybe I'm an average human girl who happens to be in touch with her supernatural side, triggered from having contact with real angels.

What am I thinking? There are signs I can't ignore. It's just that my entire life has been one lie after another. Sure, I want to be like Nathaneal so one day I can live in Avena with him, but I have to be certain before I take that mammoth step. Nathaneal is not lying, however, and he says my heart knows. But what exactly is my heart telling me?

Jordan slides his eyes from the road to me for a moment. 'Do you think your experience with angels could have unleashed some unknown psychic talent?'

This bond must work both ways! 'What are you saying?'

He switches his glance from the road to me again. 'Don't tell me it hasn't crossed your mind.'

I shrug. 'I suppose — fleetingly.'

'It's a theory that could explain a lot about you . . . should Mr Zee prove to be your biological uncle.'

I feel my forehead pucker into taut frown lines. 'I was hoping you *wouldn't* think so.'

'You know,' he says, keeping his eyes straight ahead as he manoeuvres through Cedar Oakes Valley's main round-about, 'not long ago you would have been relieved to meet your biological uncle. But then Nathaneal came into your life. And now you want to be immortal.'

'You make me sound superficial. This isn't about being immortal. I haven't even thought about that part. It's just that practically all my life I've felt as if I don't fit in.'

'Then someone tells you you're an angel.'

'Yes, quite convincingly.'

'But you don't fit their criteria, do you?'

I glance down into my lap and watch my fingers knot together. 'I don't fit the human criteria either.'

He scoffs. 'News flash, Ebony, every teenager feels they don't fit in.'

'If I am an angel I have a sister. Actually, an entire family, and I'd like that.'

'We'd all like one of those, but we don't always get what we want. You're not so unique, Ebony Hawkins.'

Nathaneal thinks I am. 'Are you saying you no longer believe I'm an angel?'

He groans. 'We're talking about family, Ebony. You already have one.'

'I know that! And I love my parents! I wouldn't swap them for anything, but they knew things and kept them secret from me. They adopted me under the condition that when I turn eighteen someone would take me away from the valley to marry a man I'd never met, and I'm supposed to comply whether I like it or not. What parents agree to that?'

'You reckon you have the world's worst parents?' He shakes his head. 'My dad's serving fifteen years for armed robbery while Mum shot herself up with heroin every day until it . . .' He stops suddenly and turns white like every drop of blood in his head has drained south. He abruptly grins even though he still looks . . . *destroyed* inside. 'You win.'

'I'm not so sure,' I tell him.

'Nah. Hands down, you do. You have two families, you don't know which one you belong to and they live in different dimensions!'

We giggle at the sudden absurd turn in our conversation. But hearing Jordan laugh gives me an idea on how to kick-start my match-making plans. 'We should have a party.'

He screws his face up in horror. 'Are you serious? We're under orders to have a quiet week. What would your fiancé think?'

Quietly it occurs to me that Nathaneal would approve, especially if Jordan ends up with a girlfriend from it. 'I don't mean a big party with an open invitation. Just a few friends like Amber and Danny and Sophie. We'll watch movies and play pool. I wouldn't mind some time to hang out with friends.'

'Yeah? Good for you. But don't count me in,' he snaps. Seeing my shocked face, he softens his tone. 'Let's just forget it, OK?'

'Jordy, what's going on?' He doesn't answer. He doesn't look at me. 'Jordan, what happened at the lockers this morning – with you and Sophie?'

'Nothing!' he says too quickly. 'Nothing at all.'

'What did she say to you?'

He laughs, his tone so cynical I get goose bumps. 'Drop it, Ebony.'

'All right, but about tonight . . .'

'It's no big deal, OK? I just don't feel like partying.'

We remain quiet for the rest of the drive home, and even the occasional glimpses of stunning valley views doesn't help lift our moods.

It's not until we're turning into the driveway that Jordan opens up again. 'What are you going to do about Mr Zavier? It's too late in the year to switch classes.'

'I don't want to ditch Physics. I just had a surprise seeing him today. I wasn't functioning at full capacity to start with, you know?' He nods. 'But tomorrow I'll talk to him, see if he can shed light on my past.'

'Good luck with that.'

'Why the scepticism?'

He shrugs. 'It's getting harder to figure out who's telling the truth about you.'

'I know what you mean. If only Mum and Dad were

58

here, I'm sure they would tell me more. They were scared, that last night, when they finally revealed how they adopted me from Zavier. They've been gone so long now. Where on Earth can they be? I miss them both so much.'

'If you ever want to talk, I'm here for you.'

'Thanks, Jordan.'

Inside the garage with the door locked behind us, Jordan switches off the ignition but makes no move to exit. I wonder again what's bothering him.

'There's something about that bond we share that I think you should know,' I say.

'Go on,' he prods.

'A Guardian and her Charge are not supposed to live in the same dimension. Nathaneal wanted to explain to you how the bond could misguide you into thinking the need to feel close to me is love when it's not a true feeling. But I thought it would only upset you more, so I stopped him.'

'I'm glad you did because that's just horse shit. He's only telling you that so you don't go thinking what you feel for *me* is love. Ebony, if you give yourself a chance, if you give *me* . . . ah, forget it! It doesn't matter since you're clearly into angels now.'

'Jordan, what's going on with you?'

'What if Mr Zavier *can* prove you're his blood niece?' he asks with a little too much enthusiasm. 'How are you going to handle knowing you're a mere mortal after all?'

'Do you know something I don't?'

'Nah. I just –'

'Then shut up before you put doubts in my head that

59

I've already dealt with and dismissed, OK?' I exit the Lambo and head for the internal door.

He calls after me, 'If Mr Zavier is offering DNA, it's the one way to know for sure.'

I go inside with Jordan's doubts chasing me all the way up to my room.

10

Jordan

I hate fighting with Ebony. It puts distance between us. And we're going to be distant enough when she leaves for good.

Man, my life sucks!

'Hey, how about I cook those yummy quiches you like tonight. The ones you said taste like pizza.' We've been home from school a couple of hours. I'm leaning my forehead on the inside of my bedroom door when Ebony comes down the hallway from her room. 'I can tell you're upset and I'm just trying to make you feel better.'

At least she's not still mad at me. But Sophie's confession is not the revelation that slammed me in the guts today. Skinner telling me my mother is alive is a big jolt to my senses. Apparently the Dark Prince resuscitated her. For the last eight years he's held her prisoner in his palace, biding his time for the right moment to reveal this news to me, knowing the accelerating effect it would have, the need I would feel to have her released immediately. Knowing my mother is alive and in the constant presence of Prince Luca is tearing chunks outta my heart.

Mum . . . Oh, Mum, you've been living in Skade long enough.

The sooner I break Ebony up from Nathaneal, the sooner my mother returns home.

'Jordy, are you all right in there?'

'Honestly, Ebony, how I'm feeling right now has nothing to do with you, so just stop trying to fix me, OK?'

'OK, I'll stop ... *after* you tell me what happened at school today.'

She's not letting up until I tell her something. I open the door to let her in but keep my profile to her so she doesn't glimpse into my lying eyes. 'They hooked up.'

'Who?'

'Who do you think? Danny and Sophie.'

There's a long pause. 'Oh. I thought she liked *you*.'

'You must have got the same screwed-up vibes I did. But ... that's not what hurts.'

'Danny didn't tell you,' she says, skimming her fingers lightly over my shoulder. 'What a coward.'

Man, her touch feels good.

'Jordy,' she says, 'I'm so sorry. Are you all right?'

'Yeah, I just ... It feels like I got no one left.'

Her fingers stiffen and go as still as four wooden pegs. 'You have me.'

'For now, sure, but what will I do when you leave this world?' I spin round. 'Who will I have then?'

11

Nathaneal

All the streets of Aarabyth lead to the Centre Square, a park of various coloured trees and vibrant gardens with pathways, fountains and play areas for the young. Communities hold gatherings there: feasts, festivals, weddings and occasionally a memorial.

Standing on the lowest platform, three thousand metres above ground, I locate Centre Square by the towering purple trees that surround it, and their magnolia-shaped blue, pink and white flowers, presently in full bloom.

The three remaining Thrones descend at Michael's command. He waits for them to land before he signals me. We dive together, head first, releasing our wings only when the ground is so close it appears to come rushing up to meet us. It's fast and exhilarating, and of the nine different angelic orders, from the highly ranked Archangels to our smallest sized Cherubs, this is a technique successfully performed only by Seraphim because our physique is the most birdlike.

Once on the road, Michael indicates the crowds beginning to gather on balconies and footpaths. 'Word is spreading quickly.'

'Do they know why I've returned?'

'There's been no official announcement, but, yes, every-one knows.'

We walk one paved road after another, making our way towards Centre Square. As we crest a hill, the Cathedral looms into view, spiralling several stories higher than most other city buildings. This is where royalty are crowned and married and occasionally remembered. This is where Ebony and I will wed, if she agrees, any time on or after her eight-eenth birthday.

I have not lost hope that Ebony's memories will return. The evidence is in her reaction the moment she saw me in her high-school car park. I was a stranger, and yet she appeared to recognise me, or felt drawn to me in some way. My unexpected presence triggered a memory; unfortu-nately it wasn't enough to identify me. I wish I knew what happened to her memories, why they're buried deep inside an area of her brain she can't reach. The logical explanation points to her sixteen years on Earth, and the way John and Heather Hawkins raised her to believe only in what she could see, feel or touch. But logical reasoning can be a sheath disguising the truth. Not everything has a rational explanation.

My eyes veer slightly east to the crown apartments where members living in outer provinces will reside for the hear-ing's duration. Adjacent is the city school with its nine border halls, one for each of the angelic orders, with their spiralling towers in their striking house colours. One of these, the Seraphim Hall, has left me with mixed memories. I enjoyed my time there, but after I turned seven my thoughts were always of Ebony, wondering where she was, who had taken her, if she was learning the skills she required to survive, and whether she was safe, happy, hurt or suffering at the hands of whoever had her. Since her abduction, I've thought of her every day.

The Courthouse swings into view on the Cathedral's western boundary. This is my destination. The hearing will take place in the circular arena that stands in the centre of this immense building. A thousand court members, representatives from all five provinces, will sit in the stands to judge my fate. And it's in the rooms beneath this colossal configuration of white stone arches and marble columns that they will hold me, a prisoner until the hearing concludes.

As our small party of five proceeds through the streets, the crowds grow and I glance at Michael with a puzzled frown.

'They are here for you,' he replies. 'You need to get used to this, cousin. You're a celebrity now.'

'Michael, this is no joking matter.'

'What's happened to your sense of humour, cousin?' he asks, grinning at me. 'Did you leave it in that lush green valley on Earth, in the hands of your beautiful violet-eyed fiancée?'

'The valley is called Cedar Oakes, and, no, I didn't leave it there. It's in the hands of a thousand court members on Avena.'

Once we reach the entrance to the Square, crowds throng to the sides in substantial numbers. Some reach out to touch me as they call out my name. The three Thrones dismissed earlier are here with soldiers from their unit helping to keep the swelling crowds in line.

Their captain, Lady Themira, greets us. She nods formally at Michael, her helmet tucked under her elbow. 'Commander, I see your mission was successful.'

He glances at me with a brief nod. 'Yes, that is correct.'

She looks at me then and a big smile emerges. It lights up her face. Her silver eyes sparkle. 'Welcome home, my prince. Wonderful to have you back on Avenean soil.'

'Thank you, Captain.'

'Please call me Them.'

'Ah . . . if you like.'

'Oh, I like!' she says, then freezes to the spot and blushes furiously.

I try not to look at her mortified face. And I don't want to look at my cousin. His tight-lipped, amused grin will not help me keep a straight face. And I would never purposefully disrespect Lady Themira, or any angel for that matter. 'Well, thank you, Lady *Them*, for that lovely honour.'

'My prince,' she goes on, 'I know I speak for every Throne when I say we are glad you have returned home, though not glad of the circumstances that have brought you here.'

Still looking at me with a smile that should have dissolved by now, the moment grows awkward. Michael is still laughing under his breath, but thankfully his need to keep me moving becomes apparent. 'My lady,' Michael says, indicating the surrounding crowds with raised eyebrows.

'Hmm?' She seems to have slipped into a daze, as if she's forgotten her reason for being here.

An angel breaks through the crowds, her arms opening as she runs to embrace me. She means no harm, but Michael gets between us, and a soldier lifts the angel and lowers her back behind the line.

'Let's keep you moving,' Captain Them says, her mind mercifully back on her job. 'I've been keeping watch since last night. As soon as I noticed the numbers swelling inside the Square, I brought my unit in to assist with court security.'

I glance at the Thrones in their impeccable silver armour, male and female, equal in height and stature, standing a pace apart on both sides. *All this is for me?* It's a staggering thought.

When Captain Them leaves us, I ask Michael, 'Why have so many come out today?'

'To send a message to the court.'

Bewildered, I shake my head. 'What message?'

'You practically annihilated Prince Luca. How long did you think news of that battle would remain quiet? The conflict on Mount Bungarra has been the main conversation topic ever since. It's caused fierce debate in the Square and in houses all over Arythea, especially here in Aarabyth.' He glances over his shoulder to where Captain Them is addressing one of her unit. 'Especially amongst our female population,' he adds with a grin.

'What message do they hope to send the court today?'

He stops and stares at me for a moment before we continue to walk towards the court's front doors. 'They support you, Nathaneal. Why is that hard to imagine? You hear the noise they're making, now listen to what they're saying. Every angel standing here today is your ally. What you did, right or wrong, you did for love. Take the politics out and it's pure romance from the people's favourite prince.'

'Now you're toying with me.'

'And Captain Themira, was she toying with you?'

I have no answer for that. He indicates the crowds with his hands. 'Does this look like a game to you?'

'When you say, *everyone* feels this way, surely you're exaggerating, yes?'

He laughs. 'They are now aware that you have multiple wings *and also* the power to annihilate our arch-enemy. Believe me; they will storm the Arena if the result of this hearing goes against you.'

'So how do you think the members will vote?'

'I wish I knew, cousin. Some members openly declare that under the circumstances you acted within the law, while some —' he shrugs — 'fear the consequences of your actions.'

'What are they afraid of?'

'War. And the losses we will incur.'

'But war is inevitable. It's written in stardust ... or is this too written in blood on stone?'

'No mention of war is ever written in anything but blood. And no one wants war to occur in their time.'

I give him a questioning look. 'If you were human, I could understand that viewpoint, but you don't live on Earth, you're not guided by mortal restrictions.'

'Everyone knows war is promised, but it's like the humans with their end-of-the-world fears. They understand it's going to happen one day, but no one wants to see it in their lifetime. Do you?'

'We don't have a choice.'

'True, but if you did?'

'Whenever there is an ending, there is always a new and better beginning.'

He nods and glances at me. 'Wise words, cousin.'

We walk in silence until the Courthouse steps. 'You're right, though, there are some who . . .'

Usually so sure of himself, Michael's hesitation is like a chill wind on my spine, the kind that forms in the High Alps of the Drifting Fjords and brings with it the first season's snow. 'What is it, Michael?'

'There are some who say you are not the *One*.'

I laugh dryly. 'You know I wish that were true. Perhaps those that say I'm not the *One* know something the others don't.'

Out of nowhere, he clasps an arm across my shoulder and draws me to him. 'Responsibility can be a heavy burden, Nathaneal, but you are not alone because I walk beside you wherever your duties take you, even if it's to the depths of Skade's darkest reaches. This is a vow, my fellow prince, my cousin and future king, a vow I intend to make public to you and to your endearing princess on your wedding day. Or maybe her crowning. Or your crowning. Whichever comes first,' he finishes with a smile.

I take a moment to digest this. 'Thank you, Michael.' Throwing my arm round him, we embrace with the warmth of cousins who trust each other implicitly.

And the crowd goes wild.

Their support is both humbling and mystifying. I raise my hands to both thank and quieten them, but the action only fires them up more. Their cheering grows to such an extent that several court officials appear on an upstairs balcony.

'It seems you have a welcoming party,' Michael says.

'"Welcoming" might not be the word I would use.'

'Thane, you have nothing to fear.' As an afterthought he adds, 'Remember, half the voting members are female.'

'That's not funny. I will still need the other half.'

His grin grows wider while the crowds continue to cheer. But when I step on to the first of twelve steps, the crowd's energy changes to a volatile mix of uncertainty, mistrust and fear.

Michael puts a staying hand on my forearm. I glance back to see a crowd of thousands bursting through security lines. Michael orders the nearest Thrones to eject their wings and form a circle round us while he shoots out his own wings and curves them round the two of us in a protective inner circle.

What's going on, Michael?

He's too busy to answer, but I see the truth for myself. It surprises me. Even shocks me.

Tell me, Michael, I ask, *has the commander of all Avena's armies taken a hiatus from his duties to serve as my personal body-guard? Why? Who commanded this? For your sake, I hope the pay is worth it.*

He swings round so that he's standing directly in front of me, his hands bearing down on my shoulders to stop me from moving. His eyes burn like the leaves of a liquid amber tree on fire. Around us is chaos but he doesn't seem to care. 'Listen to me, Nathaneal, being your friend, your minder, your defender, is not a chore, never has been, and no payment is involved. You are the *One* who will defeat Prince Luca, self-appointed King of Darkness, whether you choose to admit it, or not. Being commander of Avena's armies for the past three thousand years has been my training. Protecting *you* is my destiny.'

12

Ebony

Jordan stays in his room all night. I haven't seen him like this before. Sure, he's down some days, but this feels different. Before I go to bed, I fix him a sandwich with a cup of green tea and take the tray to his room.

He doesn't answer my knock. I try again and after a moment I hear his footsteps, slow and heavy, approach the door. His hair is wet and he's wearing only a pair of black boxers. Bare-chested, I can't help but notice how built he is. His frame has broadened, his shoulders widened, and his upper body is now muscular and strong. I try not to stare, but the improvements are remarkable. He watches me checking him out and the air thickens with a sultry kind of heat.

'I thought you might be hungry.' I lift the tray in my hands.

He turns away and pulls on a T-shirt.

He's sad and angry and drowning in self-pity. I place the tray down on his desk with the intention of leaving when I notice an open bottle of vodka, partially consumed. I find myself burning with a need to make Jordan better, to lift him from this downhill spiral.

He runs his fingers through his hair in an attempt to tame it, but only musses it up more. Our eyes connect. His are dark, streaked red, and filled with reckless menace. His heartbeat accelerates, and for the first time since we met he looks dangerous. Something resembling fear settles in the pit of my stomach. It stops me from instinctively taking his hand and telling him everything is going to be OK.

A better idea would be to leave.

Used to relying on my instincts, and recalling Nathaneal's advice to trust my heart, I head to the door.

He reaches it before me, and with a raspy voice, somewhat slurred from the vodka, he whispers, 'Stay for a bit?'

'I, ah . . . don't think that's a good idea.'

'No strings.' He lifts both hands into the air. 'No expectations. I could just do with some company.'

Against my better judgement, but knowing I *can't* walk away when he's pleading like this, I nod. 'OK, but only for a few minutes.'

He falls against me like a frightened child. I stroke the back of his head, smoothing down his damp hair. 'It's all right, Jordy. Everything will work out in the long run.'

He scoffs.

'Your friends didn't purposely set out to hurt you.'

'It's not . . .' He squeezes his eyes shut, takes a moment to gather his thoughts, then nods. 'I know. Sophie just got me by surprise. It was the last thing I expected. I actually thought she was gonna ask me out, like a date, you know?'

'What would you have said if she had?'

He looks straight at me. 'No, of course.'

My heart sinks.

We sit on the end of his bed side by side, my hands clasped in my lap, wondering what to say next. I have to be so careful around him, especially now when his senses are slurred by alcohol.

'Stop drowning in worry,' he says. 'I'll be all right. I'm just pissed off.'

'Danny should have had the guts to tell you himself. I didn't think he was a chicken.'

'He's not usually; he's just caught up in the spell.'

'What spell?'

Vodka stamps his face with a silly grin. 'Love.'

'Oh.'

'It makes people do strange things.'

He winds a long curl of my hair round his finger. I shift my head back and he stops. 'Jordan, I want to comfort you, but I don't know how without making things worse.'

'Don't say that. Just being near me is comfort enough.'

'Listen, me being near you is counter-productive to your state of mind. Unless we can get past this problem, I'll have to keep my distance. I might even have to move back to Amber's place.'

'*No!* I couldn't stand that. Isn't it enough you'll be leaving for good one day? Besides, this is where you're safe and that tops everything.'

His whole body shudders suddenly. 'Jordan, are you all right?' I look into his eyes and search for the answer but find something else altogether. Something I'm not expecting to 'see'. I begin pulling away immediately. 'I . . . ah, I should go.'

But my hair catches on his finger and I find myself staring into his eyes again. I glimpse deeper inside his soul, or mind, or whatever this is I'm looking at. I don't usually see such vivid images and it throws me at first, makes me want to look deeper. His heart is a hollow well with a boundless capacity for love, a love he needs returned to feel whole. But at this precise moment he has love confused with desire. I see him push me down on the bed and climb on top of me. It's such a strange feeling as I watch myself reaching my hands up into his hair, pulling his head down so his lips press into mine and ...

I blink, only to find his face right up close to mine, his dark blue eyes intense with his need to kiss me. I feel the touch of his lips on mine and I gasp. He misreads it for a moan and presses his mouth to mine. I freeze. If I pull back now, I'm afraid it will break him. But to give him hope will be wrong. Dead wrong.

Damn this Guardian bond!

It's screwing with his brain!

It's screwing with mine!

With his lips moving over my frozen mouth, oblivious to everything except his surging desire, I bring my hand up between us and apply enough pressure to separate our faces. 'I should go,' I tell him softly, wishing I could wipe from my memory the images I saw in his eyes, images that still linger in his thoughts.

'Shit. You're seeing inside my head?'

I nod.

'Oh, man. You should go. Yep, you should run.'

I tug my hair out of his hold and bolt for the door.

13

Jordan

I'm prepared to grovel, if that's what it takes for Ebony to talk to me again after last night. What have I gotta lose? My dignity? Pride? Self-esteem? I can't lose what I don't have. The deal Prince Luca manipulated me into making takes care of that.

No angel will save *my* soul when I die. They'll let the Death Watchers take me.

When Thane learns about the lies I'm going to be telling his fiancée, he'll probably hand me to a DW on a silver platter, glad to let me spend eternity in a place where souls are slaves, work hard physical labour, live in extreme temperatures and are regularly tortured.

Man, I have so much to look forward to!

I've seen Skade through my dreams, and I know what I'm seeing is real because Skinner is now in them. He starts back at school today, and I still haven't come up with anything to tell Danny and the others. I gotta check my schedule when I get up, but I have a sinking feeling I have another free period today, so I'll be meeting Skinner again to update him on my progress with breaking Ebony up from Thane.

I used to love my free periods. Now they're just another facet of my life that sucks.

After Ebony left my room last night, I wanted to sleep and forget the day I had. But when I closed my eyes I slipped straight into a dream where Skinner was waiting to take me on a guided tour.

He showed me the capital, a city of high-rise buildings with a river running through it, where the enslaved souls work for dark angels. Whatever skills the soul had when it was living stay with them when they die. If a dark angel could use your skills, you could be lucky enough to live with his or her family. But if you don't have any you get sent to one of many factories – the one kind of place you don't wanna end up.

The air in the capital stinks with the horrible stench of decaying flesh from any number of dying animals. Wild beasts, in particular, will jump off cliffs in their constant hunt for fresh food. On a calm day, the pungent odour of toxic smog settles over the city courtesy of endlessly erupting volcanoes that plague the wider landscape. Two deeply coloured moons illuminate the night with purple light, while in the daytime, if you're lucky, you might catch a glimpse of a dull red sun.

Man, I can't wait to get there. Where do I board the train?

I get outta bed and take a long hot shower. It helps my mood a bit, so I throw my uniform on and head down to the kitchen. Ebony is already there, standing at the bench wrapping a sandwich.

'I made lunch for you,' she says, handing me a bulging paper bag without making eye contact.

'Thanks.' Cautiously, I ask, 'Does this mean I'm forgiven?'
She shrugs. 'Maybe.'

'Are you saying you're OK with what happened last night?' I lean forward enough to check out her face. 'You saw things, didn't you? Things I was imagining us doing together?'

Two bright spots of colour appear on her cheeks as she looks up and our eyes fleetingly connect. 'You have quite an imagination,' she says, wrapping her sandwich for like the tenth time.

I can't believe how easy she's making this for me. No yelling, screaming or even throwing sharp implements at my head. I don't deserve her leniency. I'm the one planning to have her heart crushed. 'I'm not thinking those things all the time.'

'Whoa, that's good to know. Thank you, Jordan, I can go to school now and not think you're imagining me naked all day.'

I'm not missing the sarcasm; I'm ignoring it because I don't wanna fight and lose her friendship. And, well, when she dumps Thane, she's gonna need a friend. 'Does this mean you can read my thoughts now like Thane does?'

She waves her hand in the air dismissively and pops her lunch in her backpack. 'I wasn't reading your thoughts last night. I saw images, and I think that was because we were sitting so close together when we were . . .'

'Kissing.'

She flicks a glance at the opening to the dining room as if checking for the quickest exit. 'I was going to say "touching", but . . . look, about that . . . kiss.'

'I know. I get it. The Guardian thing.'

'It did things to your head last night, and since your mind was already pliant from the vodka . . .'

She leaves the rest hanging, but turns to me with a determined look on her face. 'I'd like to forget what happened last night.'

'Sure.' *At least she's still talking to me.* I lift her backpack from the bench, but she takes it from me. 'Ebony, can I ask you something?'

She tilts her head to the side. 'What is it?'

'Do you *really* believe you're my Guardian Angel?'

Her forehead creases as she pierces me with a hard stare. 'Where is this going?'

I woke this morning knowing only that the darker my thoughts get, the more vital my need to keep Ebony in my life, and there are two things standing in my way – Thane, who's going to have her for the whole of eternity, so why shouldn't I have her for a few years first? And the other is Prince Luca, who wants her too, and who blackmailed me into helping him.

My mother is the innocent one in the middle of all this. She's the one who's suffering right now, imprisoned in Prince Luca's palace. He gave me the chance to free her. If I break the lovebirds up my mother can be where she belongs – back on Earth, living out the rest of her life as she should.

But my love for Ebony won't let me just hand her over. So how do I break the lovebirds up – and consequently free my mum – while keeping Ebony safe from Prince Luca?

Only one solution comes to mind.

Get Ebony to fall in love with *me.*

'Is there something you should be telling me, Jordan?'

I reach for the car keys hanging on the wall. 'You know, Ebony, Thane has an amazing physical presence – *when he's here,* but without him as a constant reminder that this other dimension exists, all the supernatural stuff seems surreal. Even a tad *unreal.'*

She follows me down the hall to the garage. 'I don't know what you mean. Angels exist. That's a fact.'

I try a different approach. 'He promised he'd be back, didn't he?'

'Yeah, so?'

'I'm sure he doesn't want your memories fading to the point that *his* world feels like a dream.'

'Nathaneal will never feel like a dream to me.'

She would say that.

We get into the Lambo and when I reverse out Ebony gazes into her lap. 'I'm sorry, Jordan, I don't mean to mention his name every five minutes.'

'It's every four, but who's counting.'

We glance at each other and grin.

'Thane's absence will pass before you know it.' I really wish Thane would stay away longer. I could do with three weeks to win Ebony over. 'What about those wings of yours? Any signs they're emerging yet, 'cause that would be proof, right?'

'Wings would definitely be proof, but there's no new sign . . . yet.' She shakes her head and frowns. 'And since no one except Amber saw those first growths I can't confirm what they were. I have no evidence to take to a lab for testing.'

I throw my head back and laugh, imagining a feather in a sterile container. 'I'm not sure a lab would be helpful. But, hey, you must have freaked out when you saw them.'

'They were just bumps of tough skin. I thought I had a disease.'

'Your wings have to appear before you turn eighteen, don't they?'

'Yeah, or apparently I'll never be able to fly.'

'Living on Avena and being the only one permanently grounded, *man,* that would suck big time. Can you even make the trip through the Crossing without wings?'

'They have to put you inside a kind of bag made from impenetrable fabric they call a *lamorak* and carry you, at least until they find solid ground.' She sighs and opens her window, letting the wind blow her hair back. 'Anyway, I have heaps more training to do before I can go there.'

'Before you leave, you mean.'

'Pardon me?'

I point out the difference. 'When you say "go there" you mean "leave Earth forever".'

'That's harsh, Jordan. I could always return through the Crossing for a visit.'

'Immortals don't count time. They don't use calendars. They don't grow older than eighteen. They never look older than twenty-something. Think about it, Ebony: months, years, decades could pass that you wouldn't be aware of, up there in your love nest.'

'Jordan!'

'What? You think this is going to be easy on your friends, on your horses, on your parents when they return? When you remember to visit us mortals, we could be really old. I'll probably be dead. Amber could fall off a horse, or get cancer and die,' I chuck in for good measure.

Her eyes become stunningly violet just before she turns her face back into the wind.

I pull over to the roadside where a small parking bay gives some great valley views. We sit without speaking for a few minutes.

'That won't happen to me. I won't forget anyone.'

'You don't know that for sure.'

'And neither do you!'

She has me there. 'True. I'm just saying, look how quickly time passes for humans. Imagine how inconsequential time is for angels who live in a world where they don't even count it. You get busy with the things you have to do. Before you know it, a whole lifetime on Earth will have passed.'

She sniffs. 'Jordy?'

'Yep?'

'That won't happen with Nathaneal,' she says, trying hard to keep her voice steady, 'will it?'

'You said he loves you, right?'

'Isn't it obvious? Don't you see it when we're together?'

I shrug. 'Not really.'

Her face drops.

'But I'm not looking, you know.'

She glances in the direction of Amber's place. From here, with her amazing eyesight, she can probably make out the charred remains of her own house next door. She's been through a lot. Not just the fire but losing her parents too. I remind myself that I'm doing this for my mother. No other reason than to free Mum. And because I love Ebony, making her fall in love with me will keep her out of Prince Luca's grasp.

At least now I can tell Skinner I'm making progress with planting serious doubts in her head. Hopefully he'll get off my back for a while.

'Jordan, do *you* think I'm an angel?'

I try not to react. It's the most vulnerable I've seen her yet. But Thane will be home soon. Who knows, maybe even tonight! I can't miss any opportunity to forge a gap between them. 'Everyone makes mistakes, Ebony.' I start the engine and get us back on the road before we end up late for class.

'So you're saying Nathaneal made a mistake in thinking I'm an angel?'

I have to swallow hard not to choke on the lie that sticks in my throat. 'Well, Jezelle did bring up a valid point about your eyes not being vivid enough to be angel eyes.'

She stares straight ahead. 'I remember.'

'No one's perfect,' I add, giving her more reason to doubt herself. 'Not even angels.'

14

Ebony

My compulsory twice-a-week counselling session is so unproductive Rebecca Vaughn lets me go early rather than risk me falling asleep in the chair.

'See you on Thursday,' she says, while running her long manicured fingers across the keyboard as she sums up another dismal session in my file. 'Same time, OK?'

I pick my backpack up and head to the door. 'Sure, if I still have to?' I glance at her hopefully.

'You still have to.' She looks up. 'Ebony, you're a powder keg waiting to explode.'

'Excuse me?' She's never been this direct before. 'Rebecca, I don't feel like a powder keg.'

'And there lies the problem.'

I frown.

'You don't believe your parents died in the fire that destroyed your house.'

They didn't. But I can't exactly tell her how I know this.

'It's been months, Ebony, and until you can accept that your parents passed away –' she pauses as if she's changing her mind, tucks a stray black curl behind her ear – 'you will keep seeing me twice a week.'

I stifle a groan and open the door. Her voice stops me from escaping into the corridor. 'One more thing.' I glance over my shoulder. 'If you need to skip class again, drop in here first and let me know. I won't stop you, but we can have a quick chat, all right?'

Does nothing slip past this woman? 'It was just one class at the end of the day,' I say. 'Anyway, how did you find out? Did Mr Zavier report me?'

She adjusts her reading glasses higher up her nose, giving me a grim smile. 'It's my job. See you on Thursday.'

By the time I visit my locker, I'm late for English and walk into the middle of a lively debate about celebrity laws. Taking a seat in the middle row next to Sophie, I watch with a growing sense of disconnection until the buzzer sounds.

Third period is Physics.

Amber is waiting outside Mr Zavier's lab, the first of six in the Science Block. Sophie sees her and waves, walking straight in behind a group of five boys, seemingly in a hurry to find her front-row seat.

'Are you OK?' Amber asks. 'Shall we skip class again?'

'And have to report to Rebecca for extra counselling sessions? Thanks, but I'll pass, though it sure is nice to know you'd do that for me.'

'I'd take a bullet for you,' she says. 'And, before you say anything, I know you would for me.' I love how she trusts without having to think about it. 'Just nod or wink or something non-physical and I'll get you out, pronto.'

We walk in looking for two seats together. 'Why non-physical?'

She points to the back row. 'Because if you pinch me I'm more likely to scream than sneak us out unnoticed.'

A boy is already sitting in the corner spot. As I slide on to the middle stool I glance at the boy to say hello, and quickly have to restrain myself from choking in shock.

I swing my head to Amber, dragging my ponytail over to the side nearest the boy. A boy I never thought I'd see at this school again.

She frowns at my odd actions, so I point at the boy with my finger tucked behind my hair. Cautiously, she leans back for a peak. Even though I've tried warning her, she still gasps and calls out, 'What is *he* doing here?'

She stands up, kicking her stool over backwards. 'Sir!' It bangs against the back wall. I catch it before it falls and set it right. Everyone turns and stares at her. She realises Mr Zavier hasn't arrived yet and glances at me, uncertainty flitting across her face.

I wave with my hands to indicate she should sit down. Jordan didn't mention Adam Skinner was coming back. If anyone should know, it would be Skinner's victim. The last time I saw Skinner he left burn marks on my upper arms where he grabbed me at the bus stop. *I thought he was expelled*, I write on the inside cover of my diary, *while awaiting trial*.

Amber sits and writes underneath my words, *OMG! We have to warn Sophie and Jordan*. She stretches up to locate Sophie, spotting her in the front row, eyes riveted to Mr Zavier as he walks in and immediately starts writing on the board. *I'll text Sophie*, she scrawls.

I write underneath, *I'll do Jordan*. She reads it and giggles, so I quickly cross out 'do' and write 'text' instead.

After sending my text, I keep my phone in my hand. When Jordan's reply comes, I stare at his message in disbelief.

> Principal's office called 1st thing this morning. Skinner reinstated without privileges on bail. Charges reduced 2 Assault. Helps 2 have a criminal lawyer 4 a step-father, solicitor 4 a mother! His life is back 2 normal. Mine still sucks. C u in the break.

Adam tries to gain my attention, but I busy myself writing up the notes I missed from the last lesson that Sophie emailed Amber and me last night.

I grow nervous when Mr Zavier starts asking questions from yesterday's set homework. Shocked by Skinner's presence beside me, I haven't thought about Mr Zavier or the questions I have for him. I can't even put a name to what I'm feeling right now. My head's a mess. It's like I'm being attacked from two sides and don't know which is the more perilous.

Mr Zavier walks around the room, randomly pointing his whiteboard marker at someone for an answer. He comes down our aisle talking about how the only significant fundamental force of physics when measuring astronomical distances is gravity. Asking for the explanation, he starts to point his marker at our table. I don't want to answer his question so I don't make eye contact. The marker continues past me to Adam, who gives a perfect response, reciting the entire paragraph, word for word from the textbook that sits closed on the desk in front of him.

'Well done, Adam,' Mr Zavier says, then shifts his eyes to me and waits. I have no choice but to look at him. When I do, I'm not prepared to see his face softened with a smile. He leans in and says, 'Hello, Ebony, glad you could make it today. Would you mind staying back after class? I have something for you.'

It's not until he moves away that I remember to breathe.

When the buzzer sounds, everyone rushes to pack up for morning break. But Mr Zavier calls out for everyone to freeze. My stomach drops for no reason other than I'm suspicious of this man. 'Since I'm new to this school,' he says, 'to assist me learning your names, the seats you are in today will be your seats for the duration of this semester. You may go now.'

Amber and I groan.

We pack our things slowly since we're not rushing out with the rest. I notice Adam slide off his stool and I hold my breath while I wait for him to pass. He leans down between us. 'Hello, girls,' he says, 'I've been trying to say hello all lesson. I can't believe my luck, sitting next to you two for the whole semester. Freakin' awesome!'

'What are you doing back at school?'

He makes a clicking sound with his tongue on the roof of his mouth and doesn't answer, just looks at Amber for a long unsettling moment before he leaves.

Speechless, we stare after him as he makes his way out of the door.

Amber says, 'There's something really off about that boy.'

'If you ever find yourself alone with him, run. OK? I mean it. Run.'

'Oh, I will! But that goes double for you. If he still wants to hurt Jordan, he'll have you on his radar for sure. Principal Eckard must have reinstated him. Can you believe that?'

I show her Jordan's text, and she murmurs something inane under her breath.

As the last boy walks out, Sophie meets us halfway down the middle aisle. 'Hey, are you girls coming? I'm starving.'

I touch Amber's arm. 'Looks like Sophie didn't get your text.'

Sophie says, 'What text?'

'Why don't you go ahead and fill her in.'

Hesitating, Amber says, 'Are you sure?'

Until I know more about Mr Zavier, I don't want Amber near him more than she has to be, just by coming to class. 'I'll be fine.' She still looks reluctant to leave, so I push the two girls towards the door. 'I'll meet you at our usual table in a few minutes, OK?'

'Okaay,' she drawls in her worried voice. 'Be careful.' She hooks her arm through Sophie's. 'I got bad news for you, kiddo,' she tells her. And as they pass through the doorway I hear Amber explain how our principal reinstated Adam Skinner, and that he was sitting in the back row in class today.

Sophie shrieks and utters a few swear words at the top of her voice. But the rest of their conversation fades away because Mr Zavier walks over to where I'm standing with a document in his hand. 'Are you ready, Ebony?' he asks.

'Pardon me, sir? Ready for what?'

'The truth.'

'I'm always ready for the truth, sir.'

He smiles. 'Good answer. But are you ready to know the truth about who you are, and how you came into this world?'

Wow, straight to the point! 'How do I know that what you tell me will be the truth?'

His smile fades and he frowns. 'John and Heather Hawkins did a good job, but I'm starting to wonder if they took my meaning too literally.'

'What do you mean by that, sir?'

'When I asked your adopted parents to raise you in a manner that ensured you would not foolishly believe the first thing anyone told you, I didn't mean for you to grow into a cynical young lady, only a learned one, a girl who would ask questions, who checked her facts, and who didn't leap to unsubstantiated conclusions. There are many fraudulent scammers in the world, you see, and since I wasn't going to be around to protect you, I wanted to know you would be able to protect yourself and not be taken for a fool. I hope they taught you more than simple scepticism.'

'I had a broad range of lessons, Mr Zavier, including self-defence classes.' I let him know, in case he has some funny business planned.

'Hmm, well that is good to hear.' He holds his hand out. 'This is for you.'

'What is it?'

'A family photograph. Your mother is the one in the centre. She gave birth to you three weeks after this photo was taken.' He smiles sadly. 'Take it, Ebony.'

I take the photograph. Noticing my hand tremble, I inhale a sharp breath and remind myself how I don't really know if this is a picture of my mother. It could be anyone. Nathaneal told me that my biological mother was a tall redhead with creamy skin, purple eyes and magnificent, snow-white wings. And when she entered a room, she commanded attention not only for her beauty but also because of her mesmerising presence.

'Are you going to look at it?'

Deep in thought, I stare at him blankly.

'The photograph of Rachel.'

'Rachel?'

'That was the name of your biological mother.'

I lift the photograph to eye level. It's a colour photo of a young girl in the centre of three people, with blue eyes, brown hair, a black cap, and wearing a big shirt with buttons down the front. The young man on her right is clearly Mr Zavier, while an older, sour-looking woman is standing on her left. 'This girl is my mother?'

He nods, and that sad smile is back. 'If you want to know more of the truth, then come to my place,' he says. 'You know where I live.'

15

Jordan

The old white toilet block has one close neighbour: the windowless brick wall of the school's recently extended Drama room. There's a high set of stairs on Drama Block's southern side to access the uniform shop, which is only open in the mornings. But I still make sure no one is looking before I slip inside the hoary female toilets.

Skinner is waiting. 'You're late. I got classes too, you know.'

'So I heard. Everyone reckons it was your "connections" that got you reinstated. They're saying your mum and stepdad pulled strings – illegally. Doesn't that bother you?'

'Not at all.'

'Just because you're back doesn't mean anyone's forgotten you're guilty of murder.'

He smirks. 'They can't pin homicide on me, Jordan, because you're not dead. The fact that you weren't breathing for a few minutes doesn't count.'

'Twenty-six,' I tell him.

'*What?*'

'My heart stopped for ... never mind, what do you want?'

'Speaking of connections, have you met our new substitute teacher, Mr Zavier, yet?'

My blood runs cold. I plonk myself down on the same bench as Skinner, leaving as much space between us as I can.

'I take your reaction as yes?'

'Ebony wants to go to his house after school on Thursday.'

He smiles and stands, brushes down his trousers and makes to leave. 'Good,' he says. 'I'll want a full rundown of Ebony's reaction to what he tells her.'

'Hey!' I call out as he nears the exit. 'Who is this dude?'

'You, my friend, are on a need-to-know basis.'

'Not good enough. Amber's coming too. I gotta know if there's a chance the girls might get hurt.'

He grins. 'You got a thing for Ms Amber Lang, don't you? I gotta say, you got good taste. Amber's a beautiful girl.'

I jump up and lean over him, my fist pulled back.

He jerks his head to where I was sitting. 'Get out of my face, Jordan. Zavier's not going to hurt the girls.'

Not sure why, or even if I should, I believe him. I sit and he says, 'This isn't about Amber. This isn't even about Ebony. Where you're concerned, it's about your mother. Do as you're told, and she will return to the valley.'

'All I have to do is break up Ebony and Thane. That's it, right?'

He nods. 'That's your role. Why?' He peers at me, his dark eyes perceptive. 'Don't try to alter the plan, Jordan. It's bigger than you. It's bigger than all of us. What's happening to Ebony has been in motion for a long time. Just do your part, and there'll be minimum collateral damage.'

'Collateral damage? Is that what happened to my mother? And Ebony's parents? Or is this about Amber? If she turns out to be collateral damage, you better watch out because I'll come after you.'

'Really?' he says with a smug smirk that says he's not worried in the slightest. 'This isn't a game, Jordan. Believe it or not, I'm looking out for you.'

Laughter bursts out of me.

'Zavier is on your side, Jordan.'

'What?'

He gives me a minute to think about it. I get it in half the time. If Mr Zee convinces Ebony she's human, she'll break up with Thane pretty quick smart, and that's when I'll step in and help her put her life back together – as an ordinary human girl, falling in love with an ordinary human boy – me. Yep, that does help. By the time Ebony realises she's immortal, she'll have been my girlfriend for ages. By then Mum will be home. Dad gets outta prison in a few years, who knows what could happen?

I look across the bench to Skinner. 'What do I have to do?'

'Keep your mouth shut. Don't make it obvious you agree with Zavier, or Ebony will get suspicious of your motives.'

'Don't worry; she won't get suspicious of me.'

16

Jordan

'We shouldn't be doing this.' With Amber in the back seat reading a play for English, Ebony in the passenger seat beside me, I try to sound convincing without pushing too hard. Whatever I tell Ebony will probably not change her mind, but I can't have her figuring out whose side I'm on.

I hate the sound of that – *whose side I'm on*. I won't let Ebony get hurt. The only way Prince Luca is getting his hands on her is over my dead body. I realise I'm walking a thin line here, something like a double agent I suppose. But I *have* to do this for Mum, and eventually, when Thane's gone home to Avena and Ebony is over him, she'll turn to me for comfort, and I'll love her until my last breath.

'You don't understand,' she says. 'I'm not going to see Mr Zavier because I want to.'

'Why don't you wait until Thane gets back?'

'Jordan, I need to know *before* he returns.'

'He's not going to like this.'

'I know,' she murmurs.

'If something goes wrong, he'll hold *me* responsible. He ordered me to protect you.'

'Nothing will go wrong.'

'Yeah, well just remember the sun sets early these days and Thane wanted us indoors by nightfall just in case.'

Amber looks up from her book, meeting my eyes in the rear-view mirror. 'In case of what?'

'Dark angels and demons,' I clarify.

'Oh, right.'

'They're used to living under dark skies on Skade so when they come to Earth they find our bright sunshine intolerable.'

'There's plenty of daylight left,' Ebony says. 'Nathaneal will understand my reasons for doing this.'

'Really? What reasons?'

'If it turns out I'm not . . . of his kind, he can stop wasting his time thinking he's found his abducted angel.'

OK, she's not going to turn round with this mindset, so I can relax a little.

It takes forty minutes driving fast, longer than I was imagining. So we can't stay long, but even with this in mind, when I turn into Willow Tree Lane, I find myself cruising along in a low gear. It's the only way to take it all in – statuesque trees in deep reds and orange colours, massive flower displays and a brick-paved road all the way to black iron gates.

It screams wealth.

The girls exchange a knowing glance and a giggle at my gawking. They've been here before. I glance at Ebony. 'Your uncle is rich.'

'He's not her uncle,' Amber snaps. 'At least, we don't know that yet, so don't go jumping to conclusions, or I'll think you're more of a moron than I already do.'

'Thanks for clearing that up, Amber.'

She shrugs. 'No problem.'

Standing in front of the gates, I glance around for an intercom system, but Ebony just turns a handle and the gate swings open. Before I realise what I'm doing I grab her wrist. She looks at me, waiting for my objection, or my question, or something. 'Ah, that's the same door-handle technology Thane has at his place.'

'I know.' Her eyes look sad, and guilty, like she knows she could be walking into a trap, or taking the path to hell, but can't stop herself.

'So, Jordan, what do you reckon it means?' Amber asks once we're all through and walking along a sweeping driveway.

I shrug. 'Heaps of wealthy people probably have that technology.'

'Well, I've never heard of it,' she mutters.

'Stop worrying, you two,' Ebony says, 'I'm aware that Mr Zavier could be a dark angel, but it's not going to stop me hearing what he has to say. Since Mum and Dad told me they adopted me, my life has been a crazy jigsaw puzzle. I'm finding pieces in all sorts of places, and while some fit, a lot don't. But the man who owns this house is the man who brokered my adoption. He knows exactly what happened. Who I am. I will listen to his story, and then I'll try to figure out whether he's telling me the truth or not.'

'Be careful,' I warn. 'It might not be easy to tell when he's lying, and when he's not.'

She smiles at Amber, then at me. 'That's what I got you two for, isn't it? To watch my back?'

My stomach twists into a knot. 'Yeah, of course!'

She doesn't notice how uncomfortable I've grown. Her mind has already shifted. 'I want you both to listen carefully to what Mr Zavier says in case he knows something about my parents and drops a clue. I can't sleep from worrying about them, wondering where they are and if they're even alive any more.'

Tears spring to her eyes and Amber gives her a hug. 'I'll be listening, I promise,' she says. Over Amber's shoulder, she catches my eye.

'Yeah, of course. I'll be listening too.'

'The angels haven't found them yet or they'd let me know, right, Jordan?'

'Straight away.'

'It's been so long, I don't know if they ever will find them, or when they do, if it will be too late. So please, you two, will you help?'

And just like that, she melts my defences and I wanna tell her the truth about my mother and Skinner and the whole blackmail thing. But of course I can't. 'Don't worry, Ebony, I've got your back.'

She gives me a spectacular smile that has her trust in me written all over it. And I feel like the biggest bastard in the world.

17

Jordan

A paved footpath spears off the driveway, shortening the distance to the house by slicing through a rainforest instead of having to go round it. Streams trickle over rocks while lizards skitter through the undergrowth. Above us, glossy oversized foliage and colourful parrots and lorikeets fly from one tree to the next, hunting out nectar and cracking open seeds. The forest is so alive with animal sounds and the fresh smell of moist earth that it's easy to forget what we're doing here.

But once we walk out, and the house is right in front of us, our reason for being here catapults back into my brain. I glance at my watch and gawk at how much time has passed.

I pick up the pace, making the girls walk quickly to the house, a huge building made of sandstone and red brick, with multiple garage doors at the southern end and a covered veranda on three sides with white shutters on too many windows to count.

Mr Zee opens the door as soon as we step on to the veranda. Dressed casually in a navy polo-neck pullover with tan trousers and shiny black shoes, he looks more like a banker than a teacher.

It might be my imagination, but his eyes seem to linger on mine as I walk in, like he knows my life story backwards. Since he's in cahoots with Skinner, he probably does. 'We don't have much time, sir.'

Ebony flashes me a scolding look.

His eyebrows lift, then he nods, his face moving into a warm smile. 'I'm glad you told me,' he says. 'Come this way. I have tea waiting.'

He shows us into a white-tiled foyer with a high roof and an elegant, swirling staircase with polished rosewood rails, then into a living room with white leather couches set facing each other in front of a brick fireplace with a warm fire blazing.

The three of us sit on a couch together, Ebony in the middle, while Mr Zee pours steaming hot tea into delicate-looking teacups and makes small talk. He focuses on the girls, asking them how long they've known each other, have they always been friends, that sorta thing. He swings the conversation round to Ebony's missing parents, asking if she's heard anything. Then, after refilling our cups, he gets to the reason Ebony is here.

His version of Ebony's birth completely contradicts Thane's version. 'Rachel had only just turned fifteen when she discovered she was pregnant.'

Amber gasps, '*Really*? That's like me having a baby in Year Ten!'

'I was in my final year of a Bachelor of Science Degree. It was exam week of second semester with my last exam set down for the following day. Rachel wasn't due for another two weeks. She hid her pains so not to bother me while I

100

studied. The night was cold and wet, an early taste of winter. I had a fire going. When I went to start dinner she couldn't hide her pains any more, but by then it was too late. She had started bleeding and though I didn't know it then, her fate was sealed.'

The memories – if that's what they are – continue pouring out of him. 'I pulled the mattress off my bed and laid it before the fire. I called an ambulance, but a head-on collision on Mountain Way occupied both paramedic teams that night. It was going to be too long before one made it to my place.'

He looks directly at Ebony for a long moment, drawing her in, before slipping back into his story. 'You arrived drowning in a pool of your mother's blood. I severed the umbilical cord, cleaned you up a bit, slipped you inside a pillow slip and wrapped you in the first warm item my eyes landed on – my black rug. When the ambulance came it was too late for Rachel. But I wouldn't let them take you too, so I hid you in the middle drawer of a chest in the garage and told the paramedics that Rachel had given birth in the forest only moments before she staggered to my door, crying that her baby was dead. I told them, "She was shivering and bleeding terribly, so I made her as comfortable as I could, but she died soon after I called you".'

'And they believed you?' Ebony asks.

'They didn't have any reason not to. It had started raining heavily, hampering their search for a foetus. A later search proved futile.'

Amber asks, 'Why didn't you let the paramedics take the baby?'

He shifts his eyes to her. 'They would have made Ebony a state ward and I would have lost all track of her.'

'So that's why there's no record of my birth,' Ebony volunteers, sounding as if she's believing his story.

He shrugs, lifting his palms. 'I'm afraid that couldn't be helped. The truth is, Ebony, after losing Rachel, I thought your grandmother would raise you. I had to keep you out of the system to give her time to come round.'

'But she didn't, I gather,' I say.

He shakes his head.

Ebony says, 'And you were too busy.'

'Unfortunately, true. I knew as soon as I finished my degree I would be travelling, so I found you good parents who were suffering with the loss of their own newborn. As soon as I met them, I knew they were the right ones. It was important for me to keep you in the valley so whenever I returned from my trips I could see for myself you were being well cared for. I made it an adoption stipulation that you were not to leave the valley, not even for a day, until you turned eighteen. I couldn't risk coming home for even a few hours and not be able to see how you were going.'

'Ahh,' Ebony says. 'A lot of this tallies with what my parents told me, but, still, it's a lot to take in, Mr Zavier, because there's another version of my birth.'

He leans forward and looks straight into her eyes. 'I don't know what you've heard or been told, but I swear to you, Ebony, I am your uncle.'

She stares at him hard. 'So you're saying that I'm human.'

His face registers surprise. He gives a short laugh, looking puzzled and amused at the same time. 'What else would you be?'

'I don't know. An angel?' It's a gutsy thing to say. If he has any reaction, she'll register it, looking at him the way she is.

But Mr Zee's only reaction is amusement. 'Let me assure you, you were not born under a rock. I didn't find you in a cabbage patch. There is no wicked witch about to break down your door, or dwarfs with a prince in tow, waiting for you to fall asleep.'

Ebony laughs. Whether she's just being polite, or analysing his every comment, I can't say.

He smiles back gently. 'You have had a tremendous amount to deal with, but you appear to be doing very well. I want you to know I'm here for you now. My travelling days are over.'

Man, his story is convincing. He's so believable I don't know what to think. Is he an angel? Is he human? Whether it's the truth, partial truth, or total bullshit, I can't tell. Maybe because he's a teacher, or just a damn good storyteller, I don't know, but it won't take much for this dude to convince anyone his version is the truth.

Either way it doesn't matter to me – it's Ebony who has to believe this man is telling her the truth.

Maybe angels really do make mistakes.

'I'm sorry for your loss, Mr Zavier,' Ebony says.

'Thank you, Ebony, but you had the greater loss.'

She looks unsure about what he means. 'Pardon, sir?'

'You never had the opportunity to know your birth mother. You would have liked Rachel. Though she was young, she was kind and friendly and loving.'

Amber sits back, frowning. 'How old were you at the time, sir? You don't look much older than a university student, but if you were here delivering a baby sixteen years ago, that would have to make you at least –' she shrugs – 'fifty?'

He chokes on his tea. When he composes himself, he explains, 'Surely, I don't look *that* old, Ms Lang. People tell me I'm quite young-looking. I've always taken care of my skin. That might sound strange coming from a man, but you would be surprised at how many men protect their skin from the sun's damaging ultra-violet light rays. I was twenty when Rachel came to live with me. Sixteen years later, I'm still asked for ID sometimes.'

Ebony laughs. It's just a light, friendly sound, but it could mean she's softening towards him. I should be glad. Instead, I feel crummier than ever.

'You have a nice house.' Amber makes a show of appreciating our surroundings. 'You were living *here* when your sister gave birth. Alone. A uni student.' She stares at Mr Zee with her eyebrows raised.

His eyes seem to burn into hers for a moment. But she doesn't flinch and he flicks his gaze very briefly to me.

I get it. He wants me to help him with this. It turns my stomach, but I do it because I have to. 'I suppose the house was much smaller then, sir? You know, before you renovated?'

His mouth twitches with a microscopic smile. 'Yes, it was,' he says, words flowing out now as smooth as warmed syrup straight from the pan. 'My eccentric great-uncle left me this property, a mere shell of what you see today. I renovated using money I made selling off parcels of land on the riverfront.

104

'My sister was too trusting,' he continues. 'She fell in love with a boy who attended boarding school, and whose parents wanted to broaden his horizons on a working farm for six weeks. Rachel worked weekends in the supply store in the village. They met on his first day when he came to pick up provisions.'

Whether it's a load of crap or God's honest truth, Ebony is starting to lean forward more and more.

'Rachel knew she would never see the boy again once he left. He had plans to become a doctor like his grand-father. He had no mind for a pretty young country girl who dreamed of love.'

Amber catches my eye with a look that's asking for my opinion. I wish I knew what to tell her. Is he lying? I don't know! I can't say for sure! But I don't trust him. And as long as Prince Luca has my mother trapped in Skade I can't do anything to discredit Mr Zee's story. So I lean round Ebony's back and whisper, 'He sounds genuine, don't you think so?'

Amber stares at me like I'm an escapee from a mental hospital.

'They agreed they would never see each other again unless fate intervened,' he says. 'The boy was gone before Rachel learned she was pregnant.'

'How *romantic*,' Amber mutters. 'But she knew his first name, right? Even a naive fifteen-year-old would get that out of a boy she's having sex with for six weeks.'

When Mr Zee remains quiet, staring at Amber with cold eyes, Ebony sits up straighter like she's waking from a dream. 'What was his name, sir?'

He still doesn't say anything.

'What's the problem, sir?' Amber drills. 'It's a simple question.'

'Maybe Mr Zavier wants to be sure of his facts before he releases any personal information.' The words just roll out of my mouth. I don't even know where they come from. Lying isn't so hard after all. It just makes me feel dirty inside and out, like a pig rolling in mud and then eating it.

'I made a mistake once before,' he says, his gaze fixed on Ebony. 'I don't want to risk losing your trust because I didn't validate the facts first.'

'What-*ever*,' Amber mutters, stabbing me with her eyes.

'When I heard of your recent tragedy,' he says, 'I realised I needed to make contact. I never stopped thinking of you all those years. You are my niece by blood, and nothing is closer than that. I wanted to tell you everything that day we met at the burnt shell of your family home, but after seeing how distraught you were I decided to wait until you'd had time to adjust to your situation. In an attempt to set things right between us, I promise you that I am going to find your biological father, regardless of how long it takes.'

'Really?' Ebony says.

'Please feel free to call me "Uncle", except in the class-room,' he adds, smiling with just the right degree of compassion.

This dude is smooth. But time is getting away from us. I tug on Ebony's arm and point to my watch. 'We should get going.'

She glances outside and frowns. 'OK, but, um, I haven't asked my questions yet. A few more minutes won't hurt, will it?'

'It's winter. Today is shorter than yesterday.'

'I won't say a word if you speed all the way home.'

I scoff at this. Ebony is a speed freak. She begs me to drive faster. Amber, on the other hand, *will* freak and I sure don't want to be driving home with *her* screaming in my ear. 'It's not *you* I'm worried about.'

She flicks Amber a look, smiling to herself.

I take Ebony's hand to tug her up, when I notice the picture. She holds it out for us to see. It's a photo of three people. The older woman looks constipated. The girl in the middle bears a strong resemblance to Ebony but with darker, browner hair and a big baby belly. The older boy is definitely Mr Zee.

The photo looks like the real thing. Knowing Ebony she'll test it herself. All she needs is a good microscope and she can check for things like conflicting illuminations, shadows that aren't right, pixel differences and paper aging. If it proves fake, it's the one thing that could blow Mr Zee's credibility. I doubt she'd tell him, so I bring it up myself, 'Hey, would you mind if I borrowed that photo? I won't need it for long.' I turn it over; make it look like I'm search-ing for a date or something.

'Sure,' she says.

Mr Zee catches on. 'Don't concern yourself if something happens to it, my dear, I have the original stored in my safe.'

Amber's dagger eyes shift from me to Mr Zee and back again. She must have been thinking of doing the same thing 'cause she's looking really pissed off now.

The outside light drops again and this time I grab Ebony's hand and keep it. 'We're leaving now.'

She glances through a window and jumps straight up. 'Let's go.'

Mr Zee follows us out. 'Next time you should stay for dinner.'

'Keep moving,' I whisper. 'No small talk, OK?'

On the veranda, Ebony notices thick grey clouds swooping in and looks for Amber, finding her at the door drilling Mr Zee. 'Oh-ho.'

'Keep going. I'll get Amber.'

I literally pick Amber up by the waist and drag her away in the middle of her sentence. 'Hey, moron, what's your problem? I almost caught him in a big fat lie, which is a lot more than you did in there. By the way, what were you playing at? You sounded like the devil's advocate!'

'I have to get Ebony home before dark. Nathaneal's orders.'

She hits her forehead with an open palm, making a loud smacking noise. 'Oh my God!'

As soon as we're outta Mr Zee's sight, we sprint to the car.

18

Jordan

Nobody complains at the high speed I drive on the way home. It's mostly straight road and an easy run. At the corner of Teralba and Gunalda Roads I pull up to let Amber out. She insists on walking the last one and a half kilometres to save us time, but I don't like leaving her alone on an isolated country road with sunset approaching.

She notices my hesitation and slaps the Lambo's rump with an open palm. 'Get going – you still have a mountain to climb!'

She's right. It's still ten kilometres just to the town centre before the climb up Mountain Way. Forty minutes would be a dream home run. Thane would do it in half that time, but I'm no angel with supernatural handling skills.

I keep my eye on Amber through my mirrors until she's outta sight. Ebony notices, and makes a big deal out of it. 'You're checking out Amber!'

'Don't insult me.'

'Well, what was that all about?'

'I'd do the same if I left a dog on that corner.'

She gasps and goes quiet. After a minute I shrug. 'She's your friend, that's all. Besides,' I say under my breath, 'she can't stand the sight of me.'

'I wouldn't be too sure about that,' she murmurs.

We get a good run right through to the last roundabout heading past the town centre, but as we leave the valley behind street lights flicker on. 'Shit!'

'What is it?'

'Lights.' I point them out with my chin. 'Sunset is mere minutes away.'

As always, Ebony is more optimistic. 'Nathaneal didn't say demons would come out precisely at sunset. It could be closer to midnight, or three in the morning, if at all.'

'You know, that makes sense.' The knots inside me loosen up a bit, but I still keep alert just in case.

'He was just being cautious,' she says, but her eyes remain as glued to the windows as mine do. 'You should switch our lights on now.'

But that would be admitting they're necessary, so I wait until I *really* have to.

We catch up to a struggling bus, attempting to drive up a steep incline on Mountain Way. Grey smoke pumps out of its exhausts and blows all over us each time it changes gears or accelerates.

I thump the horn. 'Move it, will ya!'

A space opens up on the passenger's side. I glance into my mirrors, then overtake the bus on the narrow shoulder. It's not a smart move. Not even legal.

But getting Ebony home fast is my only concern right now.

With a clear road in front, I breathe easier. The familiar landscape changes shape around us as shadows lengthen and darkness closes in, but we're more than halfway now, and before long I'll have Ebony tucked safely inside Thane's glass fortress. Obviously he knew what he was doing when he built that place, nestled right next door to the Holy Cross Monastery on grounds still within the monastery's protective stone walls.

Ignoring speed limits, and hazard signs warning of loose rock walls and kangaroos leaping in front of cars at dusk, I concentrate on staying on the road as every steep hill, every twisting, turning climb, brings us closer to the summit.

As we approach the turn on to Ridge Road, my heart starts slowing down and a sense of euphoria begins to kick in. I damp it down. We're only minutes away from home, but we're not there yet.

'Can you hear that?' Ebony cocks her head to one side.

'Hear what?'

It takes a few more seconds before I hear the siren. 'You gotta be kidding me.'

'It's a police car and it's moving really fast,' she says.

'Aw, crap.'

'Hey, who says they're after *us*?'

I glance at her sideways. 'With my luck?'

With her lips pressed together, she gives me a pitying smile. Damn, I hate that! I try to sound more positive. 'OK, so they're cops. Doesn't mean they're after us.'

She smiles. 'That's better.'

And, strangely, it does feel better. It's as if by saying it aloud I convince my brain to believe it. Making the turn, I slide the Lambo quickly through the gears, picking up acceleration to a hundred in just a few seconds. If cops are after us, they'll have to catch us first.

The bus driver probably called them, but I suppose anyone who saw us tearing up Mountain Way could have ratted me out.

'They're catching up.'

'I'm not pulling over. I'm taking you home.' I give Ebony an encouraging look. 'They're not going to catch us.' I see their blue lights flashing in my mirrors, but as my eyes adjust, I spot something big and dark zooming up behind them. 'What's *that*?' I peer into the rear-view mirror until my eyes blur. 'Ebony?'

'I see it.'

A shiver goes through me, leaving the hairs on both my arms standing on end. 'What in God's name *is* that?'

Ebony twists her upper body round to look through the rear window, but doesn't answer.

Impatient for her opinion, and freaking out at what *I* thought I saw, I ask again, 'Ebony?'

She slowly shifts her eyes to mine. 'I have no idea what that is.'

I look again and notice flashes of electric currents sparking here and there, like lightning bolts. 'Shit, Ebony. It's bigger and faster than anything I've ever seen move on land before that wasn't mechanical.'

'It moves like a storm cloud. The whole bottom half is a swirling tornado,' she murmurs.

'But it's not a tornado, is it?'

'No.'

I need her to say it. 'How do you know? I mean, we hear about tornadoes hitting the mountain sometimes.'

'It's not a tornado, Jordan. It's not a storm or a cloud. It's a living thing. I mean … it's breathing,' she says, looking

112

closer. 'And it has a beating heart with lungs filling up with oxygen.'

'*What?*'

She nods.

'And?'

'And I see a head with an upper body. Massive arms. Fingers. It's like it's still forming its shape.' She glances at me. 'I know. It's bizarre.'

By now the cops are so close their headlights blind my rear vision, but at the same time their lights reveal massive amounts of debris in the air. 'Could it be a demon?'

'I don't know. I've only ever seen Aracals,' she says.

I force myself to concentrate on the road. There aren't many properties up here, and once Ridge Road turns into Monastery Lane Thane's driveway will be close. I can't miss it. That would be a disaster. The monastery is approaching fast on our right, then it's Thane's place, then the national park, which is forest land all the way to the ridge's abrupt cliff end.

Ebony shields her eyes with her hand as she continues watching the strange dark force looming behind the cop car. Suddenly, she calls out, 'Go faster, Jordan.'

'What's going on?'

'Just go faster! Hurry, Jordy!'

'I'm trying! I *am*! What did you see?'

'I . . . I'm not sure.'

'I'm going as fast as I can. I don't want to miss the lane.'

'It's gaining on us. It's going to catch us!'

'*What's* gonna catch us?'

'I don't know exactly, but I'm hearing it now too. It has the roar of thunder booming out of it. And . . .'

'And what?'

She turns back fleetingly, 'The tornado half is taking the road with it, lifting it up and spitting it out in crushed pieces.' She looks back and I hear her suck in a deep gasping breath. '*Shit! No way!*'

I look into my mirror and gawk at the cop car in the air. This powerful dark force picks it up with its giant hands and holds it over the top of us. 'Are you seeing this?'

The cop car seems to hover above us, its wheels spinning in the air. 'What the hell is that thing?'

While not in slow motion, it seems like the longest few seconds of my life when the hands toss the cop car to the right. It's now I realise this force is after us. The cops were just in the way.

I blink hard to clear my eyes when suddenly Ebony screams. The cop car comes down on the right side of the road at the same time as the stone monastery walls swing into sight. We're driving so fast we pass the monastery's main buildings in a blink. But the cops don't gain control in time. The car hits the road hard, rolling twice before smashing into the wall, where it explodes instantly.

The burst of flames from the collision shoots across the road after we pass, but we don't escape the shockwave. It hits us with so much force it shoves us clear off the road. We miss the unfenced cliff edge by mere centimetres, then skid on loose gravel for about fifty metres more, before finally gaining the road again.

And now our speed has slowed to half.

Ebony checks our rear and yells, 'It's still there! It's coming after *us*!'

'*Sh-i-t!*' Like a Tsunami outta nowhere, this powerful, living, breathing force folds over the top of us.

'Floor it, Jordan! Faster! It's reaching out to pick us up!'

Our rear wheels suddenly leave the surface as the lane's top layer breaks up beneath us and the dark force catches the car's rear in its hands. And then we're being lifted into the air. 'This is not happening. It's *not* happening.'

'There!' Ebony spots the first natural marker, the tree left bare by lightning, its right-angled branches pointing to Thane's driveway.

'Good work,' I murmur, concentrating hard on turning, but the dark force is still tilting us higher.

Ebony shouts through the loudest thunder I've ever heard. 'Go, Jordan. *Go!*'

My pulse jumps as adrenalin pumps through my body. Acting on impulse, I switch off our lights. Using only the front tyres, that, incredibly, are still gripping the road, I push the power button Thane told me was for extreme emergencies only. With the steering wheel held firmly in my hands, the Lambo bursts forward at a speed that would rival a Rolls Royce jet engine, shooting flames from the rear exhausts.

The dark force drops us.

Released from its hold, our tail end drops with a grating, grinding thud just as the piano rock, the second marker signifying we're about to pass Thane's driveway, flashes into view. But with four wheels on the ground now, I finish making the turn. The gates open with the dashboard's remote-control switch, closing fast behind us.

'*Phew!*' I swing round in time to see the dark force's lower tornado half chewing up Monastery Lane as it passes Thane's property. Hopefully, it will roll right off the ridge, crash into the rocks at the cliff base far below, and die.

'Do you think it will notice we're not on the road any more?' Ebony asks.

'By then we'll be safe inside.'

'Hurry, Jordan. Please hurry.'

With no headlights, the driveway seems to take too long. We both keep checking behind us. Ebony starts to tremble. But once we hit the clearing, the house swings into sight. Ebony depresses the garage door remote switch and I drive straight in, hitting the brakes hard and stopping just in time to prevent us slamming into the opposite internal wall. I hold my breath until the garage door automatically closes behind us.

Exhausted and shaken, we sit in the dark and just breathe.

19

Ebony

We escaped death tonight because of Jordan's remarkable driving skills. But the police officers' tragedy had nothing to do with skill or lack of it. I can't see how they could have survived that explosion. They were in the wrong place at the wrong time, caught up in something bigger than them, bigger than the laws of this world. I can't help feeling responsible. Though I don't know what that dark force was, I know it was after me.

If the police come looking for answers, I'm afraid of what I will tell them.

I had dealings with detectives when my house burned down and my parents went missing. They ask the most intrusive questions, trying to catch you in a lie. I don't lie. I can't seem to even when I want to, but I learned that to tell the whole truth sometimes isn't wise, and can cause more harm than good.

There are nasty storms up here, history will attest to that, but will anyone believe a tornado touched down on Ridge Road and tore up most of Monastery Lane? Maybe the Brothers saw something that could help explain what happened.

And where is it now?

Sitting in the Lambo in the dark, locked in our own thoughts, neither of us seems in a hurry to go inside. I just saw two people slam into a wall and explode. The image will give me nightmares for a long time. 'Oh, Jordy, what a terrible thing to happen.'

'I know,' he says, his voice thick. 'Come here.' He reaches for me and I shimmy over. He cradles the back of my head with his hand, murmuring caring words and stroking my hair in a steady rhythm. After a few minutes our hearts settle down from their wild, adrenalin-fuelled ride and he pulls back to peer at my face even though it's too dark for him to really see it. He holds my face in his two hands and kisses my forehead. 'I'm so relieved. Thank God you're OK.'

It feels amazing being this close to Jordan. It's like this is what I was made for. I lay my head on his chest and he goes back to holding me and stroking the back of my head.

And for the first time since we met I'm not worried he'll misread our physical closeness for something it's not.

After what we just experienced, nobody would.

Suddenly, blinding white light floods the garage. The shock makes us jump apart. We stare out of the front windscreen where the source of this blazing light appears to be coming from, waiting in silence as it slowly loses intensity and our eyes adjust. Knowing that only an angel can make a room light up like this, my pulse races as I think for a second it might be Nathaneal.

Except the warmth and serenity Nathaneal emanates is clearly absent. Instead, an icy chill leaves my skin tingling with cold.

As soon as Jordan recognises Nathaneal's brother, Prince Gabriel, he grins and jumps out. 'Hey, dude, am I glad to see *you*.' He offers his hand. 'You have no idea what just chased us . . .'

Gabriel stares down his statuesque nose at Jordan, lips curling in a sneer, and ignores the offered hand with a look that has Jordan stopping in his tracks.

Even from here I can tell Gabriel is livid.

I suppose he would be. We didn't make it home before sunset. Before he left, Nathaneal made sure we understood how important that rule was to our safety. And now two people are dead.

I take the photograph Mr Zavier gave me, slot it inside my skirt pocket and collect our backpacks. 'Hello, Gabriel.'

He nods at me, then makes a short sharp motion with his head towards the living room. 'In there. Now. Both of you. We need to talk.'

I know Gabriel doesn't like me. He made that clear the last time we saw each other. That Nathaneal chose to stay with me on Earth only made Gabriel's aversion more obvious.

As soon as the internal garage door closes behind us, Gabriel turns on Jordan. Though he's still big, he's more slender than I remember, in figure-hugging black trousers, long grey jacket with white shirt underneath. He cuts an elegant, commanding figure, especially with his yellow hair slicked back in a ponytail at the base of his head. If he came to my school, girls would swoon; guys would step out of his way.

'Do you have any idea what you've done? How could you remain out after dark when my brother's explicit instructions were to have Ebony inside *before* sunset?'

'I know I stuffed up. I'm sorry. Gabe, I'm really sorry.'

'Nathaneal trusts you. We don't understand how or why he has such faith in a human teenager, but there you have it.'

'Gabriel, is this necessary?' I ask, but his need to reprimand Jordan has turned this angel's ears to stone.

'Is his trust in you warranted, boy? And, after what I just witnessed in my brother's own car, I need to ask you straight out –' he leans down until their faces are only millimetres apart – 'are you keeping Ebony safe *for him*?'

I thought he was a tad *too* angry. He saw Jordan and me comforting each other in Nathaneal's car. No wonder he's upset. At least *that* is a misconception I can clarify – if he'll simmer down enough to listen.

A sudden blast of hot air shoves Jordan backwards into the wall.

'Wait!'

Shocked at Gabriel's show of power, I squeeze between them. 'Gabriel, back up. Move back now!' I'm surprised when he does. '*I* pressured Jordan into driving me to my science teacher's house. Jordan knew I would go on my own if he didn't come. The whole time we were there, he was conscious of time passing. He kept reminding me of our curfew. But dark clouds swept in and there was a long path back to the car and darkness arrived sooner than expected.'

Gabriel stares at me in silence, his eyes darkening ominously like angels do when they're drawing on their powers. I force myself not to cower before his intimidating look. 'If you need to blame anyone for this terrible tragedy, Gabriel, make sure it's me. I made the mistake.'

While Gabriel continues to stare at me with unnerving silence, I search into his eyes as Nathaneal has been teaching me, but before an impression develops he looks away, shaking his head.

'I was in the Watchtower at the time,' he says. 'In their duty as Gatekeepers of the portal, the Brothers of the Holy Cross Monastery keep the Crossing entrance safe for angelic movement through the dimensions. Brother Timothy was briefing me on recent demonic activity near the portal when an undefinable energy, stronger than anything the Brothers have measured before, appeared on their radars.'

Jordan steps out from behind me. 'It came out of nowhere, Gabe, and started following us when we made the turn on to Ridge Road. It chewed up the road like a tornado with lightning bolts streaking and booming inside it. Man, it was crazy. It lifted the cop car chasing –' He stops abruptly, his eyes shifting to me.

'That police car was after *you?*'

I jump in quickly, 'We don't know that for sure.'

'When Brother Timothy pointed out that my brother's car was on the same road as an unidentifiable dark force that was annihilating everything in its path ...' He shakes his head. 'I raced outside and saw a police car exploding, with no idea what had happened to you two until you drove into the garage. And when you didn't exit immediately I didn't know what to think. Jordan's thoughts were chaotic – I couldn't make sense of them – and yours, as usual, were closed.'

'We were just taking a breath,' I explain.

His eyebrows rise, his eyes widen. 'You were taking more than a breath, my lady, unless the breaths you took were each other's!'

'You're wrong. You got this wrong.'

He laughs, mocking me. 'I saw you clutched in each other's arms, gazing in each other's eyes. I heard your whisperings and promises of love.'

'*Love?* What you saw and heard were two people comforting each other after a terrifying experience. The rest your creative mind imagined.'

His demeanour suddenly changes. He straightens his back and starts walking around me, studying me as if I'm an insect from an alien world. 'You lie, and you do it so smoothly even your micro-expressions give no clues. You don't tighten facial muscles, alter your blinking rate, or break eye contact. For an angel, that's impossible.'

'What are you saying? That I'm not an angel?'

'All I'm saying is that I'm sure of what I saw – young lovers, clasped in each other's arms. And your denial makes you a liar.'

He's so arrogant and self-assured that it will be hard to convince him of the truth. He'll tell his brother, and Nathaneal will hate me. At the least it will upset him and cause him undue worry, especially if Gabriel tells Nathaneal he caught me lying. But if I ask Gabriel not to tell Nathaneal that would look more incriminating.

'Dude, you are *so* wrong. Ebony does *not* lie.' Jordan is so angry on my behalf he may do something he shouldn't. I can't risk more people getting hurt because of me, especially Jordan.

'Arguing with Gabriel is pointless, Jordan. Don't bother. His mind is closed and there are more important things to worry about right now.' I glance up at Gabriel. 'So you saw the accident.' It's not a question, but he nods anyway.

After an awkward silence, Jordan clears his throat. 'What if it comes back? I mean we can assume this dark force is looking for Ebony, right? So do you think this house is strong enough to stop even *that* thing from getting in? I'm not saying your brother didn't do a good enough job when he built this place. We all know how strong he is, but, dude –'

Jordan is babbling. My hand wants to reach for his shoulder to calm his rattled nerves. But after Gabriel's insinuations I know how it might look and stop myself just in time.

Gabriel notices I'm struggling, however.

'A Guardian and her Charge should *never* reside together,' he snarls, his piercing eyes directed at me. 'It's unheard of! I don't know what my brother was thinking leaving a pair of teenagers alone in his house for an indefinite period,' he rants. 'As I understand, you two pleaded for the opportunity.'

'I beg your pardon?'

'You heard.'

Looking frantic, Jordan rakes his fingers through his hair. 'Dude, you got it wrong! Michael said there was no one available to stay with us and –'

'Did you inform my brother that you did not need babysitting?'

'*I* said that,' I try to explain, even though it's probably pointless. 'Nathaneal was becoming distressed.'

123

He laughs. 'That does not sound like my brother.'

My skin grows hot. Gabriel seems intent on misunderstanding everything I say. I just want this all to go away, but now Jordan won't let it drop. 'That's not how it went down. Talk to him. Thane'll tell you how Ebony offered to go testify for him, even though she doesn't have wings to survive the Crossing.'

He scrutinises me and, when he speaks, surprisingly it's without the sharp, cynical edge. 'I'm afraid humans are not known for their restraint. And you, Ebony, think like a human. Left alone together, anything could happen between you.'

But it didn't! And it wouldn't! And . . . I'm starting to think less like a human and more like an angel every day.

I want to set Gabriel straight, but if he can think this badly of me, nothing I say will change his mind. The only person that needs to know the truth is Nathaneal. And he already does.

I calm down a little at this thought. But Jordan is a long way from calming down. His face is darkening by the second. Oh, no! I hope he's not recalling his fantasy from last night. Gabriel will see it play out in his head like a movie with an 18 rating. In their role to protect humans, it's second nature for angels to tune in to human thoughts, and I'm not sure that in Gabriel's mind-frame he'll be able to tell the difference between Jordan's reality and his make-believe.

I start to feel as if my blood and sweat are mixing together, like a chemical reaction bubbling up through my pores. I clench my hands into fists but it does nothing to stop the escalation of adrenalin.

Gabriel doesn't miss the red-hot colour spreading under the skin of *my* face as well as Jordan's and, as I knew he would, he misreads it completely. He becomes livid all over again and points his finger at us. 'If either of you disrespect my brother, it won't only be my brother you will have to contend with. We are a big family and we look out for each other. Do you both understand?'

'Back off, Gabriel, nothing happened!' Jordan yells out.

'That sounds like a threat,' I murmur, fed up with Gabriel's accusation. What if Gabriel works on Nathaneal until he convinces him that Jordan and I *are* up to something? Who will Nathaneal believe, the brother he's known his entire life, or . . . ? How can Gabriel . . . *Ooh!* I can feel anger tightening the muscles of my arms.

'Are you up to the task my brother set you?' he now asks Jordan.

'Of course I *am*.'

'Do you need reminding of your agreement terms?'

Jordan's face drops. 'No. I don't.'

'We angels take our contracts seriously. Whether forged with words or signed in blood, we're honour-bound to them. There are consequences if a promise is broken. Am I making myself clear?'

'Gabe, *I get it*.'

I start to see everything through a reddening haze. As I look from Gabriel to Jordan, my eyes pass over a vase sitting on the hall table, an antique from France in potent blue that I love because it reminds me of Nathaneal's eyes.

Suddenly, the vase shatters, with pieces flying through the air and scattering halfway across the living-room floor.

When the dust settles Gabriel and Jordan are staring at me. 'Well, I didn't see that coming,' Jordan says. 'Did you, Gabe?'

Gabriel gives Jordan a withering look, lifting his hand to his forearm, where blood appears to be dripping to the floor in fat globules. 'If I did, I wouldn't be standing here plucking shards of pottery out of my arm.'

20

Ebony

Gabriel looks aghast and stares at me as if I'm that alien insect again, while Jordan just looks stunned. He lifts a hand to his brow like he does when he's thinking hard.

Ignoring Jordan until I see how hurt Gabriel is, I move towards the disgruntled angel when he lifts a hand in the air. 'It's nothing. I'm healing already.'

'Can I get you anything in the meantime, like a bandage or something?'

'I require nothing from you,' he says with forced politeness.

I head over to help Jordan clean up the shattered vase pieces. We put them in a bag that Jordan takes to the garage.

'What a shame,' I murmur, watching him walk down the hallway. 'I really liked that vase.'

'Maybe next time, my lady, you should think twice before you lose your temper.'

I spin round at Gabriel's accusation that I somehow caused the explosion, bringing my hands to my hips. The red haze is still hanging around, making my head fuzzy, and Gabriel's tone raises my frustration levels. But before I can challenge him, Jordan returns and I turn to include him in my questioning.

But as I shift my glance from Gabriel to Jordan the room swirls and the two of them swirl with it. Scraping and groaning noises sound too loud and I lift my hands to my temples.

I blink hard, trying to clear my vision of this annoying redness. 'What is going on?' I yell through the noise. 'What's happening? Why is the furniture moving? Someone tell me what is happening here!'

Finally everything stops and the room falls silent. I take a deep breath, still holding my head. Jordan's mouth is open. He sets a lamp on the ground and rushes over. 'Ebony, you should sit down.'

I would if there was somewhere to sit. I look around at a living room with furniture in complete disarray. Couches, tables, lamps, books, are all over the place.

Gabriel is staring at me again. Not only is it unsettling, it's plain rude, and I yell at him, '*What?* Why are you staring at me like that?'

I'm not used to being this angry. My whole body feels as if it's buzzing. I use my hands to try to disperse the reddish haze in front of my face, but the scraping and banging noises keep distracting me.

Suddenly strong arms swing round my waist and I'm being carried across the room at lightning speed. It's Gabriel, and just as he lowers me to the ground the chandelier shatters over the spot where I was standing.

Meanwhile, my legs want to give out and my arms feel weightless yet heavy at the same time. 'What's happening?'

Gabriel spins me round. 'Ebony, look at me.'

I lift my head to find him staring down at me, and I remember he just saved my life. 'Thank you for, you know, saving my life.'

'You're immortal, Ebony. You would have survived.' He tilts my head back with his thumb under my chin and looks into my eyes. 'Ahh! I thought so.'

'What is it?'

'Nathaneal will be thrilled when I tell him.'

'Tell him what?'

'How you redecorated his living room.'

I glance around. 'Do you think I —'

'Your powers are emerging. Now, if you could learn to harness them while maintaining a calm state of mind, we will all be safer around you.'

Is he laughing at me?

'Close your eyes,' he orders.

'Why? What are you going to do to me?'

He frowns. 'I thought my brother exaggerated your trust issues. Clearly, he underplayed.' A hint of a smile changes his face completely, banishing all the harshness.

He lifts his hand to my forehead, then lowers it over my eyes. 'Ebony?'

'Yes?'

'Breathe.'

'Oh!' I do what he says and my skin immediately begins to cool. When I open my eyes the red haze is also easing away, and I sigh with relief.

I notice Jordan tidying the living room, setting tables and chairs on their legs again. He sees me, and smiles. Except his smile looks a little sad. I don't understand. I thought he would be happier to hear I'd tapped into my powers, even though it was by accident.

'Feeling better?' he asks.

'I think so.'

He lifts a large chunk of chandelier into the air. 'It's pretty much wrecked,' he announces, collecting all the pieces and carting them to the garage to join the shattered blue vase.

Gabriel helps us reorder the room, and when we're finished he sits on a lounge chair and motions for the two of us to join him. 'We need to talk about what happened tonight. It's imperative you tell me everything so I can figure out what this entity is, and deal with it before I leave. Regarding the tragic loss of human life, there will undoubtedly be an investigation. I will do what I can to keep your names out of it. When I'm gone, you will need guards here.' He looks directly at me. 'And I don't want an argument over that.'

Sitting on the couch opposite Gabriel, I'm listening attentively, but what I really want to know is how Nathaneal is holding up, how the hearing is going and when I can expect his return. It's been several days. By now there should be some idea of when it will end. I'm dying to ask him about the message Nathaneal said he would send me at his first opportunity, and if Gabriel knows anything about my parents.

'Gabriel, do you know when Nathaneal will be coming home?'

He stiffens suddenly and closes his eyes, the livid look I saw earlier evident in the tightly clenched muscles of his unearthly-beautiful face.

When he opens his eyes a moment later, they're ice cold and staring straight at me. I hurriedly try to work out what I said to spark this reaction. But he tells me himself before I get a chance, 'My lady, my brother may not be in an ideal place right now, but he *is* home. Home in Avena.'

'Oh! Of course he is! I didn't mean ...' I don't know where to look. His eyes are too condemning.

'I know *exactly* what you mean,' he says coldly.

He might be intimidating, but I need to know how Nathaneal is and I can't let his attitude get in my way. 'Gabriel, I just want to know if he's OK. Has something happened to him?'

He pats the couch beside him, but I don't move. He reaches out, and in a swift seamless motion lifts me into the seat beside him. He's warm, strong, masculine, and so much like Nathaneal that my chest aches.

'I apologise for handling you, my lady,' he says, 'but I have to tell you something and I'd rather do it without having to reorder the room again. I simply don't have the time.'

'Okaay ...'

'Something quite mundane has come up that will retain my brother for a while longer.'

'Mundane?' I wasn't expecting that. 'For how much longer?'

'At least another week.'

'That sucks,' says Jordan. But for a fleeting moment I think I see his head nod as if he approves.

To my way of thinking there's nothing positive in this delay. Sure, somehow I'll get through another week as long

as I know Nathaneal is all right and still intends to return –
to me. 'Is he . . . um, is he ill?'

'No.'

'Is it family business?'

'I'm not playing this guessing game with you, Ebony.'

'Then tell me what's going to keep him away at least
another week? Did the hearing not . . .' My heart trips, skips
a beat, and I whisper, 'Not go well?'

'It could have gone better.'

'Don't be ambiguous with me, Gabriel. Not now.'

'He's not ill, he's not in prison – that's all you need to
know, my lady.'

That's not enough! I want to scream at him. I want to grab
him by the shoulders and shake him. Why is he being so
vague? Why can't he just tell me what's going on? 'Gabriel,
where did the court send Nathaneal?'

His soft gasp is one of surprise. Grudgingly, he says, 'The
court decided my brother needed to make retribution
for his crimes against Earth's environment and for revealing secret tactical information to the enemy. The punishment nominated meant that he would spend a minimum
of two years and no more than two hundred years regenerating the Rievre Forest, recently devastated by a cosmic
storm.'

'Two to *two hundred years?*'

'But my somewhat clever brother, horrified at the prospect of being away from *you* for that long, took it upon
himself to offer up an alternative punishment. He had some
convincing to do, and conditions to accept, but he sold the
idea to enough voting members to pass it.' He stops suddenly.

'How long will this alternative punishment take?' I press.

'Knowing my brother, he will keep going until he completes the task, or extinguishes his existence doing it.'

Did he just say 'extinguishes his existence'? Like . . . like . . . he could die?

Gabriel stretches his long legs out in front of him before he looks up again. 'I'll stay the night to deal with this dark force and ensure it doesn't return.'

Jordan asks, 'And if you can't get rid of it?'

'Let's not worry about that until we need to.'

Gabriel has succinctly changed the subject, but I need more answers. Maybe there's something in Nathaneal's message. 'Gabriel, do you have a –'

He cuts me off with an open palm in front of my face. He's so rude, but I won't get answers if I lose my temper again. 'No more questions tonight,' he says.

'But –'

'No more questions, Ebony!'

'What are you hiding from me?' I persist.

His lips purse together, his jaw clenches. 'You have a problem with trust. You might take it the wrong way.'

'Try me. Not knowing is far worse.'

'Fine. But don't come crying to me when you can't handle what I tell you.'

'Okaay.'

'Nathaneal does not want you to know.'

'Pardon me?'

'He does not want you to know what retribution the court has agreed to, or where he is going, how long it will

133

take, who is with him, or what he must do. Is that clear enough for you?'

To say I'm floored is a massive understatement. 'I don't understand. Why not?'

'All I can say is that he made me swear not to tell you the specific details of his mission. As for his reasons –' he shrugs – 'purely supposition. You will have to trust him.'

I sink into the soft couch, stifling a gasp. Why does Nathaneal not want me to know? There's only one reason I can think of. 'How dangerous is this place he's going?'

Gabriel's eyes meet mine with the directness of a challenge, like a medieval knight laying down a gauntlet. If there's one thing Gabriel *wants* me to know it's how dangerous this mission is. 'Extremely,' he says.

'Skade.' My voice is barely a whisper. 'He's going into Skade, isn't he? But why doesn't he want me to know who's going with him, or what he's going to be doing there?'

He slices the air with his arm. 'Enough! Nathaneal will be distraught when he discovers how much you dragged out of me.'

Jordan lays his hand on my shoulder. It feels good, and I don't care what Gabriel makes of this innocent comforting touch. 'He'll be all right, Ebony. It's Nathaneal. Remember how powerful he is.'

Sure, I've seen Nathaneal's powers in action. And, yes, he is *utterly* amazing. But . . . 'Whatever he's doing, Gabriel, do you believe he will be successful?'

Gabriel's face contorts with rage as he springs off the couch and stares down at me. For a moment I don't understand, but then he says, 'If you really knew my brother, if you believed in him a mere fraction of how much he believes in you, you wouldn't ask that question. Perhaps the question you should be asking is whether you are worthy of that devotion, of that irrefutable loyalty and illimitable love. If you are – indeed – worthy of him.'

21

Jordan

When my alarm goes off on Friday morning, my first instinct, other than to smash my fist into my phone, is to wonder if Gabriel is still here. A door down the hall opens and shuts. That'll be Ebony returning from her morning ride.

I swing my legs to the floor and head into the shower. It'll be a relief to know Gabriel has gone. I can't think straight when he's breathing down my neck, accusing me of not being a good enough human being, that his brother made the wrong decision giving me a second chance.

Thane treated me like an equal from the start. But with Gabriel here I can't be free with what I say to Ebony. And now she's come into some of her powers, I may have to rethink my plan. How am I meant to convince her she's not an angel when she's destroying furniture without lifting a finger?

I hate it that I might have to ask Skinner for his opinion.

Ebony is sitting at the breakfast bar with her standard muesli and orange juice when I walk into the kitchen.

'Sleep well?' I ask.

She waves her hand in the air from side to side.

'That bad, eh?'

She shrugs. She doesn't want to talk, so I set about cooking up two slabs of ham with eggs, a tomato and mushrooms. I'd never get away with this if Thane were here. Halfway through cooking she comes over for a look and turns green round the edges. 'I think you'd better sit down,' I tell her, half joking, half not. 'You look pale.'

'I don't know how you can eat those little chickens.'

I glance at my eggs, the bright yellow yolks bubbling away in hot oil. 'You do know they're not fertilised. They were never going to be chickens for real.'

'And you don't think that's a tragedy?'

'Sorry,' I mutter under my breath.

'I just prefer to eat what grows naturally,' she says.

Hmm, well, this is one area of Avenean life where she'll fit right in, not that I'm going to tell her. I need to come up with ideas on how to keep her here, not encourage her to want to live in Avena.

Plate loaded, I dig in. 'Have you seen Gabriel yet?'

'Not this morning.'

'Maybe he's gone, yeah?' I suggest hopefully through a mouthful of ham and dripping yolk. 'If we're lucky, he will have dealt with that "entity" and gone home already.'

'I hope so. The crash is all over the news this morning. Both policemen in that car last night were men with wives, families, children, parents, sisters . . .'

'Hey! I get it, Ebony.'

She stops and sighs.

137

'There was nothing we could have done for them. Even if we'd stopped to help, called Triple Zero, banged on the monastery doors, they wouldn't have made it.'

She nods, then rinses her breakfast dishes, sniffing. Damn, she's really upset over the ... I was about to say 'accident', but that's not exactly right.

She turns round and leans back on the sink. 'Will you be ready in ten ...' She stops and tilts her head.

'What is it?'

'He's still here. I can hear him.'

My appetite dwindles. I toss the last few bites into the bin and load the dishwasher.

'Morning,' Gabriel says in a tight voice as he strides into the kitchen. 'I hope you both slept well, something I didn't have the pleasure of doing.'

'How did it go last night?' Ebony asks.

He pours himself a glass of orange juice and drinks it. 'I chased that thing all the way to Alice Springs.'

'Seriously?' I ask. 'That's like a couple of thousand kilo-metres from here.'

'Did you catch it?' Ebony asks.

'No, I did not. It hid in the dunes, and just before dawn it slunk into a rock cave, one of many in an area of high cliffs and deep gorges. I checked them all and detected nothing but its odour.'

'Odour?' Ebony asks with a frown.

He turns his face to her. 'Yes, indistinguishable from rotting flesh in the putrefaction stage of decay, when gases diffuse through the body, and amines like putrescine and cadaverine are released. Dense, wet, vile, almost shockingly

138

sweet, like the vomit of a drunk, or the rancid breath of a hyena after it has gorged itself on a dead mammal.'

'*Jeez,* Gabe, I just had breakfast!'

He stops and stares at me, then goes on, 'The odour was in the air, in the soil, everywhere it had passed, making it impossible to differentiate between old and fresh scent.'

'Could you determine its composition?' Ebony asks.

'I didn't get close enough to take a sample. It fed on insects first, and then a sheep, a goat, a llama, even a camel, the poor thing.' He shudders. 'I tried to save it, but the entity had drained its blood.'

'So this "thing" eats!' Ebony gasps. 'And it drinks blood?'

Gabriel shrugs. 'It's learning how to survive in a world where it obviously doesn't belong.'

'Dude, who created this monster?'

'Jordan, that's one of many questions that still needs answering. And I can't leave you two unprotected until this force is no longer a threat.'

'Are *you* going to stay here?' Ebony sounds as if she's querying a death sentence.

'Can I trust you both to be home before sunset?'

'Of course!'

Ebony's rapid response makes me grin. 'Gabe, I'll never bring Ebony home late again. I swear, man.'

He nods. 'All right. Then I'll return at dusk each evening. From what I learned last night, this creature moves freely at night and slinks away into a cave at dawn. Like all dark creatures, it doesn't appear to tolerate sunlight.'

I collect the car keys hanging from a hook on the wall. 'Well –' I glance at Ebony – 'we should probably get going.'

'In a sec,' she says, and waits while Gabriel draws out last night's leftovers and piles them on to a plate.

He notices her watching him. 'Ebony, can I help you?'

She replies, 'Yes. Actually you can.'

Weirdly, the two stare at each other for another minute. Ebony's breathing quickens while Gabriel's slight frown deepens. 'Since I can't mind-link with you, my lady, you're going to have to say the words aloud.'

'Of course. I know that. It's just ...' She breathes in deeply, releasing it slowly. 'Did you see Nathaneal before you left?'

He puts the loaded plate in the microwave and sets it for three minutes. 'We talked. He asked me to watch over you both. I refused and he ordered me, pulling rank. He's never done that before. I wanted to be in the team he selected for his mission to Skade. Instead, he ordered me to babysit a pair of horny teenagers. So here I am.'

Whoa! No wonder he's annoyed. Youngest brother pulling his princely rank over the eldest sibling obviously hit a nerve.

'So, Nathaneal sent you.' Ebony's violet eyes burst into an amazing deep purple for a second. I wish they reacted like that when she thought of me.

'I believe we had established that already, my lady.'

'Did Nathaneal ...' she starts but stops, then blurts out in a rush, 'Did he give you a letter for me?'

He holds her gaze without speaking and across the room the air crackles with electricity. 'No. He did not.'

The microwave pings. He turns his back on her to open it, but Ebony is not having any of it. She calls out, 'Wait!'

Gabe's shoulders straighten and the muscles under his tight shirt bunch into tense knots. He turns round slowly. 'Yes, my lady?'

'It might not be a letter. I'm not sure how angels do this, so I guess it could be in *any* form,' she says, controlling her breathing as she tries to keep calm. 'Gabriel, did Nathaneal give you a message specifically for me?'

Gabe growls, the sound coming from deep inside his chest. 'If my brother gave me a message specifically for you, do you really think I'd wait until the following day to give it to you?'

'I don't know you well enough to make that assumption,' Ebony says. 'I do know that yesterday you were angry and unapproachable.' She shrugs, leaving the accusation that he might not have felt like passing on his brother's message from spite to hang awkwardly between them.

When Gabe remains silent, she picks up her backpack and storms off to the garage. The message Thane promised to send her at his first opportunity hasn't arrived. Gabe was obviously that opportunity.

Ebony gets into the Lambo and slams the door.

I jump in behind the wheel and our gazes meet. She presses her lips together as she blinks back tears. One escapes down her cheek. Then another. She swipes at them viciously with her blazer sleeve. 'Something's happened,' she says, sniffing. 'Before Michael took Nathaneal away, I was afraid that once Nathaneal returned to his homeland he would reacquaint himself with his family and friends and forget that I exist.'

'You don't know that happened.'

'I'm pretty sure it didn't,' she says. 'It's something else. I can't put my finger on it, but Nathaneal hasn't forgotten me. He nominated this particular, more dangerous mission so he could return faster.' She takes a deep breath and uncurls her fingers. 'OK, so I know he's in Skade, just not why.'

'He's doing penance for his crime of saving you, remember?'

'Yeah, but what form does this penance take, and who's with him? He hand-picked a team.' Almost as if she's reasoning with herself, she adds softly, 'Why doesn't he want me to know who his team members are?'

She lifts her eyes to me. They're so vivid, so deeply violet, if she looked into a mirror now she would never doubt her origins again. God, she's beautiful.

I notice her hands tightening and flexing. I hate seeing her like this.

And yet, I could put her mind at rest so easily. Last night in the kitchen while Gabe helped me prepare dinner, he told me that everything Thane is doing in Skade is for Ebony's sake, and that he has loved her since she was still an infant in her mother's womb. 'It's a rare phenomenon,' he'd told me. 'Some say it's a gift, or a blessing from the High King, and it only happens to those destined for greatness and eternal love.'

An image of Mum comes to mind, the one Prince Luca showed me when he came into my dream once. Mum was clearly in pain from physical and mental torture, and when our eyes connected she seemed so real she could have been right in front of me. I wanted to reach out and take that

142

pain out of her eyes. Now I know I wasn't looking into the eyes of a dead person's soul, but my living, breathing mother.

This helps me get back on track.

I start the engine, open the garage door using the remote and reverse out.

'Without knowing, my imagination is going wild,' Ebony says, and I can see she's making headway with calming her temper with deep slow breaths. 'What do you think, Jordan?'

Man, what a loaded question. If only I had a choice, but I don't. I *really* don't. I have to swallow my spit to force the lies out. 'Well, you know Jezelle is in love with him, right?'

She peers at me sideways. 'Yeah, I guess. Go on.'

I muster up an empathetic look. 'She was the first he picked for his team.'

Her face drains of colour. 'How do you know that?'

'Gabe told me in the kitchen last night. You weren't around.' I pick up pace as I drive through Thane's winding driveway, caring little for the fledgling flowers and shrubs springing up again after Thane's drying winds burned them to their roots.

'Who else?'

'That's the part I didn't want to tell you.'

'You'd better tell me now.'

'There are five more, but Thane doesn't want them to join up with him and Jez for a few days.'

'Pardon me?'

'It's like the two of them are on some secret mission together . . . or something.'

'And you're sure about this?'

I swallow deeply. 'Yep. Positive.' And then I add for good measure, 'Apparently, Jez found out that if you don't return to Avena by the time you turn eighteen the court will select someone else to be Thane's princess.'

'*What?*'

'And you know who that'll be, right?'

'Jezelle?'

I nod. 'She's already made a petition to the court and, once the voting members agree, all Jez will need is Thane's approval. That's what this secret first part of his mission is about, to work out what he's gonna do.'

'You mean, decide whether to dump me for Jezelle?'

'I'm sorry to be the one to tell you, but Gabe didn't have the guts.'

'That's why he was so vague and secretive,' she considers aloud.

'Don't tell him I told you. Ebony, you have to promise you won't mention any of this to him. You saw how angry he can get with me.'

She waves a hand in the air. 'Sure. I won't say a word.' She then looks down into her lap at fingers clutched together so tightly they're white to the bone. When she lifts her head, she stares straight ahead. Her silence and stillness is unnerving, like the instant before a grenade explodes.

Seeing her torn up like this is hard to take, especially knowing I'm responsible. I hate myself more than ever. But Ebony is gonna live forever. She'll get over this. Mum is mortal; her time will run out.

All the way to school Ebony stares at the road, hardly moving a muscle. And I can't do anything but watch because today I've done my job. When I meet Skinner in my next free period, I can report not just on how well yesterday's meeting with Mr Zee went, but also on my new plan to break the lovebirds up, and how quickly it's taking effect.

22

Ebony

It's two in the morning and I wake from another dream, gasping for breath and clutching my chest.

It's been three weeks since Jordan told me the real reason behind Nathaneal's mission. At first it shook me to my core, but I'm not going to believe it until Nathaneal tells me himself. To keep from thinking about him with the beautiful angel Jezelle, I keep busy with riding, school and training in the downstairs gym.

But it's at night that I struggle most. My dreams are becoming more realistic and vivid.

Like the one that just woke me. Prince Luca took me to his world again, this time showing me decrepit factories with broken windows. The workers were shivering human souls overlorded by dark angels and grotesque whip-wielding demons.

My thoughts go straight to Mum and Dad, wondering if they could still be alive after so much time, and if they're right now in one of those factories.

With a groan, I slide my arms into my warm white dressing gown and head downstairs to make a hot chocolate. I become aware of Gabriel's heart beating too late to turn back. Though he's still staring out of the kitchen's glass wall when I walk in, he knows I'm here, so I continue walking in and pretend his presence doesn't affect me.

He turns slowly. 'Can't sleep either, my lady?'

'I had a bad dream.'

He nods, and I fill the electric kettle with water. Only the low light over the hob is on, casting eerie shadows into the room.

I take a breath. 'Have you heard anything, Gabriel?' Not a word in three weeks is hard to take. As I wait for him to answer, the uneasy feeling in my chest sharpens to a knife point.

'I have nothing new for you, Ebony. I'm sorry.'

His eyes don't quite meet mine. Since I'm *supposed* to be able to tell when someone is lying, or avoiding or twisting the truth, by their eyes, I can only assume Gabriel's heard *something*. It might not be new, but there is definitely something he's avoiding telling me. 'Whatever it is, Gabriel, please tell me. Not knowing anything is driving me crazy.'

He studies my face as if he's deciding what and how much I deserve to know. His mouth opens as he draws in a small puff of air. 'He's travelling to Skade's darker, colder side to descend into an underground world that exists deep beneath Skade's highest mountain.'

I definitely did not want to hear *that* news. 'How will he get through the mountain? Are there roads leading down to this underground world?'

He laughs, but not to mock me. 'Ebony, like most of Skade's disagreeable landscape, this particular elevation was once a volcano. My brother and his team will find a way down through vents, pipes and tunnels carved by lava and cooled many centuries ago.'

'Sounds terribly dangerous. But I want to know –'

'It *is* dangerous, and we should leave it at that, my lady,' he says, cutting me off in the rude style to which I've become somewhat accustomed. 'Nathaneal is young but it's as if his soul is as old as our angelic beginnings, as if he has been watching, learning, preparing for his time on this Earth.'

'That's all very nice, Gabriel, but it's not telling me what I need to know.'

He takes just two strides to reach me and lean down into my face. 'What is it you want to hear? How much my brother is willing to risk so one day you may grace us with your presence on Avena?'

He begins to walk away so I grab his arm. 'You've hardly told me anything. I've heard more from Jordan.'

'Such as?'

'Please, just tell me what he's doing there.'

He says nothing, doesn't even glance at me.

'Why did the court sanction such a dangerous expedition? Why, Gabriel?'

'Because he convinced them that should his mission succeed *you* would be more willing to return home with him – that's home to *Avena*, my lady.'

Why would Nathaneal say that? 'And if I don't return to Avena with him?'

'His penance will be deemed a failure, and he will spend the next two hundred years regenerating the Rievre Forest.'

'What does this mission have to do with me? Why did

Nathaneal risk a dangerous mission on the chance I would be ready to leave Earth on his return?'

He tilts his head and his eyes bore into mine. 'Do you *really* need to ask? You know he's besotted with you.'

Gabriel doesn't think I'm worthy of the risks his brother is undertaking for me. I stare up into his face, taken back by how much he doesn't like me. Is it because he believes someone else would make a better partner for Nathaneal? Does he think I'm not beautiful enough, or smart, or . . . or powerful? Like Jezelle! The thought hits me like a brick thrown at my head.

I turn away, forgetting the boiling water, the empty mug in my hand, the tin of hot chocolate powder I just put on the bench. I need to be alone, to run to my room, to bury myself under the covers.

'Ebony, wait.' I hear Gabriel call as if from a great distance. 'He's my youngest brother and I've protected him from everything and everyone as if it were my duty or –'

He stops with an abruptness that makes me look back. He's standing utterly still, his head tilted slightly towards his left shoulder.

'What is it?'

But before he answers I hear it too – a whooshing sound around the house's front side. It turns the corner and runs down the south side. A moment later there's another. We follow the sounds with our eyes until the silvery, shadowy form of a very tall man whips past the glass wall we're standing behind, followed a second later by a female shape.

My startled gaze finds Gabriel's. 'What are they?'

The shadows flick past again, but this time they turn and disappear deep into the backyard.

Gabriel says, 'I know what they are.'

'Yes.' By now, so do I. 'The dark force, except now there are two of them.'

'So it appears.'

'Could they find a way in here?'

'The house my brother built could withstand an earth-quake. It withstood *his* power, didn't it?'

'It did,' I reply softly.

'I'm going out there. Ebony, under no circumstances are you to leave this house before sunrise, no matter what you hear or see, or how long before I return. Do you understand?'

My mouth goes dry. I nod and he releases me from his gaze. On his way through the back door he switches on the floodlights.

I watch through the windows but lose sight of him almost instantly. Then I spot him zooming across the yard so fast he's just an elongated sphere of brilliant white light. He goes straight to the yards, making my heart leap into my throat. 'Shadow,' I whisper. '*No! Please* don't hurt my horses.'

Shadow bursts through the barn doors with his mother, Lady Elsa, close behind. They jump the outer fence and cross the backyard in blind panic, galloping straight past Gabriel. I throw my hand over my mouth, biting down hard on my palm to stop myself from running out there.

Someone – some ... *thing* – is making my horses crazy with fear. Leaning my forehead against the cool glass, I splay my hands against it. Shadow stops suddenly, lifts on to his hind legs and paws the air. Lady Elsa follows, and the whites of their eyes reveal the full extent of their terror.

I can't stand it!

Not my horses! What do they have to do with any of this?

Tears begin trickling down my face. 'I have to go to them.'

Under no circumstances, Gabriel's words reverberate in my head. *No matter what you hear or see, or how long . . .* He could be standing right beside me. *Do not go outside.*

'But this is *Shadow*,' I plead with myself. 'And I have to keep Lady Elsa safe for Dad.'

I hear Jordan calling my name from his room, then his footfalls pounding the stairs. 'Ebony, have you seen what's going on out –' He stops when he sees me at the window and runs over. 'What's happening?'

'It looks like the dark force is back and has morphed into two beings.'

'*Shit!* Really? What do they look like?'

'Well, kind of like us.'

'*What?*'

'They resemble a man and a woman, very tall and fast, though still a little shadowy and fuzzy around the edges. They're as dark as ever, and lightning still streaks through them. They've made quite an evolutionary leap.'

'I'll say!'

Shadow and Elsa come back into view. They look lost, confused, terrified. Suddenly Shadow slides to a stop, raises his head high, blows smoke from his lips, and looks straight at me.

'He can see me.'

Jordan shakes his head. 'Not through this glass.'

'I'm telling you Shadow can see me.'

'And I'm telling you that's impossible.'

'Then explain *this*!' I rest my forehead on the glass again. Shadow raises his forelegs, pounds the ground, stamping hard, and starts galloping straight at me with Elsa following blindly behind. 'Oh no.'

'*Shit!*'

Suddenly Elsa squeals, baring her teeth, her gums, and the whites of her eyes. It's then I make out two figures circling her, taunting her. Shadow comes to a sliding stop, turns and starts striking the air around his mother as if he can fend off the dark forces whipping around them so fast they appear as moving shadows. They circle both horses once before Gabriel reaches them and they run off in different directions. How is Gabriel going to keep both forces away from the horses when there's only one of him?

I run for the door.

Jordan charges after me and grabs my arm. 'You can't go out there. The horses will be OK. Gabriel will take care of them.'

We hear Shadow shriek – a horrifying sound that horses almost never make. I clasp my hand over my mouth to swallow the scream lodged in my own throat. Then both horses take off on a wild gallop towards the river. 'I'm going, Jordan. I can calm them while Gabriel goes after the dark forces.'

He spins me round, putting himself between the door and me. I give him *that* look and he lifts his hands into the air. 'I know. I know you're stronger than me. Tonight you're gonna have to use that strength to get through this door.'

The fear in his eyes gives me pause, and it's in this pause I hear Shadow's frantic, distressed squeal. I rush to the window to see him galloping up from the river. 'He's coming back.'

'And Elsa's not far behind. Look,' he says.

I lean on the glass and see Shadow heading straight for me again. 'Stop, Shadow, *stop!*' But he doesn't. I step back from the glass, but he keeps coming. 'Slow down,' I whisper. 'Baby, please stop.'

'Come on, boy,' Jordan joins in.

Helpless, we watch Shadow gallop at full speed across the big yard like a bird escaping its cage for the first time. *Stop. Shadow, please stop. Please, baby, stop!*

I want to turn away, shut my eyes, save myself the pain of seeing him smash into this solid glass wall, but I can't do that to him. It would be like abandoning him when he needs me most. We're best friends who have stood by each other all our lives.

So I keep still and silent, eyes open, tears streaking down my face, and wait.

Gabriel appears in the air beside him, looking like Pegasus with his wings outstretched and radiant white light beaming out of his body. Flying alongside, he reaches his hand out and touches Shadow's neck. Immediately, Shadow begins to slow down, digging his hoofs into the ground, churning up clods of grass and soil. But he's still too close.

Jordan wraps his arms around me from behind. 'It's OK,' he murmurs. 'It's going to be OK.'

We watch together as Shadow hits the wall, his head and long neck forced sideways, his solid chest flush against the glass directly in front of us. Amazingly, as he takes a step backwards, raises and shakes his head, he appears unhurt. He blows hot air out of his lips and nose, which condenses into frost on the cold glass. I lift my hand and his eyes follow it, proof that somehow – quite inexplicably – he *can* see, or at least *feel* where I am. 'I'm here, baby. I'm here,' I croon, 'and I'm never *ever* going to leave you.'

Still holding me, Jordan murmurs, 'Don't make a promise you can't keep.'

I shake my head, fighting back another wave of tears and wishing I could rub behind Shadow's ears and put my face in his mane and smell his goodness. 'If I go anywhere I will take him with me. *That* is my promise to Shadow.'

Gabriel's still-glowing palm glides with a feather-light touch across Shadow's neck and down to his pounding heart. He's checking Shadow for injuries. His hand stays over his chest until Shadow's heart finally calms down. Then Gabriel turns to the glass wall and nods. He's OK. I release a long breath in relief.

Gabriel's impeccable white wings sway behind him as he moves to Elsa to check her out next. Seeming satisfied, he turns to face the glass once more and salutes me with two fingers to his forehead before leading the horses back to the stables.

Jordan and I sit on kitchen stools and wait for Gabriel to return. I get restless and start pacing while Jordan downs a second mug of hot chocolate.

'Gabriel was amazing tonight,' he says.

'Yeah, he was incredible.'

'Well, he is an angel.'

And it occurs to me that I am too! Somehow I just know it and this feeling is coming from somewhere deep inside my core. A red haze appears before my eyes. I try to brush it away with my hand like I would if a wad of hair fell across my eyes. But it doesn't go away.

Gabriel finally comes in. We inundate him with questions. He looks weary and lifts both hands in the air. 'As you saw, the horses were extremely disturbed, but they're fine now. They're safe.' He plonks down on to a stool opposite us. 'I'm confident the dark forces won't return tonight.'

'What happened out there, Gabriel?' I ask. 'I thought the stables were as safe as the house.'

He takes the glass of water I offer him, downs it, and motions for another.

'The internal mechanisms on all the locks were seared as if someone took a blow torch to them. I don't know how they did it, but I've changed them now so they will only open with the touch of your hands.'

'Gabriel, why would the dark forces want to hurt my horses? They were trying to lure me outside, weren't they?'

'I believe so.' Annoyingly, he doesn't elaborate.

But I need answers. 'You've been watching them for weeks now, how is it that you still know so little about them?'

'I understand your concerns, Ebony, but the best I can do right now is update the Brothers with the information I've gathered, so they can assist me in figuring this out.'

Jordan strokes my arm. 'Take it easy, Ebony. Shadow and Elsa are safe now.'

'I know that!' I practically screech at him. The red haze is turning purple at the edges and my heart is beating in overdrive. I don't like the sensations coming over me. I like to stay in control and this feels like I'm losing it. It's then I notice both Jordan and Gabriel holding on to things, while their hair whips around their faces.

On some level it should occur to me to wonder why it's windy in a house with no windows and no open doors, but I'm exhausted and don't pay the thought much attention until Gabriel walks round, turns me to face him and takes my shoulders in his hands. 'Ebony, take a deep breath. Your powers are untried. We don't know how strong you are yet, but apparently your emotions trigger them.'

'Yeah,' Jordan cuts in, 'like when you're angry and about to explode.'

'Pardon me?'

'He's right,' Gabriel says. 'Your powers could quite possibly blow this roof off.'

He's saying I made this wind happen. Just like I did a few weeks ago in the living room.

I am an angel!

And no one gets to tell me that I'm not!

OK, so I don't have wings, I'm not as tall, or as beautiful, and my eyes are pale, but I can make wind inside a closed room, I can trash a room full of furniture and I can feel something powerful brewing inside me, pushing up from the centre of my core, pulsing through my veins, and pushing at my skin with an urgent need to escape.

They're both staring at me. I probably look wild and freakish, but I don't care. I just have one thing to say to them: 'Nathaneal did not make a mistake.'

23

Jordan

Ebony is amazing. She's standing in the doorway to the dining room in the middle of a wind she created that's blowing her incredible long hair, the reddest I've seen it, around her shoulders. Her normally violet eyes are vivid purple. Her skin has a golden glow. She seems taller than usual, if that's possible. And her confidence, her self-assuredness, is stronger than I've seen it before.

She looks like a goddess.

'How do I turn it off?' she asks Gabe.

He walks up to her with a big smile on his face and lightly grips her upper arms. 'Think calm, gentle thoughts.' He shrugs. 'Think of me.'

She laughs a little, then closes her eyes, and pretty soon the wind disappears.

'Way to go!' I call out, forcing a happy grin. In reality, Ebony's surging confidence and belief in her angelic origins is bad news for me. Skinner is not going to like my next report.

I'm gonna have to change my plan – again.

'So what *are* those dark forces?' Ebony asks Gabe, oblivious to my plotting against her happiness. 'Demons?'

157

'Possibly, but they have abilities beyond what demons and even what most angels can do. They don't appear connected to Prince Luca, though I'm sure he's involved somehow. I just don't know in what way yet.'

My mood starts to plummet. I recognise the signs – a sense of approaching gloominess that descends over me like a second skin. A feeling that I'm losing control, that I can't cope, that I'm a loser, and all alone in a hostile world.

It always happens when my plans don't work out. Huh! When do they ever? 'You don't sound too sure of yourself, Gabe.'

'Unfortunately, I'm not, Jordan. What I do know is that this powerful dark force hasn't finished evolving. In only three weeks it's become two almost identical entities, and they're violent, constantly hungry, destructive, and don't belong on the Earth. Their stench is still intense but receding. And I suspect they don't feel pain.'

'So they have no weaknesses,' I snigger. 'Great.'

'Why do they radiate to me?' Ebony asks, returning to the bench to sit beside me. Her eyes narrow as she looks me over and asks softly, 'Are you OK?'

I nod while Gabe answers her question. 'I'm working on that, my lady. In the meantime you will need to be vigilant – both of you.' His eyes flick to me. 'These forces can think for themselves, and they're growing smarter every day as they become more human or angel in shape.'

He walks to the wall and peers into the yard. 'It's as if they're trying to become one of us.'

'Seriously, Gabe, that can't be good.'

'With eight billion humans to hide amongst, no, Jordan, that's not good at all.'

'What are you going to do about them?'

The angel takes a deep breath before he turns round. 'According to what I've witnessed these past weeks, taking into account how rapidly they're evolving, their indiscriminate ravaging of Earth, their increasing understanding of mortal life, the possibility of entering unnoticed into a human community one day, and the way they appear focused on Ebony –' he shakes his head – 'I'm left with only one option.'

'Destroy them!' I roar, smashing my palms together. When they both glare at me, I shrug. 'What else is there?'

'Destroying them is not a simple task, Jordan. It will require careful observation to avoid collateral damage. Angels are accountable for every act that affects human life.'

'Or its environs,' Ebony adds.

'That's right, and if we can't identify their elemental life force, we can't know what will happen when we destroy them.'

'You think they could blow up?' I ask.

Ebony suggests, 'Or leak bacteria or disease.'

'Until we know more, anything is conceivable, including the prospect that *nothing* can kill them.'

'Man!'

'Once I'm able to capture one, or take a sample of their cells, I'll know precisely what we're dealing with and how to eradicate them from this world. It's the plan that offers the most protection to humans.'

I ask, 'How long will it take to catch one?'

Gabriel scoffs, 'Finding their base is like searching for a pebble in an ocean.'

'Dude, if I can help, tell me what to do. I'm in. I'll be your assistant, whatever you want.'

Those penetrating blue eyes bore into me from across the bench. 'Until Ebony is trained to use her powers safely your job is to protect her. That's all.'

'I *know* that.' I say through clenched teeth, staring back at the angel and trying not to flinch. This cocky dude needs to reassess his attitude. It stinks.

'So what about you?' I ask. 'Can you handle these dark forces on your own?' I scoff loudly. 'No offence, Gabe, but if you can't find where they sleep, and can't keep up when they're awake, how are you going to catch them, or hold on to one long enough to extract its cells?'

The angel replies, 'Tomorrow I bring reinforcements.'

24

Ebony

The weeks pass, sometimes in a blur, other times so slowly I think time is moving backwards. Nathaneal has been gone now for seven weeks, and it's moments like this, as I look up at the stars from my bed just before dawn, that are hardest. I have to keep busy to stop from thinking about the dangerous place he's in, whether he's been hurt and suffering injuries in whatever task he is nominated to do. And the longer it takes, the more I go crazy thinking someone else is making him smile the way he used to with me, someone like the stunning angel Jezelle, the one he hand-picked first for his team.

And no matter how much I ask, Gabriel refuses to tell me anything more. When I ask about my parents, he always promises he'll let me know as soon as he has information. But there's still no word.

He's worried about the dark forces' rapid development. He says they now resemble ancient warrior angels from the first rebellion. The two figures are now four, and they've grown an exterior shell shaped to their bodies that he suspects to be titanium armour. They have gold hair. Two have bright green eyes, the other two yellow. Their skin is more natural-looking these days, but occasionally he still spots a lightning flash of raw energy.

The dark forces come to the house almost every night, and each time Gabriel chases them back to their 'base' – no longer caves around Alice Springs, but a variety of sheltered areas like caves and abandoned cottages on and around Mount Bungarra. They still move incredibly fast and have not yet adapted to moving in daylight hours, but he thinks that too will come in time.

At least for now this gives Jordan and me the freedom to be 'normal' teenagers during the day. I need this time, and I'm pretty sure Jordan does too. He's more miserable than ever lately, and whatever I try doesn't seem to help.

Gabriel is working on a plan to trap the dark forces inside one of their habitats. To help him he has enlisted soldiers from the military unit he commands. Sometimes he brings two angels to the house with him. One is his brother Jerome, the other a beautiful female named Samarial, who has amazing light-coloured eyes with just a hint of aqua, and a head of silver curls she trims every day.

I always know when the angels have had a difficult night: reports of destruction make headlines the following morning. Last week, a farmer from my old valley neighbourhood had a chunk of his cornfield destroyed. He told a reporter it was as if a herd of elephants had trampled the patch. Two nights ago, the Wheelers, who own a restaurant in Mount Bungarra's village centre, had both their guard dogs stuck in mud up to their ears after chasing four intruders into the forest. Mr Wheeler said the intruders moved 'faster than lightning'. Both dogs survived, but only because angels pulled them out and blew their airways clear.

When I return from my morning ride, I get ready for school and head down to the kitchen. Gathered around the dining table and digging in to a big dish of vegetable paella, Jerome, a slimmer, darker-haired version of his brothers, waves me over. 'This is awesome, Ebony. I love your cooking.'

Though it's still early, I'm surprised to see them here. I've grown used to their night-time comings and goings. I pour myself some muesli and juice and join them in the dining room. 'How did it go last night?'

Sami, as she has asked us to call her, sets her coffee down with long slender fingers and perfectly manicured nails. 'It was like we were chasing silver laser beams and never quite catching up.'

Gabriel explains, 'They're not slowing down, though their stench is reducing.'

'You can still smell them coming from far away.' Sami shudders, and curls flop down over her eyes. Jerome leans across to tuck them behind her ear and smile at her. She smiles back lovingly, her eyes only for him.

Gabriel groans. 'Oh, come on, you two. Anyone would think you were newly-weds.'

'How long have you been married?' I ask.

Gabriel's chest rumbles with laughter. I don't understand why until Jerome turns his head to me and says, 'Three hundred and seventy-two years, eleven months and fifteen days.'

'What, no hours?' Sami chides, running her hand over his thigh with a mischievous grin on her face. She leans in to him, and in the blink of an eye he lifts her out of her chair and on to his lap so she ends up straddling him, her long legs dangling down each side of his hips.

Gabriel clears his throat.

'Sorry, you two,' Sami cries out while scooting back into her seat.

'That's OK. I'm sorry to spoil the, um, moment.' I snag my lower lip into my mouth and bite down to stop from thinking this should be Nathaneal and me. I give myself a mental shake. 'I was just wondering . . . the dark forces seem capable of changing form and multiplying almost at will. Sometimes they're angels, sometimes humans. Now there are four. What happens if their smell disappears completely and they end up blending in with human beings in large numbers?'

I can't help fearing the possibility that they could assimilate into communities around the world. 'How would you find them?'

Gabriel reassures me: 'We won't let that happen, Ebony.'

They finish eating and clean up after themselves. I tell them not to worry about the dishes, but they insist. Once they stack and switch on the dishwasher they leave. At the front door Gabriel gives me a lingering look filled with regret. It's the same one every time, two fingers tapping his forehead in a kind of salute.

25

Nathaneal

We stop to make camp in the early hours of each third morning, packing up and taking flight again at dawn, hoping to avoid running into any dark angels, demons, aggressive beasts and hostile souls that patrol or roam Skade's less hospitable countryside.

My team of seven is the strongest I could make and I'm thankful the court gave me leeway to select my own members. I would of course go nowhere without Michael, the greatest warrior Avena has, commander of all our armies for three thousand years, presently taking time off to be my bodyguard, for want of a better description. He is always my first choice.

Then there is Isaac, who was my mentor, teacher and friend for all the years we searched together for Ebony.

Jez was my next pick. The two of us were born in the same town and grew up together, sustaining a strong friendship. But I selected her for this mission not because we're friends, and not only because she is skilled in seven different combat techniques and proven in battle, but because of her amazing healing abilities, especially with humans.

I chose Uriel next. A captain of his own unit, Uri is like

a brother to me. He is an outstanding warrior, ranking alongside Isaac and Michael. I could not anticipate conducting a mission such as this without such a powerful warrior on my team.

My final two members, Tashiel and Solomon, are non-Seraphim. Tash is from the Order of *Sensitives*. The smallest of the angelic orders, they are also visionaries, renowned for their accurate insights and predictions, but mostly for their communication skills across all species. And Sol, an extraordinarily strong warrior, on loan from the Order of Dominions, physically big soldiers with hearts rich in compassion. A Dominion would never kill for the sake of killing, as a Throne might. Sol's presence is intrinsic to the success of this mission, with links to both Earth, in his Guardian work, and Skade, where, during his search and tracking missions, he has established informants who leak information to him through mind-links.

We cross three of Skade's provinces, known to humans as continents, before we reach Mount Mi'Ocra – a volcano that has been extinct for the last hundred thousand years.

For a few hours now I have led my team in a gradual ascent, giving our lungs time to acclimatise to the thin, freezing air at this exceedingly high altitude. Usually our bodies tolerate extreme temperatures well, but Mount Mi'Ocra's elevation can cause ice to build up on our wings and freeze them even while still in motion, creating the painful and slow-healing condition of wing-burn.

Finding a safe place to camp is becoming imperative. Since crossing the Magenta Sea, we have flown over numerous mountain ranges. Without even one of Skade's moons visible tonight, and with an icy blue mist clinging to the cliffs below, it's almost impossible to make out a suitable landscape.

The volcano that formed Mount Mi'Ocra erupted only once in its history — its birth. The eruption churned out sulphur, ash and magma for many centuries. As the vast amounts of molten rock cooled, rugged basalt ridges formed, with channels that led to surface vents from which endless streams of water and mud carved pathways, circumnavigating the volcano from top to bottom. These circling paths formed a maze. For thousands of years the Dark Prince used the maze to punish souls. There are stories of souls who spend unending years searching for an exit, or a loved one.

Flying in our usual arrow formation, the seven of us scour the snow-covered cliffs below for a suitable area wide enough to set up our camp of two tents. *Solomon, do you see anything?*

Nothing yet, my honourable lord and prince.

Sol, must you?

Sorry, my prince. I mean . . . what am I supposed to call you? Sunshine?

Jez laughs bitterly. *I wouldn't try that one, if I were you.*

Thanks for the heads-up, beautiful.

Or that *one on me,* she snaps, all humour voided. *Where did you learn your manners, soldier boy?*

Excuse me, darling, for not attending that fancy-pants Seraphim School you all did. I'm just your regular low-life GA, blessed with a warrior's body and endowed with tracking skills everyone wishes they had.

Michael makes a rare scoffing sound that erupts through the team's mind-link as a bitter laugh. *There's nothing low-life about having the soul of a human being in your care.*

Thanks, Michael, but that only relates to Guardians who don't *fail.*

That you still mourn your one *loss shows the true quality of your heart, Solomon,* Michael says. *With hindsight we all have something in our pasts we would have handled differently. I know I have.*

I really don't want to stop this conversation, but finding a campsite soon is becoming vital. *Listen, everyone, I'm sorry to interrupt, but our immediate priority is finding a place to camp for a few hours before tackling the summit. I need you all to focus on this.*

There, Solomon calls out a few minutes later, *the ledge at zero-two-hundred.*

He indicates a mantel of rock wide enough to set up at least one tent, possibly both.

I'm pretty sure that's a solid ledge.

To what degree of certainty does 'pretty sure' fall under? Jez asks.

I've seen these cliffs in the warm season, babe, Solomon says, risking his life with that last endearment.

Jez screeches through the link, *What did you just call me?*

Trust me, my prince, under that snow is a mantel of solid rock. Sorry, Jez, I thought it rhymed with Soldier Boy.

Everyone laughs, except Jez, who grumbles. Usually in this mood she would fling her shining black hair around, suffocating any male within sniffing range of the scent her hair puts out.

Isaac gets us back on track. *I think Sol's right, Thane. That ledge looks as if it's a side shoot from the main maze.*

But if we camp in the maze, Uri says, *wouldn't we be vulnerable to dog attack?*

Wherever we camp on this mountain we're vulnerable to wild dogs, Michael remarks.

We haven't encountered any yet, but their reputation is that of fierce, three-headed fighting machines that flourish on living flesh – when they can get it, and when they can't they make do with the flesh of the souls that have the misfortune of being sent to live here. Living flesh sends them into a frenzy. With luck, this blizzard weather will make them reluctant to leave their snug dens. *Take the lead, Solomon.*

He nods as he flies past me. Once in position, he banks right and slows our pace. To move too fast could shift a snow bank and cause an avalanche, threatening all kinds of creatures living in side caves and tunnels.

But Solomon guides us with expert precision, allowing just enough of his own glow to show the way.

26

Ebony

Lately, I seem to be hearing bad news or no news at all, so I'm not sure what to expect as I walk into school on Tuesday morning and Mr Zavier hails me over wearing a big cheesy grin. Amber has her ear buds in, listening to some new songs from our favourite band while texting, and doesn't notice. But on my other side, Jordan does, and mumbles, 'Wonder what he wants.'

'My soul?'

'Huh! When did you start believing you had one?'

'From my dreams,' I answer honestly. *Otherwise, how can I see the things Prince Luca shows me?* Jordan is still staring, so I shrug and brace myself as Mr Zavier wades through a group of Year Eights to get to me.

By now, Mr Zavier doesn't bother being secretive about our connection. He tells anyone who will listen, including my entire Physics class (who have no choice but to listen) and pleads with me almost every other day to call him *Uncle* Zavier, not *Mr*.

But I won't. I can't. It doesn't feel right.

So now the whole school knows how Mum and Dad adopted me after their own infant died, and that Mr Zavier is looking for my biological father.

'Ebony, I have news you're really going to want to hear,' he calls out. 'Come down to my office right away.'

I grab Amber and Jordan. When the three of us get to his office, two other science teachers are busy at their desks, so he takes us to the library where we wait in the foyer while he checks the vacancy of a conference room.

'This way. Come on. Hurry, people, I have a class first period.'

He unlocks the door to a dark room with blinds drawn, flicking on fluorescent lights as we walk in. The room is bare of furniture except for a whiteboard fixed to the wall at one end, a single desk and computer chair at the other.

Mr Zavier walks over to the desk and rests his butt on it. Still grinning, he says, 'Ebony Hawkins, today is the day.'

My heart skips a beat.

He watches me, his grin fixed in place, while I prepare for his announcement. Facing Mr Zavier on my right side, Amber tugs out her ear buds. 'What's going on, sir?'

'Well,' he pauses to look back at me, 'I have located Ebony's biological father.'

'You did *what?*' I screech. *No. No. This can't be true. I can't be human.* This thought makes my knees go weak for a second. Amber hooks her hand under my elbow, but I straighten quickly and whisper, 'I'm all right.'

'He's a doctor working in partnership with his grand-father, and you will not believe how close his practice is to where you are living these days.'

'Really?' My head starts spinning with so many thoughts at once. I don't trust this man. He's a brilliant Physics teacher, but, outside of that, I doubt everything he tells me. 'What's his name, sir?'

Before he answers he glances at Jordan, who is being strangely silent. 'His name is Dr Adrian James West, and he is willing to meet you and have a DNA test performed, as long as you are willing to meet with him for the same purpose.'

OK. Here it is. The chance to prove with *absolute certainty* what I am. I should do it, right? But . . . Nathaneal says my heart knows the truth. My heart doesn't need a DNA test to know that I have powers that humans don't. Nausea hits. I hold myself steady and just breathe for a moment. Do I have a choice but to have the test? Nathaneal deserves to know if the girl he loves is the one he's supposed to be with for eternity, doesn't he?

I take a deep breath and lift my head. 'Yes, sir, I'm willing.'

Amber and Jordan exchange a quiet glance behind my back. I only catch the end of it, so I'm not sure if they're happy for me or not.

Amber notices my confusion. 'I bet you never thought coming to school today could result in meeting your, um, possible biological father.' Her voice sounds odd, tense, like she's saying all the right words to support my decision, but they're not coming from her heart.

'Do you think I should?' I whisper.

She doesn't hesitate. 'I think you have to. Honey, even if you have only one doubt left, you need to put it to rest.'

Mr Zavier says, 'I met with Dr West last night.'

If he wanted my attention, he got it with this.

'I had to ensure I wasn't making a mistake. This is why it has taken me all these weeks to confirm the facts. I needed to be sure. You have suffered so much already, dear girl.'

Jordan rolls his eyes and crosses his arms over his chest.

I pull him aside and hiss in his ear, 'Do you think I'm doing this for fun?'

'Hell, no. I wish you didn't have to, that's all. But I agree with Amber, you need the truth and DNA will give you that.'

'So you agree I should do it.'

'Absolutely.'

I drag him further away and whisper more softly, 'You don't think this is a scam the Dark Prince concocted to have me abducted again?'

He doesn't answer right away; his frown tells me he's putting a lot of thought into it. 'You need this proof, Ebony. I'll be with you all the way. If I see anything suspicious, I'll get you out of there fast. You trust me, don't you?'

I don't know why I hesitate. Of course I trust Jordan. He and Amber are the two people I trust with my life.

'I have more news, Ebony,' Mr Zavier calls out. He waits for us to return. 'Having a sixteen-year-old daughter has understandably come as a shock to Dr West. He had no idea Rachel had fallen pregnant. And since he has a young family now, at this initial stage he would like to move forward with discretion.'

Now that I've made my decision this is disappointing. 'I understand. How long does he want to wait?'

'Oh, he doesn't want to wait. He's requested an immediate paternity test to settle the matter today.'

'*Today?*' Amber yelps, and squeezing my hand she leans over and whispers in a barely audible voice, 'Are you sure you don't want time to check Dr West out on Google first?'

'Dr West will perform the tests himself in a private consulting room at his clinic,' Mr Zavier says. 'It will be off the record so there will be complete privacy for both of you, and he will expedite the pathology, as long as you accept these terms.'

I glance at Jordan and find him staring at me with a look in his eyes that's so miserable it's like the world is ending. I haven't seen this look since the day we first met outside the nightclub Chill. 'What's wrong? Is there something you're not telling me?'

He pulls me in for a hug. 'I'm just happy for you.'

Mr Zavier says, 'Ebony, I must first assure myself this is something you positively want to do.'

I take a deep breath. 'OK. Yeah, I want to do it.'

'Do you confirm you wish to meet this man willingly?'

'Sure. I mean, yes, sir.'

'Excellent. And just to be one hundred per cent clear, do you confirm no one is coercing you into attending this meeting?'

Jordan scoffs. 'What's with the twenty questions, Mr Zee?'

Mr Zavier gives him a scathing look. 'If you don't like what you're hearing, young man, the door is over there. No one is forcing you to be here.'

They stare at each other with neither backing down. Amber whispers, 'What's with those two?'

I shrug and slide my hand into Jordan's, linking fingers. 'Relax, Jordan, it's all right.' I tell Mr Zavier, 'No one is coercing me, sir.'

Jordan squeezes my hand. 'Ebony, wait, I . . . uh . . . I gotta talk to you about this.'

Mr Zavier glares at Jordan. 'You heard my niece. Now be quiet, or leave, Mr Blake.' And to me he says, 'Since Dr West lives nearby in Ferndale —'

'Ferndale?' Amber gasps. 'That's on Mount Bungarra, on the north-east slopes.'

'That's correct, Miss Lang, about fifteen minutes by car from the monastery on Ridge Road.'

'He's *that* close?' I tug over the computer chair and flop into it.

Mr Zavier smiles down at me. 'Dr West hasn't always lived in Ferndale but his grandfather is a long-time resident of the picturesque town. It's why young Adrian West spent time in the valley. He has fond memories, especially of Rachel, his first love.'

He hurries on excitedly: 'Ebony, I took the liberty of checking your schedule for this afternoon. You have a free study period followed by double English Extension. According to your teacher you're ahead of other students and would have no problem catching up.'

He stops to give me a moment to absorb what he's saying. 'We would have plenty of time, but I suggest we leave at the start of lunch so I can return you home before your curfew.'

'How do you know about our curfew?' Jordan asks.

'The afternoon you came to my house I noticed how concerned you were with the time. And over the past

175

several weeks neither of you have attended any evening school events. I recently learned your legal guardian is overseas. That's when I figured he must have set you a curfew in his absence.'

Jordan's hand squeezing mine hasn't let up. He's starting to breathe faster too. And his heart is racing. Something isn't right. He looks . . . *tortured*. Under his breath he mutters almost soundlessly, 'What am I doing? What in hell am I doing?'

I pull him aside, giving our profile to Mr Zavier. 'Jordan, what's going on?' I whisper.

He sighs. 'Nothing.'

'That's not true.'

He laughs, or tries to, but the laugh is off. 'Ebony, you know I would never lie to you, right?'

I don't answer. I'm starting to get strange vibes from him.

'Come on,' he says. 'Let's get this trip organised. I just have one request.'

'What is it?'

'That I come with you.'

Amber hears this last part, and as we turn back she says, 'And me too.'

I put Jordan and Amber's request to Mr Zavier. He gives Jordan a long-suffering glance before he tells me, 'If you're sure this is what *you* want, Ebony, then of course your friends can come. The problem is my car seats only two.'

Jordan says, 'Then we'll go in mine. It seats four.'

'My car is specially configured for my long legs,' Mr Zavier says, searing Jordan with a fierce look. 'We will make the trip with mine.' He shifts his glance to me. 'You understand, don't you, my dear? Of course, your friends are welcome to follow.'

'Ebony rides with Amber and me,' Jordan persists.

'That's a very powerful car you drive, young man. Fast. Italian. Supercar. I would feel more comfortable if Ebony rode with me.'

'It doesn't make sense when my car can fit all of us.'

Then Mr Zavier says, 'Do you have a licence to drive that vehicle?'

'This is starting to sound like blackmail.'

'Just looking out for my niece.'

Jordan accepts the terms. 'We leave at the same time and drive in tandem.'

'Agreed,' Mr Zavier says, already rushing off to his first class for the day. 'I'll see you girls in the lab in fifth period.'

27

Nathaneal

Jez offers to take the first shift. Without waiting for my OK, she leaps on to the ledge above and disappears over the snow. About to enter a tent, Michael notices I'm not following and frowns. 'Are you coming in?'

'Soon. There's something I need to do first.'

He glances to the ledge above where the snow Jez dislodged still trickles down. 'Can I give you some advice, Thane?'

'About what, in particular?' I tease, knowing exactly what's coming.

'Fire,' he says, 'of the black-haired-turquoise-eyed kind.'

I can't help but laugh. 'You mean, Je–'

He claps his hand over my mouth, his eyes darting to the upper ledge. I continue in a mind-link. *I don't need the burning wrath of that black-haired-turquoise-eyed fireball coming down on me, thanks, cousin.*

Thoroughly amused at the Great Prince Michael, whose legend precedes him everywhere he goes, cowering at the thought of offending one young female angel, I lift my hands in the universal surrender gesture to assure him I won't mention her name aloud. *Michael, I don't need your advice on this.*

He links, *I know. I simply suggest you use a mind-link rather than a face-to-face conversation. That female Seraph sure knows how to dig her claws in.* He shakes his head and grins.

I appreciate your concern, cousin, but it's not necessary. This conversation won't take long, I assure him.

His eyes flicker to the overhanging ledge so quickly that a human being wouldn't catch the movement. *The people of Earth have a saying: if you play with fire, you will get burned.*

That happens to be true, but, Michael, fire of the black-haired-turquoise-eyed kind doesn't interest me.

Good, because I promised your red-haired-violet-eyed fiancée that I would bring you back to her in one piece.

I remember, and I can't help but smile at the memory of Ebony making Michael swear on our holy High King.

He pats my shoulder. *Remember, you need your rest too.*

As he turns to enter the tent, I can't help one last attempt to tease him. *Yes, Father.*

'You don't have to babysit me,' Jez says, by way of greeting when I return from a brief scout around and sit beside her on a rock wall covered in ice.

'That's not why I'm here.'

'Then why are you here? Can't you sleep for thinking of what your sweet little high-school girlfriend is doing to fill in her nights while you're away?'

'I came to thank you for accepting to join this difficult mission; I needed another healer on board. But if you insist on hurling your hatred of Ebony at me, I'll leave now.'

She grips my arm to stop me rising. 'Please, stay. I apologise, Thane. I'm sorry.'

'Do you even know what you're apologising for?'

'Don't get me wrong, I'm not apologising for hating *her*. Don't expect me to ever apologise for that.' Realising what she just blurted out, she closes her eyes. 'I can't help what I feel.'

'We're not made to feel hatred, but apparently *you* do.'

'What are you saying? That I'm a dark angel in disguise?'

'No, Jez, but you need to know I love Ebony. That's the way it is.'

'But, Thane, *why*? I don't understand. For all those years before I met the girl, I had images of what Ebrielle would be like, and I imagined someone stunning and talented, intelligent and suited to you in every way. But Ebony is none of those things. She's such a . . . a . . . *nothing.*' Her eyes turn to me, pleading. 'Thane, do you feel *anything* for me?'

Giving myself a moment to simmer down, I close my eyes and count. Her description of Ebony as a '*nothing*' incites rage inside me of a kind I've felt only once before, when I faced the King of Skade in battle.

I don't have time for this distraction, but I don't want to hurt Jez either. Born in the same year, same province, to parents who were best friends, we became good friends too. So, taking a deep breath, I choose my words with care. 'I have never felt for you what you wanted me to, Jez. I'm sorry that hurt your feelings.'

Looking down at her boots she whispers, 'Was it something I did?'

I peer at her sideways – and her stunning turquoise eyes flutter up at me. She has not stopped trying to get my attention since we were babes in our cribs. Intelligent, talented, a skilled healer, known across the provinces for her exotic beauty, why can't she let go of her obsession with making *me* her life partner? What is the real reason? Angels take partners for eternity. Wouldn't she want someone who wants her as much in return?

'Did I push you too hard,' she persists, 'to make you love me?'

'Yes, you did, but that's not the reason. I don't know why any of us think and feel certain ways. I only know that we do. Jez, I have loved Ebony for far longer than you can imagine.'

Her head snaps up. 'What do you mean? You only met recently.'

'She forged a mind-link with me from her mother's womb just before she was born and subsequently abducted, letting me know she was coming, that the seven years that had passed since we'd been together in Peridis were almost over and we could finally be together again, but in our corporeal bodies at last. I was so overexcited I ended up ruining everything. The time came for her birth and the midwife Myrinda, hurried me out. My fingers fumbled in the silk strands of the protective birthing chamber. One ray of light beaming out from the Lavender Forest that dark night was all it took to alert the enemy to her position.'

She inhales a sharp breath. 'I didn't know any of that.' She stares into the darkness and the swirling snow that has begun to fall again. 'You really knew her in the spirit world?'

'We were lovers for three thousand years.'

She gasps, her mouth gaping open. I lift her chin with my finger, closing her mouth with a smile. 'Are you OK,

Jez? Do you understand the torture it's been to come so close to being together again, only to have Ebony stolen and hidden away from me? I was only seven at the time, but my soul was much older.'

'Why didn't you tell anyone?'

'I wanted to tell *everyone*, to shout it from temple balconies all over Aarabyth, but the enemy took her away that night, and left behind so much grief. My father's soldiers hid in the trees not to give away the position of the birthing chamber. The enemy attacked from the sky with fire and explosives. I can still remember the scent of soldiers' flesh burning as they fell to the ground. I still see the flames corroding their wings in my nightmares.'

'So you kept it to yourself.'

'No one knows other than Ebony's parents, who still can't recall anything from that night. I suspect Michael knows something, and recently I told my brother Gabe. And now you know.'

'You must hate me!'

I take her hand and place it between my two palms. 'I don't hate you, Jez. I don't know if I can hate. But that doesn't stop me from determining right from wrong, or being able to act and make harsh decisions when they're called for. I can still get angry. From Peridis, Ebony and I saw the wars, both of angels and of men, and, unable to do anything, we wept.'

Tears flow freely down her face, freezing like twin glaciers before they fall away. I pat the top of her hand. 'Jez, I would like us to remain the friends I believe we were always meant to be, before you fell in love with my adorable eyes.'

She giggles, as I hoped she would, but her creamy skin flushing bright pink is a surprise. 'How did you know about that?'

'We're Seraphim. Our words rumbled through those school halls from one set of ears to another's without much thought for consequences in those youthful days.'

She laughs and adds softly, 'I'm sorry, Thane.'

'What for?'

'Everything,' she says, and this time, for the first time, she looks as if she truly means it. Suddenly the smile dissolves, she pulls her hand from mine, grasps the hilt of her sword and cocks her head.

What do you hear?

The wind picks up and it starts snowing heavier. She relaxes her stance slightly. 'It's just the wind.'

On our feet now, we both listen to the darkness, searching for the sound of movement. Snow whirls around us. After a while Jez sighs. 'We did have fun in those school halls.' She smiles to herself. 'It's a shame Ebony missed that.'

'Yes, it is.'

'Does she recall the mind-link she forged with you?'

I take my time answering. 'Not yet.'

'So you think she will in time?'

'I'm hoping she does.'

'And if she doesn't?'

'That will make no difference to me.'

'Thane . . .' she starts, and stops when she sees the look in my eyes.

I don't want to hear it, but until she asks she won't be satisfied. 'Go on. Spit it out.'

'Since Ebony has no memory of a vision she *supposedly* experienced, isn't it plausible the girl you found is not the infant Ebrielle sixteen years later? How do you know with certainty Ebony is the same Ebrielle you knew in the spirit world?'

I don't answer. First my brother has doubts, now Jez. I don't dare ask my *father* for his opinion.

She misreads my silence for an invitation to be candid. 'What if the real Ebrielle is still waiting for you to find her?'

'*Real, Jez? Real?*'

'What if the Ebony you found is part of an elaborate plan to keep you away from the real abducted angel?'

'Ebony is not a decoy.'

'How can you be so sure?'

'I just know, all right?'

She lays her hand on my arm as I prepare to leave. 'Think about it, Thane. Just promise me you'll think about it.'

28

Jordan

After spending my first two periods ditching classes and searching the internet on a library computer, I don't find anything that connects Mr Zee to Dr West. I find loads about Dr West, his home town, where he went to boarding school, his achievements and placements in research and medicine in Brisbane, Melbourne and London.

At least *he* looks legit.

Just before morning break I have a free period and meet Skinner in our usual disgusting conference room, but once I start asking questions about Dr Adrian West he gets in a foul mood and is no help at all. He rambles on about how behind I am on my mission. 'Get a move on,' he says. 'You're taking too long, dude.'

'I'm doing the best I can,' I shout.

He moves fast, lifts me off the ground, and shoves my back up against a timber post between stalls. 'Listen to me, Jordan, if you don't make your move on Ebony now, or tell her something that will end her relationship with the prince right away, it will be too late and your mother will rot in Skade.'

He lets me go and storms out. Shoving my hands in my pockets I stare after him, wondering what's got him all worked up. My pockets start vibrating. Strange, as I only have one phone. I pull it out and see it's not my phone at all, but both my hands trembling. I shove them back in my pockets and go to fourth period.

Before I walk into class I meet up with Danny. 'Hey, Jordy, you look like death. What's going on?'

'Long story. Don't worry about it.'

'Are you sure I can't help?'

I think about how two heads are supposedly better than one, but there's so much I haven't told him and don't have time to explain now. 'Nah, but thanks anyway.' A sense of urgency comes over me and I change my mind about going into class. 'If anyone's asking for me, tell them I'll be in the library.'

'Sure. No worries,' Danny says as he watches me leave.

Back in the library I get straight on to the internet. I research Mr Zee again, but come up empty, like he doesn't exist – in this world at least.

I have better luck with Dr West, finding an image of his wife with their two young sons. The kids look just like him, but nothing like Ebony.

All morning I've been freaking out that I'm helping Ebony fall into a trap. Skinner was no help. But there is someone who knows the truth.

It's like he's expecting me. He opens the door before I finish knocking. 'Come in, Mr Blake. Take a seat.'

Of the four science teachers that share this office, Mr Zee is the only one here. The office is a mess with over-stacked bookshelves, bags on the floor, jackets draped over chairs, computers blinking on desks, in-trays buried under piles of papers, red pens scattered everywhere.

'Nice,' I murmur sarcastically. He points to a desk in the far corner. It's Mr Zee's and it's nothing like the rest of the room. It's immaculate. Not a pen outta place. The desktop is polished timber, with a black laptop open in the centre.

I sink into his visitor's chair while he walks round to the other side, sits, closes his laptop and looks directly at me. 'Let us be civil about this,' he says in his deep, smooth, foreign accent. 'You and I want the same thing.'

'Ebony is not a "thing".'

'No, she's my niece.'

'You can turn off the bullshit now.'

He peers at me too long. 'What would you like to know, Jordan?'

'If Ebony goes with you today, will I ever see her again?'

'Straight to the point,' he says, nodding like he approves.

'Answer the question!'

But he just stares at me with his penetrating dark eyes.

'I take that to mean a big fat NO.' Pissed off, I get up to leave. 'I knew this was a trap when you made sure no one would be in the car with you except Ebony.'

Oh, man, he really is a dark angel. He really is working for Prince Luca.

'So what are you going to do?'

'What do you think? Warn the girls. Stop Ebony from going with you. It won't take much. She suspects a trap anyway.' My voice lowers with the muted sounds of my own self-contempt. 'She was only going because I assured her it was what she needed. *I* pushed her.'

'Be careful, Jordan, there are dire ramifications for breaking an angelic agreement, and you have your mother to consider.'

'Don't bring my mother into this! All I had to do to fulfil my end of the deal was break the lovebirds up. That's all. I checked with Adam Skinner. And don't try to deny the two of you are working together.'

He lifts both hands into the air like it's a done thing.

'According to angelic law, no human can be taken against their will. So how do you explain what you're doing to Ebony?'

'You're absolutely right, Jordan. But what does the law say about angels?'

Oh, shit! I take a punt, 'The same. Why would it be different?'

'With angels there are many variables.'

'Stop with the bullshit and just explain.'

'A soldier has no Free Will. They do what they are ordered. There are more angelic soldiers than any other kind.'

'But Ebony's not a soldier.' I remember how Mr Zee pressured her to say certain words this morning, and suddenly I get it. 'Why did you manipulate Ebony into saying no one was coercing her?'

'My employer is thorough. He likes to cover all possibilities.'

'Like what?'

'A defence in case the enemy suggests that since Ebony was raised human, she may have still thought like one at the time, suggesting the Free Will law should apply.'

Man, he really is thorough. What chance does Ebony have against this monster's sharp mind, or his lies?

The thought barrels into my head – she has Thane on her side. It ignites hope inside me. But who knows where he is? Or if he can even return in time?

I gotta get word to Gabe.

'Jordan, do you really think I'm going to let you go now?'

He's reading my thoughts. Shit! I should have been scrambling them. My hands tremble. I ball them into fists. I can't lose my cool now. I have to warn Ebony.

'Remember your mother is depending on you for her freedom.'

'I have until Ebony turns eighteen. *He's* the one not waiting. That's not my fault. Prince Luca can't punish my mother for changing the arrangement midstream.'

'You had months to do your part. You were naive to think he would wait more than a year. That was your mistake. You should have realised that right *now*, with Nathaneal indisposed, the timing was perfect. Remember, Jordan, you had Ebony all to yourself for weeks. Did you think we did not know that? If you could not make her fall for you in that time, it's clear you were never going to make it happen.'

'What are you saying? What happens now?'

He makes a steeple with his fingers. 'That's not up to me. Maybe there's time for the two of you to work something out. My employer is not averse to negotiating.'

'You mean, do something else for him? Work for him? And become like you, and Adam?' I wonder what hold Prince Luca has over the two of them?

He doesn't say anything but watches me carefully over the top of his fingertips.

'OK, Mr Zee, tell me this, if Prince Luca was planning to kidnap Ebony all along, why bother getting me to break her up from Nathaneal?'

'He has his reasons.'

I inch my way towards the door. 'So ... he wanted her single, unattached, maybe even heartbroken for a reason. Why? Is he worried Nathaneal can claim some form of legal rights as her fiancé? Or, isn't Luca allowed to marry Ebony if she's still engaged to someone else?'

I can tell by his darkening eyes that I'm close. 'There's an angelic law that condemns an angel from stealing another angel's future bride,' I venture. 'Especially since Nathaneal is a royal prince. Is that it?'

I feel the door handle behind me and slip my fingers round it. 'You know, it wouldn't matter if Ebony broke up with Nathaneal because *nothing* would stop him coming after her even if she walked into Skade willingly.'

With a firm grip I turn the handle, getting ready to run.

Only, when I pull, the door doesn't open. He locked the damn thing while I was talking, from the other side of the room! I spin round and he's right in my face, grabbing my arm and pulling it up behind my back.

'Did you really think I would just let you walk out of here?'

'What do you want from me?'

'Just a little more of this.'

190

'*Arghh!* Shit, man, let me go!' I bend down as far as I can to loosen his hold and make a better angle to extract my arm from his lock, but he's too strong and yanks my arm up higher. My shoulder kills. I can hardly breathe through the pain. 'You're gonna miss your favourite class,' I gasp.

'So nice of you to care, but I have that covered, just as I have your situation under control.'

'You don't have me under control. You never will.'

As if he knows my breaking point, he lifts my arm up over my head and thumps on my elbow, dislodging my shoulder. Excruciating doesn't cover it, and I scream. He covers my mouth with his hand. I bite down on it, but pain is making me weak.

He pushes my shoulder back into its socket with a click. The pain is like nothing I've felt before. I would take five broken fingers over this.

'Would you like me to do the same to your other arm? Pull out your shoulder, pop it back in again?'

'What kind of stupid question is that?'

'I can do the same with elbows, hips, ankles.' He bends my wrist and twists it. Pain burns in the joint and everything goes fuzzy like I'm about to pass out.

He stops just before I get to that point. 'Tell me now, Mr Blake, are you under my control yet?'

He tightens his grip, twisting and pulling at the same time. I swear he's wrenching my hand off my arm! 'Stop. *Stop!* I'll do whatever you say. I'll get Ebony. I'll take her to your car. Just let me go.'

'You don't have to bring Ebony to my car.'

'What? Why not?'

I catch a glimpse of a tight-lipped grimace just before his fist connects with the right side of my head. As the room spins and everything goes dark, I hear him say, 'Slight change of plans.'

29

Ebony

Sophie catches up as Amber and I cut across the seniors' quadrangle on our way to fifth period Physics. Half of Year Eleven has science next, while most of Year Ten are exiting from their fourth period in the labs.

Sophie is bursting with news. As we enter the Science Block via the middle doors, she says, 'Ms Paully's back!'

Amber flicks me a look. 'Did you know about this?'

I shake my head as I pull my backpack off my shoulder and hold it out in front of her. 'Can you take this for a sec?' An uncomfortable feeling has started up inside my ribcage.

It takes Amber like half a second to notice. 'Are you OK?'

Goose bumps break out over the smooth surface of my arms, while a swirling sense of anxiety settles in my stomach. I shake my head and she makes me sit beside her on the bench opposite our lab.

Sophie sits on my left. 'Are you feeling sick?'

My right shoulder becomes stiff and I rotate it, wondering why this is happening, when sudden, penetrating pain stabs the joint. Now I know something is going on. I turn to Sophie. 'Are you sure Ms Paully's back today?'

'Yeah, she's walking with the help of a cane, but apparently she's well enough to return to her classes.'

'That's great news,' Amber says with a smile that dims the longer she looks at my face. 'Or is it? Ebony, do you know something? Mr Zavier didn't mention this when we saw him earlier.'

'Something is going on, but I haven't figured it out yet,' I confide in her, and as my shoulder pain eases we start walking towards our lab door. Sure enough Ms Paully is inside, greeting the boys with big smiles as she waves her cane at them with a cheeky warning that makes them laugh. She looks happy to be back, but I can't shrug the feeling her return has something to do with Mr Zavier and our trip to Ferndale this afternoon. The back of my neck feels like someone is jabbing me with pins. I pull the girls over to the side before we enter. 'Have either of you seen Jordan today?'

Amber shakes her head, but Sophie says, 'Danny saw him last period. He said Jordan looked stressed.'

'Do you know where he went?' I ask.

She nods. 'Yeah, the library.'

Oh, Jordy, why didn't you come to me?

Amber grips my arm. 'What's wrong? What is it?'

'My Jordan alarm's gone off.'

'What did you say?' Sophie asks, looking worried. But then she gasps, breaking out in one of her most dazzling smiles. She's clearly jumping to the wrong conclusions. 'When did it happen? Oh my gosh! I knew it! Just the two of you in that big house together, *whoo hoo!*'

'My relationship with Jordan is *not* like that,' I clarify emphatically. 'All I mean is that I know Jordan is in trouble.'

Disappointed, she peers down the corridor. 'I'll pull Danny out of class. He'll want to help.'

I grab her arm before she takes off. 'You know what, Sophie, I remember where Jordan is now. And he's fine! Sorry I worried you. But I do need to talk to him. Would you mind taking notes for me in class today? I'm going to have to miss it.'

'Me too!' Amber quickly adds, giving me a look that warns not to even try stopping her.

'Are you sure Danny and I can't help?'

'There's nothing to worry about,' I reassure Sophie and nudge her inside before she gets a detention. 'You remember how frequently Ms Paully hands them out, don't you?'

'Oh yeah.'

As Sophie walks into the classroom, Amber and I hurry out through the front door.

'You should add acting to your growing list of angelic talents,' Amber says.

'Thanks, I'll make sure *not* to keep that in mind.'

'Where do we start? Mr Zavier's office?'

'Let's check the car parks first, starting with the hill. I think I know what's happening. Mr Zavier wanted to take me up the mountain, and now that his plan is foiled, he's using Jordan to get me there.'

'How do you know that?'

'The bond I share with Jordan tells me Mr Zavier has already hurt him and has no compunction to hurt him again to get what he wants.'

'Oh my God. So when your shoulder hurt, that was Mr Zavier hurting Jordan's shoulder? And he knew you would feel it?'

I nod, and try to explain, 'Because we're Guardian and Charge living in the same dimension, everything between us is exaggerated, and much more intense than it should be. But the feeling in the pit of my stomach is different; it makes me think Jordan is in really big trouble.'

'What do you mean? Like Mr Zavier is going to kill him and dump his body?'

'Uh ...' I shrug. My every instinct is screaming at me to hurry, that Jordan's life is in grave danger, but there's nothing to gain by scaring Amber. 'I'm new at this, Amber, so I don't really know, but I think you watch too much television.'

'You're probably right. I have another scenario to run past you.'

'Shoot.'

'Is Mr Zavier using Jordan to lure you out so he can abduct you and take you to the Dark Prince in Skade?'

'I'm pretty sure that's the case.'

'Oh my God!' She stops. 'So are we just going to walk into a trap?'

'No, of course not. I have a plan.'

'Which is ...?'

'I haven't thought it right through yet –' She gasps, but I take her hand and start moving again. 'My first step is to find Jordan and get him away from Mr Zavier.'

'And then ...?'

'That depends.'

'On what?'

'Let's just find Jordan first.'

'Ebony, I want to find Jordan too. I believe you when you say he's in trouble. But I don't want you getting hurt, and neither would Jordan.'

'I won't get hurt.'

She gives me a look like she doesn't believe me.

'All right,' I say, 'I'm going to *try my hardest* not to get hurt, but I can't turn my back on Jordan. My bond with him won't allow it. I can do this, Amber. I'm an angel, remember?' I try to reassure her with a smile.

'Yeah, well, apparently so is Mr Zavier, an evil one, and he's had a lot more practice at being one than you.'

'Amber, I totally understand if –'

'I'm coming!'

'Jeez! OK, well, they're close. I can feel Jordan's presence growing stronger the nearer we get to the hill.'

'Do we know what type of car Mr Zavier drives?'

'Only that it's small and fast. I should have asked Sophie before we left. She watched him like a hawk.' It's too late to run back to class and ask her now. Or text and get her into trouble. Ms Paully hears a phone and confiscates it on the spot.

We skirt the hill's perimeter, keeping a low profile and scanning every car we pass.

'How does it work?' Amber asks. 'You know, the bond.'

'I'm not sure.'

She gives me a puzzled stare.

I shrug. 'I'm learning as I go.'

I take her backpack in case we have to run fast. I never realised how big the school car park was until now. Does every student in Years Eleven and Twelve drive to school these days? Frustration at not finding Jordan quickly starts eating at my new-found angelic confidence.

So I stop, close my eyes and breathe, cocking my head to the side to pick up any sound that might give me a clue to his location. I hear something almost right away. It's Jordan moaning. I *feel* it, and then, amazingly, I *see* it inside my head. 'The car is green and low to the ground.' I try to zoom out like a video camera. It works, and I see the shady melaleuca and wattle trees of the far corner.

When I crest the hill, Mr Zavier is closing the driver's door of a slick green car that has part of its engine pushing up through the hood. Jordan is in the passenger seat, his head leaning on the tinted window. He touches the right side of his face and winces.

Amber drops down beside me. 'They're leaving,' she remarks.

The small green car, a Bugatti, according to the red insignia on the car's front panel, drives through the front gates, making an absurd amount of noise.

'What do we do now?' Amber asks.

I spin round and get my bearings, then reach into my pocket for my keys. I'm so glad Jordan insisted I take a car key with me everywhere I go in case we got separated. 'We're going after them.'

We dash to Nathaneal's beautiful white Lamborghini. I'm so used to Jordan driving that I inadvertently run to the passenger door before I realise where I am and run round the driver's side. Inside, I latch my seatbelt and start the engine.

Amber fumbles with her belt. As I quickly help her, she asks, 'You do know how to drive this thing, right?'

I've always found it hard to lie, even before I learned that angels find it impossible. But sometimes the truth isn't the right thing to say. 'Do you want to get out here and return to class? I completely understand if you do.'

'Thanks, but we're wasting time. Let's go. And, by the way, you didn't answer my question.'

I slip into gear and amazingly drive out of school without a hitch. I then give Amber the most confident look I can. 'I grew up on a farm, didn't I? Loads of vehicles there.'

'You still haven't answered my question.'

'OK, let me put it this way: I'm learning as I go.'

30

Nathaneal

I wake shortly before dawn with Uriel's warning resonating in my head: *Dogs coming! Large pack racing down the maze. Tash is up here with me. We will hold as best we can.*

Tugging on trousers, I'm out in an instant. The freezing air bites into my bare torso as I jump on to the ledge. Michael's a second behind me. He tosses me a jacket. 'Uri, which direction?'

As Uriel replies, I link with Isaac, Solomon and Jez: *Dogs approaching from the east on upper level. Jez, check the west end of camp and report back. Isaac, stay where you are, protect the tents and supplies. Sol, get up here on the overhang. Bring stakes.*

By now we're all hearing the thundering rumble of paws slamming into the ice, cracking and even shattering it. It's a large pack making its way around the defunct volcano, and there's no doubt the dogs are coming for us. With three heads each, their deadly multiple jaws could cause extensive damage very quickly.

Sol arrives with the stakes. He holds them up as Michael lights the tips with an arrow. We take several each and position ourselves on the path.

The dogs come to a screeching halt as they round the curve and hit our firewall. The flames won't hold them back for long, but it need do so only until our plan starts working. *Tash, any luck yet?*

Her deep frown and the struggle revealed in her eyes give me her answer – it's just not the one I want.

What should I do, my prince?

Keep trying, Tash.

But they're shutting me out and I don't know which one is the Alpha.

Three at the rear jump up on the backs of others like sheep. Two manage to hold on for a few seconds and a fight erupts. A sharp bark from the centre head of a red dog in the front row ends the squabble.

I glance at Tash and she nods. *I'll try again. But their walls are strong and their minds virtually blank.*

In a way they are blank, Michael says from my left side, as he continues jabbing his fiery stakes into the aggressive front row. *They're a pack. They don't think for themselves. They need to be led.*

Tash, I mind-link with her quickly, *I don't know how you do this with the animals on Avena or Earth, but with these beasts I suggest you forget about befriending them. Make the Alpha listen and submit to your will.*

I'm trying, Nathaneal, but the Alpha is the strongest and I can't even break through the runt's wall.

Tash, forget the runt. The Alpha is the one you need to control. She will pick up even the slightest hint of weakness.

I just think it might be better if I help fend them off.

You're a Sensitive, Tash, not a warrior. By nature, you can reach into the minds of animals and control them. That's why I wanted

201

you on my team. Don't waste a moment doing anything else. Do you understand?

Affirmative, my lord prince!

Tash . . .

I'm sorry, Thane, I'm frustrated. I'll try again.

But she doesn't get enough time before the Alpha dog suddenly howls. The unnerving sound silences the pack.

Uh-oh, Tash murmurs into our minds.

Like soldiers snapping to attention, all twenty-two dogs turn their heads to us. *Michael, suggestion?*

We don't have a choice, Thane. You know what we have to do.

No! Tash cries out. *It can't come to that.*

Just keep trying, Tash. I don't like this any more than you do.

The Alpha barks twice in rapid succession and the dogs spring into action. They lunge for the stakes, wrenching them from our hands, their movements so rapid they blur the air. Their heads swing from side to side, salivating and grunting as they shred the stakes into twigs and trample the fiery remnants into the snow.

Finished destroying the stakes, they come at us.

Everyone, lift!

For our own safety, we eject our wings and hover out of their range, though it doesn't stop the dogs from trying to reach us, gaining height with each leap.

We need to move camp, Uriel proposes.

They carry our scent now, Michael says. *As long as we're on this mountain they will chase us indefinitely.*

And prevent us from doing what we came here for, hangs in the air unspoken.

As much as what I'm about to do distresses me, I can't

come this far and abort the mission. I've been away from Ebony for too long already. At least she has my message and I take comfort from that. *Tash? Anything?*

I'm trying, Thane.

Do you have a sign? An inkling of something giving way?

She takes a moment before she answers, *Nothing.*

What about a weak spot?

I'm sorry I failed you, my prince.

You haven't failed me. I failed the dogs. And with that I reluctantly give the command to destroy them.

Michael sets three arrows in his bow then glances at me. Just as I'm about to give him the nod, the dogs figure out how to leap to our level, forcing us higher. Except Solomon isn't quick enough, and on his downbeat, his left wing drops within reach of a large brown dog. Sol shrieks as two of its heads latch on to his wing and drag him into the pack where several of them converge on him.

Tash screams. Michael shoots his arrows. Uriel and I jump into the pack's centre, reaching for our knives.

Michael's arrows strike vital arteries one after another. Defenceless as their blood empties out on the ground, other dogs begin to feed on the injured and dying. It's a horrible sight.

But a more horrible sight is Solomon, the biggest of us all, struggling to get out from under a frenzy of wild dogs. We hear his wings cracking, ligaments snapping, feathers tearing out from their roots.

With a knife in each hand we start stabbing, yanking heads back and slicing throats. Uriel severs three heads in one slash, spurting blood everywhere.

Isaac arrives with stakes. As Michael lights them, Isaac jumps into the narrow space we manage to clear around Sol. He tosses Uriel half and, while they work at widening the space around Sol, I reach down, wrap my arms around his broken body, and lift him out.

I lay him on a fresh snow bank a safe distance away from where I can still survey the situation, choosing the soft snow to cushion Sol's injuries while I heal him. Inspecting his wings, I gently tug out canine teeth caught in his feathers, counting breakages as I go. To my surprise, I come across a whole dog's head, its jaws still locked around Sol's lower arm. I find I have to cut the head completely in half before it releases its deathly grip.

Sol's left arm and both wings are a mess, jutting out at odd angles. In this freezing air, soaked in his own and several dogs' blood, his broken wings are in danger of wing-burn. Except for his damaged lower arm, his other injuries are minor enough to repair themselves unassisted, so I focus on repairing his vital wings first.

Solomon's pain is excruciating, but when he opens his eyes he doesn't do more than grimace.

Jez, take Isaac's position protecting our equipment. Let me know the instant you notice movement heading your way.

What's going on up there? Jez asks. *It sounds as if you need me. Who cares about two lousy tents? We can sleep under the stars.*

Stay where you are, Jez. That's an order.

She goes quiet, but I sense her seething at the thought that she's missing the action.

By now there are only twelve dogs left. *Prepare to destroy the Alpha*, I command.

Michael draws an arrow and locks it into place.

Tash, listen to the Alpha's voice while she has a few moments left. Imitate her tone, her nuances, even her body language. Learn her commands. Learn the eleven remaining names. They will be looking for a new leader. It's either you, or we must destroy the entire pack.

She closes her eyes. Tears trickle out that quickly turn to ice.

Michael watches Tash for a sign before shooting his arrow directly into the dog's heart. It's a quick, clean death.

Isaac sets up a fire barrier while I continue healing Sol's wings. With his strength returning, Sol sits up. 'How bad are they?'

'Relax, I could do this in my sleep,' I say, downplaying the extensive damage.

Whimpering sounds creep into my thoughts. I push them aside and concentrate on keeping Sol's wings warm while I finish healing them. It seems to take too long, but finally I'm done and help him stand. He flexes his shoulders, spreading his magnificent wings to their full width. He catches my eye and a big smile forms. 'Thanks, sunshine. I owe you one.'

'You owe me nothing. But should you call me "sunshine" once more, that's another matter entirely and we will deal with that in a boxing ring as soon as we're back on Avenean soil.'

It's then we notice the silence and turn round.

Solomon jerks at the sight. 'Is she for real?' Though impressed, he's also understandably cautious seeing Tash caressing the heads of one dog after another, crooning soothing words to them. 'What is she doing?'

We stroll over and join Michael and Isaac, who are listening with awe to Uriel as he introduces the dogs. He grins at us and continues, 'This black one with a red star on her flank is Neftah.' He moves his hand along to a big grey male he calls Kirsh. 'And these two –' he pats the backs of two brown dogs – 'are sisters Adette and Elura.'

The last is also the largest, a male with a sleek wine-coloured coat. He holds his three heads up higher than the other dogs, giving us a good look at his enormous white chest.

'What's his name?' I ask.

'Oryth,' Uriel says. 'Elegant, isn't he?'

Solomon scoffs. 'Elegant?' He lifts both hands into the air. 'That dog looks hungry to me.'

I have to agree. 'The delicious evening meal they had planned has just slipped off their menu.'

The others laugh, except for Tash, who gives Uriel a furtive look. He grimaces and mumbles, 'OK, I'll go find them something to eat.'

Under Tash's control the eleven remaining dogs guide us through the maze, saving us from the high-altitude climb over the volcano rim. It's a lucky break that will cut many hours from our journey, and make our return trip much easier.

The dogs will remain loyal to Tash for as long as she maintains her Alpha status. However, as a Sensitive this can't be easy for her. Sharing their minds, their emotions, understanding them, and knowing she will soon have to release them back to an uncertain existence, must be exhausting.

Releasing them will be even harder.

On our third night with the dogs we set up a camp on a narrow stretch of maze, blocked at one end by a recent landslide. Uriel is on guard duty at the opposite end, taking over from Tash, who returns to her 'family'. She settles them around her, away from the fire. They nuzzle in as close to her as they can. A fight breaks out which she quickly brings under control. She then closes her eyes and sighs.

It's not forever, Tash. She catches my thought and waits while I approach from across the campsite and hunker down beside her. 'The air is already warming. Any day now we will reach the main funnel. Before we head off in the morning, take the dogs to a quiet place to select a new Alpha and train it to take over.'

'You're giving me time to do that?' She sounds surprised.

'It will give the dogs a chance to make it on their own. Over time, they will build their numbers and be strong again.'

Her eyes glisten and she smiles. 'Thank you, Thane.'

Tash's attachment to these animals is already strong. The break will be timely – for her sake.

'The one you select will need to be the strongest both physically and mentally. Take comfort in knowing you have done your best for them, but, remember, you can't change what they are and nor should you alter their nature if you want them to survive.'

She nods and looks up at me. 'May I be candid, my prince?'

'Ah, I'm not sure,' I reply with a dubious smile, 'but go on.'

'As a Sensitive I find myself, for better or worse, aware

of the nature of angels, humans, animals and other beings.'

I nod slowly, wondering where she's going with this.

'In the two thousand years I've been alive I've seen many who want to be king come and go, including your father. But you're not like any other who covets a throne.'

At my frown she adds, 'What makes you different are traits that make me proud to be an angel.'

'Thank you, Tash.'

'Unfortunately, not everyone feels the same way.'

'It's the benefit of Free Will.'

She runs her hand through her shoulder-length hair. 'In some instances, my prince,' she says, locking her emerald gaze with mine, 'it should be outlawed.'

'Is there something you want to tell me, Tash?'

She looks troubled and as she holds my gaze her eyes roll back and she slips into a trance. '*Someone you trust will betray you*,' she utters in a strange breathy voice.

'Who?' I ask instinctively, but she's starting to seize and instead of pressing her for more information, I call out a mind-link: *Uri!*

Michael, always watching and hovering nearby, hunkers down beside me as I catch Tash and lay her gently on the ground. 'What's happening?' he asks, helping me shift the dogs to give her room.

'She's having a seizure. Where's Uri? He'll know what to do for her.'

Michael looks back at our camp, then stands. 'I'll find him.'

But Uri flies over us, touching down on Tash's opposite side, stirring snow and ice with his coat. He drops to his knees and gently strokes her face. 'Breathe, my darling,' he whispers with feather-light kisses across her forehead. 'It will be over soon.'

Jez and Isaac arrive, bringing a blanket and covering her with it. Then Jez crouches beside Uriel. 'Can I help?'

'There's nothing except to wait it out.'

'She's had this happen before?' Isaac asks.

'A few times, and always after a vision.'

Tash stops seizing, her eyes roll back to normal, and as she attempts to sit up she moans and asks, 'What happened? Did I say anything?'

I remember her warning, *Someone you trust will betray you*, but since most of those I trust surround me now, I decide to say nothing.

31

Jordan

When Mr Zee shoves me into his Bugatti I get a feeling that this is the end. This is where I lose the game.

I've been through some serious shit in my life, *really* serious. My life sucked from my first breath. A crack baby, I had to go through detox the day I was born. They didn't give me back to my parents until my mum and dad proved they could stay clean for three months. By the time I was four they were both using again. They soon became desperate and all went downhill from there.

But I've never felt like *this* before, so useless, wasted and helpless.

The two most important people in my life are gonna suffer big time because I stuffed up. Mum will live the rest of her mortal life in Skade, and when she dies her soul will stay in that toxic dark world for eternity. She will *never* be at peace.

Prince Luca will probably kill her now just to punish me.

Why didn't I listen to Skinner when he said I needed to hurry? This morning wasn't the only time; he's been pushing me for weeks. And I thought he was just being a prick.

In hindsight everything is always clearer.

There's Ebony now. I spot her driving the Lambo through my side mirror. She's about half a K behind us, and catching up fast. How can I tell her to go back?

When I chose to save Mum, knowing it meant I had to break Ebony up from Thane, I really believed I could still protect Ebony from the Dark Prince. I shouldn't have been so naive. I should have read the contract's 'fine print', the part Prince Luca didn't mention, the part that said it didn't matter if I failed – he would just move on to Evil Plan B – using me and the Guardian bond to bring Ebony out in the open.

Damn him to hell!

I hold up my chained hands. 'Is this necessary?'

'If it stops you texting a warning to Ebony, then I would have to say yes, it is necessary.'

'You're a monster.'

'It was your job to break her heart not so long ago, so don't go judging me.'

He has a point. I don't like that he's right. I close my eyes and entertain myself with thinking up a hundred ways to end Mr Zee's life.

32

Ebony

We're halfway up Mountain Way before I'm close enough to start putting my plan into action. Fortunately, there aren't many vehicles on the road today. But there are still a few, like a bus with two passengers, a family in a hatchback, a minivan with camping equipment stuffed in the back, a truck delivering store supplies, and a silver, late model sedan with a thirty-something couple inside.

Except for the sedan, I overtake them all, one at a time, and as steadily as I can so I don't freak Amber out.

She's handling the drive better than I thought. A high-speed fatality in front of her home when she was eleven left her with chilling memories. I've seen her when her father is running late: her skin is always ashen, while her hands gripping her arm rests are squeezed tight.

She keeps her eyes focused ahead the entire time, searching for the green Bugatti. Maybe this is helping to keep her mind off the sharp bends and increasingly steep drops. I flick her a quick look. She's spotted the Bugatti about a hundred metres in front of the silver sedan and sighs with relief. 'I think I see them.'

'Yeah, that's them.'

Keeping her eyes on the car, she says, 'You did a great job catching up. When are you going to make your move?'

'Soon.'

'So how are you going to make Mr Zavier pull over?'

I take a deep breath. 'I'm so sorry, Amber.'

She turns her head and frowns at me. 'What are you apologising for?'

'I've been trying to figure this out, and the only manoeuvre I can come up with that also gives us a chance to escape, is to bump the Bugatti's rear side and force them to lose control.'

Her big brown eyes swell as she stares condemningly at me. 'You're going to make them *crash*?'

'It's a manoeuvre police use sometimes, and if it goes to plan the Bugatti will end up sideways in front of us. And, while stationary, I will distract Mr Zavier, giving you time to help Jordan into the Lambo. Then the three of us take off and live happily ever after.'

'Has this become a game to you?'

Her sarcastic tone surprises me. Amber is never usually testy. 'Of course not. I was just trying to keep it light.'

'And if your scenario doesn't play out right, what then?'

'I don't have a back-up plan . . . *yet*,' I add quickly.

We're quiet for a few minutes while I navigate through a winding stretch of road.

'Honey, you've really surprised me with how good a driver you are.'

'Thanks, Amber. But . . .?'

'Have you performed this manoeuvre before?'

She knows I haven't. As I open my mouth to answer, she lifts her hand. 'I get it – you're learning as you go.'

'I won't let Jordan get hurt. I physically can't. I would throw myself in the line of fire every time for him.'

'Yeah, yeah, I get it, the G Bond.' Her uncharacteristic sarcasm is starting to worry me. 'But have you noticed we're on a steep, narrow, windy road and you're driving unbelievably fast?' She glares at me. 'Jordan is in the car you plan to make crash, you know!'

'Are we fighting, like . . . *now*?'

'I don't know!' she screams, and covers her face with her hands.

I notice then how much they're shaking. *Shit.*

'Amber, the manoeuvre is what I'm saying sorry for,' I tell her gently. 'Are you going to be OK? Do you want me to turn around and take you home?'

She lowers her hands, revealing red teary eyes. 'You would do that? Even with your bond and everything?'

I don't have to think about that for long. Amber is like my sister. We've been friends all our lives. 'Yeah, I would.'

She folds her hands in her lap. 'OK.'

'OK, what?'

'Keep going.'

'Will you be OK?"

'Yeah, I'll be fine.'

'Are *we* still good?'

'Of course we are.' Peering ahead, she gets back to keeping watch, murmuring under her breath, 'God help us all.'

A straight stretch of road gives me the chance to overtake the sedan. To distract Amber I keep her talking while I increase the car's torque and shift into the oncoming lane,

'You know, once I'm living in Avena, the bond won't have the same power over Jordan.'

She glances sideways. 'Really?'

'Really. So my leaving Earth is going to bring some good things too. You wait and see.' Smoothly, I accelerate past the silver sedan and slip back into the appropriate driving lane. Now there's nothing between Mr Zavier's car and mine.

'You sound more accepting of your angelic roots today, even of your move to Avena.'

'I don't *want* to leave, but it's important for Nathaneal that I do. It will be hard, though, especially if Mum and Dad are not found by then. I can't stand the thought of being so far from them when they return. They'll think I abandoned them for my "real" family.' I glance at her and ask, 'If it happens that way, will you make sure to let them know how much I missed them, worried about them, love them?'

She nods and gives me a watery smile. 'Of course. But you're not going away for a long time yet.'

'I would like to finish school here.'

'That would be great.'

A thought suddenly occurs. 'I know where Mr Zavier's taking Jordan.'

She looks at me, confused. 'Where?'

'The portal!' Still wearing a blank look, I explain, 'You know, the entrance to the Crossing, deep inside Mount Bungarra's forest.'

'Why would Mr Zavier take Jordan to the portal?'

'The Crossing is the only way back to Skade or Avena. And there are only two portals to access it. One is up there.' I point to the northern ridge tip, which is just becoming visible. 'The Brothers built their monastery there, setting the Watchtower on the highest point so they could keep an eye on any angelic or demonic activity.'

'So where's the other portal?'

'Alaska. There's a community of dark angels that live there and keep it safe for Prince Luca and his kind to come and go. It's where Luca and his elite force of twelve Prodigies made their entrance last time he came to Earth.'

'I remember how all the birds of the world flew in the opposite direction.'

'And freaked your mum out.'

'Not just Mum! Do you remember how Dad went looking for his last will and testament?'

I smile at the memory, though at the time no one was laughing.

'So what happens if Mr Zavier manages to take Jordan into the Crossing?' Amber asks. 'Can we go in after them?'

'Not without wings. The landscape moves around too much. According to Nathaneal, when you enter the portal, you only get a glimpse to prepare yourself, not enough time for a human mind to make the decision whether to stay or go. That's why we have to stop Mr Zavier *before* they reach the summit. It will be much harder to escape once we're on the ridge because it's too close to the portal.'

By now Mr Zavier is aware I'm behind him and closing in fast. He exerts more power and takes off, flames shooting from his exhausts.

It's time to take charge and do this my way.

I catch up to his tail, then fall back a little as we take a sharp bend. Once clear, I move up again and brace myself for action. There's a waterfall coming up just past the next hill with a pull-over bay for tourists who want to stop and take photos. The wider roadway will help make this manoeuvre a little safer. I keep close behind the Bugatti while we climb.

At the top of the hill the road sweeps sharply into a right angle. We both go round screeching sideways. When I exit the curve, I'm relieved to see the road ahead is clear of oncoming traffic. I depress the power button Jordan used when the dark forces chased us home from Mr Zavier's house, the button Nathaneal told him was for emergencies only.

'*Shi-i-i-it!*' Amber cries out as the Lambo projects forward like a jet on take-off.

'Hold tight, Amber.'

'Oh, I am!'

Mindful of the high speed we're both going, and with the waterfall now in my sights, I shift into the oncoming lane and hold the wheel as steady as I can. Then, when my front tyres are parallel with the Bugatti's rear ones, I turn the wheel towards the green car, tapping it gently with the Lambo's front passenger end, then swiftly drop back.

Instantly, the Bugatti spins across the road in front of us. It's almost a perfect move, except I didn't take into account the soapy effect that the waterfall spray would have on the road. The Bugatti hits the slippery stretch and slides all the way across the other side, its rear end hitting the guard rail meant to stop vehicles from dropping down an incredibly steep cliff.

My heart stops.

Amber screams relentlessly.

I pull over, and we watch in horror as Mr Zavier tries but fails to gain control of his vehicle. The Bugatti pings off the guard rail, leaving a deep V dent in the centre, but mercifully it holds. The small green car then careers back across the water-sprayed road, spinning in a full circle twice before crashing head first into a rocky pond at the waterfall's baseline, leaving its front wheels spinning in air.

'I know this looks bad, Amber, but we still have to do what we came for. I'm not sure how, but you have to get Jordan out of that car and into this one. Go! Hurry!'

I jump out too, but before I take off I notice the silver sedan pulling up behind us. Oh no, helpful civilians I could do without right now.

The couple start running to the crash. I run in front of them, lifting both of my hands into the air. 'Stop. *Stop!* If you value your lives you will both turn round, get in your car and drive away without looking back.'

'What? Why?' the man asks, looking past me.

The woman says, 'I'm a nurse. We can help.'

I glance over my shoulder and see Mr Zavier getting out. He slams the door and thumps the roof, denting it. He's looking for me, his face screwed up, his body language stiff and full of rage. 'See that man? I know him. He's dangerous and will hurt you if you get in his way.'

The man stares at me like I'm insane, but the woman reaches out, one hand touching her partner's arm, the other circling her lower belly. While there is no rise or swelling yet, her instincts are to protect her growing family. 'Come on, Kyle,' she says, flicking her head towards their car.

'Are you sure we can't help?' the man asks again.

'The best you can do for me is to leave and warn anyone coming not to interfere.'

'Can you handle that man alone? He looks kind of ... crazed.'

'I'm not alone. There are three of us. Only one of him.'

Just then Mr Zavier decides to roar, whether to scare these innocent human beings away, or out of sheer frustration, I don't know. But he sounds like a beast that belongs in a jungle.

The couple retreat, and while jumping into their vehicle the man yells, 'We'll call for help!'

When I turn back, I see that Amber has helped Jordan out of the car, their legs knee-deep in water. Jordan is limping with his hands chained together, right shoulder slumped and a whopping big bruise on the side of his face.

A red haze appears before my eyes. I feel my anger beating like a drum at my ribs. Looking at me, his head shaking from side to side, Zavier says in conversational tone, 'Why did you do that?'

The haze deepens. 'You hurt my Charge.'

'Apparently not enough since he's still walking,' he says. 'I should have dislocated his knees.' And in a beat he's standing before me.

He lunges for my arms. I manage to block him, but his hold on my left wrist is so tight he's cutting off my circulation. Reacting on instinct and my lessons with Nathaneal, I concentrate on shifting energy to the palm of my free hand, then shove it as hard as I can into Zavier's face.

He releases me instantly, yelling something foreign and probably quite foul. When he turns back, his nose is oozing blood from both nostrils. 'Who taught you that little move, niece?'

'Cut the crap and stay away from me. I don't want to fight you. I've come for Jordan. That's all.'

He looks at me with pretend pity. 'I'm sorry, my lady, but I can't let you go. You see, my employer is waiting for you. And he's not particularly patient. It's my job to take you to him, and that is what I am going to do. So why don't you come along quietly and I will consider letting your friends go.'

My friends make it to the car.

'Don't listen to him, Ebony,' Amber says.

The red haze turns purple at the edges, and I'm sure this haze has to do with the energy I'm feeling pulsing inside me right now. I remember how I trashed the living room and brought down a chandelier.

I squeeze my fingers into balls, imagining I'm holding poisonous darts.

Reading his body language, I can tell Zavier is about to attack. He lifts into the air. In the split second before he lands on top of me, I fling my hands at him, imagining I'm releasing the darts at supersonic speed.

Purple flashes of light fly from my fingers into his chest, flinging him backwards at least ten metres before he drops on to his back and slides a bit further away.

Jordan whistles and cheers, annoying Amber, who is completely focused on getting him in the car. 'Come on,' she yells, lifting his injured leg inside before slamming the door closed after him. Then she yells at me, 'Get in, honey!' She jumps into the back seat. 'Come on, come on!'

I get the driver's door open only to find Zavier already behind me. 'You are not getting away from me this time,' he says, pulling me back by the waist, and trying to wrap his arms round mine.

I manage to keep one arm free, and kick him. But my legs feel weak and my foot only reaches his thigh when I was aiming for his head. I don't know why I come up short, but I don't like it.

Amber climbs over Jordan into the driver's seat and grabs my free arm. Zavier backhands her. She slumps, slithering downwards until her head comes to rest on the steering wheel.

'What did you *do* to her?' I feel the pulsing anger of my power build again, but the red haze is fuzzy and I can tell it's not as strong as before.

Zavier pulls me towards him far too easily. I latch on to the car door and grip it with every skerrick of willpower I have. Suddenly we hear sirens in the distance. They're still a fair distance away, but there's no doubt they're coming here. The couple in the silver sedan must have alerted them.

From the corner of my eye I see Jordan making his way round the front of the car, just beyond Zavier's scope, his hands still in chains, and wincing silently with each step. I force myself not to look at him in case it gives his position away.

I hold my breath as Jordan, who is now directly behind Zavier, raises his arms, and in one fluid movement brings the chain down across the angel's neck, pulling it with as much strength as his injured human body can summon.

I can tell right away that Zavier is too strong for Jordan. I need to help out, but to do that I will have to step further away

221

from the car. Amber stirs and starts to come to. Relief gives me extra momentum, but before I use it the sky darkens overhead and my stomach sinks at the sight of twelve dark angels circling us like hawks zeroing in on their prey. I recognise Prince Luca's Prodigies, the same team he brought with him from Skade the last time he tried to take me away with him.

They touch down without making a sound.

Interestingly, I notice how they're all wearing black wrap-around sunglasses. This must be how they're tolerating the intensity of the Earth's bright sun. So how long have they been on Earth? I have a sudden terrifying thought that they've been here since Nathaneal's battle three months ago.

By now Zavier has flung Jordan's chain off. Amber stumbles out and helps Jordan get back into the car, motioning to me to hurry.

Meanwhile the soldier I recall being Luca's lieutenant strides past Zavier with an arrogant look and turns to me. I've ended up a metre from the car door, a metre too far from the protection I need right now, and I start taking tentative steps towards it.

The lieutenant smiles at me. It's the lazy, lecherous look of a predator confident his prey has nowhere to run. I can only imagine the perversion his soul would reveal to me if he were not wearing block-out sunnies and I could look into his eyes.

The sirens grow louder. It sparks the lieutenant into action, calling out four names and giving them orders to get rid of Zavier's car and fix his mess. He then points to two other soldiers. 'Ezekeal, Tobias, you take the boy. Now!'

'*Take?*' Zavier queries. 'Saul, I have orders for the girl *only.*'

'Your orders have changed,' Lieutenant Saul says.

Amber cries out, 'Ebony, get in quickly.'

But Amber doesn't understand who these twelve angels are, nor what's about to happen. As Ezekeal and Tobias reach into the car for Jordan, I swing round and make Amber look at me with one hand on either side of her face, stopping her from seeing Jordan being yanked out of the car and carried away. 'Listen to me, Amber. Listen! You have to leave *now.*'

She whimpers, 'Why can't you just get in?'

I glance at the two dark angels lifting Jordan higher and higher into the sky. 'They have taken Jordan. And they're going to take me.' Tears sting my eyes. 'But I can't risk them hurting you. I couldn't bear it.'

We smile grimly at each other as tears run down our faces. Behind me I hear Lieutenant Saul command another member of his team, 'Sarakiel, you and I will take this one.'

'Amber, I need you to go the monastery.' Four arms start dragging me backwards. I call out to Amber, 'Wait there for Gabriel. Tell him what's happened.'

She doesn't move and I have to yell at her. '*Go! Amber, go now!*'

I hear the engine click over and then the sweet sound of the Lambo reversing. Relieved she's getting away unharmed, I spin round and start fighting. First I break their holds on me, shoving my assailants off with a kick to Sarakiel's groin, and a well-aimed punch to Saul's jaw.

They fall back, their massive chests heaving. The lieutenant holds his hand out towards Zavier. 'Did you bring it?'

'Yes,' Zavier says, 'but, Saul, we don't need it yet.'

'Give it to me!' the lieutenant commands, grumbling, 'Obviously she hasn't hammered you in the head yet.'

'Ebony,' Zavier calls, ignoring Lieutenant Saul's command, 'you're a very smart girl. You can see that you're not getting away today, can't you?'

'Where have you taken Jordan?'

'Come with us calmly and I'll take you to him.'

How can he even think I would trust him now? 'Tell you what, Zavier, you bring Jordan back here, *now*, and after I watch him leave I'll go with you calmly.'

He groans, shaking his head. The lieutenant folds his arms over his chest. 'Now will you give it to me, Zavier?'

Zavier remains quiet.

'Give me the damn syringe!'

'All right!' Zavier snaps. 'But I'll do it.'

'Wait!' I start moving backwards. 'What are you talking about?' If I can distract them long enough for the police to arrive, maybe they will fly away so they are not seen.

'What's in the syringe, Zavier?' I ask.

He pulls out a hypodermic needle like the vets give to horses. 'Just a sedative, my lady.'

'Stop calling me that!'

The sirens are so close now. I glance over my shoulder and spot two police cars with flashing blue lights tearing up the hill behind me. I turn and run in their direction. Obviously a stupid idea since these guys can all fly. Where are *my* wings when I need them? Two come down behind me, two directly in front. I aim my left foot into one angel's face, knocking him backwards. I throw my right fist into another's gut, misjudging my aim a little too high. He doubles over anyway so I must have hit a tender spot. I spin round to do the same to the two soldiers behind me, but more of them come down, and now they completely surround me.

It takes six of them to hold me still long enough for Zavier to stick his syringe in my neck. '*Damn you, Zavier!*' I scream at him as the cold liquid enters my bloodstream.

'Sarakiel,' the lieutenant calls. 'Quickly, the humans are arriving. Help me collect the girl so we can finish this.'

My hair is all over my face, practically blinding me as Lieutenant Saul and Sarakiel come to collect me. I manage to make a few more kicks and punches connect before two arms swing round my waist. The swish-swishing of strong, fast-beating wings fills my ears as I rise up into the sunlight, my limbs becoming wearier by the second.

'Stop squirming, my lady, we are already high enough off the ground that should you fall you would seriously injure yourself.' I recognise the voice, the familiar accent and smooth deep tones.

I shove the hair from my face and look at the angel holding me. '*You!* What happened to the other two?'

'I overruled them,' Zavier says.

'But I thought Lieutenant Saul was in charge.'

'Where you are concerned, my lady, the only one to carry you will be me.'

33

Nathaneal

A sudden cloudburst of acid rain cascades down the main vent from the crater opening high above us. Our stinging eyes send us scurrying back to an abandoned cave we recently passed.

Solomon remains by the opening to check in with his informant inside Prince Luca's city palace. When his mind-link concludes, he enters the cave but waits at the entrance, standing still and quiet, as if gathering his breath.

He walks past Jez, Tash and Uriel. They glance at him, eager for news, but he ignores them, making us all uneasy. Especially when he continues past Isaac, sitting on a boulder attempting to replait his knotted hair, and then Michael, whose golden gaze, once upon you, is difficult to ignore.

But Solomon doesn't utter a word until he is standing directly in front of me.

By now my heart is pounding like a wild beast running for its life. 'What is it, Sol?'

'My prince, no one has seen him.'

'Can you be more specific?'

He twists his fingers, a strange activity for such a robust angel. 'No one has sighted the Dark Prince since your battle with him on Earth.'

For a beat there is nothing but silence, punctured with the sounds of our breathing and hearts beating fast.

'Of course there's been no sight of him,' Isaac says, finishing his braid though he's only halfway through it. 'He can't have recovered so quickly from *those* injuries. He would still be in hiding, and probably for months to come.'

Jez comes and stands between Michael and me. 'No one's seen him because he's recuperating outside the capital with only his close medics on hand. He won't go public with this battle because his losses would demean him in the eyes of his people. And we all know what appearances mean to him.'

Michael seems to agree. 'He has a secret fortress in the Hyactyn Mountains. His minders could have diverted him through underground tunnels.'

Isaac's eyes suddenly widen. 'Hold on, everyone.' He glances at each of us with a look that asks why we haven't thought of this already. 'It's a long journey to Alaska from Mount Bungarra. That would have been a tough flight in Prince Luca's condition. For his team too. How far did the Brothers track their movements after the battle?'

I explain what I know. 'The Watchtower was damaged during the attack. It wasn't operable until the following morning. By then, the Brothers couldn't pick up a trace of Prince Luca, or any of his team. Somewhere in that forest they disappeared. We considered that since they knew the tower was out, and surrounded by flocks of Aracals to provide them cover, Luca and his team used the nearest portal to return to Skade.'

'*Our* Crossing?' Jez squeals, shaking her head in disgust and nearly suffocating us with the scent her long black hair always throws out.

'That makes sense,' Michael says, coughing and spluttering. Collecting himself, he gives her a scathing look.

'What?' she yells.

'Do you have any idea how lethal your scent is? We should register it as a weapon of mass destruction.' At her outraged gasp, he clears his throat. 'Never mind.' He quickly shifts his gaze back to me. 'The Alaskan portal would have been too far away for them to reach in their condition, right on the cusp of dawn. But they could have crawled to Mount Bungarra's portal from where we left them.'

Tash moves to the cave's entrance, concerned that our heightened emotions could cause her harm. 'Solomon has more news.'

Everyone looks at him and he nods, his face remaining grim. 'The Gatekeepers have reported that the Dark Prince has not returned to Skade yet.'

'At all?'

'Correct, my prince.'

'In *all* this time?'

'That's right. His Prodigies haven't been seen either.'

'But there is only one way into Skade.'

Everyone is suddenly keeping their thoughts to themselves, but I know what they're thinking, and it makes their silence all the more alarming.

Michael lays his hand on my shoulder. 'Don't jump to conclusions until we learn more.'

I point out three facts that terrify me. 'Prince Luca is still on Earth. Ebony is on Earth. And I am halfway down a volcano inside *Skade*!'

I glance at the worried faces of my team. They watch me, alert for signs. They're concerned I will lose control. They have every right to be. The powers surging inside my body continue to intensify as my struggle to regulate the volatile mix of emotions begins to unravel. Love, anger, frustration and fear that Ebony and Prince Luca's paths will cross, that *he* will make them cross, is tearing up every last vestige of my control.

I grab Michael's arm. 'She pleaded with me to return safely.'

'I know. She *threatened* me. She's stronger than you think, cousin.'

The image of my sweet Ebony standing up to the commander of all Avena's armies sends my emotions on a spiral of pride and panic. 'I cannot be this far away from her,' I call out. 'She does not know our world, or the deviousness of *his*.'

Michael places one hand on my shoulder and another across my chest in an attempt to keep me immobile. 'Stay calm, cousin.'

'How am I supposed to do that, Michael? How do I stay calm? I'm burning up inside!'

A sudden jolt of energy explodes from within, and my powers plunder right through me, pushing and straining against bone and muscle and skin, yearning to escape a body that has suddenly transformed into a prison. 'Leave, all of you! Go now!'

'Save your breath, my young prince,' Isaac says. 'I've been beside you since you were seven years old. I'm not going anywhere now.'

Blood rushes into my veins. My lungs fill with air. My wings shoot out, sending Michael flying. Around us the cave shudders.

Tash screams as she feels my pain. Jez, Uriel and Solomon throw themselves over me, wrapping me in their arms as they try to hold me still, even while my powerful wings thrash at them.

Tash looks at me from the entrance, trembling with tears in her eyes. 'Go, Tash! Get out of here!'

Uriel encourages her with a sharp nod. She steps outside the cave where she slides to the ground and hugs her knees.

'Keep still, cousin,' Michael murmurs. 'We will figure this out together.'

I have felt each of my powers before, just not all at once. Every cell in my body feels as if it is in danger of exploding.

The cave walls shudder and fill the air with dust and rock particles. Images of Ebony, her gentle touch, her feisty spirit, her true, tender heart, and eyes that see the good in people first, look up at me pleadingly. Another surge plunges through me, flooding my senses. 'I'm supposed to protect her, not put her in harm's way!'

'I know,' Michael murmurs.

He will crush her!

We will not let that happen.

'Think calm!' Isaac orders in the voice he used when I was seven. 'Tranquil thoughts can help you reverse this.'

How do I think calm when pure evil walks where my beloved walks? Someone tell me how!

My heart is beating too fast, pumping massive volumes of blood through lungs and organs struggling to handle such intense pressure. 'I have to warn her. I have to –'

'You can't go back now, Thane,' Jez says. 'You persuaded the court to give you *this* task. What do you think will happen if you don't complete it?'

'But –'

'She's right,' Michael says. 'Besides, you didn't leave Ebony and Jordan alone.'

What are you talking about, Michael?

Through a mind-link he sends me an image of my brother Gabriel arguing with me after I asked him to watch over Ebony and Jordan in my absence. It took some convincing, but ultimately he agreed.

Recalling that Gabe is with them right now gives me an instant sense of calm. I take a deep breath and exhale gently, feeling the urgency inside me ebb away. As I explain to the team, my body and mind slow to a comfortable level. 'How could I have forgotten the arrangement I made with my own brother?' I chastise myself.

Smiles break out as tensions ease. Even Tash grins, though wisely still keeps her distance. 'Prince Gabriel can call in his whole unit if he needs reinforcements,' she says.

I will owe my brother for this, and, knowing Gabe, he'll make the payback gruelling and distasteful, but he will have my unending gratitude.

Now I can return my energies into completing restitution for my crimes. 'Has it stopped raining yet?'

Tash replies, 'Affirmative, my prince.'

'Then what are we waiting for? We have a very important mission to complete.'

34

Jordan

The two Prodigies lift me so high above the ridge the properties in the valley take on the appearance of a chessboard in shades of green. Wind blows around me from their two sets of wings beating hard while expertly keeping apart. I don't dare move in case they drop me.

Eventually they bring me down in a thick part of the forest, but nowhere near the portal like I was expecting. They lower my feet to the ground first. I glimpse a dry creek bed, dense shrubs and a rocky hill before they shove a hessian bag over my head and push me into a cave.

We walk at a steep downwards angle for a kilometre or more. It's so dark the only light comes from the Prodigies' own glow.

A second tunnel with a left turn keeps us descending. By the time they stop and make me sit, we're deep underground. It's cold, moist and smells like wet dog fur. I hug my knees to my chest and wonder what happened to the girls.

Pulling the bag off my head, the angels leave me here while they walk into a tunnel opposite where I'm sitting. When their light fades from view, it becomes so dark I can't see the tunnel entrance or even my fingers held in front of my eyes.

This has to be an old mine. The valley is littered with them from the gold rush days. I bet Thane doesn't know it's here, and yet it's on the ridge and can't be too far from both his property and the monastery.

Sitting alone in the cold and dark, I get time to think.

I got it wrong. I got it *so* wrong. I should bury myself in a deep hole and never come up for air. I grit my teeth and squeeze my eyes shut while I swallow down my anguish.

I aligned myself with the enemy. I *trusted* the enemy.

But I did it for Mum.

What an idiot!

Mum was my weak point and the prince knew it. He was in my dreams enough times to see how I longed to have her back in my life. 'I'm sorry, Mum, I can't help you now.'

I hear footsteps. Enemy angels pour in, their faces glowing around their sunglasses. They walk straight past me into the tunnel like I don't exist. If they forget about me, maybe I can sneak out when they go to sleep. I count twelve, including the first two and not counting Mr Zee. That's how many Prodigies Prince Luca brought with him when he almost abducted Ebony the last time.

That battle practically annihilated them. According to Thane and Gabe, they shouldn't be capable of doing something like this yet. They thought Luca would lie low and build his strength to make a final attempt just before Ebony's eighteenth. But that's still more than a year away.

So why did it take *two* of them to carry me when one should have been plenty?

The amber glow of a lantern appears inside the tunnel and grows brighter quickly. I jump to my feet with the sense that whoever's carrying that lantern is coming for me.

I'm not wrong. I stare at Mr Zee's face with words leaping from my mouth: 'We thought Prince Luca had returned to Skade. Everyone did.'

'Really?' His voice drips sarcasm. 'In the condition your prince left him?' He rubs the back of his neck. 'He couldn't walk. He could hardly breathe. How was he supposed to fly to Alaska? There was no one to help him since his entire team were left equally as damaged.'

'So . . . what . . . you just happened to come along?'

'I was keeping an eye on things.'

'You brought the angels here and looked after them with tender loving care?'

'Someone had to get them off the street and out of the gutter! It wasn't long before their self-healing began, but they needed to be out of public sight. Your prince unleashed his powers without any thought of the consequences!'

'Don't get me started on consequences,' I snarl back. 'Thane did what he *had* to that night. And he'd do it again to protect Ebony. Just wait until he hears about this. So what have you done with the girls?'

He takes too long answering. Sweat beads across my forehead even though it's freezing down here. Finally, he says, 'Amber escaped.'

'Yes! Yes!' I punch the air. My shoulder kills but I hardly feel it because Amber got away! 'And Ebony?' I swallow to bring moisture back into my mouth.

'She is here.'

'Shit! Is she all right? Can I see her?'

'She's sleeping.'

'What? *Now?* Why would she be sleeping in the middle of the afternoon just after being kidnapped?'

The ensuing silence makes me suspicious.

'What did you do to her?'

'Ebony is fine. Leave it, Jordan. We have other things to discuss.'

If I could throw something at him I would. 'How did you know about this place?' I ask. The more I learn the better chance I'll have of helping Thane when I get out of here. 'Well?'

'Drained of practically every drop of fluid from his body, Prince Luca told me about a cave he'd used when he created his first demons thousands of years ago. The cave was nearby, and though mortals built a mine around it to find gold the cave remained undiscovered. So I brought them here to regain their strength.'

I look up into his face, so close I can smell mint-flavoured mouthwash on his breath. He's so human-like, and yet he's so far from being human it's not funny. 'You should have let them die in the gutter. That's what I would have done.'

'You're forgetting their immortality. Unable to control their dark powers in their weakened state, it would have leached out of them and caused unimaginable damage to the Earth. Loose and free and without form, it would drain into the soil, poison the fresh waters, passing disease into crops and livestock.' He lifts his shoulders and lets them fall. 'Who knows, perhaps even the air would fill with bacteria or worse.'

Mr Zee's words are like puzzle pieces plopping into place. 'Some of their evil leached out before you found them.'

His surprised look is genuine. 'Explain.'

'On our way home from your place something dark and powerful chased us. It tore up the road like a tornado and killed two cops. It was all over the news.'

He listens. If he's breathing, I can't tell.

'This dark force started evolving. First it split into two parts and took the form of a man and a woman, then it looked more like a pair of armoured angels and became four. In the beginning it hid in outback caves by day and fed from the valley at night, but now the two pairs stay close to Ebony day and night. Prince Gabriel says they're drawn to her.'

His eyes impale me. 'This is equivalent to opening the gates to Skade's deepest prisons where the worst human souls transmogrify into beasts.' He flicks a glance at the tunnel, then leans right in and whispers, 'They must be stopped. Tell your angels to destroy them even if they have to bring a legion of Throne Warriors to accomplish the task.'

'They can't do that.'

'Mixing with angels has given you leeway to order them around now, has it?' His eyes burn with indignation. 'You don't understand what Prince Luca could do with them if he learns of their existence.'

237

'But if angels bring an army that big to Earth, there'll be mass hysteria and the world will never be the same again.'

'Perhaps the time has come for change, Mr Blake, before there's nothing left to save.'

'Why did you bring Ebony here?' I ask.

'I had no choice. Just as I have no choice now.'

'Everyone has a choice, even if it's one they don't wanna make.'

'For your own sake, you must forget Ebony. Her fate is sealed. You cannot help her now.'

'Screw you! I don't care what excuses you make up – you have to release her!'

Mr Zee grabs my arm. 'Stop yelling, or they will hear you. I've talked Prince Luca into letting *you* go.' He points with his right arm. 'That way will lead you to a small cave with a heavy door. It's unlocked. Leave, Jordan, while you still can.'

'I'm not going without Ebony.'

He glares at me. 'I know about the deal you struck with Prince Luca.'

'He tricked me.'

'I thought as much,' he mutters. 'I wondered why you allowed him so much control.'

'What control?'

'Jordan, you forfeited your right to choose the time the contract ends – the day, the hour, the minute of your death.'

'*What?* Bullshit! I didn't forfeit that! I told you he tricked me.'

'Listen, Jordan, Prince Luca has no need for you yet. This is why he is allowing you to leave. Go now and live your life while you still have one.'

'But I *don't* have one, not without Ebony.'

'Don't be so selfish! What about your family, or friends that will miss you?'

'I don't have family or friends.'

'There's Ms Lang.'

'What about Amber?'

'That girl will need you now. She lost her closest friend today. Who else but you will understand her pain?'

'You're wrong. She thinks I'm a moron.'

A flood of light puts an end to any further discussion as Prince Luca, self-appointed King of Skade, walks in. Dressed in sleek, tight black clothes, he might not be at peak health yet, but to look at him you wouldn't know it. He still has a powerful presence, an aura that announces him. When his penetrating green eyes fall on you, you feel as if he's extracting your whole life, every event you've experienced, every thought you've had. Just as he's doing now with each step until he's standing right in front of me, peering down his nose.

'Jordan, my young friend.' His velvety voice slices into me, bringing a chill to my soul. 'Don't you want to leave?'

'He's leaving now,' Mr Zee says.

Prince Luca shoots Mr Zee a look that should freeze his heart, that's if Mr Zee has one. 'Is that correct?' he asks me.

My head is nodding, but no words are coming out.

'Jordan!' Mr Zee hisses. 'Leave now.'

Prince Luca tilts his head as if he's peering at a bird in a cage. It's so unnerving my teeth start chattering. 'C-c-can I see her first?'

Mr Zee closes his eyes, then says softly, 'My lord, I need a moment to talk to Jordan.'

'Your talk is finished,' the prince declares in a tone no

239

one would argue with unless they were insane. Still looking at Mr Zee, he inclines his head at me. Mr Zee shudders before he shifts his eyes to me with some sort of warning in them. I brace myself, but barely finish the thought before Mr Zee grabs my arms and twists them up behind my back.

'Argh! What are you doing?'

'What I should have done,' he says, 'before our futile conversation.'

His grip is as strong as steel. I suppose it *would* be, considering he's a dark angel, after all. I try to think positively like Ebony does. It works for her. The least I can do is try, so I remember my training with Thane and drop as low as I can, turn and keep turning until I get enough leverage to knee him in the gut. He releases my wrists. My shoulder is in agony but I have to keep going. I unfurl and kick his thigh. Amazingly, he crashes to the ground. But he gets up in one fluid movement and wraps his arms round my chest in a hold that feels unbreakable. I try to twist. I try everything Thane taught me, and everything Ebony and I have been teaching each other, and somehow I slip out of his hold, sliding between his long legs and out the other side.

With Prince Luca looking on, Mr Zee comes after me. I let my instincts take over and spin round to gain momentum and put energy into my next hit. Jumping up with the flow, I land a kick to his jaw, knocking his head sideways. His eyes widen and he makes a frustrated grunting sound, but with a piteous look in his eyes as if he's been holding back this whole time. It fires me up.

'Jordan, submit,' he says.

'No way, *sir.*'

'I will admit your strength and agility surprise me. For a human being you are exceptionally strong. You have recovered remarkably from your injuries this morning, or you are hiding your pain very well, but you must know that if you don't give up, I will hurt you.'

His eyes flicker to the prince as if checking his orders are still the same.

'You're like an obedient dog,' I tell him. 'All you do is follow orders.'

He growls, 'Jordan, let me take you down quietly.'

'No chance, *sir*. You want me, you fight me. I might surprise you some more.'

Prince Luca claps in that slow mocking style arrogant people use. 'You are either ludicrously brave or exceptionally stupid. Either way, I'm not amused any more.' His eyes shift sideways to the tunnel for a moment and four soldiers run out.

Oh crap.

More soldiers follow, Prodigies I recognise from the battle on Thane's front lawn. Prince Luca barks orders in a language I have no hope of understanding and the first four start kicking me. I drop to the ground, instinctively curling into the foetal position, but it doesn't stop them.

I catch Mr Zee's eyes from the floor, but all he does is watch with an unreadable expression.

The prince barks another command and the soldiers drag me down the tunnel. About halfway along, a lantern marks the entrance to another tunnel breaking off on my right, and another on my left further down.

This place is starting to resemble an abandoned underground city. Eventually a short tunnel leads to a door in a rock wall. It opens into an enormous cave. Roughly circular with a high ceiling, there are candles and lanterns burning on shelves, on tables and in nooks around the walls, giving the place an unsettling fairy tale look.

A fairy tale from hell.

There's furniture that's mostly iron, like a table with thirteen chairs, and screens that create private areas along the sides, like bedrooms or something.

I absorb this all in one or two glimpses, because once I spot Ebony looking unconscious on a reclining chair with her wrists cuffed, there's room for nothing else in my head.

A hit of adrenalin helps me kick my way free. Still, it's not as if I can grab Ebony and make a break for it, at least not while she's out cold with her hands chained to the floor. So the first thing I gotta do is wake her.

They jump me just before I reach her. I kick and punch my way free again. 'Ebony! Ebony, wake up!'

With the help of another two soldiers, they drag me to a solid rock wall. They remove the remnants from my previous chain that Zavier destroyed when he stopped me from choking him. Two Prodigies hold me up while another pair locks my wrists into wide metal cuffs attached to chains bolted into the wall behind me.

Shit, this really sucks!

I pull hard on the chains, but I soon figure nothing will budge these. My body aches everywhere from the beating, which will feel a lot worse when the adrenalin stops. I start to feel hopeless again.

242

But I can still wake Ebony. If she can make a run for it, this might be her only chance! 'Ebony. *Ebony!*'

Prince Luca lands in front of me, so close his body heat burns the soft hairs on my face. His eyes narrowed, he stares like he hasn't figured me out yet.

'What drugs did Zavier give her?' I ask him. 'Look at her – she's out cold.'

Mr Zee runs a finger over his left brow. 'She's fine!'

Prince Luca asks him, 'What did you give her, Zavier?'

He takes a deep breath. 'Midazolam.'

The prince nods. 'Quantity?'

He doesn't answer and Prince Luca's voice grows eerily stronger. 'Zavier, you will answer the question.'

'Humans were arriving; I didn't have time to measure the dose.'

When he still doesn't answer, rage flares up inside me so great all I can think of is killing him. I yank on the chains over and over, willing my hands free. Stuff the fact he's immortal. Stuff the fact they chained me to a cave wall. I want to jump on him and strangle him with my bare hands.

Obviously he's given Ebony too much Midazolam. That's why she's unconscious. I've seen a drug overdose before. I remember the colour draining away from my mother's face when I tried to wake her to take me to school. 'You killed her!'

'Jordan, listen to me,' Mr Zee says, 'Ebony is not dead.'

'If Ebony doesn't survive this overdose, I *will* kill you. I'll find a way.'

'It was necessary.'

Prince Luca walks over to Mr Zee. 'You don't have to explain your actions to the boy.'

Mr Zee goes silent and glances away. But just then Ebony stirs. Seeing her eyes flutter open makes me go weak with relief. 'Hey!' I call out. 'Ebony, over here.'

Two soldiers approach her carrying a black garment. 'What are you doing with that?' I ask, chills running up my spine.

Mr Zee comes closer. 'It's all right, Jordan. It's called a *lamorak* and it will protect Ebony in the Crossing.'

I gotta wake her up. 'Ebony!'

Her eyes open. 'Jordan? Oh, Jordy, are you all right? Do you know what happened?' I yank on the chains. 'Why are you . . . ? Who did that to you?' She looks around the cave.

'You!' she yells as she lays eyes on Mr Zee. 'You brought me here?'

'Ebony!'

She drags her eyes back to me. They soften like melting butter. 'Jordy, I need to tell you how . . .' She swallows, licks her dry lips and tries again, 'I'm so sorry. I tried to save you.'

She spots the two soldiers opening the *lamorak* near her feet. 'What's this?'

Prince Luca crouches beside her. 'My sweet young princess, this may not be a gold carriage to whisk you away to your new world, but the *lamorak* will protect you in the Crossing. It is imperative that you wear it.'

She peers at him through eyes narrowed to slits. 'Where do you think you're taking me?'

'Don't be afraid, Princess. Now that you're moving into your destiny, I take full responsibility for your protection.'

I shout out, 'This isn't her destiny. You're forcing her. And that's against the rules.'

At that, he leaps over Ebony, grabs my chin and forces me to look up into eyes so angry they flash a glowing yellow colour before turning black.

'Stop!' I shout. 'I mean, whatever you're thinking of doing, just, eh, stop for a sec. Hear me out.'

Amazingly, he does.

'Ebony's lungs aren't ready for Skade's atmosphere. You know that. It's why you stashed her on Earth in the first place. It was supposedly for eighteen years, right? She's nowhere near that yet and . . . and . . . as future queen she'll need to be in perfect health. Right?'

It hurts to hold Prince Luca's gaze. Finally he reduces the intensity of his glare and his eyes turn green again. 'What do you propose, Jordan?'

'Give her the time she needs, leave her here until she turns eighteen, and take me instead. You're going to take me eventually anyway, so why not now?'

'I already have you under contract. No one can take *you* from me.' He looks pointedly at Ebony. I notice loose skin around his neck, and a reckless thought runs through my mind that he needs to concentrate on his appearance more if he wants to impress his new 'princess', as he sickeningly calls her.

He hits me. A slap across my face with an open palm. Ebony screams while I swallow a tooth and some blood pooling inside my mouth.

'For your own sake, Jordan, let Ebony go,' Mr Zee yells.

'Screw you,' I hiss at him, clutching my aching jaw.

245

The Dark Prince runs his fingers through my hair, making my skin crawl. 'Your hair is just like hers.'

He's obviously talking about my mother, but I've had enough of his manipulating tactics. 'You can stop lying now. I know she's dead.'

He frowns. 'You don't believe your mother is living in my palace? She was so looking forward to seeing you soon. You are quite the disappointing son.'

He spins away, leaving me stewing over his comments. While I try to figure out whether he's telling the truth or not, a cheer erupts, followed by applause and back-slapping. It's annoying to see the Prodigies so revved up.

So *happy!*

Prince Luca lifts his palms and they fall silent. 'Prodigies, your patience has only made you stronger. Today the wait is over. We're going home.'

They're leaving?

And while the soldiers are momentarily distracted with this *joyous* news I try to get Ebony's attention, but she's fallen asleep again. 'Ebony!'

She opens her eyes and murmurs, 'I'm sorry you're in this mess because of me. I'm so sorry, Jordy.'

My heart melts. Man, it just dissolves into a puddle inside my chest. I want to tell her to save her strength, that there's no way I'll let the Dark Prince take her to Skade. But I can't lie. 'Don't give up hope. Promise me you won't.'

She nods. 'Tell Nathaneal that I will never stop loving him.'

I yank on the chains until the cuffs cut into my wrists. 'How can you still love *him*? He was supposed to come back for you.'

Her fingers reach out to me, but stop when the chains restrain her. She yanks on them to no effect. 'I was your Guardian,' she says, lowering her hands. 'Things didn't go to plan and I couldn't save you. I can't forgive myself for that.'

'This would all be different if Thane had sent you the message he promised. This is *his* fault. *All* of it.'

She shakes her head. 'Don't blame Nathaneal.'

'Don't stick up for him. He made promises and he broke every one of them. He doesn't deserve your love.'

Prince Luca orders the two soldiers to place Ebony in the *lamorak*. They start with her feet. She kicks out at the pair, knocking them both backwards, then half climbs out of the chair, but as she's still sluggish, with chained wrists, they overpower her. She puts up a heck of a fight but they finally get her legs and hips inside. She stops struggling and just breathes for a minute.

Thinking she's giving up, they release her chains. But this appears to be what she's waiting for. She punches the soldier on her left first, and while he's dropping to the ground she slugs the other one, knocking him out cold. Prince Luca, watching silently, shifts his eyes to Mr Zee.

'Ebony,' Mr Zee says as he approaches her, 'you can't fight us all.'

'Watch me,' she says through gritted teeth.

But three soldiers move in behind him, with another two flaring out at the sides. I wrench the chains as hard as I can. There's no way she can do this on her own.

Mr Zee holds a hand out in a pacifying gesture. 'Ebony, let's do this peacefully.'

Quick as a snake, she snatches his hand, twisting his arm up behind his back while wrapping her other arm round his throat, a defensive move she executes brilliantly.

But Mr Zee doesn't have Midazolam slowing his brain and muscles. He grips her arm with his free hand and gives it a hard yank that must hurt like hell. She doesn't cry out but her eyes blink fast and her lips press tightly together.

She doesn't give up, even when the other six Prodigies move in and hold her down, shoving her into the *lamorak*, limb by limb. She bruises them all before they finally draw the *lamorak* up to her neck and hold it there while they catch their breath.

She gasps and calls out to me, 'Tell Amber I love her like a sister.'

It sounds too much like goodbye and a sob forms in my throat. But she hasn't finished yet. 'Jordan, tell Nathaneal that my heart will always be his, no matter what happens. You tell him, OK?'

She sees me shaking my head and her eyes open wide. 'Jordan!' she cries out, her voice husky and urgent. 'I need to hear you say that you *will* tell him.'

I take a deep breath. 'All right, but he doesn't deserve your love.'

They yank the *lamorak* over Ebony's head and all I can do is watch. The cave takes on a surreal effect, as if none of this is really happening, as if I'm in a terrifying nightmare. But it *is* happening, and I can't do a thing to stop it.

Mr Zee walks over to me, stops about an arm's length away, and gives me a pitying look. Then, without saying a word, he turns his back and starts walking away.

'Hey. *Hey!* Where are you going? What's going to happen to me? You can't just leave me here. Come on, Mr Zee, don't walk away. At least take me with you!'

He stops and glances back at me. 'I tried to stop you. I tried to have Ebony alone with me. But I underestimated the courage of the human spirit and the bond of human friendship. I'm sorry, Jordan, now there's nothing I can do.'

For a second I hold out hope, but he walks away.

'Bastard!'

He goes to where Ebony is on the recliner, completely enclosed in the *lamorak*, twisting and punching away inside it. He says something to her. But his words only make her more incensed. He speaks to her again, not for long, but whatever he says this time seems to work.

And then I get it. Why he won't help me. Why he's gonna leave me here to die. *He's* the dude that reaches down and lifts Ebony into his arms. It's no effort on his part. He hoists her up and cradles her like a child.

Mr Zee is the *only* one strong enough to carry Ebony through the Crossing. And all the way to Skade. Since I'm doing nothing to block my thoughts, I'm sure he's hearing me. All he has to do is refuse and maybe she could walk free.

We both know this is true.

He shuffles his weight as he settles Ebony in his arms more comfortably for the long journey ahead, then gives me one last lingering look before he turns and follows the others out.

35

Nathaneal

To pay for my crimes to Earth's environment and revealing my secret powers, I asked the court if I could rescue John and Heather Hawkins from the prison in which Prince Luca put them, and to my relief enough voting court members said yes.

According to Solomon's Skade informant, their prison is on a small island in an underground ocean that was once Mi'Ocra's core magma reservoir.

So far every team sent to find them has failed.

Now, after a near-vertical descent inside the dark, main volcanic vent, my team members sit in pairs on various rock ledges. Glowing faintly, they understand that resting is not a luxury we can afford any more. So after I instruct them in a mind-link, I tap Michael's shoulder, signalling it's time to make what we hope is the last jump before locating John and Heather.

Since Michael and I are the first pair to descend, we increase our glow to light the way. Then we release our wings and plunge head first into an area of Skade where no angel of light has been before. We fly down a considerable distance before we realise that our glow is becoming unnecessary. Light is exploding from a singular point. Along with this brighter atmosphere, oxygenation, heat and humidity also appear to increase. I cast a speculative look across at Michael, flying like a torpedo on my left, but even with his thousands of years of experience, he simply turns his head to me and shrugs.

Following the light source, we fly through an arched opening in a wall of volcanic rock, and find ourselves in an astonishing tropical world, a world we had no idea existed. Mountains soar above us while creeks, streams and stunning waterfalls thousands of metres deep flow into a river that's at least a kilometre wide.

Since it's an ocean we're looking for, we follow the river as it cuts through a dense jungle. The sounds of buzzing insects and the roar of ancient beasts surge up towards us. It's an extraordinary find, and I wish I could show it to Ebony.

A small but potent red sun climbs high enough to reveal a vast ocean ahead. The river hits a sand bar, slowing its force so much that the junction is practically imper-ceptible.

Michael follows me down to a glistening sandy beach. Standing side by side, we stare in wonder at this secret underground world.

Isaac lands on my right side. '*Incredible*,' he whispers as the rest of the team touch down nearby. 'We should probably work fast,' he says. 'That sun could bake us dry if we stay out here for too long.'

'Should we look for shelter?' Tash asks, glancing along the beach to where the forest meets the shore. 'Or make our own?'

'See what you can come up with,' I tell her. 'But stay close to the beach. I don't like the sounds coming from those jungles.'

'I'll help,' Uriel volunteers.

'Sol?' I call.

'I'm on it, my prince,' he says, lifting into the air immediately.

I try to follow him with my gaze, but he flies straight into the rising sun and the glare reflecting off the water makes him invisible.

On Solomon's return, I shield my eyes as I follow his directions, locating a castle-like stone structure on a small island about twenty kilometres offshore.

I leave immediately. Michael joins me in the air, while the team prepares a base for the arrival of Ebony's parents: two humans in conditions yet undetermined.

If not for Solomon's secret source, finding this prison would be impossible. The informant warned of a balancing scale on which the prison sits, triggered to explode by the slightest alteration in the prison's overall weight. It's a clever mechanism that eliminates the need for fences, and even guards.

John and Heather are apparently in a dungeon at sea level, which I hope allows them access to water for bathing and keeping their human bodies cool during the hottest daytime periods, or they would not survive this heat.

A reef surrounding the island calms the waters and ensures the delicate weight ratio remains undisturbed. Our presence could change that ratio if we're not vigilant of every movement we make.

Michael locates the entrance gate and points it out. 'It doesn't appear stable,' he says. 'Be careful with that.'

I nod. 'I'll go in first and carry John, while you bring Heather out.'

'We lift them simultaneously. I'll wait for your signal before counting down.'

I take a deep breath. 'Then we're set?'

'We're set.' Noticing my nervousness, he tries to reassure me, 'It's going to work out.'

'What if something goes wrong? Every time Ebony looks at me she'll remember I'm the one who killed her parents. She'll end up hating me.'

Michael grips my shoulders as we hover above the island. 'Listen to me. I know you better than anyone, maybe even better than your own mother, and there is no one I trust more. These doubts you have don't belong in your head. They shouldn't be there. Get rid of them.'

'I'm trying, Michael.'

'Nathaneal, the time has come to declare yourself as the *One*. All the worlds are waiting for you to take up your throne. And, cousin, we wait with bated breath.'

The lump in my throat makes it impossible to speak so I breathe deeply, and nod my gratitude at his faith in me.

'OK?'

'Failure is not an option. Today, I will not let Ebony down.'

'Good. Now, are you ready?'

I look into my cousin's golden eyes, a source of courage from which I have drawn many times already, and I nod.

36

Ebony

My first instinct is panic, and I lose it for a while when darkness closes over me and I feel as if I can't breathe. But it doesn't matter how hard I kick or punch or try to tear it, the fabric doesn't come apart. Zavier – *the fraud* – confirms my suspicions that the *lamorak* is unbreakable, and that I'm only wasting my energy trying to destroy it. So I put myself into a quiet state to conserve my strength, and sanity.

Feeling groggy, I wake to the swish and crackle of breaking branches as Zavier runs through the forest, carrying me at colossal speed. He stops abruptly and inhales deeply. Rotating his shoulders, he compresses the muscles of his upper torso and tightens his hold on me by pulling me deeper into his chest.

No! No! I'm not ready!

His wings discharge with a mighty *whoosh!* The backwards drag is powerful and jolting, like being in a car and going from zero to a hundred in one second.

It happens in a blink.

Once his wings settle into a steady rhythm, everything about him relaxes. I sense a change around me but I'm not sure exactly what. I listen keenly for sounds, but there's only the paced swish-swishing of ... thirteen, no, fourteen pairs of wings. Gradually I become aware there are no animal sounds, no insects or birds. There's no rustling of branches or leaves, no distant hum of traffic, no siren or blasting horn. It's creepy. I hate not knowing where I am, or seeing where I'm going, but this blind silence is different. It's overwhelming.

Now and then male voices sound off in a pattern: the twelve Prodigies and Prince Luca must be flying in some kind of formation around us. After a while of careful listening I catch something in the distance. It takes a moment to realise what I'm hearing is wind.

'Where are you taking me?' I ask.

'My lady, how are you feeling now?' Zavier's voice sounds different from the classroom teacher's voice I came to know so well. It's more formal, and also stronger.

'You *tricked* me. And I don't know who I'm more disgusted with: *you*, or myself for tolerating your lies.'

'Ebony, you were played, and not just by me.'

'What are you talking about?'

'You would not have entertained doubts about being an angel without your trusted friend Jordan feeding your insecurities regularly.'

'But ...' Conversations flit through my head with speed and clarity I've not experienced before. This has to be more of my angelic nature coming out. It's amazing! 'Jordan had his reasons.' *I'm sure of it, or else why would he try to manipulate me?*

Zavier takes his time replying. 'Yes, he did.'

I didn't need the confirmation, but I'm glad I got it anyway. 'Where is Jordan?' I recall the last I saw him, beaten, bleeding, and chained to a rock wall. 'Zavier, tell me Prince Luca released him.'

'Stay calm, Ebony.'

'Zavier, where is Jordan?'

'I'm sure Amber will alert the Brothers.'

'Does she know where the cave is?'

He doesn't answer quickly enough. 'The Brothers will search until they find him.'

'Like my parents? No one has found them yet. What did you do with them?'

'Ebony, listen to me.'

But my heart is frantic. My mind is frantic. Both are moving astronomically fast.

'Ebony!'

'*What?*'

'You have to calm down and stop worrying about your friends. They will find their own way now. I know this is hard to hear, but it must be said.'

'Go on.'

'You're not part of their lives any more. You need to concentrate on taking care of yourself. And . . .'

'Not that I'm interested in *your* advice, but go on. Amuse me.'

'The best you can do for yourself is to submit to the demands of Prince Luca.'

He has to be joking. 'You're deluded if you think I'm going to submit to that monster! Clearly, after months of studying what makes me tick, you don't know me at all.'

'Perhaps not, but for your own survival you need to accept that you belong to Lord Luca. You are now the King of Skade's property, soon to be his wife and the Queen of Skade.'

'Never going to happen. But thanks *so much* for setting me up with the most evil creature in the universe, who only *just* takes the title from you!'

'Don't make this harder than it need be, my lady. Think wisely. Lord Luca doesn't have to be unkind to you.'

'So, if he is, that will be *my* fault? Is that what you're saying? And why are you calling him "Lord" now? What happened to "Prince"?'

'Before the First Angelic War, Luca was a prince who held the highest rank of all the princes in Avena. After the great rebellion he became king of his own new world, but his compatriots refused to recognise his title. Outside of Skade, they still call him prince. Ebony, you must forget everything you learned on Earth. Equality and fairness don't exist in Skade.'

'If your lord or king, or whatever he calls himself, expects me to be his slave, he can just forget it.'

'He wants you to be his *queen*, not his slave. How it all goes will be up to you.'

'He may as well kill me now.'

'Ebony, even if you want to die, you can't. And it would only entertain him to watch you try to kill yourself.'

'That's sick!'

As much as I hate the thought, I probably should listen carefully in case something Zavier says proves useful. 'That story you fabricated about my birth was very convincing.

I almost believed you. At times I think I did. How I allowed myself is unfathomable to me.'

'Don't be too critical of yourself, Ebony. I'm good at what I do and there's something about me that you don't know.'

'I don't want to know anything more about you. I've heard enough of your lies.'

He goes silent, but I have questions, lots of them, and he owes me answers. 'How long have you been planning my abduction?'

'Let's see, I began planning for this day a century ago.'

'*Excuse me?*'

'To ensure absolute success I covered every possible outcome.'

'But there would have been so many variables! You couldn't possibly have prepared for every one of them. That's impossible. Life isn't formulaic.'

'Yours was. I made sure of it.'

'How? Give me an example.'

'I ensured you would be raised with a scientific mindset.'

Well, he did achieve that. Even when the subject wasn't science, in my home-school lessons Mum would always remind me to, 'Observe, propose, test and analyse. Believe only in what you can see, feel or touch.' This fact-based way of thinking had quite an effect on the choices I made growing up. It eventually became the way I selected to believe or not believe in things, like religion, near-death experiences, or anything supernatural.

'How did you know my parents would comply with all your conditions?'

'I just had to find a suitable couple.'

'You didn't answer my question.' His arms stiffen around me, and I ask again, 'Just tell me how you knew John and Heather Hawkins would follow your orders without question.'

He hesitates and I think about what type of people he needed – a couple who, once they had started to raise me, would be so terrified of losing me that they would abide by any conditions he put in the adoption contract.

Around the time of my birth, Mum and Dad were grieving for the baby boy they had lost. He wasn't even an hour old when he stopped breathing in Mum's arms. Yeah, they were desperate enough to do just about ... Wait ... No, he wouldn't ... Only a monster would contemplate something that horrendous.

The thought terrifies me and I pull at the *lamorak*.

'Stop moving,' he hisses.

But I don't. I need to see his eyes. I take a deep breath. 'Zavier, tell me you didn't ...'

His sudden erratic heartbeat reveals that it's true.

'He was an innocent baby who had just started his life! I haven't been an angel long, but I'm pretty sure that killing a human infant is breaking a damn serious law in any dimension.'

'You would be correct.'

'You're evil!'

'I had no choice.'

'No choice but to murder a healthy infant to ensure his parents would agree to *any* condition you put in front of them?'

His voice drops. 'There's no going back, Ebony. I can't change the past.'

'I hope you find it extremely difficult to live with yourself.'

'No more, no less than usual,' he murmurs.

'Why are you doing this? What does Luca hold over you?'

He sighs. 'It's a long story.'

'Then give me the short version.'

He sighs again. 'A long time ago I had to leave Avena. Lord Luca welcomed me to Skade, but . . . I disliked it there so I asked the king to cease my existence.'

'Why didn't you go back to Avena?'

'I was forbidden.'

'So you wanted to die?'

'Yes. At the time existing seemed pointless.'

'But here you are, in the flesh.'

'Lord Luca said he would do it himself but only after I managed his Death Watchers for a thousand years. It would mean living on Earth for that time.'

'So even death has a price in Skade,' I remark dryly. 'I've heard of Death Watchers. They convince the dying to choose Skade. So what happened?'

'I came to like Earth.'

'Did he let you go after you served the thousand years? Or is he charging you to live on Earth by doing his dirty work?'

He inhales sharply, as if caught by surprise. After a moment he says, 'Every hundred years I must do a job for him.'

'Aha! And this century it's me! I suppose you jumped at the chance. Did you?'

'No, I refused. I offered to do anything, *anything* else.'

'Sure you did.'

'I don't blame you for not believing me.'

'What does it matter whether I believe you or not? You're a monster, just like your employer. So what was the deal?'

'On your safe delivery to his palace a thousand human souls will be released from Mount Mi'Ocra.'

'How philanthropic of you!' I hope the coldness in my voice freezes his heart. 'So what is this mountain, a village for souls?'

'Something like that, except their housing takes the form of caves, crevasses, a nook under a ledge or even a rock, if they're lucky.'

'Zavier, the hero,' I mutter sarcastically, so angry inside my blood is boiling. The red haze descends and makes me feel claustrophobic. I try to breathe slower, lighter, calmer. 'Tell me, what was in this for you?'

In a tight voice, as if he's speaking through clenched teeth, he says, 'Ten million dollars.'

'Thought as much.'

He stiffens and says, 'In a world where money is the commodity by which all things are measured, a man does what is necessary to survive.'

'But you're not a man.'

'No more, no less than your precious Nathaneal, who lives more amongst humans than angels.'

Yeah, because he's been looking for me! 'Don't compare yourself with Nathaneal. You are poison where he is wine. Now get this *lamorak* off me.'

261

He goes quiet, and in his silence my mind ripples with a sense of familiarity about this mountain he called Mi'Orca with souls living in caves and nooks. I try to hold on to the feeling, recall where I'd heard it mentioned before, but I'm so tense it hovers just out of my reach. 'Tell me more about Mi'Ocra.'

'Let's see, Mi'Ocra began as a volcano and was active for tens of thousands of years. Its walls grew to unimaginable heights, and when the lava ran out over time the reservoir filled with water and has since become an underground ocean. But, Ebony, there is more to this place, and it's time you know it all.'

I brace myself inside this enforced darkness. 'Go on.'

He takes a deep breath. 'There's an island in the centre of this ocean with a prison on it.'

At the mention of a prison my mouth goes dry. 'This island, is it dangerous?'

'Deadly.'

'How so?'

'Altering the prison's weight ratio will trigger an explosion. The island and everything on it will sink to the ocean floor where prehistoric aquatic creatures live in perpetual hunger.'

'Zavier, why are you telling me this?'

'Because, Ebony, there's something you need to know.'

But I've figured it out, and it makes me angry and sad at the same time. 'This is the prison where Luca is keeping my parents.'

'Yes.'

How will anyone find them there?

'Try to keep calm, Ebony.'

'Calm. Who would know to look in this underground world? It's not as if I can tell anyone who might be able to help them. Obviously, this is why you're only telling me *now*. Do you have any idea how much I hate you?' I need to see his face to tell him how much. 'Zavier, get the *lamorak* off me.'

'But, Ebony –'

'Get it off now, or I'll crawl out of it. I swear, Zavier, I will keep moving until I find how to open this thing.'

He shifts position, balancing more of my weight against his chest while he tugs on the fabric at the back of my shoulder blades. As he finally lowers the *lamorak* from my head, I imagine Mum and Dad locked in this underground world, so far from home and all alone. I take in a shuddering breath as tears flow freely from my eyes.

'Are you all right, Ebony?'

Wiping my tears away, I sniff hard and take notice of my surroundings for the first time. We're flying over a violent, dark-grey ocean, while above is a muddy-coloured sky half covered with green-tinged clouds moving fast and in two different directions. Instinctively, I grip Zavier harder. 'This is not Earth.'

He sniggers. 'Technically it is. You can still breathe here.'

'You'll tell me when I can't?'

He laughs. 'Ebony, we're in the Crossing. Didn't anyone tell you about it?'

'I know it keeps the dimensions apart.'

He nods. 'In a few hours we will arrive at the Gates of

Skade. It's time for you to leave your past life behind and look towards your future.'

I look for the soldiers, surprised to see them spread across an area as wide as a football field, with Zavier and me flying in the centre, Prince Luca about a hundred metres directly ahead. Every once in a while they glance down at the wild unfamiliar ocean with frothy brown-tops everywhere, deep swirling whirlpools, and waves that surge up to obliterate what appears to be an approaching coastline. 'You won't drop me, will you?'

'Of course not!' He flicks my chin upwards. 'Keep your eyes up, not down. Ahead, not behind.'

'All my life I've had good instincts about people. Some of your story made sense to me. I even remembered things from my childhood that seemed to back up a truth I believed I saw in your eyes.'

'It was a confusing time for you, but, Ebony, let me tell you something that will make everything clearer,' Zavier says. 'You believed me because you are a reader of souls; you know when someone is telling the truth, and I was telling you the truth. So don't be too harsh on yourself.'

'Maybe at times you were telling the truth, but you lied too.'

'True, but I didn't lie about one important fact.'

'Which one was that?'

'Whenever I allowed you to look into my eyes, I was not lying.'

'I don't believe you. That can't be true. I looked into your eyes heaps of times.'

'I was there at your birth.'

'But my mother wasn't your sister, and I wasn't born on your living-room floor. On the night I was born you were on Avena, snatching me from the midwife's hands the moment she pulled me from my mother's womb.'

'Masked by magic to disguise who and what I was, the midwife saw only the evil act I was committing.'

'According to Nathaneal, she said she saw a hideous monster.'

His eyes close as if he's recalling the moment he irrecoverably wrecked my life, then he exhales a deep breath. 'I took you to my house and cared for you for three days, then wrapped you in a blanket to meet your adopted human parents.'

'Are you telling me the truth now?'

'Ebony, soon we will be standing at Skade's entrance, and from that point on we won't have a private conversation again. That's why I'm giving you all the answers you've craved these last few months, so you can enter into your new life knowing the truth of who you really are.'

He glances down at me with a look of affection in his eyes.

'Don't look at me as if you care!'

His arms tighten around me. 'Ebony, I *am* your uncle.'

'Not this again!'

'Look into my eyes. Those three days taken I kept you in my house I put you in a bedroom with a painted ceiling.'

'I remember the painted ceiling.'

'I needed three days with you,' he says.

'Needed? Why? What did you do to me?'

265

'I applied a concealing glamour to your skin so your glow would not frighten the humans I had selected to raise you.'

'That's why they put me in dark clothes. They said my skin cells couldn't tolerate the sun's rays.'

He nods. 'I explained how it was a temporary condition, and that you would grow out of it by the time you were three or four, which is the usual age infant glow recedes.'

'So what else did you do to me in those three days?'

'I . . .'

'Zavier?'

He sighs. 'I blocked your angelical memories so you couldn't recall any you had inherited from your ancestors, or remember anything that had happened to you before you arrived at the Hawkins' house. Seraphs can evoke memories of time they spent in their mother's womb, and sometimes even before that.'

I gasp, horrified by his confession, a confession that explains *so* much!

He glances up at the fast-moving clouds and expels a staggering breath. I brace myself for whatever else he has yet to confess.

'Spit it out, Zavier, before it chokes you.'

His eyes lower to mine. 'Your mother's name is Elesha, a remarkable and beautiful Seraph.'

'You *loved* her,' I whisper.

'Yes. It's why I had to leave. You have her hair colour, and her eyes.'

'Did she . . . love . . . you?'

'She was completely loyal to your father, Rhamiel, a high commander of Avena's Royal Army. And ... and, Ebony, I really am your uncle. I know you don't believe that, but the truth is ... your father is my brother.'

37

Nathaneal

I descend in a silent glide, quickly confirming that, at least on the outside, there are no guards. I hover above the prison a moment to study the gate, mind-linking the image to Michael. It's a perplexity of criss-crossing bars of obsidian and iron. Dissolving the bars with my powers, a portion at a time, I gradually lower my weight to the solid stone floor.

The interior is dark and blessedly cool. With my wings tucked close by my sides, I find the two humans who must be John and Heather in a cave at the end of a long tunnel of yellow rock. There are no bars, locked doors, or guards in sight, but also nowhere for these prisoners to go.

They lie on stone beds covered in damp, filthy straw. Their sluggish beating hearts and shallow breaths reveal their tenacity to live.

But Heather is in better shape than John.

Moving closer slowly, I allow a brief moment to observe my surroundings. A fire pit in the cave's centre holds only cold ash and scraps of a charred animal. There is no indication that anyone has been here for several days. Whoever is responsible for John and Heather's wellbeing has left them to die, alone, with no answers to the many questions they must have.

'Heather, can you hear me?'

She stirs and sits up, her eyes fluttering open as she searches for the source of the voice. She sees me and scoots backwards into the wall.

I smile at her and gently move my wings. 'Don't be afraid. I'm not here to hurt you.'

'Am I dead?'

'No, you're not dead.'

'But I've been here *so* long ...' she sighs. 'Oh my God, you're different to those other angels.' She squints as she peers at me, then bursts out laughing. When she catches her breath, she wipes a tear and says, 'I'm hallucinating, aren't I? No one is *that* good-looking.'

Michael's sniggering laughter lets me know he's behind me. Then Heather sees him. 'Oh my Lord, there are two of you and you're *both* spectacular. The other ones were brutes and scary.'

'Heather.' I try to get her attention. 'Please don't speak for a minute.'

'Oh!' She covers her mouth with both hands, and then says through them, 'Sorry, it's just nice to have someone to talk to. I have so many questions. My daughter, do you know her? Do you know how she is? Oh, God, tell me she's all right.'

I hear Michael's laughter building. Before it bursts out, I mind-link, *Don't even think it.*

She's all yours, cousin, he mind-links back.

'Heather, my name is Nathaneal.' I point to my left. 'This is Michael. We're here to take you and John home to your daughter. And, yes, the last time I saw Ebony she was fine. She never gave up hope that a team of angels would find you. Several search attempts have tried but your prison is well hidden.'

A sob of pure joy bursts from Heather's lips. Taking a deep breath, she wipes her eyes with trembling fingers. 'Does Ebony know what happened to us?'

'No one knows what happened to you. And now is not the time for a briefing. We need to get you both out of here fast.'

She glances sadly at her husband, still lying on the bed, unmoving. 'It's only me. John passed a couple of days ago. Ebony will be crushed.'

'Heather, John's heart is still beating.'

'Really? *Really?* Oh thank goodness.'

'How long has he been unconscious?'

She shakes her head. 'I don't know. Two or three days. It's hard to tell time here.'

'Let me try to wake him.' Swiftly, I slip into his dream. *John? I am the angel Nathaneal and I'm here to take you home to Ebony. Open your eyes, John. See that I'm really here with you.*

John struggles to open his eyes. His left is swollen and badly bruised, but when he sees me he pulls himself up to a sitting position. Then, to the amazement of Heather, who starts crying again, he gets up and stands on his feet.

But he's clearly in bad shape with a fractured fibula just below his left knee, another fracture in his spine, C5 and maybe also C6. At least his spinal cord remains strong. There is bruising with swelling on both sides of his jaw and some internal injuries. But those I would need to lay my hands on to assess accurately.

He was tortured, but carefully kept alive, I link with Michael.

He nods. *He was worth more alive than dead*, he says, *until now.*

John's injuries are grave, making his chances of surviving the journey across Skade's vast landscape, *and then* the pressures of the Crossing, slight at best. Thank the stars we still have the two *lamoraks*, or returning John and Heather to Earth would be impossible.

I scour the prison for signs of a Death Watcher's presence, but apparently even the reapers will not risk entrapment beneath this improbable ocean for the sake of one or two human souls.

John's partially opened eyes study me. He sees Michael, notices our wings, and a sense of wonderment fills him. A light switches on inside him and a tear escapes as he reaches for his wife's hand. This is what I admire most about the human race, their perpetual capacity to endure trauma and tragedy without losing hope.

'Tell us what you need us to do,' John says.

With golden wings pulsing lightly, Michael positions himself beside Heather. 'Don't fear us,' he tells them.

I indicate I'm ready and on Michael's count of three we lift the two human beings into our arms and move quickly into the tunnel.

A series of clicks warns us that we've triggered the explosives.

Michael makes it into the outer passage at the first rumble from below. John and I are not so fortunate. Though I'm right behind Michael, the floor breaks apart between us, forcing me back into the cave while he continues to move towards the gate with Heather. I quickly lose sight of them when, behind me, the cave wall starts to collapse and big slabs of rock crash down on each other. Another explosion sends a fireball rushing towards us. I spin round in search of another way out, but there are only collapsing boulders everywhere.

I decide to take my chances with the fire since it's the fastest and probably our only way out. Beating my wings gently, I lift us off the ground. Then, curving my body round John's torso, I throw my hands over his head. Taking a deep breath, I fly into the flames.

The prison sinks into the ocean, dousing the flames as it drags us down along with enormous rocks that have become threatening projectiles. I glimpse sunlight fleetingly above my head. As boulders smash into each other all around us, I avoid those I can, taking hits from those I can't. Focusing upwards through the dark waters, I search again for glimpses of sunlight, but all I see is an ocean strewn with disassembling boulders, intent on pushing us further down.

38

Ebony

Zavier shifts my weight in preparation to land. Setting me on my feet, he peels the *lamorak* off, supporting me while I step out and firm up my wonky legs.

I take a deep breath and allow some moments to adjust to my new surroundings. We're standing on a mountain peak covered in green-tinged ice with winds blowing at us from two directions and making my hair a chaotic mess. As I hold it down, I take in the astonishing series of ranges with ridges, valleys and ice-covered peaks for as far as I can see in every direction, the ocean now far behind. 'Wow.'

'Don't mistake beauty for safety,' Zavier warns.

The Prodigies start landing one after another, the whoosh of their wings as they touch down scattering pale green snow into the air. One Prodigy immediately distributes dried-food snacks and water flasks, and while everyone partakes, another flies to a peak higher than ours.

'So this is the Crossing.' Saying it aloud helps to keep me grounded in reality because it would be easy to talk myself into believing I've gone mad and this is a delusion on a grand scale.

But this is not a delusion. It's not a dream. I'm standing in another world, a nothing world, an in-between space that links the four dimensions that are all bound to Earth – the four dimensions that *are* Earth.

Curiosity aroused, I watch the Prodigy on the higher peak lift his arms out wide and turn his face up to the sky, where ice-green clouds move fast and in two opposing directions.

While I watch, I untangle the *lamorak* and start folding it. 'What's *he* doing?'

'Gamorn? He's taking a weather report.'

'Really? I didn't think angels bothered with that sort of thing.'

Zavier says, 'Normally we don't, but we're taking the long route to Skade today.'

I look at him. 'Why is that?' But then it comes to me. 'Because we entered the Crossing at the opposite end of the world to where dark angels usually enter; so now we have a longer journey and have to worry about things like weather.'

He stares and I ask, 'What?'

'Your mother had a quick mind. You must get it from her.'

'Don't, Zavier.'

'Don't what?'

'Mention the mother I will never know because of you.'

Gamorn returns, flying low over the peaks, his massive charcoal wings beating fast and blowing up a storm of green snow where he passes. He heads straight to Prince Luca, standing alone on the next peak over, while the

Prodigies, mostly sitting on this wider peak with us, turn to listen.

It's then, when everyone is still, I notice the silence again. Other than Gamorn's foreign words, and winds whistling through valleys, it's completely and utterly empty.

Nothing lives here.

When Gamorn completes his report, some Prodigies groan in low voices. One soldier makes an obscene hand gesture at the sky. Prince Luca turns his head and stares at me with a frown.

'Zavier, Prince Luca looks worried. What's wrong with Gamorn's forecast?'

He massages his left shoulder. 'Er, we're heading for some rough weather, that's all.'

'Either Prince Luca and his soldiers are overreacting or you're seriously underplaying. Which is it?'

He sighs. 'There's a three-system low pressure event up ahead.' He glances at my confused expression. 'In other words, a hurricane. We're heading straight into it.'

'So what do we do now? Go back?'

'We go through it.' He shakes out the *lamorak* I just folded. 'You will have to keep this on for the duration.'

'But I want to see what's happening.'

'My lady, it's not safe for you to be exposed to those elements.'

'You don't understand how I ...' Just in time, I stop myself from revealing how frightened I am of storms at night. With the *lamorak* on, it feels like night all the time.

OK, so I have to grow up fast now. I can't avoid what scares me any more. That doesn't mean I should simply do everything I'm told. 'An angel should not be hidden away in a bag.'

'About the *lamorak*.' He holds it up. 'You have to trust me. You need to understand that the dangers in this nether-world are real. You've seen the clouds move in two directions?'

I nod.

'Well, in this place, *everything* moves in different directions. If a cyclonic gust should snatch you from my arms, it could conceivably carry you across mountains and oceans before it weakened enough to release you. Ebony, there's a reason no one lives in this world. To be lost here means to be lost for ever. And when you are immortal . . .'

We become aware of Prodigies falling silent, their eyes shifting to us as they tune in to our discussion.

'I won't let anything happen to you,' Zavier whispers.

The staring soldiers remind me that I'm their prisoner, and I spit out the word, '*Pity!*'

The muscles around Zavier's mouth and eyes tighten. Lines appear where there were none before. 'What would you prefer,' he shouts, unable to contain his temper any more, 'to be burned to ash by the strike of a lightning bolt? To be swept up by violent winds and never seen again? To live in perpetual hunger, scavenging on what little seeds you are able to dig up out of frozen soil or dry baked mud? Waking each morning to a different landscape than the previous night?'

I don't respond, except to release a weary breath. He softens his tone. 'The storms that circulate the Crossing are nothing like you've experienced on Earth.'

Through clenched teeth, I mutter, 'But I can't breathe inside that thing.'

'Ebony, you're stronger than that.'

'Have you been locked in one before?'

His eyes soften. 'No.'

'Then you have no right to lecture me.'

Prince Luca appears in front of me. He glares at Zavier, dismissing him, then it's just the prince and me, and an audience of Prodigies looking for entertainment.

'You will wear the *lamorak*,' he says in his velvety voice, and with the speed and stealth of a snake Prince Luca grabs the back of my neck. Heat sears into my flesh but I try not to react. Then, at a much slower pace, he runs the fingertips of his other hand lightly down the length of my hair.

'Step back from me, Prince,' I say evenly.

No one speaks, though the Prodigies' expectations fuel the air like a dozen rockets lined up for take-off. They're waiting for something.

Prince Luca tilts my chin up with the long nail of his thumb. Our eyes connect and a bridge forms from his mind to mine. I'm not expecting this and the suddenness and openness of it shocks me.

I see that he wants me in a way that he's never wanted any other being before – to possess me completely, from my physical body to the innermost thoughts of my mind. And though he knows he should wait until I'm eighteen, he's acknowledging that to do so would be virtually impossible. He wants me now.

The invasion is too personal. Intimidating and violating. I try to push him out of my head, but he doesn't move so I'm either not doing it right or he's too strong for me. I remind myself how I'm still learning. Inside, my blood throbs through my veins. I notice the red haze at the edge of my vision and I reach for the energy that always seems to accompany it. 'Get out of my head, Prince Luca.'

His eyebrows rise. *I will leave when I'm ready, Princess.*

I focus on his words, holding on to them even though they feel heavy like bricks. I draw on my anger, then shove his words back at him, imagining I'm hurling hot rocks off a bridge.

He cries out, stepping backwards and shaking his head. A chorus of gasps erupts from the Prodigies.

I've hurt the Dark Prince and now I don't know what to expect. Will he strangle me in retaliation? Beat me to a pulp?

He stares at me, his eyes flashing the colour of autumn leaves. *You have hidden talents, Princess. I look forward to exploring them in a more intimate environment,* he links.

Sniffing my hair, he runs his fingertips down the length of it again.

'When Nathaneal learns you've kidnapped me, he'll bring war down on you. Is that what you want? Another war? You've shown me your cities through my dreams; I've seen your people. Do they deserve to have their homes and lifestyles destroyed?'

'You *care* about my people?'

I shrug. 'I don't know them, but it seems to me they're innocent bystanders. Do you want them to end up as collateral damage?'

278

'Are you suggesting I release you?'

'Well . . . yes.'

He chuckles as if I've cracked a funny joke. He glances at his Prodigies, still laughing, and they laugh with him.

'Don't laugh at me!' I spit.

'Ebony, I will not release you, so you should dismiss that thought from your head. If war is waged because of my actions –' he lifts his hands – 'then so be it.'

He strokes my hair again. The watching soldiers seem to all breathe in at once. 'Your hair and the setting sun are the same colour,' he says, with a degree of gentleness that surprises me. 'Once you are queen, no one but your maid-servant and I will touch your hair again.'

Oh, Nathaneal, where are you? When you *touch my hair, the strands curl around your fingers of their own volition. But now, here, with Prince Luca, they lie flat and pretend they are dead, just like my heart is without you.*

My hair draws away from Luca's touch, strand by strand. His left eyebrow lifts and he makes a growling sound deep in his throat. His green eyes blaze with those gold flecks again, but this time they turn glossy black almost instantly, and a sudden pounding ache throbs inside my head. *You will not always yearn for him!*

I dig my heels in, determined not to break eye contact first.

Then Luca amps up the power, making my head feel heavy, compressed.

Damn it! I won't be able to take much more. He'll turn my brain to mush. 'OK, stop. Stop! You've made your point – you're stronger than me!'

Amazingly he does stop, but I can't let him walk all over me. 'You might be physically stronger, at least today, but you will *never* own what's on the inside.'

It's the wrong thing to say. A Prodigy, the young one with black shaggy curls, called Sarakiel, gasps and moves as if he wants to intervene. Lieutenant Saul slaps an open palm on his chest, stopping him.

I brace myself for Prince Luca's retaliation. But all he does is lean down so that his mouth is equal with my cheek, his heat scalding my ice-cold face. 'On the day you turn eighteen you will become my queen. Skade is where you belong. It is written in stone with the blood of dead warrior angels,' he says. 'One day you will understand, and that is when I will own your body, your soul, and your mind.'

He lifts his head and motions to Zavier with a sharp nod. 'We take off soon. Make sure she's wearing the *lamorak*.'

'Yes, my lord,' Zavier says, and, lifting me into his arms, flies us to an unoccupied peak where he sets me down and begins lecturing me. 'Are you insane?'

My head still hurts and I mumble, 'I'm sorry, what?'

'Now is neither the time nor place to prove your strength, Ebony, or reveal the force of your inner will.'

I give myself a mental shake. I can't let Prince Luca's creepy words affect me.

'Ebony?'

'What?'

He peers down at me. 'Are you all right?'

'Yeah, I'm brilliant. Fantastic! Never felt better!' I look him straight in the eyes. 'I know I sound like a child right now, but for what you have done to me I could kill you.

The fact that you deceived your own family disgusts me, and I feel stronger hatred than I think an angel is supposed to feel.'

He stares down at me, his brown eyes wide and unblinking, his big chest expanding as he draws in a deep breath. Then he nods in a kind of weird slow motion and says in an exquisitely gentle voice I've not heard him use before, 'As you should, my lady. Precisely, as you should.'

39

Ebony

We take to the air again with Zavier carrying me in his arms and the black *lamorak* confining me to darkness and oblivion. The storm is too wide for us to skirt around it, so we fly directly into its path.

Hours later prevailing winds continue to pound us, bringing pelting rains with them. And with lightning tearing the sky in vertical and horizontal patterns, we gain ground with painful slowness.

'How long will this last?' I ask in a rare moment of calm.

'It stops when it stops,' Zavier snaps. I don't ask again because, even though I can't see his face, I can tell by his brutal hold that he's maintaining fierce concentration to keep the gales from snatching me from his arms.

Then, abruptly, everything stops. Even the winds are silent. The sudden stillness makes my skin itch. This strange calm in the midst of a violent storm would never happen on Earth unless we were in the eye.

'Zavier, are we in the –'

He cuts me off. 'Don't say it, Ebony.'

I can hear his heart beating. 'Zavier, are you afraid?'

'Yes, my lady.'

His admission surprises me and makes my own heart beat faster. 'Of what?'

He takes too long to answer and I have to prompt him, 'Zavier?'

'Dropping you.'

'Oh. *Really?*'

'You don't have to sound so surprised. You are my niece.'

'Who you sold to the King of Skade.'

'Point made.'

'Is there a soldier who can give you a break?'

His answer is decisive. 'No.'

The moment we fly back into the storm, Zavier takes a deep breath, tightens his arms round me more intensely than before, and hisses near my ear, 'Hold tight, niece. With luck, we shall be through the worst quickly.'

It's as if the sky opens up and throws everything it has at us. Every lightning strike generates an explosion of energy that scatters the Prodigies in different directions. More than once, a lightning bolt strikes so close, the hairs on my head stand on end and I scream from the depths of my lungs.

Hot chocolate always soothed me when storms struck at night. I close my eyes and force myself to visualise my mother bringing me a cup to drink. But this is a bad idea. My heart wrenches at the knowledge that I'm never going to see Mum and Dad again, never feel their loving arms around me, or hear their voices, or watch their proud faces when I graduate from high school.

My tears flow and, at least for now, I let them.

I don't know how long we ride this storm, but eventually

the winds die down, the rain stops pelting us from different directions, thunder ceases to deafen us, and I'm still safe in Zavier's arms. That's when I think I doze off for a few minutes, so weary I can't force my eyes to remain open.

I wake when we come to a sudden stop and the only sounds are fourteen pairs of beating wings hovering beside us.

A lump forms in my throat. 'Have we, um . . . arrived?'

'Not yet,' he says. 'But at least the storm has passed and the way ahead is clear. We'll make better time now, my lady.'

'There you go again. Zavier, don't call me, "my lady". It's medieval and just plain weird coming from someone who used to be my science teacher.'

He laughs. 'As you wish. But now I don't quite know what to call you. Perhaps, "your highness"?'

'I certainly won't answer to *that*.'

'How about "Princess", like Lord Luca prefers?'

'Not that either.'

He sighs. 'If only it were that simple, my lady.'

'Stop it right now! My name is Ebony.'

'All right, all right, simmer down, niece. Is that better?'

'I suppose.'

'Once we're in Skade, I could have my tongue cut out for disrespecting you.'

His words send a sickening zing down my spine. Zavier already thinks of me as the Queen of Skade.

A Prodigy suddenly calls out an order and Zavier banks left. They all do, and I get the sense we're making way for something to pass.

I listen carefully, and before long I hear voices, a few at

first, and then hundreds, chattering away in languages I recognise as belonging to various nations of Earth.

'What's going on?'

'What you're hearing are human souls on their way to a special dimension where they will live in tranquillity for eternity.'

'Do you mean heaven? Are you telling me there's an entrance to heaven nearby?'

There is a long pause before he answers. 'It's called *Peridis*.'

'Can I see these souls? Just in case, you know, my p–parents are amongst them.'

He snaps, 'I told you where your parents are!'

'Yeah, in a prison that will explode if anyone tries to rescue them. The explosion will kill them too, right? And when they die their souls will go to … to …' I choke on the word. Thinking about Mum and Dad in a place that's only for souls, a world I will never see, is too much to handle right now.

'Ebony, even in death, no one escapes Mount Mi'Ocra. Souls live in the tunnels and caves there, hiding from the three-headed dog packs and … other wild things.'

'But the souls you freed as part of your payment for me came from that mountain. You said that.'

'Yes, but I had to bargain for those. There's no other way out for the souls who are sent to Mi'Ocra.'

'That's hardly fair.'

'Brace yourself, niece, because where you're going you will see unfairness every day. It's the way of life for the souls who end up in Skade and the angels born there, through no choice of their own, generation after generation.'

He groans. 'So for the last time, Ebony, heed my warning

285

and forget your old life. Forget everything about the human world. Forget you ever had human parents. Forget Nathaneal, and Jordan and Amber, and your horses, and your farm. They are all dead to you now. Remember, your entire life on Earth was a lie. But the truth is you were destined to be a queen long before you were born. Soon you will become one. Embrace the position and all that it brings.'

'Does it ease your conscience that I hate you?'

'Nothing will ease my conscience, dear.'

'You left Avena because your love for my mother went unrequited. You tried to live in Skade but hated it. Now you get to live on Earth where I want to be. Why do you get a choice when I don't?'

'You're too smart for your own good. That's going to be a problem for you in Skade. *Damn!* Your talents will be squandered in that miserable forsaken world,' he mutters angrily.

Suddenly, a soldier wrenches me from Zavier's arms.

Whack!

Someone – I'm guessing Prince Luca – just hit Zavier. I hear the whooshing sound of him flying through the air. His scream goes on and on, receding slowly as I assume his body hurtles further away.

'Why did you do that?' I yell, trapped inside the *lamorak*.

The human voices are gone, but I still need to see what's happening, so I try yanking the fabric down over my head. By now I've figured the release mechanism is somewhere between my shoulder blades.

The Prodigy holding me mutters a string of words in his

foreign language as I move around trying to release the *lamorak*. He sounds anxious and suddenly shouts out what sounds like a plea for help.

'Hold still!' Luca commands, which I ignore, wisely or unwisely. My guess is that land is not far below. And since I'm immortal, even if I were to break both my legs, they'll heal themselves – eventually.

I try again to yank the *lamorak* down from my head. I pull and tug and try poking it with my nail to get a grip, yanking it over my face with my teeth. It's such a tight fit it sticks in all the wrong places. But I haven't tried everything yet. So when these attempts fail, I try rotating it the opposite way, rolling the fabric down my back with curled toes.

Suddenly Prince Luca bellows in a thundering voice, 'Zavier, I command you to return immediately!' He ejects a burst of energy that blows us sideways. I assume this is supposed to break Zavier's momentum, not send the Prodigy holding me into a backwards spiral.

Prince Luca yells, 'Thorian, do not drop her!'

He doesn't – yet.

'Gamorn, Sarakiel, hurry,' Prince Luca yells.

Gamorn and Sarakiel beat their wings hard.

Suddenly I slip from Thorian's hold and begin to fall. One pair of arms almost catches me, but fails, while the other one's beating wings sound too far away.

Strangely, I thought free-falling would feel better than this, but with no room to spread my arms or legs, it's a nightmare. And now I'm not so sure land is close below me.

I drop for the longest time, what must be thousands of

metres. The wind whistling past changes and becomes sharper, ear-piercing. Soon I'll be hitting the ground. Even an immortal will have a hard time recovering from a drop this high.

It's then that I hear the familiar sound of Zavier's wings. He seems to take too long to reach me, but finally his strong arms wrap round me, and I feel safe again.

He squeezes me until I'm breathless, murmuring words that I don't understand, but which are thick with emotion. I clear my throat, 'Uh, Zavier, you do realise we're still dropping?'

He lifts his head off my shoulder. 'On purpose. Don't fret. You were moving very fast.'

'So were you.'

He slows the beat of his wings, gradually coming to a complete stop, and we simply hover for a few moments. 'Thank you, Zavier,' I murmur, and press my face into his shoulder.

'I'm sorry this happened, Ebony. I should have been more careful. I know better than to speak against the kingdom. It's the one sure way to antagonise the king.'

'Do you *have* to take me back? Prince Luca just attacked you. And you know what he wants to do with me. Can you turn round and fly us back to Earth? The Prodigies are still weak. You would out-fly them all.'

'Ebony, there is no place to hide on the Earth if Prince Luca is looking for you.'

'If you took me back, Nathaneal would protect you.'

'Nathaneal would destroy me!'

'Like Prince Luca just tried to do? Come on, Zavier.

This is my only chance, and I need you to help me.'

'Ebony, I have a contract with the King of Skade.'

'I know – me, in exchange for a thousand souls and ten million dollars.'

'It's not that simple. Contracts are *covenants* between angels. The only way out is by mutual agreement or a battle to the death.'

'That's barbaric.'

I feel him shrug. 'It's the way these things have been done for thousands of years.'

'Well, it's stupid.'

'Perhaps as queen, you could have that ruling changed.'

'Sure. And Prince Luca will simply let me.'

'It won't be his decision to make. That would be a matter for the high court to decide, and only a royal ranked as high as king or queen can submit a law for review. You wouldn't need the king's permission to submit.'

We reach the others, and Prince Luca starts yelling at Zavier, his voice still magnified with a strange echo. 'Should one more traitorous word pass your lips, I will throw you into outer space where you will be crushed to dust for the cosmic winds to spread throughout the universe.'

He barks out a command in his own language and I hear the Prodigies moving around, falling into their standard formation around us. We start flying again, but this time Prince Luca remains right alongside us.

And now I'm not sure who I hate most – Luca for wanting me to be his queen, or Zavier for making it possible.

40

Nathaneal

Searching for light between descending boulders, while carrying John, is becoming a losing battle. John's injuries are critical. Oxygen deprivation could end his fragile hold on life.

Ebony, my sweet love, if I should fail you in this, please find it in your heart to forgive me.

Swimming against the explosion's powerful downward drag starts taking its toll on my strength. I need to break the surface, quickly. A glimpse of white light high above looks hopeful, but a massive boulder plummets towards us.

Too large to deflect, I swim with the drag until I clear it. And now I have taken John into deeper, darker depths.

I'm sorry, my love.

Michael and Heather are nowhere in sight. Until I know otherwise, I will assume they became airborne before the downward drag took hold, and are now safe.

So far I have shared oxygen from my own lungs with John, but now I'm struggling for air too, and beginning to doubt that I will make it to the surface before losing consciousness.

I can't afford for John to slip from my arms, so I have to find a quick path to the surface through plunging boulders, rocks and other debris. But the last of my air floats up in a series of bubbles and I'm starting to lose focus.

It's then that I see Ebony's face as if she were right in front of me, her rich red hair floating in the water like a silk cloud. Her deep-violet eyes are pleading with me to follow her. I reach out and grasp her arm. *Ebbie, don't go.*

I'm not going anywhere without you, she says. *Come. I know a way.*

Still clutching John, I follow her, relishing the sound of her hauntingly beautiful voice, her spirit voice from our time together in Peridis. *Stay strong, my handsome prince, and we will be as one again soon. Promise me you will not forget me once you have grown into your corporeal body.*

I could never forget you, sweetheart. Never ... But, Ebrielle, you have forgotten me.

She frowns. *Don't tease me.*

You don't remember you're an angel.

That's impossible. My love, don't say such things.

But, Ebbie, it's true.

No! I could never forget you.

She begins to fade. I reach out for her, but she disappears, and in her place I see a bright white light. It becomes three lights. Angels, in maximum glow, descending like torpedoes.

Uriel reaches me first. He takes my shoulders in his hands. *Are you all right, my prince?*

I nod. *John needs air.*

He lifts him out of my hands, and with Isaac and Solomon clearing a path through the debris, we soon break the surface.

By the time I land on the beach, Jez is already clearing John's airways and breathing life back into his lungs under a makeshift shelter of palm tree fronds. But the heat is too much for any human, so as soon as John is breathing again we fly out of this extraordinary and somewhat bewildering underground world that exists where nothing should.

In an abandoned cave about midway up we lay John and Heather on blankets. Everyone waits outside except for Jez and me, giving us space to tend to the humans and prepare them for transport.

After some urgent healing of John's more critical injuries, Jez explains how we're going to transfer them. 'You'll be in a deep-sleep state until you're back on home turf, at which point we will bring you out of it.'

'My home?' Heather asks with a hopeful look.

Jez links with me: *They don't remember the fire!*

It appears their abductors lit the house after taking them.

What should we tell them?

Nothing yet, Jez. I think it best for Ebony to break the news to them, when they're further along the healing process.

Jez smiles at Heather. 'That's right, Heather. We'll have you home before you know it.'

John stirs, his eyes fluttering open. Heather gasps, lifts his hand to her mouth and kisses it gently. 'Hello, my darling. We're going home.'

Weak and far from well yet, John smiles. 'Can't wait, love.'

Tears cascade down Heather's face. 'The angels are going to put us into a deep sleep until we're back, so that we won't feel anything.'

John glances at Jez and me. 'Will we still hear things as they say coma patients do?'

'No, you won't hear, see or feel anything,' Jez explains while wiping a tear from her own cheek. 'And you won't remember anything either, except maybe a strange dream. We have to prepare you for your journey home now, but don't worry – it will soon be over.'

I work on John while Jez works on Heather. When we are sure the two are in their deep-sleep state, and coping with their enforced slower heart rates, Jez and I sit back on some rocks and reach for our flasks and energy snacks.

Tash rushes in with the *lamoraks*. As I help her put them on the humans, I ask if she's seen Solomon.

'I'm here, my prince.'

As soon as I hear his voice I know something is wrong. Uriel, Michael and Isaac walk in behind him. Their disheartened expressions are not what I need to see right now. 'Is it Ebony?'

They exchange glances. My pulse races while I try to stay calm. 'What is it, Sol? Tell me what your source has learned. All of it. Now.'

'I'm sorry, my prince, but Ebony has been captured.'

My body shudders with dread. 'How do you know this? What proof do you have?'

Michael puts a steadying hand on my shoulder, encouraging me to sit on the rock.

'Prince Luca sent a message ahead to his palace staff announcing his imminent return, and to make preparations for the arrival of Skade's future queen.'

'Tell me more, Solomon. Tell me every word.'

'Not counting Ebony, Prince Luca travels with thirteen others, all male. Twelve are his Prodigies. My informant doesn't know who the thirteenth is. There was no name mentioned in the message the palace received.'

'Where are they now?'

'In the Crossing.'

'Could this thirteenth male be Jordan?'

'No, my prince. The unidentified male is the one carrying . . . Ebony.'

I stop a moment to take this in and try to stay calm. 'You've done well, Sol. Do you know if Ebony is wearing the *lamorak*?'

'Yes, my prince, she is.'

I look up at my team. 'I should have aborted this mission.'

Isaac drops down in front of me. 'Thane, we wouldn't have made it back in time anyway.'

I look directly into his eyes. 'I would have.' And then I look at the others. 'We all would have.'

In their silence I ask, 'Any ideas who this thirteenth male could be?'

It seems no one has any. I have no doubt of Jordan's courage or devotion; he would defend Ebony to the death, which is why I'm worried about him too. I pray he is home safe and under Gabriel's protection.

Solomon still has that burning look about him. 'Speak, Solomon, what else do you know?'

'The Crossing hasn't exactly been kind to them.'

'What do you mean? Has Ebony been hurt?'

'They've flown into a hurricane and are making extremely slow progress. What should have taken hours has stretched into three days.'

Having all experienced difficult Crossings, we remain silent at this news. I can't imagine how horrible it would be for Ebony, inside a *lamorak* for all that time.

Uriel's hand comes down on my shoulder. 'This could be good for us.'

I cast him a questioning glance and he explains, 'When Prince Luca's team left Earth they may not have been *completely* healed yet. So they're already weak. Then they enter the Crossing and battle a hurricane. So by the time we meet up with them, their energy should be drained.'

This is both good and troubling news because Prince Luca has Ebony in the Crossing, and a storm could cause great harm if they're too weak to protect her. But the hurricane will also slow them to a crawl, giving us the time we need to apprehend them *before* they lock Ebony inside Luca's city palace.

I take a deep breath as I stand and meet the eyes of each member of my team. 'Michael, you will lead us to the Gates of Skade. Take the most direct route possible. Everyone: we fly without stopping, day and night, and we rotate carrying the humans every eight hours. We have a long flight ahead and we will grow weary, so we travel as light as possible. Leave the tents, bring only essential items. Tash, process what is left of our food and water supplies and ration them out. Everyone carries their own. Isaac, you take the first rotation with Heather. Uriel, you carry John. We don't have time to deal with demons, so outside this cave we mind-link only. No one speaks again until I say so. Is everyone clear?'

Expecting a barrage of objections, or at the very least questions, I'm quietly overwhelmed when no one says a word.

41

Ebony

Days turn into nights that turn into days again. Last night we camped at the top of a hill near a crater-sized hole in the ground that shoots out shimmering blue light high into the atmosphere. We started seeing the light two days earlier, and now I understand why. The hole in the ground is so immense it's breathtaking, and the light that pulses out of it is like the aggregate of thousands of lighthouses.

Now, after the Prodigies packed away our camp and consumed a meagre breakfast from supplies that should have run out two days ago, everyone is preparing to jump into the light.

Zavier starts walking towards the hill, stopping once he realises I'm not beside him. He looks back with a querying frown, but ... well, apparently after we jump we're only minutes from the Gates of Skade.

And suddenly it's all too real. I don't want to go to Skade. I didn't choose this. As for marrying the Dark Prince, I would rather die.

I want to scream: *This isn't supposed to be happening to me!*

Tears stir behind my eyes and I fight them ferociously. But the image of Nathaneal's tortured face when those giant Thrones ripped him from my arms appears before my eyes, bringing with it emotions that threaten to undo my resolve to be strong. The reality is that I may never see him again.

Suddenly Prince Luca appears in front of me, smiling. He looks different when he smiles, like the first time he came into my dream – elegant and handsome and charming.

'You have held up exceptionally well through a harrowing journey. Well done, Ebony,' he says, his voice filled with . . . respect.

I nod, not sure how to react. 'Thank you.'

But nothing has changed, and slowly, he brings his mouth down and moves his lips over my face in a series of disturbingly tender caresses. He looks at my trembling mouth and a low rumbling purr escapes from somewhere deep inside his throat.

'Luca . . . step back please.' Revolted, and seeing red, I push against his chest, but he just moves his mouth closer to mine. I slide my hands up between us, flatten them on Luca's chest, and before he realises what I'm doing I shove him backwards with the fury of a lightning bolt striking a thousand-year-old gum tree.

To my surprise, he flies through the air, falling amongst his soldiers. They help him to his feet. His face contorts in rage. I stand my ground, bracing myself for whatever punishment he wants to inflict.

He walks over until he is standing before me, his hands by his sides. 'I have waited through the ages of all existence for your birth,' he says. 'I've watched thousands of others marry and have sons and daughters, but you are the one I choose, the one I will honour with the title of queen. Understand this, Princess, as queen you will enjoy many liberties, but you will never escape Skade. Or me. Whatever you attempt, or however hard you resist, you *will* be my queen on the day you turn eighteen. Tomorrow I will make the formal announcement from my palace balcony, and you will stand beside me wearing the garments I select, the hairstyle of my choice. And if I deign to kiss you, you will not flinch no matter how hard I press my mouth on yours.' He raises an eyebrow to ensure he's making his meaning clear. 'One more thing. Until you learn to control your temper and conceal your thoughts from others, you will train yourself to think only of me. No one will hear my queen pining over the enemy's prince. Do we understand each other?'

I nod slowly, suddenly so tired I just want to lie down and sleep until I die.

He turns on his heel and walks away, barking orders to his Prodigies. They scatter immediately, with three of them – Periel, Josiah and Sarakiel – scooting straight over to me. Josiah, with dark skin and mustard-yellow eyes, rushes to my right side. Sarakiel hurries to my left, his masses of black curls bouncing on his collar. Periel, a bronze god-like soldier bows his head formally and indicates the blue light with an outstretched arm. 'We will be escorting you through the light, my lady,' he says in a deep voice.

The boy Sarakiel gives me an impish grin, 'It would be my honour to carry you down, my lady.'

Periel shakes his head. 'Not on your life, little girl. I'm carrying the princess.'

Not to be outdone, Josiah scoffs loudly. 'You can both forget it. I'm the most senior one here.'

'You're older but I'm in charge,' Periel counters.

'Let's draw swords.'

'How does that work?' I ask.

Zavier rushes back and plucks me from their centre. 'You don't want to know.'

'Yes, I do.'

'It's a childish game involving slicing each other's hands and whoever is first to heal, wins.'

I give all three of them a disapproving look. They try not to laugh but can't seem to help themselves, especially Sarakiel, who I learned recently is only eighteen human years old.

Zavier picks me up and settles me in his arms. 'Are you ready, niece?'

Feeling dizzy suddenly, I glance over his shoulder at the three soldiers who won't take their eyes off me. If I make a run for it, I doubt I would get very far. 'Do I have a choice?'

Pity pours out of his resigned sigh, 'Ebony . . .'

'Don't stress, Zavier, I'm ready,' I spit the words at him, 'but don't expect forgiveness any time soon. Selling out your own blood is a crime that deserves the death penalty. Maybe I can submit *that* to become a new law.'

He deploys his wings. 'If I were of royal blood, I would second the submission, my lady.'

His wings form a kind of parachute as first we fly upwards a little, and then we drift down for hundreds of metres into the blue light's centre.

We touch down inside a tunnel of cosmic proportions; Mount Bungarra from base to peak would easily fit inside it. The distant walls give off their own white light and are, apparently, dangerous to touch. The solid crystal floor cuts across the centre, slicing the tunnel into two domes from wall to wall. Specks of light from the lower sections beneath the bridge shoot up like sunrays through occasional gaps.

It's so amazing that I can only stare with my mouth open and my eyes huge as I look all around. And while it's *all* astonishing, it's the twelve Gates of Skade at the end of the bridge that blows my mind to oblivion.

'There are six pairs,' Zavier explains, 'operated by twelve Gatekeepers, who carry the honour of being Skade's finest soldiers.'

I close my mouth and swallow. 'Are the gates moving, or is that an illusion?'

'It's a chemical reaction occurring on the surface between microscopic particles that constantly ram each other and create light and the illusion of movement. The gates are solid and stronger than titanium. If you touch them, you will burn.'

'Good to know.'

The remaining nine Prodigies fly over our heads. It's then I notice they've donned uniforms. Even Prince Luca, flying proudly out in front, is wearing the same tight black uniform of his soldiers, except where their hair is contained inside helmets with twisting horns up the sides, his flows around his shoulders in gleaming waves of golden brown.

'Why are they dressed in war clothes?' I ask Zavier.

He frowns, staring after them. 'I don't know. Prince Luca is big on impressions. He's returning home with his future queen.'

Luca brings his soldiers almost all the way to the gates, then orders them to form two straight lines. They hold their heads high while they wait, I assume, for the gates to open. You wouldn't know how excited they are from looking at them, but the spark in their eyes gives them away.

The opposite is true for me. I'm numb inside, though it feels more as if I'm dead.

Twelve Gatekeepers stride out from six booths that seem to disappear once the doors close. Surprisingly, they seem genuinely pleased at their king's return. They form a horizontal line in front of him. As we move closer, I notice four of them are female. Their tight-fitting uniforms give them away, the same ones the Prodigies wear – ankle-high boots, leather trousers that look painted on, sleeveless shirts revealing bulging biceps, metallic vests and the intimidating silver gladiator helmets the Gatekeepers hold under their left arms.

They give their reports one after the other, maintaining an unnatural stillness until it is their turn, while Prince Luca listens attentively, drills them with questions, and occasionally even makes them laugh, smile or blush. Sometimes their conversation becomes serious and Luca fastens his eyes on them with a look that should burn holes in their eyes. Yet they all seem enamoured of him, and this piques my interest. 'Zavier, can you translate?'

'They're welcoming home their king.'

'I get that much. Some specifics would be helpful.'

He stalls. 'OK. Well ... let's see ... they're informing the king of visitors and other goings on in his absence. Don't ask me why they're bothering him with such trivial details.'

I feel my brow pinch into a suspicious frown. 'Can I have a word-for-word translation?'

He stares at me with his mouth open before finally relenting. 'You will find out soon enough anyway,' he mutters. 'Better hearing it from me, I suppose.'

'Hear *what*?'

'Nathaneal came through these gates several weeks ago.'

I gasp. 'I was told he came to Skade, but I didn't know how, or that he had passed through these gates.'

'There is no other way in or out. Apparently he made a big scene, burning holes in the gates, which, by the way, is impossible, even for Prince Nathaneal with all his fancy powers. Allegedly, he knocked out a couple of Gatekeepers.' He shrugs. 'But I have my doubts.'

'You don't believe Nathaneal was here?' I ask, my heart pounding.

'I believe *that* part,' he whispers. 'It's the part about burning holes and knocking out Gatekeepers I don't. It's more likely the Gatekeepers accepted a bribe.' Still whispering, he adds, 'Pink diamonds are highly valued in Skade. With their volcanoes spewing up lava every day, the pink ones still remain elusive. And, of course, what you can't have, you tend to want more of –' I squeeze his arm and he cries out, 'Hey!'

'Stop babbling! Tell me what Nathaneal was doing here.'

'*Is.*'

'Excuse me?'

'This is the part I didn't want you to know.'

'Go on.'

'He came to Skade with a team of six, and . . . hasn't left yet.'

It starts to sink in. Nathaneal has been here all this time. It's what Gabriel hinted at but wouldn't tell me for weeks. I go over conversations I had with him and try to put together why Nathaneal came – *is still* – here. The Courts made him pay restitution for his crimes in the form of good works. They wanted him to regenerate a forest wiped out in a cosmic storm, but Nathaneal nominated his own form of restitution. He was to descend into an underground world beneath a . . . Oh! *Oh! Oh no!*

'He's looking for my parents, isn't he?'

Before Zavier confirms or denies this, I remember something troubling. 'But you said my parents were stashed on an island that will explode at the slightest weight change. Is that why Nathaneal hasn't returned to Earth? Did he . . . ? Has he . . . ? Zavier, is Nathaneal at the bottom of some bizarre underground ocean?'

'Try not to worry, Ebony.'

'Try not to worry! Are you insane?' My head begins to ache. This can't be happening. While I've been safe at home, snug in my bed, complaining about *everything*, Nathaneal has been in a horrible place searching for my mum and dad. *My mum and dad!*

'Where is he?' I glance at the Gatekeepers. 'Do *they* know?' I start to run over, but Zavier drags me back with a stern warning in his eyes and a brief glance at our three guards, who follow every step I make with their eyes.

'If the Gatekeepers know anything,' he says, 'they're not going to tell *you*.'

Meanwhile Prince Luca moves on to hear the last Gatekeeper's report.

'Do you think Nathaneal is all right, Zavier?'

'The truth is, Ebony, I don't know.'

I point with my chin at the tall female Gatekeeper practically preening herself before her king. 'What's *her* name?'

'Lailah.'

'What is Lailah telling Luca now?'

He sighs. 'She's just flirting.'

'You're kidding! Well, she can have him!'

'Ebony, *shush!*'

The prince notices. He stops and turns his head to me. His eyes meet mine and I scramble my thoughts like Jordan told me works for him. Thinking of Jordan makes me wonder where he is. The last time I saw him was . . . was . . . in the cave, chained to a wall. Thanks to the sedatives, I have scant memories.

The Gatekeepers' reports over, Prince Luca selects two Prodigies and snaps orders at them.

'He's sending them on ahead to notify the palace of our imminent arrival,' says Zavier.

'And . . . ?'

'He has asked for the handmaiden Mela to prepare a room for you in the north tower, and to have a warm bath waiting, along with the kinds of things you like.'

I raise my eyebrows at him. 'Such as?'

'Your favourite toiletries. Shampoo. Clothing.'

'How does "Mela" know what toiletries I like?' I sneer.

He shrugs. 'Mela is very intuitive. You will be safe in her hands.'

Safe? In Skade? 'What did Luca mean by preparing a room for me?'

'Your own bedroom, of course.'

'I won't have to share *h-his?*'

'I assure you, Ebony, he won't share your bed until you turn eighteen and are married.'

'Goodie, I have a whole year and a bit.' I glance down at the bridge, the very same bridge Nathaneal crossed an unknown number of weeks ago. If only he were here now. 'Prince Luca has warned me he *is* going to share my bed, if not tonight, then tomorrow.'

Zavier stares at me, and is quiet for such a long time I think he's not going to say any more. But then he shakes his head. 'No, I don't think –'

'Zavier, I saw his intentions. I *felt* his obsession. He wants to own me and *he* doesn't think he can wait.'

Zavier turns me so my back is to the prince, our profile away from the guards. 'Listen to me,' he whispers. 'I've noticed the way he looks at you. It's just that after waiting thousands of years to choose his perfect bride, why would he take risks that might endanger the health of his unborn children? Making a mother out of you before you're ready, before the law allows, could result in an illegal marriage or, worse, imperfect babies that he would drown like a litter of unwanted kittens.'

My stomach churns. 'Zavier, help me. You can't leave me with this monster.'

His eyes fill with shame, regret and pity.

And I know then Zavier isn't strong enough to fix this.

His inability to protect me, his gutlessness, makes me so angry it's no surprise when I see a red haze in front of my eyes and feel my power begin to pulse inside. I hammer at his chest with my fists. He does nothing to protect himself and the sad thing is this doesn't surprise me. 'You should be defending me, guarding me, saving me, not handing me to the vilest creature in the universe in exchange for ten million dollars. It's despicable. You are despicable. I hope, for as long as eternity lasts, I never set eyes on you again!'

Prince Luca suddenly appears between us, and taking my wrists he covers my fists with his hands. 'Enough, Princess,' he says calmly.

Over the top of my head he barks orders at the three perplexed bodyguards. Bringing my hands together he holds them gently, warming them while his hungry eyes burn into mine.

For the first time I notice he's taller than Zavier. He might even be taller than Nathaneal. His hair is like Nathaneal's too, except a few shades darker. For someone recovering from horrific injuries, his hair and skin are in amazing condition. His face is a vision of unblemished perfection, except for some minute areas of loose skin around the eyes and neck.

'Come,' he says, turning me towards the gates. 'So that you may see your new kingdom, I have ordered the gates be thrown open.'

Hearing this, Zavier shrugs off the bodyguards. 'All twelve, my lord?' He sounds shocked. I flick him a glance, but he's not taking his eyes off Prince Luca. 'Is this wise, sire? We're a small group. We could pass virtually unnoticed.

It would give Ebony time to rest and freshen up before her first public appearance tomorrow.'

The prince's green eyes glow. 'You have lived so long amongst the humans you've picked up their ways of questioning their superiors.'

'My lord, I assure you, my words are borne out of concern for Skade's future queen. If you recall, it was the plan.'

'Are you questioning my memory now?'

'No, not at all, my lord.'

The gates are heavy. Spaces open up between each pair slowly. My first sight is of a dark sky with bulbous grey clouds, streaked blue and red. It could be dusk or dawn, I wouldn't know.

I start to tremble. This is really happening.

A dark purple orb, maybe a moon, sits high in the sky but is so large it looks as if it might drop at any moment.

This is certainly not my beloved Earth. I'm so far from home! A sob rises into my throat. I take a deep breath and force it down. Now is not the time to come unstuck.

As the gates open a little wider, I find myself walking towards the edge, where I catch my first glimpse of a city far below, though I can't see much because of a dense layer of grey fog obscuring almost everything. The top portion of a high-rise building and the towers of a white palace are the only structures tall enough to rise above it.

But it's the sky that tells me so much. I lift my eyes and fall backwards with a gasp as a second orb comes into view, low on the horizon. Another moon? Or is this the sun, obscured behind the toxic grey clouds that apparently surround this world?

Oh, Thane, where are you? This place . . . This place is so strange.

While dwelling on Nathaneal, I miss what's going on behind me. Prince Luca has ordered Zavier to leave, and not just for now, but for all time.

'Your job is done to my satisfaction,' Prince Luca announces formally. 'But from this day forward you are forbidden to pass through the Gates of Skade unless I summon you.'

'But, sire, the arrangement was to deliver Ebony to your palace and see that she settles into her new surroundings.'

'You're not listening!' Luca bears down on Zavier with an arm outstretched, staring at him and pointing down to the blue light. 'Leave now!'

Zavier stumbles backwards, cowering and wincing with pain. Prince Luca is squeezing his brains.

'My lord, what has changed?'

The prince stops right in front of Zavier, but doesn't speak.

Zavier moans and grips his head with both hands.

I run over and help Zavier to his feet. 'You should go. I'll be all right.'

'It appears I have no choice but to leave you, my lady.'

Zavier takes my hand as he straightens to his full height. 'My lord, I ask permission to say goodbye privately to my niece.'

Luca's eyes narrow as he stares at Zavier without speaking.

'After all I've done to ensure she becomes your queen, don't I deserve this one request? My lord?'

309

Prince Luca assesses us both with a look that chills my bones to the marrow.

Sensing defeat, Zavier growls, 'No one else could have pulled this off for you, my lord, and you know it.'

Prince Luca peers at the gates, nearing half open, and looks at me. 'Do you wish this foolishness too, Princess?'

Not sure why, I give the Prince a slight nod and he says, 'You may say your goodbyes until I call you.'

Zavier scoops me up in his arms, shoots out his big brown wings, and whisks me off to the solitary southern end. 'Listen carefully,' he whispers as he sets me down on my feet. Keeping his back to the prince, he grips my shoulders. *Something has changed. I don't have time to explain how I know this. Blink twice if you can hear me.*

I blink twice without realising it, startled by how clear his thoughts are in my head.

This is a trap. I don't know what shape, or form it will take, but I'm sure of one thing: right here on this bridge is where he wants Nathaneal. Now that he has you, Luca will use you to lure his one true enemy into an ambush.

I start to gasp but pull myself up quickly, close my mouth and try with all my might to forge a mind-link with the person, who until recently I have hated with all my heart. *Why?*

Nathaneal is too powerful. When he revealed his powers are strong enough to annihilate a king, he became too great a threat.

So Luca is luring him here to . . . to . . .

Destroy him.

How do you know Nathaneal will come?

Zavier tilts his head and a small, coy smile forms. *For you, Nathaneal would walk through fire and ice. Luca is counting on it.*

But, Zavier, I don't know where Nathaneal is. You said no one could survive rescuing my parents from Mi'Ocra.

That was before I knew it was Nathaneal who led the rescue.

Why are you telling me this?

He shrugs. *I don't know, Ebony. Perhaps finally I am developing a conscience.*

'Zavier! Time is up!' Prince Luca yells. My three body-guards approach with a purposeful stride.

Ebony, Zavier says in my head again, *now is the time to have faith, to believe unconditionally in what you are.*

You don't know what you're asking of me.

Yes, I do. I'm the one who created the environment that ensured your distrust would germinate and blossom.

But I've only ever heard Prince Luca's thoughts in my head clearly enough to have a conversation. Once or twice I saw Jacob's thoughts, but in images.

And now you're communicating with me.

I nod. *Is it because we're blood relatives that I can hear you?*

Ebony, it's because you can! *You must believe in yourself for your powers to believe in* you. *Why do you think Lord Luca goes to such lengths to ensure you are the one he weds, that your blood will run in the veins of his heirs? He is desperate for you.*

The three soldiers close in. *Zavier, what should I do?*

You must convince Nathaneal to abort his plan to rescue you. His destiny is to be a king, and once crowned he won't need permission to extinguish the existence of another crowned king. He is the hope of –

The soldiers grab Zavier from behind and start dragging him back towards the blue light. 'Leave me be, I'm going!'

He shoves them away all at once, lifting into the air with the solid beating of his wings.

I call out to him with my thoughts, *What if I can't convince him to stay away?*

He glances over his shoulder. *You must! The world cannot lose its one hope for everlasting peace!*

42

Nathaneal

We find a perch on a high mountain ledge with a north-easterly view of the shimmering Gates of Skade. Below, an impenetrable fog blankets the capital. The sun, rising in the distant east, lightens the dark sky with streaks of indigo and crimson, staining the fog below with splotches of purple. It's a dull morning in the capital, which is starting to awaken from its long slumberous night. One of its moons, the smaller Thoran, on the last day of its elliptical cycle before it swings out into space, appears low and intimidating on the horizon.

Solomon assures me there's been no sight of Prince Luca or his Prodigies at the palace yet. No sight of Ebony. So for now I've ordered my team to take a much-needed rest.

How are John and Heather faring? I ask Jez in a mind-link.

Heather's heart is strong, she says. *She's doing well. The deep sleep we put her into, in that cave on Mount Mi'Ocra, is helping her body to repair itself.*

And John?

He's holding on. The deep sleep is helping him too, but he's still critical and needs more healing before I can be sure he's going to live.

Do what you can for him, Jez. His traumatic journey is nearing its end, and when we wake him he will see that he has many reasons to live.

Isaac hunkers down beside me and peers between one of several rocky outcrops providing cover. *How long do we wait?*

Until a gate opens.

Why don't you get some rest while I keep watch?

I glance at my exhausted team. How many days and nights have we flown with so little to sustain us? Since finding Ebony's parents we haven't stopped until now, and without a whisper of complaint. I couldn't be prouder of my team, who have become close as family to me. That Tashiel had a vision that one of them could betray me is as improbable as the sun falling from the sky. *Thanks, Isaac, but there will be time for all of us to rest soon.*

Solomon approaches with his eyes cast downwards.

What news, Sol?

Reports of extensive troop movement are filtering into the palace. My informant is trying to find their location. The official word is that soldiers are preparing the streets for the return of their king and his new, ah . . . future queen.

But?

So far, my informant can't see them. They're not anywhere near the palace. He shrugs. *I've asked for a wider search.*

Good idea. And, Sol, when your source says 'extensive', how many soldiers does this mean?

Solomon rakes his fingers through his wildly knotted hair. *A legion, my prince.*

A legion!

Hearing Solomon's disturbing report, Michael crawls over. *That's a lot of 'missing' soldiers. Could your informant be exaggerating?*

No, Solomon says. *Not about this.*

If they're not ground soldiers, and they're not airborne, where are they? Michael asks the question on all our minds.

Keeping low, the four of us spread out along the ledge to look for signs. Skade's capital is rather unique in that volcanoes, dormant for millions of years, surround it on three sides, making a defensive barrier like no other city I know.

It's a trap!

I look across to Michael, Sol and then Isaac. *Did any of you hear that?*

They each reply in the negative. My pulse jumps, and a frisson of anticipation courses through my heart.

So no one heard that warning?

They look at me with blank expressions, and my hopeful hunch that this voice belongs to Ebony has my heart yearning to break free and shout it from the mountaintop.

Michael returns to where I'm crouching with a smile and a golden eyebrow arched high. *So what did the little one have to say?*

Unable to remove the grin from my face, I lift my hand as another mind-link enters my head. *You must leave! Nathaneal, if, by the grace of our High King you're hearing this, please . . . please do not come for me.*

Is this really you, sweetheart?

Nathaneal, you're alive! You can hear me! Are you all right? Are you anywhere nearby? No! Don't answer that. I have a message you must abide by – do NOT come through the gates.

315

You need to find another way home, or wait until he's gone. Please, Nathaneal, you have to stay away from the entrance.

She bears grave news, and she's worried and scared, but . . . I'm hearing her voice! She is so close! We made it back in time! Moisture rushes my eyes, overflows, and the salty tears of relief are sweet on my lips, so, *so* sweet.

Michael squeezes my shoulder, while Isaac and Solomon inform Uriel, Jez and Tash.

Ebony, are you injured?

No. But, Nathaneal, don't worry about me. I'll be all right.

Where are you?

Just inside the locked gates with twelve Prodigies and twelve Gatekeepers, but you can't set one foot on this bridge, Nathaneal, do you hear me? I can't stress this enough. Prince Luca wants to destroy you. I don't know his exact plan, but he'll probably hurl you into space from the Crossing, or some other way angels can be destroyed.

There are a few other techniques.

Are you taking me seriously?

I hear the fear from her heart, woven into the fabric of her words. *I'm sorry, Ebony, hearing you is such a relief after so long without you.*

She's goes quiet and I ask, *Are you all right?*

For now I am. Nathaneal, promise me you will NOT enter this tunnel.

The only promise I'm willing to make, my love, is that tonight you will sleep safely in my arms.

I want that so much, Nathaneal. I even dreamed of you three nights back. You were drowning in an ocean and you told me that I'd forgotten you.

Ebony, I don't know how it happened, but it was not a dream. You saved my life that night.

Really?

You told me to be strong, and now I'm telling you the same thing. Be strong, my love, it will all be over soon. Where I have failed you in the past, know that this is one promise I will not break.

Nathaneal, you have never failed me. It is I who let you down. I let Jordan get captured and now I don't know where he is.

We will go and look for him as soon as this is over.

She remains silent for a beat and my heart burns for her. Finally she links, *Nathaneal, I need you to stay alive. Just to know that you're breathing gives me strength. Nothing else matters.*

What are you saying?

If you love me, and I know you do, you m-must leave.

Ebony, don't ask me to abandon you. It would be easier to hurl myself into space.

Don't say that! I know this is hard. It's hard for me too. I'll never see Mum and Dad again! But you and I, we have no choice. You cannot die, because if you do then there is no hope for the future of this world.

Without you, I don't have a future. And about your —

Nathaneal, listen to me. If you can't do this for my sake, or for your own, then you must do it for Avena, and the world where you will be king one day.

Ebbie, no, please . . .

How can I live with him *if you don't exist? I would have no reason to believe that one day — somehow — I'll escape and see you again. And, Nathaneal, I want you to . . . go on and live the life you're meant to. Even if that means finding —*

Don't say it.

. . . someone else to share your life. A king needs heirs.

Ebony, let me give you something to think about that might change your mind.

She remains silent.

I have your parents.

There is a pause before she links again, and her thoughts are splintered and thick with emotion. *I didn't know . . . I'd heard things. I . . . I imagined terrible things. Oh, Nathaneal, are they all right?*

They've been through more than any mortal being could normally bear.

She gasps.

But I'm confident that once they see you they will recover with astounding speed. Ebony, your parents need you now more than ever before.

I don't know how you did it, or why you would risk so much for me. I've heard terrible stories about the prison they were in, but . . . but you made it happen and I'll never be able to thank you enough.

Ebony, you must know by now that I would do anything for you, face any threat that keeps us apart.

I know that.

Now I need you to listen to me. When you see us, as soon as it's safe, run to Isaac. He will be watching for you, and will take you home with your parents –

I'll be with Mum and Dad again?

That's right, Ebony, with your mum and dad.

But . . . you can't ignore this threat. It's real.

I've had worse in my past and will face worse in my future.

Nathaneal, I want to go home with Mum and Dad, but I want

318

*to be with you too. Prince Luca has almost completely recovered,
especially his mind.*

Thank you for the warning, my love.

Nathaneal, take me seriously, do NOT *enter this tunnel until
he has left. I'm telling* him *you're not coming. Wait, he's . . .*

Ebony, what's happening?

*I have to go. I won't be able to link when he's right next to me
in case he hears us, but, Nathaneal, whatever happens today, promise me you will go on –*

Ebony, wait.

Nathaneal, I love you.

Ebony. Ebony?

Too stunned to move, it takes Michael, pointing at the
gates. *They're all open.*

All twelve?

He frowns. *He could fit a thousand soldiers in that entrance.*

*Why would he open all twelve gates if not to fit a thousand
soldiers?*

I gather my team together to brief them. Not long after,
horns start blowing their warning of war across the city,
alerting the populace of an imminent battle.

I crouch near the edge to survey our surroundings one
last time. While peering into the fog, I catch a flash of silver,
a reflection of something glistening. I spot another, and
then another. And now that I've noticed those I see
hundreds of glittering reflections hidden beneath the fog.

Uriel. Our weapons. Now!

Michael takes his golden bow and swings it over his
shoulder. *What do you see?*

Down there. Look. I take my sword from Uriel's hand and

slide it into its casing, then a dagger for my belt, and a knife for each boot. I indicate the fog below with a jerk of my head. It's dissipating quickly now, unveiling more and more rows of perfectly aligned soldiers, their shields catching glimpses of sunlight.

What are they doing? Solomon asks.

Preparing for war.

In the split-second it takes to forge the mind-link, a stream of shadows pass over the top of us. 'On your guard!' I warn my team as a dozen soldiers touch down in a semi-circle round our camp and draw their swords.

43

Ebony

The Dark Prince takes my hand and drags me to the edge of the balcony. Keeping close beside me, he shows me his city spread wide and far below, pointing out landmarks such as his palace and where the beasts come at dusk for feeding. But since fog blankets the city I can hardly make anything out.

Normally, I'm not afraid of heights. I don't have a problem with standing at the edge of a cliff and looking down. It doesn't make me dizzy, or nauseous, like it does Amber. Height to me is like speed. It makes my heart surge with a faster beat, reminds me that I'm alive.

But this is different. It's like standing in the open doorway of an aeroplane at three thousand metres.

A flock of six large birds sweep into view as they fly over the top of a mountain then disappear into dark clouds. At first glance they appear a dull grey colour, but when they emerge a few moments later I see striking crest feathers of red and gold, with flecks of fluorescent lime on the undersides of their wings. I wonder if this is a symbolic trait of this world – a dark, dull exterior, but on further inspection surprising colour emerges from within.

Somehow, I don't think so.

The birds have slender bodies with long beaks and elongated necks. I can't stop looking at them. There's nothing like this on Earth, except in prehistoric imagery. As they sail toward us their considerable size becomes more apparent. They're starting to resemble small aircraft!

The flock banks left suddenly, and as they sweep in close they flap their mighty wings and blow a gale. Instinct has me move back from the edge. Prince Luca wraps an arm round me, and the next thing I know he has me locked in a tight grip where I can't move either of my arms. From the outside I must look like a damsel in distress.

I can't let Nathaneal see me like this!

I'm certain now Prince Luca has me standing here as bait to lure Nathaneal out of his hiding place. Zavier warned me. The Dark Prince plans to destroy the angel I love. And now I understand this fog is hiding something – something big.

'I don't know about you, Luca, but I can't see anything through this fog. What do you say you blow it away and give me a better view of your city?'

He ignores me, but I know he's listening since his entire body tenses each time I speak.

Minutes pass and he grows irritated, but not because he's weak or tired. He's itching for a fight. Except, without Zavier around to help, he has the annoying task of having to keep an eye on me.

'What are you waiting for?'

He brings his face down to the side of mine and sniffs the hair around my ear. 'Is patience not one of your virtues,

Princess?' He seems to consider his own question. 'I like that. You will fit well in my palace.'

'How? Like a rug?'

He laughs, and his hot breath on my cheek burns and makes me shudder.

'You're cold. I'll send for a coat immediately. It will be waiting when we land.' Strangely, he sounds as if he cares.

'You haven't answered my question.'

'If I'd known you were in such a hurry,' he says, 'I would have taken a short cut to the palace.'

I can't believe I'm going to say this, but if I'm going to pull it off I have to at least sound as if I mean it. 'Luca . . . er, is it all right if I call you that?' His eyebrows shoot up but he eventually nods. 'Well, um, I was thinking, why don't we leave now? You could release your soldiers. They're keen to go home anyway. And with Zavier barred . . . well, it would leave just the two of us.'

He examines my face for the longest time. I meet his gaze without flinching, and for a heartbeat I think he's going to accept my offer. 'Tempting. But there is a small matter I must attend to first.'

'By "small matter" you mean Nathaneal.'

'It will be worth the wait, I promise you.'

'Promises are just words.'

'I assure you, I keep mine.'

He must be referring to his promise of revenge. 'If you're waiting for Nathaneal, you'll be waiting a long time because he's not coming.'

His fingers dig deep into my arm, cutting off my circulation. I glare up at him. 'Do you mind?'

He doesn't loosen his grip, but shakes me. 'Explain yourself.'

'It's not rocket science. I warned him with a mind–link.'

He shoves me away, barking orders I can't understand, and my left foot rolls clear off the edge. Swaying like a gymnast about to topple off a balance beam, I suppress a scream in case it alerts Nathaneal to act irrationally, which is probably Prince Luca's Plan B.

Fortunately Sarakiel is watching. He opens his wings and dives over the edge as I begin to drop. He catches me and sets me back down a safe distance from the edge.

When I turn to thank him, I notice how he's breathing deeply and leering at me with a look bordering on predatory.

I flick a quick glance at the prince. 'Thank you, Sarakiel, but you should now return to your unit. If you keep leering at me your king will notice and your life will not be worth living.'

But the foolish boy takes no notice. 'My lady, may I speak?'

'OK, but be quick. I don't want your king to get the wrong idea – you know what I mean?'

'Of course. I just want to . . . offer, I suppose you'd call it.'

I glance briefly over my shoulder. Though he appears not to be watching, I'm pretty sure he's listening to every word. 'Go on, Sarakiel.'

'My friends call me Sarak.'

'Then I'll call you Sarak too. Now if that's all –'

'Now that we're friends, if you ever need anything, you can come to me. I live at the barracks. Everyone knows me.'

I can't help but smile at that. 'I'm sure they do. Thank you for your kind offer. Now you must return to the others.'

His heart rate suddenly rockets. 'My lady, may I kiss your hand?'

'No. Sarak, you're almost home.' I flick another glance at Prince Luca, temporarily occupied with one of his Gatekeepers, scouring the cliffs that surround us on three sides with binoculars. 'Surely, you have a sweetheart waiting for your return?'

'No, my lady, there is no sweetheart.'

As I bring my eyes back to the soldier, he's already moving towards me. 'Sarak, whatever you are thinking of doing, don't.'

My words have no effect. In an instant Sarak is lifting my hand to his mouth. His lips touch my knuckles and he peers at me with sparkling baby-blue eyes.

Moving faster than light, Luca appears between us. He grabs Sarakiel by the back of his helmet, ripping it off his head. Masses of black curls tumble over the angel's face, making him look even younger. He peers at me through his hair without an inkling of regret in his eyes, and my heart twists for him.

To my disbelief, Prince Luca kicks Sarakiel's legs out from under him, takes the young angel's head and slams it into the bridge repeatedly until a loud crack rings out. I scream, recoiling at the sound, and look around for help. But no one is even willing to meet my gaze.

It's more than enough punishment, but apparently Prince Luca isn't finished yet. His eyes dark and gleaming, he kicks

Sarakiel's chest. I can't stand it and run over, crying out, 'Luca, stop! That soldier saved my life!'

He points at me. 'Do not interfere with how I discipline my Prodigies.'

'He only kissed my hand.'

'Maybe where you come from that's acceptable behaviour, but it isn't here. No one touches my queen without my permission, and they need to know what happens if they do.'

'So you're making an example out of Sarakiel.'

'Call it what you want.' He sears me with a warning look to shut up, then stands over Sarakiel's unconscious body. Slowly, he turns and stares at each of his Prodigies with eyes shimmering black and chillingly evil. 'No one touches the future Queen of Skade.' He points at me again. 'It means instant annihilation. Do you all understand?'

Lowering his gaze to Sarakiel, Luca heaves a heavy sigh and utters a string of swear words in the Skade language that I have, for better or worse, begun to understand.

Shaking from head to toe, I fold my arms round my waist and watch as Luca collects Sarakiel's body from the floor and, carrying him like a child, runs down the bridge to where the blue light beams up into the Crossing's atmosphere.

Shocked and horrified and disgusted, I race after him, arriving in time to see him cast the young soldier high into the Crossing's atmosphere. Sarakiel's body gains momentum the further he soars.

Horribly riveted, I watch Sarakiel's body burst into flames and hurtle higher and higher.

If it were night, he would resemble a shooting star.

The remaining Prodigies and Gatekeepers have also come to watch. With their eyes open wide, they share micro-glances, which turn into horrified gasps when their comrade slams into something. The sound is thunderous, like a jet breaking the sound barrier. The impact causes an explosion of cascading fireworks high in the sky.

I gradually become aware of something else happening. I hear a sharp piercing sound from way off, while all around me, soldiers are running in different directions.

Suddenly, Luca throws himself on top of me. His hard torso slams my back into the bridge a moment before the shockwave pounds into us.

When it finally passes, Luca lifts his head and stares at my face with angry black eyes. 'What were you thinking?'

'Excuse me?'

The longer he stares, little by little, his harsh look softens. 'You could have been hurt. Whatever comes from space can kill you. Don't ever forget that.'

'I didn't know.'

'Didn't you see everyone running?'

Now *I'm* getting angry. 'I *didn't* know! Why didn't you tell me before you threw that poor boy into space!'

'I had no choice.'

'You couldn't just put him in jail?'

He sniggers and I shout at him, 'You're laughing?'

'Princess, you haven't seen the jails here yet. They're not for soldiers.'

'What you did to that boy —'

'I know. But you gave Sarakiel three chances. That's two more than I would have. By then, I had to set an example.'

'You can't rationalise what you just did and call it reasonable punishment.' I suddenly don't know where to look and shift my eyes to a spot above his shoulder. Hooking my chin with gentle fingers, he turns my face back, tracing the outline of my lips with his thumbnail. A shudder goes through me.

'Are you cold, my lady, or is it fear making you tremble every time I touch you?'

'I'm not scared of you; it's . . . it's . . . the shockwave.' Lying apparently comes easier the closer one is to Skade.

'Princess, you are either courageous or stupid. Either way, I will have to rectify that annoying attitude. You will behave in the way I consider appropriate for a queen.' Inhaling deeply from my hair, he offers his hand.

'No thanks,' I mutter. 'Your touch revolts me.'

'Be careful, Ebony. You wouldn't want me to hurl your rescue party into space just because you sparked my temper, would you?'

'I told you, Nathaneal is not coming.'

'All seven of them are presently preparing themselves for the fight of their lives, which, by the way, they will lose.'

'Go to hell!'

His laugh is scathing. 'I can't wait. I just have that small matter to attend to before we leave.'

'We?'

'Don't tell me you're still holding out hope for your dashing young prince to rescue you? I thought you said he wasn't coming.'

'He's not!'

'In that case, where did you think you were going?'

Honestly? I was trying not to think about what happens next. 'I thought you couldn't take me anywhere against my will.'

He smiles with a closed mouth. 'You were given a choice and you said "Yes".'

'No way. You're lying.'

He dramatises a sigh, as if this is something I'm forcing him to do. Then his mouth moves and *my* voice flows out from his lips, "*Yes, sir. No one is coercing me, sir*".'

'I was tricked!'

'Really?' he says. 'What part was trickery?'

'All of it! I would never have agreed to *this* and you know it.'

He shrugs and throws his hand out again. 'It's not debatable. *Take it!*'

He closes his hot fingers round mine and spins me so that my back is flush against his chest, so close that not even a hair follicle would fit between us.

His fascination with the scent of my hair has him leaning down to breathe it in again. 'Intoxicating,' he murmurs. 'Do you always smell this enticing, Ebony?'

'I thought I was seeing Nathaneal today.' *I don't know why I keep baiting him. It's not helping.*

'Ah, but you *will* see Nathaneal today. Unfortunately, it will be an occasion you might not want to remember.'

'What are you talking about?'

'Last days are like that.' His words, like a serpent's fangs, inject venom into my heart. 'I'm not blind, Ebony. The only way you will forget him – and make room in your heart for me – is when he no longer exists.'

'If you kill Nathaneal, how could I ever love you?'

'You will learn. We have plenty of time.'

'You don't *learn* love. But, wait … listen … you don't have to kill Nathaneal. I'll be your queen willingly if you promise *not* to kill him – *ever!*'

'Princess, don't embarrass yourself by pleading. I may not be a Soul Reader, but I can tell you're lying to me now. You *can't* devote yourself to me as long as Nathaneal exists somewhere in the universe. Every day you will wonder where he is, what he's doing, who's making him smile, soothing his broken heart, pleasuring his body, giving him an heir. Admit it.'

I shake my head. 'You don't know me. I can do anything I put my mind to.' The lies flow out like spilled wine, one after another. 'I promise I will do my duty. I'll learn to love you over time like you said I could, and until that happens no one will know the difference.'

He studies my eyes. 'You're good, Princess. You almost convinced me. Our children will be brilliant Soul Readers. We'll have *many* of them, and they will pass your gifts to their children, and *their* young will infiltrate Earth and place an invisible mark on every newborn with the potential to be future soldiers of Skade.'

My knees weaken.

'We will train them from the beginning when they are most pliable.'

'You can't be serious.'

Self-righteous supremacy radiates from his glistening eyes. 'Do you have any idea how strong this strategy will make our future armies? Stronger than any armies Avena could ever amass, especially after I destroy the young prince in which they have foolishly put all their hopes.'

'So you plan to kill him no matter what I promise.'

'We understand each other perfectly.'

The eerie sound of horns blasting gets Luca moving again. He drags me to the edge of the balcony again. Fog still blankets the city, but he makes a casual waving motion with his hand and it parts like the Red Sea did for Moses.

'Look, Princess, see those people down there on the streets? They've never had a queen before and they're waiting for you.'

I stare at a broken city rising out of darkness like the arms of death clawing out of a funeral pyre. It appears to be early morning, grey clouds bleeding crimson streaks across a vast sky. Dark angels and human souls, who look just like regular people, pour out of buildings. The difference between the two species is evident in the way they carry themselves. The shorter humans wear worn-out coats, and rush around without making eye contact, carefully avoiding bumping into the taller, well-dressed dark angels who command an aura of confidence and superiority.

Both species keep glancing to the sky. They hear the horns and become more animated. The humans gather in groups while the angels keep mostly to themselves or in pairs. Apparently they've all heard their king is returning with his . . .

Jeez, I can't even *think* it's me they're waiting for.

My stomach rolls with the reality that's starting to hit me. I'm going to be living in this world for the rest of my life. Not long ago, I was an ordinary girl with regular dreams who sensed she was different, but if I think about my future now I'll go crazy.

A breeze wafts up with the unmistakable smell of sickness, poverty and death clinging to it.

Prince Luca points out his palace – a glittering white, multi-tiered structure with classic medieval turrets and spires. It sits on top of a hill at the end of a gold-paved street, a high white wall surrounding it, capped with gold tiles.

It stands out like a dazzling oasis in a barren wasteland.

I try to imagine myself living there, looking out those square windows, not just for one lifetime but for a thousand more. 'No.'

'What did you say, Princess?'

'I can't do it. I can't live there.'

He shakes me and I glare at him. 'Do you mind? I'm not a ragdoll. I'm an angel just like you. And if you expect me to be a leading figure for your people, you had better not shake me ever again!'

He stares back at me, his lips parting as if he wants to say something but can't find the words.

Not long ago I couldn't wrap my head round being an angel. And while I still don't resemble one, and I have no wings or memories like angels are supposed to have, apparently, I *know* I'm an angel. I feel it in every breath I take, in every beat of my heart.

I straighten up to my full height, not an easy task with Luca's arm clamped round me, but I do it, and raise my head. The horns continue to play out their spine-chilling notes as the fog continues dispersing. And to my horror I now see what Luca's been hiding – endless rows of soldiers dressed in black uniforms, complete with polished chest armour, glistening silver shields and an array of weapons attached to their belts. My breath catches in my throat.

This is what Prince Luca wants me to see, the power he's going to use to annihilate the angel who fills my heart with love, and leaves no room for him.

44

Jordan

I'm having a great dream. I'm picnicking with the girls at the lookout at the end of the ridge. The sun is shining, the sky is clear and sparkling blue, the view is spectacular in every direction, whether we look west over the Oakes valley, north to the ranges, or straight down the cliff where the Windhaven River separates the two ridges.

I'm whistling a tune I've never heard before, and both Ebony and Amber are smiling and clapping along to it. We're all happy and, *man*, it feels good.

Amber gets up and tries to coax me into a dance. Her blonde hair is bouncing around her shoulders, her eyes inviting and warm as she moves to the tune.

'I can't,' I say, lifting both hands into the air by way of apology. 'I can't do both at the same time.'

Sitting on the rug, Ebony looks up at me with a questioning frown. So I explain, 'I can't dance and whistle at the same time.'

'Oh!' Ebony exclaims, and still frowning she says, 'But, Jordy, you're not whistling.'

'I'm not?'

Both girls shake their heads at me. I glance up at the sun, but it's gone behind a black cloud and suddenly it's so dark I can't see a thing.

I open my eyes, my heart beating hard and fast. It's a rude awakening — realising that even in my dreams I can't get anything right. I lift my head, careful not to lean too far forward and pull on the chains. After they left me here, I tried yanking on them as hard as I could, over and over, hoping to work the chains loose from the rock wall, like they do in the movies. Huh! Reality is so different, man. The cuffs cut into my wrists, blood dripped down my arms and the chains didn't budge a single bit.

If only they'd left me a lantern. Or water! Now that would have been considerate and could maybe even have extended my life by a day or two, giving someone time to find me.

But who in hell is gonna come looking in a redundant gold mine previously used by the Dark Prince to create demons? The truth is, nobody knows where I am except Mr Zee, and he'll be in Skade by now, celebrating Ebony's capture.

My arms are beyond aching, my shoulders are pretty much gone and my hands are so dead that I haven't felt them for hours. At one point there was numbness and I tried to keep my arms and legs moving, but eventually I got too tired. Now I can't feel much of anything except for pressure in my chest that's steadily getting more intense and making it harder to breathe.

I hear whistling, just like in my dream. It stops abruptly and now I'm not sure whether I really heard anything. I've been down this tunnel so long I can't be sure whether I'm imagining the sound, or having another dream.

I hear it again. Someone *is* down here.

But who? More dark angels? The same dark angels? Have they returned to finish me off like an annoying loose end? Who else would know about this place?

Maybe this whistler isn't an angel at all. Maybe it's kids who think it might be cool to check out an old gold mine, maybe even find some gold if they're lucky.

Whoever it is, maybe they can get me out of here, or at least get me the help I need, like bolt cutters and water.

Then I can finally find out what happened to the girls.

45

Ebony

A general, wearing a gold-trimmed black helmet with two long, curved blades sculptured on either side like horns, stands before his army. He passes an order to his first lieutenant, standing on his left, who relays the command to the soldiers in a loud shout. The first row performs some kind of quickstep pivoting movement, ending front-facing and at attention. The second row follows and so on. It's an intimidating display of precision and discipline.

After showing me this, Luca drags me into the tunnel. It's here his eleven remaining Prodigies wait for his orders. He disperses them in small groups to strategic positions along the edge, then commands the six remaining Gatekeepers to form a protective unit around us.

The general flies in, retracts his wings, swings his sword across his back and lopes over on all fours like a giant spider.

My mouth goes dry. I force myself not to scream the closer he gets, but it's hard not to freak out. Instinctively, I move backwards and hit Luca's chest, who chuckles and whispers in my ear, 'He won't bite you.'

When he reaches us, the general swings his body back into standing position, drops down on one knee, removes

337

his helmet and bows his head. His long silver hair, tied back in a ponytail, flops over his shoulder. In a deep voice he says something in his native language but Luca cuts him off. 'Speak English before your future queen, General Ithran.'

He stands and nods at his king. 'Good to have you back, sire, and looking so well.' His piercing gaze drops to me. 'My lady, your beauty and youthfulness surpass the imagination. Welcome to Skade.' He glances across the short distance between where we're standing and the tunnel edge. 'Well, you're almost there. It's a pleasure to meet you.'

He seems to be waiting for some kind of acknowledgement. I glance up at Luca and he raises his eyebrows.

I can't believe I have to do this!

I take a deep breath and nod in the general's direction. 'The pleasure is mine, General.'

Luca chuckles. The noise turns my stomach. 'Have you sighted the enemy yet, General?'

'They lounge on Hornet's Nest, my lord, depleted by their travels. I dispatched a squad to shake them up. We can't have them too rested, sire.'

I look up at Luca with venom, but I bite my lip. The general is after a reaction from me that will clue him in to Nathaneal's strategy. And the way Luca's jaw is twitching, he either did not know, or did not want me to know about this latest attack.

So I do the only thing I can. I urge Nathaneal to fly as fast as possible in the opposite direction.

But who am I kidding? Nathaneal is a pure soul who loves me with his pure heart. How our love came into being isn't the question. We met, and our meeting activated a love that was ordained by destiny or something. And now separation is impossible to endure. He could never abandon me, even if he died trying to save me from this monster.

A sob bursts from my chest. I catch it in my throat and hold it, swallow it, and bury it before anyone notices.

It's then I hear his heart beating, faster than usual, but I would recognise that deep, solid, reassuring thud anywhere.

And the anticipation of seeing him again after so long, knowing he's walking into an ambush, is almost too much to bear. Sweat beads across my forehead as I force my eyes not to look in the direction of his heartbeats in case I give his position away.

He flies in, his eyes searching for me, his team behind him in the formation of an arrow. Their hair is long, and they look scruffy and unkempt, as if they've just stepped off the battlefield, but otherwise they are just as I remember them — stunning blue-winged Jezelle, golden Michael, Isaac with his silver eyes and bright copper hair, and three others, whose names I don't know.

But it's Nathaneal who has all my attention, as beautiful, as intense and as perfect as ever. I want to jump into his arms and kiss him. I want to hold him, lay my head over his heart, and stay there for the rest of my days. I would run to him right now if Luca weren't holding me with his unnatural strength.

But all thoughts of Prince Luca disappear as my eyes and Nathaneal's meet, and he lets me know he's not leaving without me.

How I've missed him!

Memories stolen from me at birth suddenly burst through their hiding place, memories of my mother's beating heart, of healing fingers splaying across her stomach, of reaching for them with my tiny hand, and feeling frustrated with the pulsing wall keeping us apart. Someone, somehow, had just shown me my future and I needed to reveal it to the boy who would share it with me, so I forged a connection between my pre-natal spirit and the pre-pubescent prince who was standing over my mother's body with his hand on her belly.

Noticing how Prince Luca's arm crosses my chest, Nathaneal stiffens; every muscle of his beautiful face hardens, and my heart breaks with the knowledge that more pain lies ahead.

From the corner of my eye I spot flashes of blue, then purple wings, beating fast into passing blurs. It's Jezelle and another female angel. They sweep across my vision carrying two *lamoraks*, surrounded by golden halos. *My parents?*

And now Nathaneal and his remaining team are going to try to bring *me* home too.

'Tell your soldiers to throw down their weapons,' Prince Luca commands from over the top of my head. 'It's not as if you are in a position to do any bargaining. You must have noticed the legion of soldiers outside awaiting my command. You're in my world now, Nathaneal.'

Nathaneal glances over his shoulder at Skade's grey sky. 'I believe I just left it.'

Luca growls like a bear. 'You know you can't win this, so why put your team through the ordeal of a battle. If you haven't noticed, I hold the prize right here in *my* arms, and this time she comes home with me.'

'Don't speak too soon,' Nathaneal says calmly, prompting another rumbling sound from Luca's chest.

'You're an ambitious young prince, but your heart is bigger than your brain. Hasn't your team done enough for your foolish romantic quest? Look at them. They're exhausted.'

When he doesn't look, Luca shrugs. 'You fell in love with the unattainable and yet you expect your friends to fight for you. Your inexperience is showing. Real kings fight their own battles.' His smirk is disturbing. He turns it on Nathaneal's team, lingering on each of the four remaining angels. 'Feeling a smidge weary after that lengthy journey, are we?'

'What's your point?' Nathaneal snaps.

'How long do you think you can hold out against an army that will keep coming a dozen, a hundred, even a thousand at a time? They have orders to annihilate you all, to do whatever it takes. Once the battle begins, there will be no mercy for your team. But if you accept my terms the four standing behind you will be allowed to leave immediately. They're good soldiers, I'm sure you'll agree. No need for them to die. Are you willing to put their needs before yours, give them the reward they deserve?'

Michael says softly, 'Remember you're negotiating with the one who talks with forked tongue.'

'Michael, my past adversary,' Luca drawls, 'I see the high court has found a new job for you as a consultant. How

341

interesting that you would accept a position so clearly beneath you.'

'What are your terms?' Nathaneal snaps.

'It's simple. You will lay down *all* your weapons.'

'What of Ebony?'

'She stays with me, I thought that was clear.'

Michael says, 'Nothing is ever clear with you. What of Nathaneal? What is your intention?'

'You ask a lot of questions for someone who is second in charge. Nathaneal will cease to exist. That can't come as a surprise,' he spits out over the team's sudden cries of outrage.

Nathaneal lifts his hand and his team falls silent. 'We didn't come here to negotiate.'

But that's not fair! Not to him, and not to his remaining team members. *Nathaneal . . .* I forge a mind-link though I probably shouldn't because I don't know yet how to select who can and cannot listen. But right now I don't care. I *have* to talk to him . . . *negotiate for your life, please.*

His eyes plead with me to understand.

But I don't want you to die!

'Perhaps you should check with the rest of your weary team before you make such a selfish decision on their behalf,' Luca says.

Michael's voice suddenly resonates through the tunnel as clear as church bells ringing, 'Cousin, I will fight alongside you until the end of days.'

Isaac follows with his own declaration, 'Bring on the first hundred!'

'Is this your view too, Uriel?' Luca asks the angel with white hair and unusual yellow irises. 'To follow a prince into a battle you cannot hope to win, a prince who is a mere fraction of your age?'

Luca gives a mocking laugh, but with each word Uriel utters, the Dark Prince's smile tightens.

Uriel shrugs. 'This isn't about age, or whether the odds are stacked against us. It's about doing what is right. And you have taken what is not yours to take.'

'What about you, Solomon?' asks Luca.

Solomon, a big angel with stunning sea-green eyes, black curly hair and chocolate skin, straightens his broad shoulders and spears Luca with a look of such deep loathing it makes me wonder what past grievances have passed between the two. 'I'll do whatever it takes to dismiss this scourge, my prince.'

A tear pushes through my determination not to cry.

Luca hisses like a snake. 'You arrogant fools! Do you really believe you can hold up against an entire legion of Skade soldiers?'

Isaac murmurs, 'I've had worse odds.'

The angel with sea-green eyes says, 'Yeah, I remember, *sunshine*. That battle lasted thirty-seven days and by the end we'd whipped their butts.'

Luca's whole body jerks. 'I have underground tombs with seals so secure I can keep you imprisoned for all of time. And there is something else you insolent idiots should know. When you are so weary and can't hold up your swords a moment more,' he glances at Michael, 'or your bow, I will separate your heads from your bodies and fling your dismembered parts throughout the distant reaches of space.'

343

'Don't hold your breath, Luca. We don't tire easily.'

Nathaneal's calm voice infuriates Luca. He screeches, and multiple voices reverberate through the tunnel. 'Have it your way, for today you will all die!'

46

Ebony

An unexpected male voice bellows into the tunnel, startling everyone, 'I wouldn't be so sure about that, Prince Luca.'

Everyone turns towards the blue light of the Crossing entrance. Most of us recognise the self-assured, somewhat cocky, somewhat arrogant tones of Prince Gabriel.

Nathaneal nods at me with that gorgeous smile-wink of his. We're not out of this by a long shot, but the odds have improved because Gabriel would not have come alone.

He looks superb as he lands on the bridge and strides down the tunnel in his war uniform with black chest armour and matching helmet, his visor raised to reveal the family's stunning blue eyes.

'I thought you might need a hand,' he says when he reaches his brother, flicking a look back to where his troops are starting to pour through the blue light and forming rows along the bridge.

'Is Jordan safe?' I call out even before acknowledging Prince Gabriel's presence. I just have to know. 'Gabriel, is Jordan all right?'

Gabriel holds my glance a moment too long, his eyes darting left, then right, as if Jordan will appear suddenly in his line of vision. With a furrowed brow he whispers to his brother, 'We thought he was with Ebony. Amber said he was kidnapped by the same angels who took her.'

'No, no, no!' I scream out. 'He was chained to a wall in an underground cave on the ridge.'

After Nathaneal gives him a slight nod Gabriel says, 'I'm sorry, Ebony, I don't know where Jordan is, but I'll send word to the Brothers to begin an intensive search of all caves in the area.'

Nathaneal sneers at Luca and hisses, 'What have you done with him?'

'Well, that would be my business.'

'You keep your sordid hands off Jordan!'

Luca laughs. 'My "sordid hands" are all over that boy. And soon he too will belong to me.'

'That's not going to happen, Luca.'

'It's too late for your paltry promises, Nathaneal.'

Losing control, Nathaneal moves as if to attack us both. White light shudders out from him in waves, altering the air between us.

But Luca raises his hand to my throat, blocking my air and burning my skin at the same time. They eye each other until Nathaneal's threatening stance eases and Luca lowers his hand enough for me to breathe again and heal.

Nathaneal shifts his eyes to mine, and the anguish I see there is gut-wrenching.

But then Luca taunts him, 'You let that boy down so many times it's a wonder he can stand to be in the same room as you.'

'What are you talking about?'

'Jordan and I have a covenant. He begged for it and I was kind enough to oblige him. What could I do?'

'Explain,' Nathaneal says.

But Luca is having too much fun. 'For the record, I don't have to tell you anything, but since I'm feeling benevolent I suppose I will.'

Luca smiles. 'It started with Solomon.' He looks at the super-big angel with coffee-coloured wings. 'Really, Solomon, how hard could it have been to protect a human girl? Ebony tried to protect Jordan and she didn't have the benefit of Guardian-how-to classes. She didn't even know she was an angel for sixteen years! Unfortunately, protecting Jordan didn't turn out well either, did it, Princess?' He glances down at me, and then grins at Nathaneal. 'Anyway, when Solomon called *you* for help, you failed the boy too. Big mistake on both your parts because the girl whose soul you missed was Jordan's mother.'

'You bargained for his life with his own mother's soul!' Nathaneal's voice oozes disgust.

'Well, not quite, but we can deal with that trivial point later. Back to the covenant, Jordan gave me the chore of deciding when he dies. I felt sorry for the boy, and since I'm more experienced in these matters than he is I agreed.'

I try to break free, desperate to attack him, but his grasp is so strong and so tight, it's like being wrapped in a steel cage. I can't feel my powers. So I resort to words and logic.

'That was a dream Jordan had in his own bed. Your covenant with him is not binding.'

'Oh yes it is, and I'll tell you why – when we agreed on the terms, Jordan wasn't dreaming.'

347

'You can't get into my house,' Nathaneal insists.

'Normally, with all your confounded protections over it, I wouldn't. But Jordan invited me into his dream and, well, I happened to be in the area.'

'You mean, you were watching and waiting like the predator you are. Still, I don't believe Jordan invited you. That would mean . . .' Nathaneal's voice trails off, and his troubled eyes scan Luca's amused ones.

'That's right. He was thinking nasty, dark thoughts about *you . . . or someone.*' He shrugs.

Nathaneal remains silent. I can tell by his serious face that he's really worried.

'Don't worry, I don't want Jordan yet. Why would I, when I have –' he looks down at me – 'my new toy.' He nibbles on my ear, an action meant, I'm sure, to provoke Nathaneal.

It does. It drives him crazy. Michael and Gabriel hold him back and talk him into calming down.

But Luca's not finished yet. He whispers at my ear, 'As soon as we deal with this riff-raff, Princess, I'll take you home like you asked earlier, like you *pleaded.*'

I shut my eyes tight. I couldn't stand it if Nathaneal believed him.

Prince Luca calls over to his general: 'I've developed an appetite to get this over with. General Ithran, deploy your legion. Send up a hundred at a time. I want them all eliminated. And start with this foolish love-sick prince.'

The general's first lieutenant flies in and the two military men converse through mind-links, their eyes flitting over Gabriel's soldiers. A moment later the first lieutenant rockets out with the sound and speed of a jet, drawing everyone's attention to his dramatic departure. And while all eyes are on *him*, the general draws his sword on Nathaneal.

'Behind you,' Michael warns, then moves to defend himself as Luca's Prodigies rush over and attack the team.

Meanwhile, Gabriel disappears in a blur of movement over our heads, promptly returning with his troops, who march down the tunnel looking and sounding just as intimidating as Luca's first hundred, who fly in and meet them halfway.

The only soldiers not moving are the six Gatekeepers surrounding Luca and me.

The battle gains momentum quickly. Everywhere around us swords clash, sparks erupt into flames, arrows soar. Michael's arrows are the most identifiable, leaving a trail of bright burning lights through the air, almost always hitting their marks.

The last time I saw Nathaneal in battle he mostly used his hands and the power that came from them. I've seen him handle a sword before, but only in training. He's a clean opponent, except, against the general I doubt that matters. As I watch the duelling pair, I'm relieved to see that in training Nathaneal was holding back his best moves.

He executes his strikes in short, quick movements. His footwork is faultless. He parries and thrusts with conviction and more precision than the general, but Ithran is vicious. It's as if he's striking everywhere at once. He keeps the pressure up even in between beats and has Nathaneal in a defensive position enough times to raise my concern. He wouldn't be a general if he wasn't an outstanding soldier – I

349

know that. But this dark angel is not just a skilled swordsman; something deeper drives him. I wouldn't be surprised if Prince Luca threatened to kill his children if he lost today.

Nathaneal counters Ithran's thrusts expertly, but I'm still scared for him. The general focuses too much on Nathaneal's hands, watching for an opportunity to strike them. And even though their parries are sometimes too fast to see in detail, each time Ithran lunges my heart stops.

Though it doesn't show yet, I can tell Nathaneal is exhausted. But, as driven and ruthless as Ithran is, Nathaneal is just as relentless.

'Your prince is too inexperienced to win this, you know.'

'So you keep trying to tell yourself.'

Luca chuckles and I hate him for it.

Suddenly the action speeds up as if both Nathaneal and Ithran are sprinting for a finish line. They move forwards, backwards and sideways, striking, blocking, cutting and defending. Nathaneal brings his sword up close to his shoulder. He holds it there for a beat, and my pulse jumps. He has purposefully opened a target point on himself. Ithran lifts his sword to attack. With meticulous timing Nathaneal steps out with his left foot, thrusts downwards, striking Ithran's chest above the breastbone, penetrating the general's seamless armour.

'Yes!'

'Don't be too hasty to celebrate, Princess.'

Ithran touches the hole, and his gloved fingers come away with blood. Beside me, Prince Luca grunts, but that's nothing compared to the look of absolute loathing he gives Nathaneal now.

Their next parry is so fast I can't maintain focus on one or the other. Behind them, I catch Michael squinting as he too tries to watch. He sets an arrow in his bow and without taking his eyes off the duel, shoots. Amazingly, he strikes a dark angel in the narrow gap of armour between his chin and sternum.

Meanwhile, the air seesaws around us with breezes generated from the hundreds of beating wings as angels clash with one another on the bridge, or in the air above it. Arrows whiz overhead, but none penetrate the protective dome-like circle the Gatekeepers have created around Luca and me.

Everywhere soldiers fall. Blood drips from swords as another hundred of Luca's legion fly in to bolster the first round.

When will this battle end? Will there even be a winner? Or will it be like the wars of Earth, where no one side is ever truly the victor?

But the duel between Nathaneal and the general comes to an unexpected ending when the general dislodges Nathaneal's sword, making it soar towards the ceiling. The crazed general quickly pounces, pushing his sword tip into the flesh of Nathaneal's throat. Smirking, he then shoves Nathaneal backwards on to his elbows, triumphantly thrusting his boot down on to his chest.

Breathing heavily, the general carefully leans forward and takes a dagger from Nathaneal's belt and a knife from each boot, sliding them across the floor to one of his soldiers. 'Raise your hands at me and I will push this blade through to your other side before you can blink.'

No! I call out in my thoughts.

Since this duel began I've kept my thoughts tightly controlled so not to distract Nathaneal, but now . . . now his eyes glance at me and tell me to be strong, that everything will be all right.

Still breathing deeply, and glowing with pride, Ithran looks to his king. 'Sire, how would you like the pieces?'

'What's he talking about, Luca?'

But before Prince Luca answers the general finds himself surrounded by all four members of Nathaneal's team, as well as his two brothers, Gabriel, who I knew was here, and Jerome, who must be in Gabriel's unit. They all have their weapons, still dripping with the blood of dark angels, aimed at Ithran.

And as other angels, both of light and dark, become aware, the fighting comes to an eerie standstill.

Wounded and incapacitated angels litter the floor, some groaning aloud, pleading for a healer; others wait with open-eyed stares for their own healing processes to kick in.

'It seems we have reached a stalemate,' Prince Luca says as he scans the disturbing sight. His sharp intake of breath lets me know, though he is a monster, that he's not untouched by the scene. 'General, withdraw your sword.'

'But . . . but, sire, I *have* him,' the general sputters.

'And his crew have you. Look around, General.'

He takes a peek and groans. 'Whether I release the prince or not, they will still kill me, sire.'

'They won't touch you as long as *I* have what *they* want.'

He means me. Finally, General Ithran understands his predicament. He sneers at Nathaneal while taking his time to withdraw his sword. I watch, unable to believe my eyes as he pushes his sword into Nathaneal's throat and twists it before withdrawing with painstaking slowness. A trickle of deep, cardinal-red blood runs down Nathaneal's chest.

And finally I feel power thrumming through my body. The red haze is back and I welcome it like I would an old friend. I imagine my hands are fists of solid steel. I would love to take the general out myself – but first I have to escape Luca's gripping hold.

In my thoughts I will Nathaneal to look at me. But Luca is tormenting him by making a show of sniffing my hair. 'Keep still, Princess. I don't want even one hair on your head harmed in this pathetic but somewhat entertaining exercise.'

His flippant sarcasm in the face of all this pain on both sides inflames me even further. The red haze deepens and I embrace it, drawing it up into my arms to make them as strong as steel too.

Suddenly Prince Luca laughs at Nathaneal, catching me off-guard. 'Well, well, my inexperienced adversary, apparently it's true – you still don't have permission to annihilate a king. On the other hand I can do whatever I want with you since you're not a King yet, and with the mistakes you're making you'll never become one.'

He looks to his general. 'I've had enough of this. I tire of it! I'm leaving now, and I'm taking Ebony with me.' He gives our Gatekeepers what appears to be a pre-arranged signal, before returning to his general. 'Order the entire legion up here and end this quickly. There's been enough bloodshed today. Overpower the enemy with sheer force, General. Leave no witnesses.'

'Yes, sire!'

'Wait, except for this lot.' He indicates Gabriel, Jerome, Michael, Isaac, Uriel and Solomon. 'Put them in the tombs.'

'And the young prince?'

'Destroy him. But slice off his hands before you shred his soul. I want to see those hands for myself.'

He wants to show them to *me*, so I will know that my love is truly gone, and in Luca's sick head that will mean I will then have room in my heart for him.

'Have your first lieutenant bring them to my suite.'

'On a silver platter, your highness?'

Luca snarls. 'I don't care if they're in a paper bag! Just bring them to me.'

'Yes, sire! My pleasure!'

A paper bag! His pleasure!

I need more power. I'm panicking, and the red haze is losing intensity. I need training to know how to use my power properly, how to draw it up and keep it where I need it, when I need it!

Where is my power?

Nathaneal told me in training once that it lies dormant inside my inner core, waiting for me to awaken it. And only I can do so by believing in what I am and accepting it in my heart.

Soldiers dressed in all-black fly into the tunnel, hundreds of them at once. Luca isn't kidding about how many he has on call. They don't stop to assess the scene – they just attack, running and leaping and flying across the spaces, screaming some kind of war cry in their dark language.

I close my eyes and concentrate on that centre part of my mind that nothing and no one ever reaches except me. It's dark in there, and so peaceful. I look around, drawn to a small light that flickers and seems to call to me.

It becomes difficult to hold the image when Luca starts dragging me towards the edge while the six huge Gatekeepers close in around us, forming a barricade with their shields in front like an Ancient Roman legion.

I take a deep breath, plant my feet firmly on the ground and focus on the flame flickering in my mind.

Luca stops. 'Princess, what are you doing?'

I don't know how long I can hold out against him, so I need him to stop talking.

'Ebony, your body temperature is rising. What *are* you doing?' he says again.

Apparently, something *is* working.

Inside, my body shifts somehow, as if it's speeding up. The flame in the quiet spot in my mind gets bigger. My arms and legs grow heavy. Luca still has me trapped in his grip, but I know that whatever he's feeling has him worried. I cast my glance around, looking for Nathaneal.

The battle surges with soldiers engaged in combat everywhere. Isaac is taking on the enemy three at a time. Gabriel and Jerome are back to back with too many enemies to count. I don't see Nathaneal yet, but I continue focusing on the flame, pulling and stretching it until there is nothing in my head but fire.

A red haze appears on the edges of my vision. A rush of heat swirls down into the centre of my chest and spreads outwards. A burning sensation flows in after it, like acid filling my veins, moving into my arms, my fingers, and down into my legs.

This is my power. I recognise it. I feel it. And I *will* it to grow, to strengthen, to deepen, to swell.

Everything burns. It's as if I'm making electricity in my core and syphoning it through all the cells of my body.

My breathing accelerates, my heart races, and I hear Nathaneal call out to me. He sounds worried. His voice punctures the air between us even while sounding far away. 'Open your eyes!' he calls. 'Ebony, open your eyes and breathe!'

I open my eyes and see Nathaneal a short distance away, his eyes more intense than ever, calling out, 'Release it! Breathe, sweetheart, breathe!'

But how? I've never come this far before.

Prince Luca suddenly stops trying to drag me over the edge. His arms fall away and he roars a deep abdominal growl. 'Run!' he orders his Gatekeepers while he leaps over them and into the air, flying away from me like a madman escaping the flames of his own fire.

And without his arms wrapped so tightly around me any more, I find I *can* breathe. I exhale all the air in my lungs.

And then I explode.

47

Jordan

I've been hearing whistling now for at least an hour. Sometimes it becomes faint and I can hardly hear it, but sometimes it sounds so close I'm sure it's coming from my cave. Just as I get my hopes up, it fades again.

And every time it sounds close I call out, yelling for help, inadvertently pulling on the chains and opening up my wounds from previous attempts to escape or make noise. Now my wrists are oozing blood again.

If nobody finds me, I will die down here. That's a fact. The angels will look for me once they realise I'm missing, but I could be already dead by then. I wonder if the girls will keep looking for me. Or will it be my dead body some- one finds first? The image of my skeleton hanging from this rock wall in fifty, or maybe a hundred years from now sucks the air out of my already struggling lungs. It's starting to feel like someone has whacked me with a sledgehammer.

The whistling becomes louder suddenly, closer than ever. At least it's someone comfortable enough this far under- ground to be whistling a jolly tune.

I think about that for a sec and a familiar face springs to mind, someone who has direct contact with the Dark

Prince and calls himself the Messenger. I start recognising his voice, and can't decide whether to be relieved or terrified.

Light from his lantern spills into the big room where they chained me. My eyes take their time to adjust. He's almost directly in front of me by the time they do.

He's dressed in boots, jeans, a knee-length leather coat and a new, expensive-looking haircut. He had a *haircut*? While I'm chained to a wall in a pitch-black cave, alone?

He lifts the lantern to shoulder height and studies my face. 'You're still alive.' He sounds surprised.

'Come to gloat?' I ask.

'I could always leave.'

'Nah, don't do that.'

He smirks with his trademark swaggering smile that the girls at school used to die for. With his free hand, Adam Skinner wraps his fingers round the cuff on my right wrist. He stops and stares at the blood, both fresh and congealed, then at me. But he doesn't say anything and while he stares, my skin grows hotter until it starts burning.

'Mate?' I tilt my head towards my wrist. 'Do something, or let go.'

He closes his eyes. I try not to scream when the skin under the cuff starts bubbling up in blisters.

He releases my wrist, but grips my arm, holding it in the same elevated position. 'Keep still, this is going to hurt.'

'How did you know where to find me?'

'Connections.'

'Who told you? Zavier?'

'Maybe.'

So Mr Zee came good in the end, or he thought I would be dead by now and wanted my body found.

Skinner gradually lowers my arm, and I stare at the mangled cuff. 'How did you do that? You got magical powers now?'

'A gift from the king for my loyalty.'

'Are you serious, dude?'

'Do I look like I'm joking?'

'Everything he gives you will have to be paid back in blood. But you know that, right?'

'Don't be so melodramatic,' he mocks, but I can tell by his grim expression that I'm not telling him anything he doesn't already know.

He then sears the other cuff off and lowers my arm with the same tender technique. With numb fingers I massage my hands and carefully rotate my shoulders to get circulation moving again.

I want to ask about Ebony, and make sure Amber got away like Zavier told me, but before I get a word out he produces a water flask and helps me hold it to my mouth. As soon as I get a few sips down my throat, I drill him with questions. 'Where's Ebony? Does the prince still have her? Did she recover from that sedative Zavier gave her? Medaza-something? What about Amber? Is she all right? Have you heard anything? Have you seen her? Why don't you answer me, dude?'

He holds up his hands. 'Amber is safe at home. But the king has Ebony. He's not going to let her go this time, so you may as well get used to not having her around any more.'

'No! No, that can't be true!' I want to grab his shoulders and shake the shit outta him, *make* him tell me that somehow Ebony got away. 'What happened? Did Amber tell Gabriel? Are the angels in touch with Thane?'

'There was a battle at the entrance gates to Skade. And there was a duel between your angel Nathaneal and a general named Ithran.'

'Thane's back?' Relief makes my tingling legs feel light as air. 'Now I know she's all right! Thane won't let anything happen to Ebony.'

'Hmm.'

'What's that supposed to mean?'

'It's over, Jordan. Face it. Ebony is gone. She's on the verge of becoming Queen of Skade and there's nothing you can do about it. Nothing your angel friends can do either. You're just going to have to get over her.'

'You're freaking cold, man.'

'If I'm so cold, what am I doing down here?'

I hang my head. 'Thanks heaps. I owe you one.'

'Yeah, you do.' Skinner collects the mangled cuffs off the ground and slips them into his coat pockets. 'And the way you're going to pay me back is by keeping your mouth shut about who set you free.'

'Sure. I won't tell anyone. Mate, your secret is safe with me.'

He grabs the back of my neck and brings my face right up to his. 'Are you mocking me?'

'Shit, man, of course not! I'm just worried about Ebony. She can't be gone like you said. If there's a battle, Thane will win it and he'll bring her back. You'll see.'

He releases my neck and starts walking out. I follow him because by now my sense of direction is shot. He walks fast, and my legs have pins and needles running through them. It's intense, but I catch up before I lose the light. 'Adam, why did you release me?'

'Because you're a loser and someone has to look out for you.'

'Now who's mocking who?'

'I couldn't leave you down here knowing how hungry the Aracals get around midnight.'

'Seriously? You rescued me so shape-shifting demons wouldn't get a feed tonight?'

He shrugs. 'What do you think?'

'I don't know because I've been down here more than one night and no Aracals came for a feed. In fact, nothing came in here. It seemed like even the rats knew it was sacred ground or too dangerous, or something. And during the time you and I spent together in the last couple of months there were moments I glimpsed the old you. I even caught you smiling once – for real. It reminded me of when we were kids. When we were best friends. And here you are now setting me free.'

He stops walking and lifts the lantern so I can see his face clearly. 'I'm not your friend, Jordan. Don't ever forget that.'

'OK. I won't forget. But . . . thanks.'

'Zavier turned up at my door this morning,' he says. 'He was raving on about being deceived and tricked, or something. He told me where you were and that I had to find you right away.'

'So where is Zavier now?'

'Gone. Far away. I don't know. Listen, Jordan, there's more to keeping this secret than you think.'

'Like what?'

We start walking again. 'When you're in *his* presence, or within hearing range of any dark angels, or any one you suspect of being a dark angel, you have to keep my name out of your thoughts.' He turns and flicks my forehead with his long index finger. 'In here. OK?'

I rub my forehead. 'Sure, man. I get it.'

'You can't tell anyone it was me who released you, or bring an image of the seared cuffs into your mind.'

Shit, how am I supposed to do that? 'What if Prince Luca asks me directly, or probes his laser-beam eyes into my mind looking for the truth?'

'Can you do this, or should I take you back and chain you up again?'

'I can do it!'

'If I find out that you broke this promise —'

'What? You'll kill me? Dude, any time, 'cause without Ebony I don't care.'

He says, 'I was going to say that if you break this promise I'll come for Amber, and I'll kill *her*.'

48

Ebony

The floor falls away around me, curving up and down like an ocean wave, spreading outwards in an ever-widening circle. The air distorts in the same way, stretching and shrinking in a manner that shouldn't be possible.

Soldiers everywhere shout or scream as the wave tosses them about like fish caught in a whirlpool. It catches up to Prince Luca in the air, carrying him southward for tens of metres before slamming him into a sunken portion of bridge.

It takes a moment to comprehend how powerful this force is. A force *I* generated, that rumbled out of me like an earthquake. I have no idea how many soldiers – of light or dark – my power has damaged. I spot Michael smiling to himself as he gets back on to his feet. He retrieves his bow, reloads an arrow and winks at me with his golden eyes.

With no time to waste, I look for Nathaneal before General Ithran tries to slice his hands off again. But I locate the general first. He's on the ground, not far away, quickly regaining his balance. Remarkably, his sword is still in his hand. He sees me while still on one knee and scowls with eyes filled with loathing. He gets up, screams and starts to run at me. I meet him halfway. Our bodies smash into each other. As he drops, I kick his sword out of his hand. He watches it soar high into the air and his face turns red with rage.

But I'm ready for him.

Fuelled by the power still throbbing in my veins, I slam my fist into his face. My punch sends him soaring over the edge, where gravity propels his unconscious body in a downward arc into Skade.

It's then I hear the horns play again. Somewhere near the entrance, soldiers have struck up another tune, but this is different – a scale of eerie notes. I shiver. I wonder what it means.

The notes continue to play and then I see why. A unit of at least fifty soldiers fly into the tunnel. They wear the same sleek black uniform as their comrades but with armour from head to foot. They have in their hands shimmering weapons of a type I've never seen before, and as they fly over the top of me it's like watching a fast-moving storm cloud. My heart races when I see them head to the blue light, where their mission becomes frighteningly clear.

And I still haven't located Nathaneal.

When I spin round, I finally spot him, and the soldiers blocking our only exit home shift to the back of my mind. He's getting to his feet from under a pair of dark angels' bodies. He sees me at the same time and smiles.

It's the single most sensational smile I have ever seen.

With no thought except to get to him, I run, but my legs feel as if I'm moving in slow motion. I trip over a body and scramble across the top of it. Then he's in front of me, helping me to my feet. I jump into his arms, wrap my legs round his waist and bury my head in his solid shoulder.

He holds me very tight. 'I've longed for the moment you would be real in my arms again, and not just in my dreams,' he says. Lifting his head, he keeps me curled up against his chest, and whispers into the top of my hair. 'There is so much I want to tell you, but your safety must come first. Ebony, I have to get you out of here fast.'

'One second,' I whisper, knowing escape is not going to be an easy task with those giant soldiers controlling the exit. 'Please, Thane, I need to know *you're* real too.'

I need to feel you, my heart screams.

His eyes lock with mine and the world holds still for us while I reach up and kiss the wound on his neck, tracing it with my fingers, delighting in the fact that he's healing already. 'I'm remembering things from my past. Zavier blocked my memories – all of them, even the ones from my time in my mother's womb, and before when we were together.'

He shakes his head. 'I suspected as much. Where is this criminal? He will pay for his crime. Is he here? Point him out to me, sweetheart. I have to arrest him immediately.'

'Luca banished him. He's long gone.' I slide my fingers up from his injured throat to his face, running them over his chin, his mouth, his striking eyes. He looks real, he feels real. 'I'm starting to remember some incredible things.'

He smiles and says, 'I belong to you, my beautiful one, and I'm never going to let you forget that.'

He kisses me then, and the chaos around us fades into a distant otherworld. All I'm aware of is Nathaneal's mouth pressed against mine, his lips tasting both salty from his sweat, and sweet from his warmth. Time doesn't exist as his mouth opens in response to urgent pressure from mine. We share breath and taste each other, and it dawns on me that we need each other in the same way as the Earth needs air and fire and water.

His hands at my back press me into him. 'My love, you were always in my thoughts.' He groans deep and low and slides those firm but tender fingers along my thighs and hoists me up higher, pulling me in so close that nothing, absolutely *nothing* can come between us. And I get what he's telling me. He confirms it with an intimate mind-link. *No one will come between us again. I promise you this, sweetheart, with all my heart. Unfortunately, we can't talk now because we must leave, but when we are a safe distance from these gates, I want to hear everything that's happened in my absence, like how much you missed me. And then I'll show you how much I love you.*

I feel the smile form on his lips as they brush against mine, which makes me smile too.

But now I have to get you out of here. Are you ready?

Um . . . of course, but . . .

What is it?

Just as I go to point out the blocked exit, Prince Luca scrambles over some wounded bodies and sees me in Nathaneal's arms. He roars, making the sound of a multitude of furious beasts. His face contorts into that hideous look of fury I witnessed when he killed his own soldier. I know what strength he can muster in this mindset. It scares me and I grip Nathaneal harder as a tremor of fear passes through me. 'I think you might be right about needing to leave in a hurry, but there's just one problem.'

'Ebony, I'm not going anywhere without you again.'

'I want that too, Nathaneal, and I agree that we should –'

He kisses my eyelids. 'So you got my message?' he murmurs.

'Message?'

'He was hesitant at first and took some convincing. He thought I shouldn't reveal so much about how we knew each other in the spirit world, who we are in the living world and our future together as destiny predicts. But I knew you needed to see it. All of it – the way in which you were raised – without me to help you bring your memory back, the truth would be the only way to eliminate your doubts and free your powers.'

Speechless, and while maintaining a watchful eye on Prince Luca's progress towards us, I pull back slightly to look into Nathaneal's eyes. He's telling me the absolute truth. I can see him passing the message through a mind-link to his brother, revealing everything about his life from when he was a little boy to who he is today, and who he is destined to become.

Around us, angels of light and dark rise up and continue to battle each other. Uriel engages Prince Luca in a duel. This will give us more time to find a way through those soldiers guarding the blue light. I catch Gabriel's eye and he goes still for a moment and frowns. He seems to want to say something, but a black-armoured soldier draws him into combat.

He had the message all this time and didn't pass it on to me, though he came to the house every night! But *why?* Did he really think so little of me?

Nathaneal picks up that something is wrong. 'Sweetheart, you did receive my message, didn't you?'

I drag my eyes back to him. 'From Gabriel, right?'

He nods and smiles his beautiful smile again, relief evident in the softening of his jaw and the slowing beat of his heart. 'I couldn't trust anyone else with that information.'

Ambiguously, as I've always done to avoid straight-out lying, I say gently, 'You were right to be careful.'

'I made you a promise.'

Arrows split the air above our heads, reminding us that this battle isn't over yet. I point out the blocked exit and he sighs under his breath. 'It's nothing we can't deal with now Gabriel has brought reinforcements, with more on the way,' he says while sliding me down to the ground.

But my legs buckle beneath me. 'Nathaneal, what's happening? I feel unsteady.'

He pulls me up against his chest, taking most of my weight. 'Using all that power in one thrust has exhausted your energies. It happens. Don't worry. You just need nourishment and rest.'

'My legs are numb. I've felt weak and tired before when I used my power, but nothing like this.'

'You'll be all right. I'll teach you how to measure out the energy you use so you don't drain yourself, but now I have to get you out of here.'

No sooner does he say this than a troop of masked soldiers wearing all-black armour that even covers their eyes flies into the entrance. Incredibly, they're bigger, taller, clearly superior to all the other dark angels here, including the unit controlling our exit to the Crossing. There are so many of them in such a tight formation that they block out almost all the light behind them. Their leader looks around, sees what he's after and orders his soldiers to move. They do so with terrifying speed. My heart races as the twenty or so massive angels head straight for us.

'Dark Thrones!' Nathaneal shouts, throwing me behind him. In one lightning move he discharges his four wings, covering me with them, and generates his protective shield. 'Michael! Isaac!'

As the wave of Dark Thrones rise over us, Nathaneal uses the force from his hands to blast them away. But as soon as they fall back, stumbling blindly, another black wave of their kind appears at the entrance. This time one gets through Nathaneal's blast and, discharging his weapon, ruptures the shield. Bones crunch and feathers fly as the Throne blindly tries to grab me. I bite down on his armoured hand and somehow make contact with his skin. He growls and goes feral in trying to get me, destroying what's left of the shield.

Through the spaces opened up in Nathaneal's wings I see Michael trying his hardest to reach us even though several Dark Thrones are restraining him. My heart thuds in a slow, thunderous beat. This is what Zavier meant. This is Prince Luca's ultimate plan for revenge. A plan he developed during the months he healed in the underground cave. Surrounded by his Prodigies, the elite of his army, they would have strategised day and night, preparing to set this plan in motion, allowing for all possible variables, while their bodies regained strength.

And the realisation that Prince Luca might win today makes my heart sink with the heaviness of lead.

Nathaneal reaches round, grabs the Throne trying to get me, and hurls him far away. He doesn't get a moment to catch his breath before another wave of Dark Thrones appears at the entrance, forcing Nathaneal to forge a desperate mind-link, *Michael, where are you?*

Don't despair, cousin. They have me contained, but not for long. I'm coming.

Isaac! Uriel!

It's an ambush! Isaac replies. *First they isolated us, then sent their Dark Thrones to restrain us. We just need a few more seconds.*

Gabriel! Where are you? I need you now! I don't have a few seconds.

I know, brother. I can see them. They have surrounded me too. But I'm almost done, so hang on both of you — I'm coming.

As soon as you can, brother! Get Ebony out of here. Hurry!

The next wave of Thrones seems to come at us faster than the first. While Nathaneal blasts them away, another row, hiding beneath them, shoots up over the top of their fallen comrades. The sneak attack takes us by surprise. Nathaneal doesn't get time to regroup. They move in, flying low over the top of us. Their many sets of beating black wings bring darkness and confusion as they tighten their circle round us. Arms, like iron braces, shoot down from a frenzy of feathers and drag me out of Nathaneal's protective wings.

I twist and turn, punch and kick, trying to free myself, but my body remains weak. I try to reach for my power, but can't focus with everything happening so fast.

Gabriel arrives at the same time as Michael, then Isaac and the others. I hear their shouts as they try to wrench me from the Dark Thrones' arms. Then Nathaneal bursts free from those holding him down. Body parts in black armour and portions of black wings fall like debris caught inside a tornado's funnel. But other dark soldiers are lying in wait, and drag them into fierce combat.

As the Thrones carry me over the edge and into Skade, Nathaneal's tortured scream rips the very fabric of the air and shatters my heart. It's the scream that tells me we lost the battle. It's over. And everything is not going to be all right ever again.

The next thing I know, the black wings part and there's enough light in this strange-smelling atmosphere to see my surroundings again. But what I see makes me sick to my stomach. I'm in the arms of Prince Luca himself.

I should have realised his strength had fully returned. There were so many signs.

With Dark Thrones surrounding us, he begins the descent into Skade.

I stretch and twist my upper body to peer behind and catch sight of dozens of angels coming for me with Nathaneal leading the charge. A surge of hope makes my heart quicken. But just as they near the edge and are about to fly out the tunnel and into Skade, the six Gatekeepers, locked in their cabins during the entire battle, activate the gates. In a mere fraction of the time they'd taken to open, all twelve gates slam down in front of them.

Devastated, shocked, unable to look any more, my body slumps and the horror of what's happening — the

371

finality – starts to sink in. A sob threatens to erupt from my chest, but I won't cry, not in front of this monster.

The air is thick with smoke; the sky is heavy with dark clouds streaked with crimson from a sun that hides itself from view. Lightning slashes the mountain ranges on the horizon as volcanoes pump toxic gases into the atmosphere. In the distance I hear the unfamiliar cries of wild beasts roaring for food. Overhead, a purple moon hangs low in the sky while, below, thousands of human souls and thousands more dark angels line the streets, waiting for a glimpse of their new queen.

It takes a heartbeat to acknowledge that the new queen they await is me.

A Final Word

Thank you to my beautiful family for all your support and assistance during the writing of this book, with special thanks to my daughters Amanda Canham and Danielle Curley for their insightful comments and critiques; and to my sister Therese Mallia who has supported this series from the start and who has not been disappointed yet!

To my good friend and agent, Geoffrey Radford, a heartfelt thank you. And to my London agent Janelle Andrew, I appreciate all you do for me.

To the brilliant editorial team at Bloomsbury's London Office – you always bring out the best in me, and I thank you for that. With special mention to Ele Fountain, Emma Young, Sam MacIntosh, Isabel Ford, Maurice Lyon, Helen Jones, Katie Everson and Katie Smith.

A big thank you to the Bloomsbury New York Office for all you do to make the Avena Series a success in the US.

And to Bloomsbury's Sydney office; what did I ever do before you set up in Australia? You are a great supporting machine with many amazing and invaluable talents. Thank you to Louise, Hannah, Elizabeth, Kristin, Brendan, Bethia and Jennie. And a very special mention to the lovely Sonia Palmisano – I promise next time you won't have to hold my hand quite so much!